Wet BONES

The Fourth D.I. Thompson Novel

MARK DENNIS

To

This book is dedicated with love, as always, to my Sandra.

I don't know where these stories come from. Life lived, in part, and imagination for the majority I suppose. Without Sandra to marshal them, my stories wouldn't be out there because, while I write the all the right words, they're often not necessarily in the right order.

With thanks to Eric and Ernie.

Cover illustration, internal illustrations and cover design

by Sandra Dennis

Foreword

Ending a novel with the first chapter of the next one is perhaps ambitious when that's all you have, an idea. When 'Spiked' closed with the discovery of a skull at Colwick Park, I had no real idea what the plot direction might take or even whether I had a plot at all, and yet here it is, the Wet Bones story.

For those new to the Thompson tales, I suggest you start with Coldhearted, otherwise you'll be confused about some of the characters and I'm really not going to tell their complete back stories in Wet Bones again, just so you can catch up. What you should know is that this is a story involving the police, the crimes they investigate and the personalities involved in one particular team. It is not a police procedural. All the characters presented are fictional, because that's how fiction works, and while some of the stories interwoven may have factual roots, I'm not telling you which ones.

Coldhearted, the first Thompson, was my first ever novel. I hope I've honed my writing skills since that first, lengthy story, I've certainly gained more insight into the skills of writing. This book, 'Wet Bones', is my eleventh.

The next question I ask myself is, will there be a fifth Thompson novel? I didn't end this one with the start of the next, but that doesn't mean I'm devoid of ideas and I didn't kill all of them off either, so perhaps. 'All of them?', I hear you wonder. Does someone get bumped off in this book and, if so, did you like them? Read on and find out.

Mark Dennis,

Clam Point, NS. March 2023

One

28 June 2017

Charlie Stevenson dragged his spinner back again, nothing. So far he'd tried just about every lure in his tackle box, but nothing was working, nothing biting, not even a knock. He was going to complain, again, but this time he'd take his complaint higher; it was those bastard cormorants that were eating all the fish, no matter what that poncy student studying them said. He didn't care what the other anglers said either, it was the cormorants that were getting the fish that the specimen pike needed to eat to grow, that and the Poles that kept nicking them to eat. It never occurred to him that if the pike were genuinely hungry they would go for his lure.

The line suddenly tightened as he slowly reeled in, but he knew it wasn't a fish, just another obstruction on the bottom of the lake. Colwick Lake was an old gravel pit that was a mass of snags that he was sure had been left in deliberately. He also reckoned that the wardens had a lucrative side-line selling recovered spinners and lures. He never elaborated exactly how they recovered the lures if he couldn't, logic was rarely at home for Charlie. He didn't trust the wardens; they kept a very close eye on him. He knew that they knew he wasn't above using creative methods to get his fish, despite the ongoing live-bait ban.

He hauled again, hoping his lure would come loose; the thing he'd hooked gave a bit more, but there was still resistance. It was probably an old carrier bag full of water and crap, or an old sack, one of the wardens' traps, it certainly wasn't a fish. He hauled again and it gave some more. He desperately wanted the lure back this time; it was one he'd bought on a trip to America, it was his favourite although he'd never caught a fish on it. A few more tugs and he felt the hooked thing finally give and, as the catch surfaced, he could see that it was a hessian

1

sack. This was definitely one of the warden's tackle-traps. He reckoned, if it was covered in lures as expected, he'd be able to photograph it to prove to the club that they did this deliberately just to piss off anglers, not to mention rob them. He was convinced that the wardens hated all anglers, and him in particular.

He reeled the sack in close to the boat then, using his gaff to hook it, swung it aboard. The sack was still in good condition but covered in silt, which stank as it splashed all over the floor of the previously clean boat. The wardens would just have to clean this one out again, not that they ever did a very good job in the first place but fuck 'em. Grabbing the bottom of the sack, he turfed the contents out into the bottom of the boat. A muddy off-white skull bounced across the fibreglass floor, rattling into the well by his feet. It was face up and smiling.

By the time he got back the fishing lodge flustered, his little electric outboard was starting to slow down and he thought he'd have to call the lodge to get towed in, again. On the jetty, one of the wardens who he knew did bugger-all but drink tea all day, was busy mopping out three new boats for freshly-arrived anglers. "What do you call this, then?" said Stevenson, pointing into the boat. "A practical joke is it? Hide some Halloween skulls in the lake and watch us silly sods shit ourselves in fright? Not me, I was in Cyprus, fighting for King and Country, I've seen worse than this".

The warden climbed out of the boat he was mopping with a resigned look on his face. He took one glance at the skull and pulled out his radio. "Jack, call the police, tell them we've got another one". Then he went back to his cleaning.

"Is that it? Is that all you've got to say?"

"Charlie, it's a skull, what do you want me to say? Should we weigh it to see whether you've caught the biggest skull this season or you could just bugger off and leave me to mop the duck shit out of this boat for another deserving customer. For you information it is 'Queen and Country' and has been since 1952. Thanks a lot for making such a shitty mess of a previously spotless boat, I'll add it to my list of things to do. Have a nice day, won't you".

Stevenson was livid and started ranting about this, that, and everything, but that had been the warden's intention, baiting Stevenson could be the highlight of a dull day. Eventually he stormed off, threw his tackle into his car and then sat at the traffic barrier because nothing was happening. After a lot of waving out of the window, the barrier went up and he sped away at somewhat above the park regulation speed limit.

"One of these days that man is going to have a heart attack", said John Fraser to his colleague, smiling.

"Was I wrong to turn off the automatic barrier and make him wait thirty-seconds, then?" asked Jack, the elderly desk warden.

"Excellent initiative I'd say, it gave him valuable reflection time, space to gather his thoughts. You probably saved him from having a nasty accident out there, keep up the good work. Serving the general public can have its rewards, if you search diligently".

The elderly desk warden agreed. "I didn't storm the beaches at Normandy, it's true, because I was too young, but if I had, I certainly wouldn't have complained about it. People today, tsk!"

Dave Thompson pulled a sheet of paper from his drawer, on it were as many of the names and contact numbers of officers he'd worked with as he could remember. It was his 'to do' sheet, following up on his old DI, Jock Charnley's, suggestion that he should be cultivating a network. Before he could start dialling, an apologetic cough got his attention. His open-door policy sometimes meant people were able to appear silently, especially if you were preoccupied.

"Boss, I need at least a couple of days off. I promised to run Marie Burns home to Liverpool and I have some personal things to attend to, they just came up". It was Joe Lawrence, one of Thompson's sergeants but formerly DCI Marie Burns' right-hand man, he seemed a bit nervous. Thompson put it down to 'new boss syndrome', he'd suffered from it himself, sometimes.

"No problem, Joe, give Marie my best and make sure she's aware that any Scally nicking your car is her responsibility. Take whatever time you need, call me if anything else happens, we'll cope".

"Thanks boss, hopefully it's for just a few days. Can you tell Jenny? I haven't had chance to run it past her, it only just came up".

Thompson said he would, but he was surprised that Joe hadn't called her himself, they were supposed to be an item now, weren't they? He wandered out into the operations room to look for her, but there was no sign. After a brief word with Liam Prosser, another of his sergeants, to let him know about Joe, he wandered back to the office.

Later that afternoon another wad of files appeared on Thompson's desk just as he was casting an eye over the clock, a sheet was on top with a skull-and-crossbones on it. They didn't have a pet name for the case yet and he didn't have much of a handle on it either. Carla Adams, one of his newer detective constables, had been the delivery system for the files and she, too, was ready to call it a day.

"More fun and games, Sir. Skulls at Colwick, what's that all about?"

"I only know bits at the moment, Carla. You know the place though, can you get me a staffing list, say everyone in the past ten years, along with current whereabouts plus all contractors, ancillary council staff and anyone with a gate key?"

"Sure, Sir, that must be about eight hundred people. Give me five minutes and I'll get it done for you". There was more than a hint of sarcasm in the delivery.

"Sorry Carla, I didn't mean now, and make it a team effort, I haven't sorted out who is leading on what yet so you can take your pick. I've inherited all of Marie's cases plus I've got Tilda to talk to and I need to get to know Marie's people soonest. Joe is out for a few days, pass it on will you, especially if you see Jenny before I do".

"Sure, I'll just mention it to Josh and he'll have the whole nick informed inside an hour, Greater Nottingham in two".

"Because he's efficient or because he yaps?"

"Actually he's efficient, I'm warming to him. At first I thought he was a complete waste of skin, but underneath the puppy that wants to please is a puppy that's completely house-trained".

"And Lorna? Had time to make your mind up about her yet?"

"Is that all, Sir? I'm heading home".

"Give her time, Carla. She's covering new team nerves with bluster. Don't forget, I've seen it before in new recruits".

Carla smiled, she knew what he meant. She herself had been plucked from obscurity by him and levered into the team.

"Maybe we'll take the children for a Colwick visit tomorrow to get to know each other, can you prepare a picnic? By the way, I've just been told that we have a new DC arriving soon. He's yours when he gets here, please don't break him on his first day".

Carla started complaining like a sixteen-year-old. "Aw, Sir, not me for the new one. It's so unfair, give him to Josh or Lorna, please Sir, I'll do anything. How about a bribe? I'll fetch you a bacon cob every day".

"My visits seem to be at increasingly inopportune moments, Detective Inspector". Superintendent Perkins had eased into the room without knocking as usual, but at least this time he was smiling. Perkins knew how Thompson's team were a pack of jokers. Serious when need be, but jokers all the same.

Carla looked Perkins directly in the eye, which was difficult given their height difference. "True, Sir, I desperately want to get out of being mother to the newbie, but I'm not making a full English for anyone".

Perkins didn't bat an eyelid. "And quite right DC Adams, women no longer need to spend time uncomfortably on their knees in order to progress in the modern police force, now bugger off".

"Sorry about that, Sir", said Thompson after Carla had skipped out of the room. "She's getting cockier".

"Everyone is on a high after a recent success, quite normal, just don't let them get too close, David. You're the boss of a bigger team now, be an ogre occasionally. Now, about the bones case, I see you have the files. Upstairs are chattering. It's in the public eye, the newspapers are talking, 'is it demonology?' they wonder. Personally, I think it might be a prank, or perhaps an obsession. Please keep me posted. Send Prosser.

"Sir, I'll cancel the picnic, then".

"Did you look at the other thing I mentioned? Sorry for the sketchy information, I'll send the file presently, I've not seen it myself yet".

Thompson recalled a hurried phone call with his superior, earlier that week, and an e-mail with some brief details appended. "I had a read through of what little we have, Sir. A theft in Leicester? I'm surprised we're being asked to take an interest, seems small beer. I'll get back to you on that one when I've seen the full file, I'm sure there must be a reason why it's on my desk".

"Recovery of the missing bounty seems to be of high importance to some people who have a degree of influence where it matters. At the moment, the newspapers don't have the details of it, but you can't have a superstar football person robbed and the news not get out. This is a 'tread carefully' situation and the details of what was stolen will not be for sharing with the team at the moment. While I'm here, I'd like your assessment of Marie's people, in writing, along with your thoughts on young Tilda. I understand that Simon Beresford will join your merry crew

soon. Confidentially, his uncle has the title 'Assistant Chief Cons|
appended to his name and emblazoned upon his door, just sc
know".

As Perkins left, Thompson heard Perkins tell Prosser that he was wan

"Boss?"

'Tomorrow, take Gecko to Colwick, speak to John Fraser and investiga
the discovery of a body part. It doesn't sound urgent; in fact, it all sound
a bit odd but it is what it is. The body part in question is a skull, another
one apparently, I'm just going through the file now. The case is one of
Marie's old ones".

"Will do, Boss. When you allocate, am I getting it?' Prosser was keen to
gather cases. As one of the newest sergeants in the team, and with
Gecko's situation as yet undecided, he felt he had to show some
enthusiasm.

Gecko was already a sergeant, but he wasn't exactly popular with
Thompson or his team. In fact, his move over from Vice was a bit of a
mystery and he'd been imposed on them from 'above'. Thompson was
taking it slow while trying to work out the reason he was there.

"Working on that too, I'll have it sorted tomorrow, or later. Don't worry,
nothing is happening with this one yet. Marie hadn't touched it so
nobody has had a real poke around. It might be something we can use
to ease people in, we've got a new DC soon. Can you send Tilda in
please? Thanks".

Tilda Jeffries strode confidently into the office and sat, waiting.
Thompson had been digging in one of his drawers and seemed to have
found what he was looking for, placing a handful of manila folders on
the desk. "Tilda, we have five minutes to get to know each other better.
I just skimmed your file, you didn't piss anyone off anywhere, so that's
good. By now I expect you've talked to the others, been told scurrilous
lies about me and been shown where the biscuits are kept. Why did you
ask to join this team?"

Ilda saw that one of the files on the desk was hers, she knew that anything Thompson had learned about her from it was likely limited. "I heard good things about your team, I like the mix. No stuffy old detectives getting in the way when they should be somewhere eating grass, and I know some of the people a bit, including Gecko – he's not a total arse, he has work to do before reaching those heady heights. I asked about you too, as a boss. None of the girls said you'd try to get into my knickers, which I take as a backhanded compliment. They say that you can be a bit naïve at times but you get results and I want to learn how to do that".

Thompson had been impressed by Tilda Jeffries, especially when he'd witnessed how quick she thought when getting him away from a call girl in a café while undercover. It had been an entirely innocent situation, but one that might have led to difficulties for him, professionally.

"Ok, good. Any preferences about who you work with? I tend to mix and match a bit".

"Nope. The straight boys will like me, the straight girls will watch me carefully and the gay girl isn't interested as far as I can tell. You're taken and I'm single by choice. I get on with everybody generally but I can be a bit forward sometimes, not a fault as I see it, more a positive in a detective. I'm also a bit of a magpie when it comes to collecting interesting, shiny new experiences. Like I said, I want to learn".

"Blimey, I wish I was as confident as you at your age. A magpie? They can be destructive too, interesting analogy. Your last assignment, what can you tell me about the Vice work?"

"Nothing".

"Fair enough, good answer. Any problems here and you go and see any sergeant first. If you have a problem with any of them, you see me and if you have a problem with me, see Superintendent Perkins".

"Got it. And if you have a problem with me, please tell me first. I know I can be a bit 'in your face' at times and being new I might try too hard sometimes".

"I got that early on. You're with Jenny initially, see what you make of our 'pickled chef' case, just a read through. I like to get as many perspectives as possible and that one is a bit static at the moment. Jenny will do a catch-up brief for everyone over the next few days".

"I was told you like to have a nickname for each case, I like that. 'Pickles' is obvious but apt, from what I've been told. I hope I can chip in with the odd bit of originality for any new stuff".

"I've filed 'Magpie' away for future reference, if we get a case involving something shiny being nicked, it's a shoe-in".

"Boss, thanks for the chat. I think I'll enjoy it here, for however long that is".

"Great, send Sham in, please".

Thompson swapped files, read as quickly as he could and got ready to make a connection with the first of several of Marie Burns' old team. It was going to be a long afternoon.

On the way home, he reflected on how things were going. He was happy with it all so far. The bosses had obviously seen something in him that was future DCI material. Whether circumstances would actually let him get to those heady heights was another question. His rise to DI had been swift, although to him the progression had seemed to drag at times. Now he was a major player and his team were on a level with the other three teams, he was finally moving up. The traffic was bumper-to-bumper as he mulled things over, but that was ok. It was also pissing down again, real stair-rods. At least a steady crawl in this weather might mean everyone would get home in one piece.

After a bit of stop-start the pace picked up a bit. He'd almost got into third gear this time before the car in front was braking hard, he followed suit. The crunch behind him sounded expensive, he put his hazards on and got out as the rain got heavier. An older Ford had tail-ended him. His own car didn't look too bad, mostly because it wasn't too good in the first place, the other one was a bit worse for wear though. The radiator was leaking green fluid all over the road and the engine making clunking noises. He walked towards the driver's door to check he was ok. Before he could react, a middle-aged man got out and swung a punch, clipping Thompson's forehead, his follow-up missed, mainly because he was now being restrained. With his free hand Thompson showed his ID. "Calm down. Now".

The puncher didn't seem to want to be calm at all, but further back a siren and set of blue lights suggested more guests would be joining the party soon enough. Thompson kept the guy firmly restrained. "That punch was a stupid thing to do. You rear-ended me, it would have been a simple insurance exchange, and now you might be charged with striking a policeman".

"You braked hard, I couldn't miss you".

"I braked hard because the car in front of me did, but I was far enough away that I could stop safely, you obviously weren't-or were there other factors?" Thompson peered into the car, on the passenger seat was a mobile phone with an active ongoing call. Behind him the occasional burst of a two-tone told him that the traffic cops had nearly caught up, picking their way nearer as disgruntled drivers objected to even more delays.

Thompson held his ID out while the wet and not very cheerful traffic cop took a look. "What happened, Sir?"

"Rear-ended me then caught me with a haymaker, but just a glancing blow. Check that phone on the passenger seat, see when the call started".

The puncher had now become a limp wet rag and Thompson realised that he was crying. "Come on, it's only a bump. You alright?"

"Sorry, it's the wife, she's had a fall and I was rushing over. We're estranged but she still calls me, you never stop caring. I took my eye off the road for a second. Sorry about the punch, glad it wasn't one of my best".

Thompson laughed out loud. The traffic cop had heard too and was trying to keep a straight face.

"Get in the car while we decide what to do with you, son", said Thompson. "And you are?" He turned to the traffic cop.

"Wade Morris, Sir. We're all getting a bit wet here and, as I see it, it's your party, you decide. Do you want him arrested?"

"No, can we get him off the road though? You can check his docs and we can swap details. Can you get someone to go and take a look at his missus? He's going have to be recovered here, I hope he's in the AA. No real harm done and you can see he's shaken". The traffic cop was happy to help but a bit surprised that a plain-clothes DI was being reasonable. In his experience they rarely were.

Between them they pushed the stricken car off the road and onto the shoulder, at least the traffic could get moving again. By now both men were soaked through and it didn't help that now traffic had picked up speed, water was coming at them from all directions. "I notice your partner isn't keen to get involved", said Thompson, pointing at a cop sat in the patrol car.

"He's a thick twat, Sir, should be sweeping streets rather than in the force, in my opinion".

"Right, I've met a few like that".

Thompson pulled his car over and pulled out a card. He swapped details with the puncher and gave him a short lecture about self-restraint before telling him that someone was going to look at his wife. Now whatever had been propelling the guy had faded and he was resigned to the tow truck. "I'm really sorry about this", he said, as Thompson left him to his misery.

"Later than I expected", said Rebecca, as her saturated partner squelched into the flat.

"I had a bump on the way, rear-ended and a bit of a fracas".

"I hope you arrested him and found some concealed drugs or something".

"No, I let him off with a strong word. His missus had had a fall and he was worried. It was nothing".

"Is the car alright?"

"I'm fine, thanks for asking".

"I can see that, although you've got a lump on your forehead. Did you bang your head?"

"Must have, anyway, here I am".

"You'll have to eat alone again I'm afraid, I've had mine and I've got to do my interior design work. I still haven't worked out how to use the programme properly yet".

Thompson wasn't that upset at the prospect of another peaceful dinner. Since Rebecca had decided to take a course in interior design, she'd been kept busy with training assignments. She'd always had what Thompson thought of as an arty bent, and he was happy she'd found something to occupy her mind. With luck she might get some commissions. The downside was that Guy had been ushered off to bed early, or was he that late? He'd take a peek in later, just to say hello.

With his dinner on a little plastic tray, Thompson sat back and watched some YouTube videos of old Forest matches. The quality was iffy at times but in one he was sure he could see himself in the crowd. When he'd done, he cleared up, went to see his sleeping son then settled in with a wad of papers to read, adding a few unpaid hours to his already busy day. After reading the notes on the skulls, he was no wiser about what was actually going on there.

Rebecca was fast asleep when he went to bed but at least she was in their bed and not in with Guy. He might not get to snuggle but at least she was near again.

Two

29 June 2017

"Good morning and welcome to Nottinghamshire's finest, you're here so often we're thinking of marking out your own parking place. Tea?" John Fraser, the Head Warden at Colwick, knew most of Dave Thompson's team after having met them more frequently than anyone might reasonably expect to. They, in turn, now knew him and that he had a peculiar sort of wit, much like their own.

"Thanks, John. You have some sort of body for us, I hear". Liam Prosser liked John, a man who was dead-pan with comments that were frequently underlaid with the sort of humour you needed to develop after years of working with the general public, although he let the hackneyed 'parking spot' joke go. "This is DS Newton, we call him Gecko, he's now with us for some unearthly reason. As you can see, Gecko here normally lives under a rock and is unfamiliar with dealing with real humans, don't mind his darting tongue".

Fraser gave Prosser a look, the one he got in return was the equivalent of a lengthy explanation.

"Welcome, Gecko. Ex-Vice by the look of you and possibly from the south of this fine country, judging by the dried jellied eel stuck to your chin. You take your tea Navvy Brew with three sugars, correct?"

Gecko was used to people treating like an unwelcome wart, but he liked being in Thompson's team and so played along. "Spot on, Squire, and if you've got any sort of build-up of dead flies on the window ledge, I'm your man".

Prosser laughed. "We'll make a human of you yet, Mickey".

14

"Any progress on these skulls, Liam? People get pretty wound up when they reel in a surprise, besides, we don't have a permit for it", said Fraser.

"Investigations are underway, I understand. You know how it works, John, diligence is our watchword", lied Prosser. "The boss has been told to step up on this one, we don't think it's a murder, or murders, but the brass hats want answers. We've only just got the case too, but with our top-class people like Gecko on it, we'll crack it in no time". Prosser was prevaricating because he wasn't sure what was actually known about the case but didn't want to show it. Fraser was a bit sharp for that though.

"You do know why you were sent, don't you?" Fraser suspected that Prosser had no idea.

"I was told a body part, a skull to be precise. Nobody is panicking so I assume we're not dealing with a fresh one, just unexplained bones. Why, is there something else? Like I said, we just got the case, things are a bit confused at work". His phone rang. "Boss?"

"Sorry Liam, I thought I'd catch you before you left. A bit more info for you. Some human skulls were found at Colwick previously, like I said, a Marie Burns case on the back burner, as was. Now some Charlie bloke has been complaining to his councillor, his MP and the Pope so we've got to be seen to be showing interest. Pick up whatever they have and bring it in, we already have some, somewhere. Give Fraser my regards".

"Boss", replied Prosser and he hung up. "Seems a 'Charlie somebody' has been in the ear of various worthies, multiple skulls have previously been found here, but you already know that. I'm here to collect the latest and Dave sends his regards".

"Charlie Stevenson is the moaner, he found the most recent one. We know him, he fishes here, a one-man complaint machine", said Fraser. "He reckons that he and the super are fishing buddies from way back. When I say 'super', I don't mean the Chief Superintendent, just a senior police officer who thinks he's super. Stevenson gets under everyone's collar. He'll moan and moan until the recipients take the course of least resistance, which for councillors is to go to our bosses who then follow suit, leaving it to us to tell him to fuck off. It's high time the higher-ups learned how to converse properly with the complaining public, it'd save time all round, we could easily run a course here".

Prosser had always found conversations with the Colwick wardens, and Fraser in particular, refreshing. They bent the rules a bit, could be overtly rude to idiots and ran the park according to their own train of thought. They also dealt pragmatically with everything life threw at them, which could vary from rocks and stolen cars to dead people. "I sometimes wonder whether this job hasn't made you a darker person, John".

"Only from day two, Liam. Right, tea drunk, world righted, we should go and get the latest additions to your collection".

"Additions, collection? How many have you got here and how many have you had so far, can you remember?" said Gecko, who'd lost the train of the conversation early on but had picked up on the plural 'additions'. At the back of his mind he was also wondering why Prosser was actively engaging with this Fraser bloke, instead of treating him as guilty of something. That was what he'd been taught when he'd joined up. Perhaps, away from Vice, life wasn't really like that?

"We now have another seven here for you, Gentlemen and, yes, I know, we should have called, but, I recently discovered that another six were found on the weekend by the diver-training people. You were coming for Charlie's anyway and it seemed silly to call again. Don't worry, we didn't assume that any were beyond saving, we tried CPR but no luck, they were all definitely dead", said Fraser. "You already have four others tucked away somewhere, Gecko, although it wasn't your group that collected them".

"Any theories, John?" asked Prosser. "I know you can be a deep thinker when the urge takes you. I assume you'd know if you had a serial killer on staff?"

"Not one of us, Liam, when we top members of the public they stay buried, we're very efficient, although one of the lads does grow fabulous roses".

"Glad to hear it. Right, lead on to those wet bones".

They followed Fraser through the park. Storm damage was all around and the Trent was lapping almost to the road below the sluice gate; any more rain and local feet would be getting wet.

"Ever been here before, Mickey?" asked Prosser, conversationally.

"Not this end, but we had operations around the bogs with the...er." Gecko stopped himself from using a politically-incorrect slur.

"You know I'm an 'er', right?" Prosser smiled to himself, enjoying watching Gecko squirm a bit.

"Yeah, but you seem alright", admitted Gecko, a bit shame-faced.

In a shabby building that they laughingly called a workshop, a pile of small boxes each held a skull in a hessian bag, in a plastic rubbish bag. After a cursory look, they were loaded into the boot, ready for transport to the pathology people. "Your boy on the desk is going to let us out, right?" asked Prosser, who'd seen the geriatric with the hesitant finger on the barrier operating switch before.

"Yes, with his history he knows not to mess with the law. He doesn't want your lot poking around, don't ask". Prosser didn't. Instead he told Gecko to call Thompson with an update.

"Boss, we've picked up the bones, seven more skulls. Gecko, boss". Prosser could just about hear Dave Thompson asking who was calling, then heard him ask 'Gecko who?'

"Gecko, boss, I'm with your lot now, remember? Mickey Newton, we've met, Boss, are you there?"

"Dave, stop pissing about", said Prosser loudly. "Like Mickey said, seven more skulls hauled out the same lake but from different spots. We'll

17

drop them off with whoever dealt with the other wet bones, let me know where. Nothing to know until Pathology have played with them. You might want to get our divers to come down for more of a look around, there might be a few more yet". Thompson muttered something about budget constraints in reply and hung up.

"What is it with him, Liam?"

"He's winding you up, Mickey, Dave does that. Play along with it, talk intermittently so he misses words, talk about something completely different when answering a question, the price of butter or something but if it's important, don't piss around. You must learn when Thompson has someone in with him too, very important to learn that. You might be on speaker and not want to make a prick of yourself".

Gecko looked confused. It had all been very simple in Vice.

"Cheer-up, Mickey, you'll get the hang of it. Team meeting this afternoon, there should be cake".

There wasn't.

Every face in the room was looking at him, every pair of ears listening as Thompson spelled out his plan for the new joint team. He'd been prepping for a while for the first full team meeting and was happy he'd come up with something reasonably coherent. At the back of the room, Superintendent Perkins watched in case he made a dreadful mistake and had to be demoted on the spot. Ranjit from HR also watched, taking notes, just in case he committed a sin against the minefield of equality. He didn't.

"Obviously I know my old team, I know what they can do and I know where their strengths are but as for you guys", and he waved a hand in the general direction of five men who now occupied their own piece of the room, as if an enemy faction. "I don't know you lot so well although, if you had the balls to work with fiery Marie Burns for so long, that's a pretty good recommendation". There was a 'tumbleweed moment' before a bit of chatter started up. "So Tim, Dan, Harvinder, Lucas, we'll be having one-on-ones, expect more in the coming weeks, Sham I already did. Now, everyone remember to mingle, please". The hubbub continued.

"Shut the fuck up, you lot", yelled Jenny Banks, her Welsh accent getting sharper when pronouncing a swear word. It went very quiet, very quickly.

"Er, thanks Jenny. As I was saying, one-to-ones until we're up to speed with each other. Any problems and my door is that wooden thing in the corner. You all know who the sergeants are, mostly, equal respect at all times, thanks. Oh sorry, one more thing, Joe's off for a few days". The room sat for a moment, then started to fragment as people went to the loo, to the cafeteria or just wandered off.

"I think that went ok, Dave". It was Ranjit, but they called him Ranji, which wasn't the least bit different, phonetically speaking. "You didn't offend any minorities or sexes and all non-binary and alternative-pronoun people seem cool with things. All in all, I think our little courses are working".

"Perhaps, Ranji, but I think I might be a bit busy for courses in the future, unless absolutely essential".

"Do you honestly think I'd send you on non-essential courses, Dave? Next up is an understanding and application of the current guidelines when dealing with Transexuals and people from Essex. I made that last bit up".

"Blokes who are girls and girls who are blokes. What's to learn? If someone wants to be something different, that's fine by me. If they want to use a different pronoun, go for it. Just don't commit crimes and you'll never see me".

"It's not quite that simple, Dave, hence the course, you really need it in your CV. I'll send up a list of ones I have planned for you, in red means compulsory, we'll make a DCI out of you yet, Dave".

"I thought I virtually was one?"

"In training for now but don't worry, you'll soon be as enigmatic as Superintendent Perkins".

"He's done all these courses?"

Ah, no, not all. 'Old dog, new tricks' and all that, but the young bucks like yourself will be the modern face of policing in this country for the next generation and we have to do it right".

Next up was the sergeants' meeting. At least that one wouldn't require him to stand in front of class telling them what they already knew.

"Just the two of us then, Joe's leave was spur of the moment?" asked Prosser, as he and Jenny Banks took their seats.

"Yes. I expected him to let me know when he's coming back by now but his crisis must be more important than he thought", and he looked at Jenny, hoping she might bring some information to the table. She didn't.

"What about Gecko? He's a DS, too. Shouldn't he be in here with us?" continued Prosser, purposely levering boulders onto the smooth path of Thompson's planning. Or at least that was what it felt like.

Thompson looked a little harassed. "Yes, Gecko. I hadn't forgotten him, it's just that I'm not sure just how he's going to fit in here. I'd rather start working with you two, three when Joe gets back, and evaluate Gecko's strengths before getting him more involved."

'I think we all know what Gecko's strengths are", muttered Jenny, darkly.

Thompson looked shrewdly at Jenny. "Right, well", he said, nearly clapping his hands together but remembering the 'Charnley mannerism' fine box, just in time. "I've got Sham sorting through Marie's cases for me, I want Marie's boys to report to both of you for now. I envisage sub-teams by case, I intend to allocate cases to sergeants to lead and will add personnel as required, any questions?"

"Sorry, Dave, but I thought we were here to discuss this, not be told what we're doing. Do you welcome input, or should we just do as the big boss says?" It was Banks, who was being tetchy.

"I'm de-facto DCI, acting or otherwise, and I'm the one who puts his head over the top of the wall every time. Obviously, if anything doesn't work we'll thrash it out between us but, for now, I came up with a starter process and that's what we'll use. What's upset you, Jenny?"

"No, you're right, sorry, it's just Joe. I'm as surprised as you that he's still away. I'm sure there's a good reason though. Liam, the plan, any comments rather than just me being a moaning cow?"

"Speaking as a fairly new DS I'm happy to be guided by our old DS in this. If I think something is shit, I'll say so but we have to get something running, so this is it".

"Good", said Thompson, glad to have got his plan out there at least. "Staffing by case then", and the conversation started in earnest. By the time they'd gone, it was later than expected and another slow ride home but, this time, without incident. Thankfully, the weekend was only a couple of days away, even if part of it was going to be hard labour.

Three

30 June-02 July 2017

"I'm just keeping my fingers crossed that nothing new comes in that's going to put a spoke in the plans". Thompson was chatting to his best friend Cliff Colman on the eve of his move, he was down for driving a rented box van full of Cliff and Elkie's, or DC Laura Knight's, possessions. He'd be going one way, and then bringing Cliff's aunt Joyce's stuff the other. It was going to be a busy weekend. In Netherfield, a few of the lads from Cliff's old fire station would be helping with the loading and unloading, but at Joyce's old place in Radcliffe, it was just him and Cliff for the heavy stuff. Joyce's new boyfriend had cited a bad back for not being around on the day, but Thompson was naturally suspicious.

Colman had noticed the look when they were told. "I know, Dave. I think he's a slimy shit myself, but Joyce is happy". Thompson decided to let it lie and be a simple grunt for the day, it was somehow liberating.

The move went very smoothly, with barely a broken vase. Not that Cliff or Elkie owned any vases. When he left his precious garden for the last time, Cliff was almost in tears until Elkie assured him that the first priority would be a pond at least five-times the size of the old one. It was late afternoon when they'd finally done and Thompson took the van back to the rental place, leaving Cliff and Elkie facing the unpacking at the other end.

"Us next, only a short time to go now, I can't wait to leave this flat", declared Rebecca, when Thompson arrived home aching. "Guess what? I might have a way into the interior design field when I've whelped. An old friend from back home got in touch via mummy. He remembers my

22

creativeness and has offered to look over my ideas for our new place with a view to perhaps putting some work my way, exciting times. I've done some preliminary designs, I'll show you later".

Thompson was too knackered to take everything in and just said 'great'. Interior design to him was about painting walls, laying carpet, putting your junk furniture where you wanted it and then relaxing. He flaked out on the sofa, but a call from work came and he said he had to go in.

"Hello, boss, I didn't expect you to come in on the strength of this, just keeping you up-to-date". It was Prosser who'd been there all day, unpaid as far as Thompson was concerned.

"What's going on, Liam?"

"A dog walker at Colwick was surprised when his little doggie carried a jaw bone back to the car with him. This was a week ago but it's only just found us. Confirmed human, I'll add it to the collection, there might be a bigger bit still at Colwick somewhere, unless we've already got it".

"Fresh?"

"No, just more elderly wet bones. I was speaking to Sham, he reckons Marie was trying to hand it off which is why she did nothing. It's clearly not murder, I doubt it even counts as serious crime, probably just an elaborate prank or maybe a weirdo". Prosser sounded disappointed at the possibility of losing it.

"All the same, we're going to have to get stuck into this one soon, I'm handing nothing off. 'Rule number one', never give things away freely if you want to keep your people happy and occupied. As I see it, we can pick at this one while sorting out the rest of the stuff. I'm more interested in getting a result with Pickles, that would be a more important case to clear up but I don't see much progress, do you? By the way, 'Wet Bones', I like it, thanks for the case name, Liam".

"You're welcome, at least now you've noticed my subtle prompts I can stop saying it now. With Pickles, I think we know it's down to Trevor

Gold, we've just got to find the necessary to back it up. I know we didn't entirely rule out Kieran Joyce, but since he's dead, we'll have a hard time questioning him, besides, the timeline is off. Have you decided who will be doing what cases yet?"

"No, still working through the staff profiles, wading through Marie's stuff, some of which is done, some needs work. Next week we'll do another sergeants' team meet and I'll pass work out. I want Josh and Lorna busy too, I don't want them getting bored and jumping ship. Perkins will expect results across the board and I want to keep a clean desk, that's why I went for three sergeants".

"Got you, boss. Jenny and I have had a further chat, we've got some ideas to supplement yours".

"You didn't want to wait and include Joe? We're a team now".

"I tried to call him, just to get some input, but he wasn't picking up. I left a message though. Ask Jenny to find out the situation, I don't really know what's going on there although I don't think she does either, it's getting to her".

"I'll follow-up. Now I'm here I'll just have an hour with a pile of paper while it's quiet".

"Before you do, Boss, Gecko. I've been working with him a bit, he's much sharper than comes across and I think he'd be ok given the chance. I've not spoken to Jenny about him though, she'd need to buy in if he becomes a consideration, he is a DS after all".

"Did he ask you to talk to me?"

"No, off my own bat, that's why we've been buddying up a bit, so I can see who he really is. He's a bit in awe of you, I think, you must have hit him hard".

Thompson preferred not to revisit that little contretemps. "I've got it on my to-do list to talk to him but for now I've got my three sergeants. Unless the team gets bigger, I can't see a fourth being added".

"I see that, Boss, just thought I'd chip in with an opinion, hope you don't mind".

"If I ever do I'll say so, Liam. I appreciate your insight. Got any on Joe, between you and me?"

"I think his absence and lack of communication is of concern but he's a big boy and can take care of himself. I don't want to speak ill of someone I barely know, it might be thought of as pushing my own case forward. If he doesn't show in a day or two, or talk to Banks, I'd be more concerned".

"Agreed, listen to Marie's lads, see if there's anything we don't know. Right, and, no, that was not a 'Charnley', to the paperwork pile, no prisoners".

Thompson sat at his desk and did some organization. He laid out all the various case papers on the floor, a temporary measure until he got the extra desk he'd decided he wanted. He surveyed his newish realm. Eight current cases, some just needed the court to pronounce on them, a couple needed some leg work, and then there was the Wet Bones and Pickles mysteries. If I don't get any more second-hand cases, it won't be long before everything is mine from the start, he thought. He checked the clock, that can't be right, but it was.

"I thought you'd run away with Banks and left us to fend for ourselves", said Rebecca, humourlessly.

"Sorry, the merger needed urgent work and I had something to deal with. I had to get on top otherwise Monday I'll be there until midnight. Jenny wasn't there".

"Midnight, you say? Oh good, you'll be home early then". It was unlike Rebecca to be sarcastic like that but she had a point. Thompson's days had become inextricably longer with increased responsibility, and maybe lengthened by just a little bit of avoiding hormone-driven mood swings.

"Once I get Marie's cases out the way and everything is running the Thompson way, things will be better and we'll have the new house to keep us busy, too". He knew that mention of their impending move to a virtual derelict in Edwalton always cheered Rebecca up. For himself, he saw weeks, months or even years of living in a hovel while they saved for more improvements.

"I hope so. Anyway, microwave the stuff in the fridge, I have work to do", and she went through into the bedroom.

Re-heated food out of the microwave is rarely great, but Thompson had some more light reading to do and eating became just a necessary function. One note in the folder he'd brought home with him was from Perkins, hand-written, giving him the heads-up that Duncan Collins was throwing random stones to see if he could hit whoever had burnt him out. He'd even bothered the Stones family, who everyone knew were naughty but without conviction, literally. For some reason, the Stones family business had been previously ignored by those who like their lives, and crime, organised. He made a mental note to look the Stones' up, just to have something to work with.

He pulled his sheet of planned responsibilities out and looked it over. Acting on a hunch, he took a red pen and ran a line through Joe Ashworth, instead dividing the cases between Prosser and Banks for now. He was sure Ashworth wouldn't like it much when he came back, but Prosser was right, it was chain-yanking time. 'Be an ogre', Perkins had said. Time to give that a go in Ashworth's case.

Dave Thompson was relaxing, reading the sports section of the Sundays, Rebecca had already grabbed the colour supplements. His arms and shoulders ached after a busy day moving furniture but he felt quite serene for a change. "Do you think we should get tattoos?" asked Rebecca, completely out of the blue. "It's very trendy. I know a few people with them, personal ones, the names of loved ones, that sort of thing".

Thompson had thought about getting the Forest badge tattooed on his left arm, it had been on his mind since he'd seen actor Sean Bean's '100% Blade' tattoo. It was a real mark of allegiance, but he'd deliberately not mentioned it because it wasn't the sort of thing posh birds like Rebecca understood.

"I always think of old sailors when I see tattoos. I get the odd discreet one, but sleeves and tattooed legs and necks leave me cold. Jenny Banks has a tattoo, a Welsh Dragon at the base of her spine, it's actually nicely done".

"Seen it then, have you?" The question was laced with daggers and ice, and changed the atmosphere in an instant.

"Yes, we all have, she showed it off when the office had this same tattoo conversation, recently".

"By your gushing 'nicely done' comment it sounds like you've had a particularly good look. Sure she's not got others for you to check out? You know, 'welcome' or 'enter here' or perhaps 'now wash your hands'?"

"Hey, come on, that's uncalled for. It was an office conversation, she has the dragon, Elkie has a tiny Gambia flag on her arm, Josh has some Chinese script, Liam has some imp thing from home, Carla has a pink bow, me, Joe, and the rest don't have anything, or at least anything they've admitted to. Gecko wasn't there, but he probably has a health warning. That's it, the whole story".

"Forget I even mentioned it, not sure I want to be branded permanently anyway. What are you up to today, flat cleaning, writing?'

27

"No, there's a match and I have some more work stuff to read up on, this change carries more paperwork than ever. I'm beginning to think a DI is just a glorified clerk".

"Well keep the TV down, I have course work to do. Guy's off too, so don't wake him", and with that she went into the bedroom-cum-office and shut the door.

Thompson was baffled, he didn't even know where the conversation had come from or why, but he was beginning to think mentioning Jenny's Welsh Dragon had been a bad idea. He was also glad that he didn't mention that it wasn't the first time he'd seen it, nor how Jenny had reacted when he'd traced the dragon outline with one finger to see if it was embossed, it did look like it was. He hadn't thought that one through either.

The match wasn't up to much, some foreign team on telly in the morning because of the time difference. Proper football in England hadn't started yet, but at least he'd almost got up to speed with all of the outstanding stuff he was supposed to have read. He still didn't quite understand why Marie Burns had had the bones case in the first place, nor why it was now his, but when his master calls and all that.

In the afternoon the atmosphere improved and they went back to the house, again. Rebecca wandered all over the outside and took yet more photos. Then they went to the DIY store, again, while Rebecca looked at decorating stuff. By teatime, both he and Guy were knackered and asleep on the sofa until Rebecca nudged him. She put Guy down then went back to work and so did he. When he finally went to bed, Rebecca was in with Guy again. He had a fitful night's sleep.

Breakfast was dry toast. The noises from the bathroom said child cleaning was taking place, which, in Thompson's opinion, ought to come after Guy had splatted food all over himself and not before. In the fridge, his haslet sandwiches looked less appealing than ever. He was almost out the door when Rebecca appeared. "Sorry about yesterday morning, I was tired. I'll be glad when we can get cracking in the new place, just got to find a man with a hammer".

"I'm still talking to people, the best, most reliable way to find a workman is via word of mouth. I have feelers out, I'll get someone. I still think we should get moved in first and let nature take its course before thinking of knocking the new place about though. And there's the cost, these things don't come cheap".

"I know, it's just that it is all up in the air and will be for a while if we don't get on with it. I know you, so I added any work to be done to the mortgage, Daddy was fine about it when I explained. Only four or so months to go until yet another Thompson sprog crawls out of my nether regions, I'm feeling anxious and I want some things sorted out". Thompson hugged her, but she was a bit stiff, he put it down to her being cramped in bed all night.

"I'll call later, hopefully with good news about the builder. Cliff told me to remind you about the match we're planning to go to, it's a few weeks away yet but forewarned and all that".

"No probs, I'll talk to Elkie. While our men are away we'll have some girlie fun". As Thompson climbed into the car, he reflected that 'girlie fun' was a most un-Rebecca thing to say. It wasn't until he was half way in that the phrase 'added to the mortgage' hit. More money begged from Daddy and without even asking him.

Four

03 July 2017

Thompson's phone light was flashing ominously when he hit his desk. On the way in, they'd played 'Puff the Magic Dragon' on local radio, talking about the supposedly risqué lyrics. After hearing it, all he could think about was the Scandi-noir film 'The Girl with the Dragon Tattoo', which he'd rather enjoyed. He'd been replaying Rebecca's tattoo blow-up in his head, trying to find the reason, but he couldn't. Was she getting bored with him, or he with her?

The office was starting to fill up, only Prosser and Gecko were missing. They seemed to becoming something of a double-act and Thompson wasn't sure he was in favour of that. He'd always tried to rotate people so everyone worked with everyone else. It stopped cliques developing and, with that, rivalries. Like Ranji had said in a recent short course, cringingly, there is no 'i' in team, but you can find it in 'dickhead'. He hadn't carried the room with that one.

"Elkie, a moment please".

"Boss, Dave".

"Elkie, you talk to Rebecca, right? You know, girlie talk. Is she ok? Only she went off the deep end about something and I can't for the life of me understand why".

"She called last night, asked me to confirm the circumstances around us seeing Jenny's tattoo, which I did. It must be hormonal, Dave. Was she like this first time? Only we've talked a lot recently and she's been a bit, well, detached".

"No, first time she was mostly knackered but excited. I'm worried, I'll talk to her later, see what I've done and how I can fix it".

Elkie gave Thompson a look that said 'good luck with that' before going back to her desk.

When Prosser and Gecko arrived back from wherever they'd been, Jenny Banks called a quick briefing. The dead boards were mostly empty, this brief was intended to be more to call a 'state-of-play' and assign tasks. Thompson took his regular place at the back, everyone settled down and Banks started.

"Ok everyone. You've each got a sheet with your actions, this means we've settled on teams for the current cases. Liam will now lead on 'Pickles', we need some evidence there, something more than circumstantial, keep digging. I've got the 'Wet Bones' and, if your name is on the sheet then so have you. Don't worry, I'm sure a still warm corpse will come through that door any minute soon".

With impeccable timing, the door opened and Superintendent Perkins entered. The room burst out laughing. "Do carry on, DS Banks", said Perkins, mystified.

Banks became a bit flustered but quickly recovered. "Resolved cases are in-hand, court dates are known so check if you're needed there. The super-team is officially up and running but, for now, Joe is absent. He's still on personal leave, so it's just Liam and me, or the boss if you want. Actions have been sorted and allocated as I said, but take a look at both active cases and get your thinking heads on"

Two groups formed around two active dead boards. 'Pickles' took pride of place on one board as the best of what most thought a dull bunch of cases. On the other, a row of grinning skulls looked like the most unimaginative identification parade ever.

Thompson looked around but Perkins had vanished, he found him waiting in his office. He signalled for the door to shut.

Perkins started in, with no preamble. "You did your homework, I presume, and so you see why the missing jewel can't be too public? That sort of valuation will spark a lot of tabloid silliness and, while the owner would like it back, it is insured. It has been suggested to me that a local firm were responsible for the removal of said item and we are naturally seeking an audience. I note no mention was made at the briefing, as I asked. Very wise, for now".

Thompson looked a bit confused, until he remembered a brief conversation about a case from Leicester from last week, or maybe centuries ago-it could be hard to tell the two apart, sometimes. "Hang on, all I really got was a photo of some necklace thing with no details, apart from a valuation on the back. I was going to bring it back; I don't see how this is ours".

"Ah, sorry. Keep hold of it for now, David. It's is a new case for you and as I said before, details to follow once I know what we're dealing with", and he left. Outside, Jenny and Lorna were hovering.

Jenny didn't wait for an invite in, so Lorna remarked that she'd catch Thompson later and departed. "How was it? I was a bit nervous in front of new people but they all seemed ok with the allocation and everything. Dave? Jenny calling Dave, anyone home?" Thompson found he'd not taken much in. Instead, he was thinking about how strange Perkins had been and how much he liked Jenny's Welsh lilt.

"Sorry, something ran across my mind. Yes, good brief. Don't worry, you'll get the next decent case, I know that the wet bones job is a bit uninspiring. Speaking to Perkins just now, I might well have something very different coming up for you, I'm just waiting for them throw the complete file my way. Jenny, can I ask your advice, as a woman?"

"You're a woman, Dave? I'm shocked, what should we call you? I see you as a Beryl, or possibly a Hilda".

"Very funny. No, Rebecca threw a wobbly when I told her about your tattoo, she even rang Elkie to confirm my version of events. I can't make sense of it; I thought you might be able to?"

"Do you mean the time I showed everyone the tattoo here, or the wet knicker moment you were responsible for on the course?"

Thompson blushed. "The first one".

"She's just being hormonal, Dave, a she-bitch defending her territory. It can't be easy for her when her man is surrounded by hot totty, even if I say so myself".

"Did someone mention me? I heard hot totty and came running. Oh, it's you, Dave".

"Very funny, Elkie, and after we've been...intimate".

"I've got work to do", said Jenny. "I'll leave you two to reminisce about moments of close proximity. Be gentle with him, Elkie, he's feeling emasculated and you, Dave, no more making any knickers wet".

Elkie looked at Thompson quizzically, so he explained about how he'd asked Jenny's advice about the whole tattoo thing too, but leaving out the whole 'knicker' scenario, he was still blushing slightly. When he'd finished, Elkie agreed with Jenny. "Hormones, I already told you, listen to your friends and be nice to her". She also told him to treat Rebecca to something she'd dropped hints for, if he'd noticed any.

"You might be right there. What I need is a reliable builder, any ideas?"

"I was thinking more a nice gift, something personal, intimate even but as it happens, we've just found a bloke, Pete Wheeler. A bit fly but does good work so I'm told and, while he's said to make a nice job, don't ask too many questions about him would be my advice".

"I can't hire a villain, especially not to work where I live. What if we have to nick him?"

"He's not a villain as such, but someone who settles disputes using the local builders' form of Sharia law. Nothing has ever been proven, no convictions, a few tickets, all paid, one assault charge, withdrawn. I checked with a mate at Carlton nick who knows him. Obviously, I thought the same as you but she said not to worry".

"We're getting desperate now, Rebecca has decided that she wants the work done before she issues, that means starting soon and being finished before the end of November. Does he do extensions, do you know?"

"Yep, roofs, extensions, the lot. We were impressed when we talked to old customers. He's not shy about letting you check, he's just a bit of a rough builder, aren't they all?"

"Why am I only hearing of your adventures in procuring someone willing to undertake house renovation now?"

"We thought you were sorted. Here, this is him, call him, you won't be disappointed", and she took the number from her phone, Thompson jotted it down. We've pencilled him in for next year. It suits us as it'll be after I issue myself although we won't be knocking holes in walls and having a roof. Be warned with Wheeler, he's in demand and might be busy".

To Thompson's surprise, half-an-hour later Wheeler was promising a home visit that evening to discuss. He said he'd had a cancellation and the job would fill it nicely. Rebecca was texted with the good news and Thompson thought her response to it bordered on the almost cheerful. Then he thought about the mess and months of having hairy-arsed builders around every day and regretted mentioning it to Elkie at all. He wandered out into the office and found who he was after. "Lorna?"

Lorna Meikle followed Thompson back into his office and shut the door. She sat and waited while he opened a file. "Sorry about Jenny pushing in front like that, she's trying to make her mark here. You wanted a word?"

"Sir, I'm looking to transfer out, Sir".

"Oh, really, sorry to hear that and I'm more than a bit disappointed, you've only been here five minutes. Who upset you?"

"It's not you or the team, Sir, Dave, it's just I can't seem to stop thinking I'm not home, you know, where I belong. I never thought it would be a problem, but I seem to be going home to London sometimes even for just half a day, and it's getting silly. Hearing we were adding a body to the team with a new DC was a catalyst for the request, I have options at home".

"I think I understand. My partner comes from the south and she still calls her parent's place 'home'. It's not something that would happen to me, I was out of Clifton as soon as I could. I won't get in your way Lorna, work provided, do you have any sort of timeframe?"

"I was waiting for your say-so, Sir. I have an interview this week so a day off would be nice".

"Go, use your day, we'll cope. Like you say, we have a new DC, when he gets here. I've enjoyed working with you, briefly. Lorna Meikle, a star in the making I think".

"Thanks, Dave. I'm really grateful for your understanding and that I didn't have to follow Carla's advice".

"What advice?"

"She said I should bring my volleyball knee-pads in just in case I had to spend time in here, er, kneeling".

Thompson laughed. "Well, Carla would know".

"Oh, sorry, Sir, I thought it was a joke, not that I don't like you and everything but, you know".

"I was joking, Lorna", said Thompson, suddenly worried.

"Me too", said Lorna laughing. "You know, I think your team have corrupted me. My friends back home say a visit to Nottingham has broadened my horizons".

"Back to work, we'll fix up a drink before you go. The new boy's first solo task, I think".

As Lorna left, another body entered. Thompson was already head-down reading when a polite cough had him looking up sharply. "Sir, are you lost?" Thompson bit his tongue; it had just slipped out unintentionally but to have Assistant Chief Constable Osbourne in your office wasn't normally a good thing.

"Detective Inspector, I just thought to pop down and put your mind at ease. I see young Simon's arrival is imminent and I want to assure you that I despise nepotism and expect him to receive no favours or special treatment. Superintendent Perkins assures me that you and your team are a good place for him to be at this stage of his career. I find him to be an able lad, very good at exams but perhaps light in terms of world experience and practicality. Do not hold back, teach him to be a detective".

"Nepotism?"

"Yes, we are related, Simon is my sister's boy, I thought you already knew".

"Yes, of course, Sir. Busy, you know how it is". Was Osbourne giving him a compliment in placing his nephew in his group, or was he being used as a dumping ground, safe in the knowledge that if he turned out to be not officer material, Thompson would be less keen to dump the big boss's relative? "Anything else, Sir?"

"No, carry on", said Osbourne and he left. As he exited the office, the hubbub outside ceased abruptly, then slowly recovered.

Thompson called Ranji in HR to find out where his baby cuckoo was. "He won't be here for a week, yet, Dave, and when we do get him we're going to hang on to him for a day or so, just to iron out the odd crease before we drop him in at the deep end. You do know about the ACC?"

"He's just been in my office talking of his hatred for nepotism, Ranji. I hope Simon is not going to make us wonder about that?"

"Like I said, Dave, a few wrinkles but nothing serious. I'm sure he'll do well with you, it's not like I suggested it or anything". *Click!*

Rush hour wasn't very rushed and Thompson got home in plenty of time for Elkie's rough-arsed builder to arrive, or so he thought. When he got in, there on the sofa was a well-built guy who was obviously used to working in the great outdoors. Ruddy-complexioned but otherwise smartly dressed, he was showing Rebecca some photos in a binder. On seeing Thompson, he jumped straight up and offered a shovel of a hand. "You must be Dave. Your lovely wife was telling me about the place you've just bought, charming, just needs a bit of TLC. She showed me her plans too, very Imaginative. I'll wander over to the house in the next day or two for a shufti and then, once you're in, we can sort out dates. Pleasure to do business with such nice people".

Rebecca got up, handed him back his binder and let him out. They heard him clumping off all the way to the front door.

"What a nice man, a rough diamond, I'd say. He showed me photos of his work, you did well there, Dave, just what I'm looking for".

Thompson felt his chest tighten. "I thought I was a part of this discussion? I wanted to feel him out, get a sense of who he is, make sure he's legit. We've not even talked price".

"All done, nothing for you to do here. I thought you'd be pleased that I keep this sort of thing off your busy plate, given all the long hours you and your sergeants seem to work. He reckons he'll be all done five weeks before I eject your child into the world, which suits me. Wash your hands, for dinner tonight I'm trying a vegetarian recipe from a friend".

"A what?"

"Don't knock it until you try it. You won't recognise anything, just open your mouth and swallow, God knows I've..."

37

"Yes, thank you very much, I get it".

Half-way through dinner, Rebecca had to do a facetime with someone from what she insisted on calling 'home'. Thompson wasn't really paying attention, something he'd eaten kept repeating on him and it wasn't something pleasant like Angel Delight. He cleaned up what he hadn't managed to blindly shovel down and waited for Rebecca to come back but she didn't, so he watched some cricket highlights and had a beer, then a second.

Five

25 July 2017

"Where are you, boys?" Ritchie Johnson was ready to move again but the car he'd been using was making a funny noise and the girl didn't have a car, she couldn't drive. Across town, another house, another bed awaited him. He'd keep moving until things quietened down a bit, until the heat was off. That thought made him laugh. Heat, that was a stupid idea, one of his worst.

"We're out Wollaton way, just picked some bits up, legit, nothing to worry about, why?"

Matt could be a nosey and argumentative sod. He shouldn't be asking why, he knew not to piss Ritchie off otherwise it would be 'Postcards from Brazil' time and waive your share of the fee, when they got it. He verbally gave Matty the address and waited. While he was in any of the houses the girls couldn't work and, while this was a big fee he'd be getting, thanks to a bit of help, it didn't make sense not to have ready cash available for when you needed it. Brazil sounded good, he'd ask his contact about that, she did business there, she should know.

The car pulled up, a decent-looking SUV for a change, they'd look like just another bunch of bored commuters once they got going. Ritchie left the house with his rucksack, it held all his personal possessions for this mobile phase, and the prize, all tucked away safe.

"Taxi for Johnson. Where to, Sir?"

"Very funny Matty, drop me at the end of the Embankment and I'll walk the rest of the way". In the back, behind his seat, was a black blanket, he lifted it up. "What the fuck are these, boys?" Under the blanket he could see a pile of flat screen TVs, boxed, expensive ones.

"Just a bit of stuff we've got customers for, nothing to worry about, Ritchie, we didn't expect to be seeing you for a while, we gotta eat". His other brother, Igor, although his real name was Christopher, was letting his annoyance at everything taking so long show.

"Find somewhere to pull over, I'll flag a taxi", said Ritchie, not at all happy to be in a car with some hot gear. "I told you we'd be good for a long time after this but you just couldn't break the habit of a life time, you thick pair of cunts".

"Hey, watch your mouth little brother, or I'll put my fist in it. You don't boss me around like you do your women", snarled Igor.

"Can't stop here, Ritchie, nearest place I can pull over is the next junction, half a mile but you won't get a taxi there. Besides, if you do and it's one of Collins', what then? Do we get to go through your possessions to divide them up? Sit tight, we'll be there in ten minutes, not much traffic this way, we'll breeze along the Embankment, drop you and be on our way". Matty was brighter than Igor, but not by much. Ritchie sat back and waited, if they went along normally and didn't attract attention, they'd be fine.

"I'll be there in twenty minutes", was all he said into his phone before putting it back in the waterproof pouch and sticking in the pocket of the rucksack. He opened up the main pack and checked, he was nervous. Everything was still there, but one of the plastic clips on the rucksack had broken, typical of designer shit.

"Do you shag 'em all, these birds of yours?" said Igor, it had been on his mind for some time. Ritchie said nothing, he wasn't willing to discuss his other lines of income, not with his thicko brothers. They were happy making a few quid knocking things off, he had bigger plans. He looked back at the white car and thought he saw something.

"Pick it up a bit, Matty, look behind you".

"Oh, fuck! Hold on", and he floored it. The SUV shot off, weaving between cars. Behind them the white car was following, catching up, a blue light had appeared.

Ritchie put his head in his hands. "Not now, please, not now". He knew his brother could drive, but some of his handling surprised even him, then they clipped the curb. There was nothing in it, but the low-profile tyres left the rims and everything was a shower of sparks and grinding noises. Some way ahead, more lights were approaching, they were going to get boxed in. "Stop here", yelled Ritchie, as the car slewed all over the road. Matty threw it into the curb and stopped. In an instant all three were out and running.

To their right the Trent was waiting. Ahead and behind there were cops, to their left another two unmarked cars with flashing blue lights had appeared. "We're going to have to jump, swim the river, get lost in Wilford, come on", and Ritchie was up and over the little black rail and gone. The cops shouted something, Matty looked at Igor and they made an unspoken agreement, they jumped.

"Why are we bothering again?" asked the uniform to his mate, the driver, as they sat in the gloom. "They'll have dumped and torched the car by now. Look at it out there, every few minutes a hundred cars have gone past, we're wasting our time here, we don't even know what sort of SUV it might be". The driver ignored his colleague. He was a known moaner, never happier than when putting the world to rights with his one-sided and frankly dodgy opinions. It was a wonder that he'd not had a good smack in the mouth before now, he was overdue. "I mean, it's only a bunch of chancers nicking a telly or something. We're supposed to be doing more important stuff these days, not sitting here hoping the arseholes come past and give us a cheery wave".

The driver had seen the Kia SUV coming their way and noticed that it was driving 'over-normally', the way people did when they didn't want to attract attention. It was like a sixth-sense that you got when you worked in Traffic, people always clinched their sphincters when they saw a cop car, it was natural. Those that didn't were the ones you were interested in because they had the balls to do breaks-ins and nick stuff, although, these days, owning a pair of balls were not always a prerequisite. He slipped the car into gear.

"Half the local economy revolves around people nicking and selling flat-screen TVs", the uniform droned on. "It's seen more as an income supplement these days, not like cyber-crime, that's where the cutting edge lies, that's what I'm aiming for. What?"

The white unmarked car pulled out briskly and the driver hoped that the SUV hadn't noticed. Within a few minutes it was obvious that they had. Speeds increased, lights went on and the yapper in the passenger seat thankfully shut up. Soon another car joined the chase as the SUV was very skillfully thrown around corners, cut through gaps and generally tried to make as much space between it and the chasers as possible. The cop car driver was quietly impressed with the driver of the chased car, a grudging respect for someone obviously able to handle a vehicle. Clarkson would have been proud.

Inevitably the SUV slipped and banged into the curb, flipping off two tyres in a shower of sparks. In moments the occupants were out and on foot, one trying to sling a rucksack on as he ran for it. It was pretty pointless running because they could see that the other cops ahead were just waiting for them to come to them. To their left was traffic and more cops, to the right the River Trent slid steadily past at the bottom of a steep wall. There was a path down there too, a painful one if you jumped for it and didn't clear it.

The three men stopped, they'd run fifty yards and clearly thought their chances of a wet landing offered better odds than those of hitting the treed bank further back. The first guy, the one with the rucksack, jumped. The other two stood for a moment as the police closed in. They didn't seem to fancy it at all.

"Come on lads, nowhere to go", yelled a voice ahead. "Give it up, now".

The two remaining men disagreed and went the only other way that there was to go, for them.

Slowly the traffic picked up speed, the police were obviously busy so people relaxed and didn't worry too much about their speed, forgetting that the cameras were always on duty on that particular bit of road. The gloom became evening and evening became night.

Distant lights played on the river surface as a boat eased under a bridge. Eventually, the boat arrived, two bright spotlights on the front scanning the surface. Joe Meade knew what he was doing, he'd been skipper on the old police launch until the powers-that-be binned the service in the 1990s and put him behind a desk to graze. His own boat, that everyone including Meade still referred to as the 'police launch' and that used the old mooring sometimes, had been regularly pressed into duty in emergencies involving the river and Meade relished the chance to get back behind the wheel. Once he retired, there would be no more boats to help out, just the divers and they usually only worked days.

Meade eased his boat into the shore and tied up. "Not seeing anything, pretty rough here with undercurrents and a lot of water. I'll work both banks a while but my bet is the fish will be having a party later, one or all of them might find the chains on the tanks at Colwick. I can probably look there tomorrow if you like but I'd tell the Colwick wardens, they'll keep an eye out. Mangled and bloated bodies tend to upset picnickers". Meade was very much old-school, with a line in gallows humour that many of the fresh-faced officers in the force didn't get. After Meade, the oldest officer there was the lead driver, Wade Morris. He got the joke.

"Thanks Joe, take your time, this was the Johnson boys, all three. With luck we've saved the world a whole load of grief in one big splash". Meade cast a look that said 'careful' but it was too late.

"Care to expand on that officer, Wade isn't it?" It was Sheila Wright, a local journalist who'd managed to sneak up close, despite the presence of officers who were supposed to stop that sort of thing. Her phone was out and apparently picking up everything that was said.

Morris looked at her as if the river was an option for her, too, but Meade stepped in. "Hello Sheila, scanning the airways for titbits? Someone will give you the details later, I expect. Off the record, three blokes wanted for a crime decided to jump into the Trent rather than give themselves up. It should all be on CCTV, God knows everything else is. You know the score with some people, the planet's better without them".

"Just doing my job, Joe, not long left now, eh?"

"A couple of weeks, Sheila, I'm ready. You?"

"Soon, I think. Another change of owners at the paper, people who only want some things reported, and others swept where they can't be seen. We stopped serving the public interest years ago".

"Care to expand on that, Sheila?"

"Touché, Joe. I'll wait for the suits to show up. No hard feelings, Wade? Got to ask, don't worry, it wasn't recording", and she waggled the phone.

Morris ignored her, he knew that tales about officers talking to the press got back to the station and he didn't want to have a finger pointed at him. Joe didn't give a flying fuck any more, he harked back to a better time in Morris's opinion.

When Morris got back to the car, his partner was telling anyone who'd listen about the exciting chase and how the blokes who'd jumped in were scum. Morris looked around, in case any other reporters might be listening in, but none were obvious. These days that often didn't matter, because every phone could record exactly what was said, along with photos and video. "In the car", he said curtly

"Yes, Sir", said his partner, clearly not happy at being spoken to that way. "I don't know what you're snappy about, we got a result there. Three shits dead, a good night's work in my book".

"Keep talking and I'll take you somewhere quiet and make it look like an accident, understand?" It suddenly went very quiet. The yapper had heard rumours that Morris could be touchy, and Morris had made sure the rumours were out there as a form of insurance against twats like his current partner.

They sat in the car and waited in silence until Morris recognized a newly-arrived detective that he'd met before, then he climbed back out to talk to him. The detective listened, made a few notes and then sent him on his way telling him that they were to talk to no one, which was odd. As senior uniform present and lead pursuer, he'd expected more of a grilling in the circumstances, but it never came.

Back at the station he wrote his report and emailed it to his boss, printing a copy for himself and slipping it into his pocket. A few minutes later his boss was there with him, telling him that he was taking a few days of desk work in the station. Not a favourite occupation, but at least he'd be shut of his mouthy twat of a partner for a while.

"All is tidy at our end, Sir, I'll send everything over now. Meade came out but he found nothing. Morris is a good lad, I'd talk to him if you want to get any sense out of anyone. Any idea why this isn't going to Internal Affairs yet? I know the Johnsons are arseholes of the first order but it all seems bit unusual". Ian Berritt was doing as he'd been told, but a bit more by way of a reason why would have been welcome.

"Wish I knew more myself, Ian, I do as I am bid the same way you do. I expect that we'll find out, eventually. My man Thompson is very reliable, a solid team too, I'm sure they'll be professional in all things".

"Thanks, Mr. Perkins, I'd appreciate being kept in the loop".

"Me, too. I'll pass on what I'm allowed but, as you know, mightier forces than we guide our hands and it is not for our level to speculate at what those of higher rank are thinking. Good day to you".

Ian Berritt shook his head and looked at the now silent phone. Sometimes talking to Chalky Perkins was like being an extra in a Jane Austen novel.

Ritchie Johnson looked up from the bank trying to figure out just where he was. His lungs were bursting, everything was cold and ached and the rucksack on his back was a dead-weight of water. Lights were everywhere and he finally figured out that he was a few miles downstream near Rivermead flats, a 1970s development that was now aged but that had fancied itself at one time, not any more. He threw the rucksack up the bank and followed it. As far as he knew, hoped, his brothers were doing the same somewhere else, hopefully on the opposite bank from the police. He was also wishing he'd not cadged a ride with his brothers. If he'd know the thick twats had done a place beforehand, he'd have stayed well clear.

Getting his breath back, he undid the one remaining clip on the rucksack and eased back the flap. Trent Water doesn't smell particularly nice close up and this was pretty close. He eased the bag over and gradually emptied out all the water. Nothing followed. He shook the rucksack a few times, nothing, everything had come out. Shit, he'd have been better off not finding his way out of the river because now, when certain people found out, he wasn't going to survive anyway. He reached for his phone in the zipped-up back pocket of the rucksack, it was still there and in its waterproof pouch, a legacy from when he'd run 'Swim with Dolphins' sessions off Penzance one summer. He dialled, but got no answer to the first number. He dialled again and a female voice answered. "It's me, get to Rivermead Flats, wait by the shop". He didn't wait for an answer.

He was feeling very cold, shaking violently. He thought he was probably suffering from hypothermia but he didn't have to wait long until the little hatchback appeared. He dived into the passenger seat, the heater already full-on. "Drive".

The day after the event, social media was busy banging likes onto a short piece of video taken by a driver waiting at traffic lights directly opposite the Johnsons launch point. He'd got all three men jumping and several police officers running forward to see where they'd gone, but not much more. A muffled toot told the viewer the clip had ended as the lights changed and the filmer had to move, the unedited video shaking as it ended. Three blokes being chased by police and leaping into the Trent was mildly interesting, but some people had to be home for their tea.

In the small house, Ritchie Johnson watched the computer screen as he and his brothers vanished over the little black fence attached to the low wall. He'd hit the water hard but was a strong enough swimmer to get control and cross the Trent, despite the rucksack, then he'd had some luck. He'd found an ancient lifebelt that yobs must have thrown in upstream, probably years ago. It was tangled in weeds right up close to the bank. He'd grabbed it and, despite the cold, kicked off further into the flow to get as far away as he could. He'd seen the boat with the spotlights coming and ducked under just in time. Luckily the bloke on board hadn't bothered to try to recover the lifebelt.

"You need to get out of Nottingham, Ritchie. You know people will be looking for you, they don't piss about, these people". The girl looked suitably concerned, but it might just have been that she wanted Johnson gone so as not to implicate her. What if the cops looked at Rivermead CCTV? She'd be screwed and, if anyone else found out she'd helped him, she'd be dead.

"I made a call, I'll be gone later. You talk to nobody, right, and if they ask you why you was at Rivermead, you tell them you was working. Make it convincing, get arrested if you have to". The girl was quiet. Ritchie Johnson could have a temper but he didn't usually hit any of his girls. Nobody buys bruised apples.

"Sorry about your brothers, they're probably hiding out too. You know what they're like, indestructible that pair".

"Not this time", was all he said, and she could see that he meant it.

Johnson was picked up by another young woman in a newish Ford. He didn't thank anyone for the rescue, the food or the place to hide, he just told the girl to earn some money. She watched him go, stripped the bed and bagged up the towels. She cleaned anything he'd used from the bathroom, then combed each room in the place for signs he'd been there. Her brother showed up an hour later, with his mates, and within two, the car and contents were well ablaze near Holme Pierrepont. Then she reported the car stolen before posting her house keys through the letterbox. This was her chance.

Six

28 July 2017

It was never not busy in the department, but that suited Dave Thompson. If he had to admit it, he'd prefer to be doing the door knocking and interviewing himself, but his expanded group was going to take a lot of steering. Like most things in life, it had just been dropped on him and he was supposed to make it work while the likes of Superintendent Perkins threw stingers into his path. One thing was for sure, he was going to do things his way now. His way had worked for him this far, there was no need to abandon a tried and tested method. The tap on the door was probably Pixie, thought Thompson, she had a distinctive knock that said 'excuse me, Sir, but I'm not fussed if you don't'. It was a good edge for an officer of the law to develop, especially in one so young. "It's open", he shouted and Carla Adams came in with a box, plonking it down on his desk.

"Another gift from above, Dave".

Normally Thompson got Perkins' distinctive voice telling him more work and worry was coming his way, there had been nothing this time which probably meant he'd get a visit in person. Oh good.

"Thanks, Carla". He was busy and didn't want any banter. She took the hint, Carla was fully in-tune with Dave Thompson and his modus operandi, although she knew that she could get his attention with a well-placed bacon cob, lightly laced with brown sauce, his Achilles Heel. The next knock, shortly after, confused Thompson. He didn't recognise it, so he decided it was either Josh or Lorna and that he was not up to speed with the rhythm of their delivery on his door yet. "Yes?" It was a yes of 'addressing a junior officer' quality.

"Ah, David, sorry to bother you. Good, I see you have the files". It was Superintendent Perkins in what was surely a first for him, actually knocking on the door.

"Sir, what can I do for you?"

"This is a new case for you to investigate sensitively, the details are in the box. I just wanted to personally stress the importance of discretion, people in society seem to be making their presence felt over this, that's all, we'll talk later", and he left, just walked out. Thompson was surprised to see him actually leave, he was almost convinced Perkins could teleport from office to office.

Thompson leafed through the case documents thoroughly. This didn't seem right, it was surely an internal, what wasn't he being told? Annoyed at the apparent cloak-and-dagger nature of the case he picked up the file and set off for Perkins' office. He wasn't expecting the ACC to be leaving just as he arrived. Osbourne stopped and seemed to be about to say something, then he obviously changed his mind and wandered off.

"Come in David, I assume you are now up to speed. I was on my way down again to make clarifications, but here you are in all your glory". Perkins was being weird. Again.

"Explain to me why this is us and not Internal Affairs, Sir". Behind Perkins, Thompson realised he was looking at a tropical fish tank. How long had that been there?

"The jewel we spoke of before and this case are related. Sources suggest that Stanley Richard Johnson was transporting a certain piece of jewellery when he went into the river, so you see this incident is a part of the jewellery robbery investigation. If you find Johnson, you might find the jewel, it's as simple as that. There will be a formal internal investigation in parallel, but your focus is Stanley Johnson. I see you are admiring my fish tank, my little hobby, it gives me peace".

"Can I assume that whoever has had an eleven million pound trinket nicked is able to exert certain pressure on senior people through various, legal means, resulting in us at ground level being charged with taking up their cause?" asked Thompson, not mentioning the fish tank because he'd decided that it was there to deliberately confuse people.

"Very nicely put, David. Remember that phraseology and sentence structure and save it for when you sit in this chair, it confuses the hell out of senior and junior officers alike".

"While I'm here, Sir, I've been wondering. Where did Tilda come from? I know she worked Vice and she's quite rightly declined to furnish me with details of that, but I need to know my officers, what they've done, where they've been, I need that information to build trust. I remember you hinted before about her chosen profession, before not choosing to tell me she was one of ours. The other girl with her when I first met her, was she one of ours, too?"

Perkins attitude changed and Thompson noticed. "Alas not. Tilda has worked in different areas and her service record has some details that she might best explain personally. I'll speak to people about the release of more information from her file. Now, if there's nothing more then, please, back to the battle. I'll feed you what else I can re the stolen jewel later. Good day".

Sometimes, after another strange conversation with Perkins where Thompson was convinced that words, or even complete sentences, had been omitted from the conversation, he could see why his old boss, Jock Charnley, had developed his paranoia. His own was shaping up nicely. No sooner had he sat at his desk than Perkins arrived, this was getting to be of farce proportions. Carry on Super!

"There's something else, I'd prefer it if you were the one talking to the officer who chased the car first. Go alone and just collect the salient details for now".

Thompson knew he only got the bits of information Perkins allowed him, but so far things had turned out ok. If Perkins wanted him, and him alone, to do a bit of background that was fine by him too. At least it got him out from behind his desk. Seizing the bull by the horns, he let people know he was going out for an hour and headed over to Traffic.

"Hello again, Dave, how's the back-end?"

Thompson did a double-take. It was the traffic cop who'd attended his rear-ending.

"Wade Morris, isn't it? How's it going?"

"It was going all right until those three dickheads leapt into the Trent. I'm correct in assuming that is why you're here, yes?"

"Obviously there's an Internal into the activity, but it's in the public domain already so a foregone conclusion. I've got a case linked to the scrotes who jumped. I'm particularly interested in the one with the rucksack".

"Scrotes, don't tell me, you were raised watching The Sweeney?"

"Something like that although I'm no Jack Regan. This is just a chat between us Wade, no tapes. That will be done during the Internal and by someone else. First question, why did you pursue?"

"We'd had a watch notice for a bunch of robbers in a SUV, it was in my 'to do' tray. I just assumed we'd had a nod from somewhere, maybe a favour. We get the odd request for cars to look out for, sometimes they're owned by another cop or relative, we had one for your lot a while ago I remember, Carla someone".

"Yes, I remember it well and it was found so all's good there. This watch then, you'll have to excuse me, I never worked Traffic. You get the heads-up and then what, if you see the suspect car you pursue and apprehend?"

"Yes, but we don't get many contacts, there's too many cars on the road".

"The one with the bad guys in, what made you pursue there?"

"I saw it coming, it was an SUV and it looked odd. Most drivers are going over the speed limit if only by a bit, fact of life, but when they see us, or even get a hint, they slow down to under, always under. This car I saw from way off, it was going steady. I checked the speed and it was spot-on, being careful. As it went past, I saw that it had three blokes in it, I thought I recognized them as a bunch of shits 'known to us', as they say, so I eased out and into traffic".

"Did they see you straight away?"

"That's what made me more suspicious, they reacted and the driver floored it. Whoever it was at the wheel, he could handle the car. Even when it threw two tyres I thought they still might give it a go, but they stopped, almost as if jumping in the Trent had been a viable option already considered".

"Interesting, but the river was in spate, it has been forever with the shit weather we've been getting. Who jumped first?"

"You know it was Stanley Johnson, the one with the rucksack. The other two heard the lads up front, even I could hear them above the traffic noise, although most of the cars were only crawling. Stanley jumped, the other two paused, then followed".

"How long between?"

"Maybe thirty seconds, they were obviously doubting the sense in jumping".

"What happened after?"

"Joe Meade appeared, somebody must have called him. I doubt he just happened to be on the river in that flow. He found nothing. Searching was next to impossible so when a suit showed up, no offence, we went back to base".

"We?"

"Me and my partner, the lemon who watched us push that car in the rain, remember?"

"Right. Then you made a report and knocked off. I looked for the report on the system and couldn't find it for the 'day of', but it was there for today. I put it down to a slow system, any thoughts?"

Wade leaned forward. "You seem straight, Dave so I'm taking a leap of faith here", and he slipped Thompson a copy of his own copy. "Just a bit of back-watching. I filed straight away, I've never had a delayed one before". With the chat concluded, Thompson shook hands with Morris and let him get back to his desk work. Since the event he'd been kept indoors but he'd been assured it wasn't for long.

Back in the office, Thompson checked the copy he had of Morris's report against the one on file, they matched, then he scrolled through his numbers but he didn't have one for Meade, so he called John Fraser at Colwick, thinking Meade might moor there. "You're in luck, he isn't here but I have his mobile", and Fraser repeated the number, clearly enunciating every syllable. Meade turned out to be working in the records office of Central Nick, so Thompson popped down to see him.

"Joe, seeing out your time in the dark?"

"Something like that. I'd prefer to be out on the river but times change. Dave Thompson, I worked with you and your team recently, I remember. Netherfield wasn't it, dead bloke under the bridge?"

"Yes, that was us. I just have one question, Joe. Who asked you to take your own boat out on the river on the night the Johnsons leapt in?"

"He has ACC as part of his title", and Meade touched his nose.

"Here?"

Meade nodded. "Sorry, if I don't get this done I'll have to be here on my own time and I don't owe them that. Good luck with this one, smells funny to me. I don't know why the ACC called, I suppose someone even higher up was pushing his buttons, and someone with money or influence was pushing his in turn, that's how it works these days, Dave. I wouldn't trust any of them as far as I can throw them and, if I did get to throw them, it would end in a splash. Stopping the police boat then asking favours, it really pisses me off".

"Any idea why someone might slow a report getting on the system?"

"Buy a bit of time, slow people down a bit, depends what was slowed and who slowed it. Was it unedited when it came up on the system?"

"Yes, that's the odd thing. I'll not fret about it, I would if it wasn't there at all though. Thompson thanked him, leaving him to his bits of paper to file. He knew exactly how he felt and he had sympathy about the police boat, binning it had made no sense, not when you had a major river to police.

The hours had ticked by and he knew it was time he was hitting the road home. As he fetched his jacket, Lorna stopped him. "Elkie tells me you're moving house tomorrow boss, good luck. Nothing quite so exciting as moving to a new house". Lorna, while at times intimidating, had a way of doling out enthusiasm so that it washed off on you. Thompson had seen the moving as a chore, something to get over and done with, but she was right, yes it was exciting, but also represented a long road of expense.

"Obviously I'm quite excited at the prospect of lugging boxes and furniture across south Notts, but this will be a good move, I hope. We'll finally be in a house and not a pokey flat. If I look exhausted on Monday, you'll know why".

"How will we tell?" she said, laughing. She had a point, the face in the mirror in the morning was starting to look like somebody else's, more and more.

Seven

29 July-30 July 2017

It took Cliff and Dave only about an hour-and-a-half to empty the flat and load the van. It didn't look much, it didn't even fill it, but Cliff kept pointing out that it was only a small flat and that they'd soon fill the new place. As the flat door closed for the last time, Thompson didn't even notice. The place had become less friendly recently and he was glad to see the back of it. He knew, in the recesses of his mind, that it was wrong to blame the flat, but it was the only cause for the recent edginess he'd been feeling that came to mind.

"Do you know what they're up to, Cliff?" Rebecca had been picked up by Elkie and they'd gone off to B&Q. "We did say we'd move in before buying stuff, that way you don't end up wasting money".

"Relax, Elkie's buying some paint, Rebecca is helping her out and pricing things up, it'll keep them busy and out of the way while we do the lugging about".

It was an odd feeling getting to the house and unloading the stuff from the flat, each item colour-coded by Rebecca to make sure they put it in the right room. In the cold light of having to live there now, the house looked much worse than he'd remembered, even though they'd been back often. Maybe the rose-tinted scales were falling off. When it was all done, Thompson was surprised at how little of the new place they'd filled. Luckily, some furniture from the previous owner remained but probably not for long.

Cliff took the van back while Thompson tried to do a bit of tidying and organizing. A lot of the stuff already in the house was dated, but next to their hand-me-downs it looked positively new. All he could see in his minds-eye was delivery trucks rolling up, disgorging themselves of expensive appliances, while their bank account shipped cash. His phone went, and he was relieved to see it was one of the lads confirming the new five-a-side league season start date and was he in?, they needed to know soon. Was he? Thompson really didn't know "I'll get back to you, I just moved house, I'm carrying boxes".

It was an hour before Elkie showed up, having picked up Cliff from the van rental place on the way back from the shopping trip. She came in for a look around, she'd not seen the house before, just photos. "Lots to keep you busy, Dave. Excited?"

"What? Yes, naturally". It didn't sound much like it.

"Don't worry, things will be better with more space, you won't keep tripping over each other like you did in the flat and Rebecca will be able to pour her creative talents into the house, you'll see". Thompson thought of how distant they could be in the flat, in a bigger place like this they'd never see each other if they didn't want to. Rebecca was moving from room to room to check that the colour-coding system had been followed. When she got back downstairs she looked how Thompson had been feeling. He didn't know what to say that would sound sincere, so he said nothing and waited.

"I thought this might feel different when we finally got here but, it just feels like we've got so much work to do", she said as Thompson was busy setting up the TV.

"Daunting, but we did say we'd take our time, follow your schedule and do rooms as and when we can. It'll look different once you've organised our stuff a bit, and when we start ordering appliances".

"About that, à fridge and a cooker were on sale so I bought them. Essential items so I made an executive decision. I'm planning on a dishwasher, a new washer and a dryer too, once I find the models I want".

In Thompson's head, a cash register ringing up five grand went 'ker-ching'.

"We'll be off then, don't forget to christen the new house tonight, just don't start until we're out of here". The laughs at Cliff's joke were a bit stilted. Rebecca had become less keen on any 'christening' these days, but to be fair she wasn't alone in that feeling.

Sunday was better and Rebecca much brighter. Even Guy was good, with minimal yowling and unplanned food redistribution. Waking up, the new place felt odd, not least because Rebecca had insisted in being in with Guy during his first night in strange place. Breakfast happened as they stepped over boxes, but slowly they were being cleared of their contents and then folded up and stored 'for next time' as Rebecca had said. By late afternoon, the house was looking like someone loved it, or had at least showed it some affection for a few hours. In the evening, after Guy had gone up, the conversation happened.

"Are we ok, Dave?"

Thompson wanted to shout 'WHAT?' They'd moved house, had a second child coming, were into her parents for enough to buy a luxury yacht and she was asking that now? What he did was play dumb. Rebecca carried on.

"We seem distant a lot of the time, you're at work a lot more too. I have to keep showing Guy photos of you so he knows who his daddy is. I'm worried. I know I've been distracted too, I've been trying to fill my time with other things besides baby vomit and worse".

"I think we have a lot to contend with. I've seriously thought about leaving the service, getting a more nine-to-five job and being with you more. I will if that's what you want". It was a peace offering, a cards on the table time. If she said do it, he would, he might.

"No, I know how much you love the job and I knew that when we got together, it's just that life is zipping along and I'm not. I loved doing the carpet business, the activity, the talking to people, social interaction. There's only so deep a conversation you can have with a baby. If it wasn't for Elkie, I think I'd go mad. James thinks I have some talent for interior design, I feel flattered, I want to run with it".

"James?"

"Yes, I told you, an old friend from home, James Poole. He runs one of those exclusive interior designer businesses, they do work for famous people, even footballers or at least their better halves".

"James, right. Sorry, I've had a head full of stuff recently. Will this affect us?"

Rebecca went quite frosty, interpreting the 'us' as 'me'. "No", she responded, tight-lipped.

"Sorry, interior design then, I can't say I know much about it, tell me", said Thompson, trying to chip a nick into the ice.

"It's the thing now, some people can afford to pay well to have an experienced eye come up with designs for their homes. James said that if I come through the various modules, I might have a placement with his company. He's well-respected, I did a thorough check this time, Elkie helped, he's legit". Thompson nearly said he hoped she wasn't using police resources but instinct stopped him. Elkie wouldn't and Rebecca would blow up if he asked.

"Good, keep the mind active. Do I get to see the plans you have for here?"

Rebecca looked surprised, it hadn't occurred to her that her partner would take any interest. "If you like, I've got modelling software on my laptop but they aren't finished yet. I can show you when they're done if you get in at a decent hour".

Ooh, there was the barb.

"I said sorry. I'm getting a lot of cases and, even though I delegate most of the field stuff, I still have to do the dotting and crossing, I'm the boss, remember?" Rebecca seemed unmoved but, worse, lacking understanding. They'd been together long enough for her to know how demanding work could be, even if he rarely provided corroborative evidence these days, such as case details.

"This guy then, the interior designer, James, how well do you know him? Not an old flame is he, do I have a rival?" Thompson was trying to lighten the mood, Rebecca's response made him curious.

"I told you, I know him, knew him back home. We always rubbed along very well together. He's just a business contact now, nothing to worry about, it ended long ago".

Eight

01 August 2017

Dave Thompson waited while the cheap-looking table was maneuvered into his office. It required much grunting and a little light swearing from those delivering it before it was in place. It almost seemed as if the architects responsible for planning out the nick didn't want their rooms sullying with oversized, or even standard-sized, furniture. Thompson shuffled things a bit to accommodate the chairs, his desk and filing cabinet, it was the cramped side of snug in there now.

"Whatever your Feng Shui consultant is charging I'd refuse to pay it. What if we get a cat that needs swinging? Poor bugger'll bang its head on all this furniture".

"Very good Liam, I need to see my workload, visually. I work better if I have things in specific piles but not on the floor where I can trip over them. I can separate the cases out by lead and drop sheets onto the right piles. It works for me. I just need to get some paperweights for each pile, every time the door wafts open I'll get a tsunami of paper and spend half the day picking and sorting again.

"One minute boss", and he nipped out, leaving Thompson talking to a bunch of manila folders. He didn't recognise one of them, the bastards appeared to be breeding on the quiet.

"Here you go, Boss", and Prosser tipped a box of metal action figures onto his desk, they landed with a thud, they were pretty solid. Thompson picked a couple up, they were certainly weighty enough for what he had in mind. "Before I accept this interesting gift, care to tell me why you had a set of what looks like a load of nicely-painted and very realistic 'dancers at a gay nightclub on leather night' figurines handy?"

"Gavin collected them, I picked them up as a gift for him but he's gone so I don't need them". It was the first time Prosser had admitted the split and explained why he did so much unpaid overtime, he was filling his life with work.

"I see. I can't even begin to speculate where you might find this sort of thing, Liam, a specialist shop I suppose?" Just then Elkie came in to see what was going on.

"Ooh, nice figurines, Dave. Hang on, I'll fetch my butt plug if we're having a party".

"Thank you, Elkie, charming as always. These are a gift from Liam, just to keep on top of my piles of paper to stop injudicious wafting".

"And for your information, Dave, I got them from a shop on Mansfield Road, they sell all manner of the eclectic".

"Really, where is that, Liam? I'm looking for eclectic for the new house", Elkie was still having a good look at the graphic toys. Prosser explained while Thompson placed a mini-Xena or an obvious Frankie on each pile.

"I see you've subconsciously put the Xenas on Jenny's piles and Frankies on mine. I won't take offence but you really should see me in my Xena costume before you make a final decision", said Prosser, while Elkie giggled.

"This reminds me of when I got the 'birds and bees' talk from mum. She saw my dolls were all laid out top-to-tail and wanted to know why, so I showed her one of dad's mags. I think I was about nine", she said.

"Thanks, Elkie, my mind is now filling in the blanks", said Thompson, laughing himself. "Remind me not to have a fancy-dress party".

Jenny had joined the squeeze. "What am I missing?"

"It's Dave's new filing process, he has a Xena thing. He sees you as a warrior princess, Jenny".

"Dave, that was between you and me. You know I ordered that costume especially for you, I'm just glad it was washable. I felt so ashamed asking in Tesco whether they had a stain remover for that. In the end I had to go to DFS and get some stuff for cleaning leather furniture, although I do still wear it on special days". Everyone was laughing when a voice cut through the mood.

"Ah, such merriment, good to see officers relaxing even when they have so very much to do. David, a moment". In the way that he had, Perkins had appeared and had thrown cold water over what had been a real laugh. The room emptied and the door closed to almost shut.

"David, I see you've been organizing, and such novel paperweights, too. I had a file dropped here earlier, it came from one of the other syndicates, although to me that name makes us seem to be optimists filling in a pools coupon. Anyway, it's the Collins file for his little brush with charcoal, they tell me it was hot enough to fry doughnuts in there, he was lucky. It's a dead-end but you have cases that seem to have a tenuous link so it's yours".

"I did wonder where it had come from. Sir. I'll get Prosser to look at the Duncan's Doughnuts file. Pity you broke the moment there, we've not laughed a lot recently".

"Think of me as a natural end to the frivolities despite my offering up the doughnut tag, it amused me too. How are you and your good lady getting on these days? It's not my business, Dave, but you're not the first and you won't be the last to find work interferes with life. Balance, Dave, you must strike a balance while you can. Sadly, many of us are too late. I hope you get more laughs soon, my door remains ajar", and he was gone. Before Thompson could process the conversation, Prosser and Banks walked back in.

"I don't see a Joe pile on here, despite me including an Invisible Man figurine especially", said Prosser, joking but also watching Jenny out of the corner of his eye.

"No, Joe is still on leave for that personal matter. You two, work out who your helpers will be for the new stuff between you and let me know. Liam, this new file is Collins's fire, this one is yours. Perkins said they'd reached a dead end elsewhere, see if you can do better. 'Duncan's Doughnuts', courtesy of Perkins".

"Boss, I'll dig a bit. I like the name, didn't know he had it in him".

"I'm out this afternoon and all morning tomorrow, a 'Responsibilities of Office' course. I'm to be reminded that a Detective Inspector needs to be spotless or something, like I have time to piss about with that shit. Don't think you two are getting away with it either, Ranjit wants you sergeants all on the same course at some point". Prosser and Banks wandered out mumbling something about time wasting, but that was modern policing, a series of courses telling you how wrong everything you did was.

"Boss". It was Gecko, Mickey Newton.

"Mickey, what can I do for you, I see you and Liam are getting along, I hope his good habits are rubbing off on you".

"He's alright, a laugh, earthy. I just wanted a word about Johnson. My mate in Vice reckons something happened between Johnson and Collins. He reckons Ritchie Johnson fancied being a player with his girls but Collins wasn't having it and had his boys explain it to Ritchie. He also reckons that Ritchie is laying low in a flat, don't know where, the tart wouldn't say and I don't think she knows either, but she said he was alive. He also said to be careful, meaning you, Sir".

"Careful, why? Is Collins thinking of having his boys explain things to me, too?"

"My mate wasn't specific, he just said for me to tell my boss to watch himself. Sorry, my mate will only give me bits here and there, once you're out the pool you don't get the same access. I'll keep asking but I wanted you to know. I've got your back if anything happens there". Thompson was surprised. He didn't much like Gecko and he thought

Gecko wouldn't be happy with him, given that he'd once been thumped by him, but he didn't seem to bear grudges.

"Thanks, Mickey, I'll watch my back as you say. Any chance of getting some names for Johnson's girls, a starting place?"

"I know he had birds in Derby and Leicester as well as here, mostly here, not many though, just enough to be a local irritation. They weren't all street girls either, mostly they were escorts, reserved for expensive events. He was also into pay-day loans too, high interest stuff for the desperate. I think he was trying to work under the radar of local businessmen but he got noticed. I'll turn over some more rocks, see what crawls out".

Thompson understood. 'Local businessmen' was just a euphemism for gangster. "I think it's time we got Johnson up on a board, tell Jenny to prepare a team brief just on Johnson, associates, girls if we have info- get Tilda on that, too. I want his known properties, his arrest record, the name of his pets, the lot. I want everyone thinking about him a bit".

"Will do, Boss. I was hoping we might chat at some point. If Joe has done a bunk will I be considered?"

"Joe we don't know about but I was always considering you, I'm still evaluating though, you came with baggage Mickey, I'm being cautious. Give it time, you're not forgotten".

Gecko seemed pleased by what he'd been told, scuttling off to do his master's bidding and leaving Thompson to his paper piles.

"Tilda, the boss wants me and you to set up a board for Stanley Richard Johnson, he said I was to draft you in to do the prossies, you know why, he thinks your recent work will be helpful", and he gave her a look that indicated he knew more about it than most. Tilda knew all about Gecko too, and from the off they'd waged a low-level conflict of sorts until a quiet chat had allowed a truce. Tilda thought Gecko was trying very hard to live in the light now, but if he slipped just once, she'd know.

"You seem brighter, I like it" Thompson had made a special effort to get home early, this had come in the form of not going back in to the nick when his course ended, that and the fact that the course was in Loughborough so getting back to the office after would have been a dogfight. Besides, nothing much had happened and Prosser and Banks had all the chicks occupied.

"Treasures have been delivered, well some of them, walk this way", and Rebecca led him into the kitchen where a shiny new cooker, upright fridge and dishwasher looked back at him. I got a local chap to fit the dishwasher, you know, 'no job too small'. Fifty quid, the pipes were already in. What do you think?"

"That didn't take long. I was expecting a week of phone calls and a lot of whistling through teeth".

"I used their priority service, we needed this stuff. To celebrate, I present Chicken Balti with Garlic Naan and Kingfisher beer, for that full curry house experience". For the first time since moving, that evening the place felt more like a home. If buying kitchen appliances was going to have this sort of effect on their relationship, it was worth it. It felt like they'd done something positive, invested. Only the money, or at least the source, was worrying Thompson.

Nine

02 August 2017

The early morning light backlit the curtains as the alarm went off. Close by, a snuffling was reassuring. Guy had slept through, again and was still sleeping when Thompson checked. Padding downstairs, he looked at the kitchen and wondered whether they still owned a toaster. Nobody else stirred as he ate some cereal and grabbed his files, the one's he'd meant to read the night before. Loughborough was a bit of a drive and part two of the course started early, so he slipped away.

Outside he could smell petrol, but put it down to someone having a mower on the go. He'd noticed that some of their new neighbours got up at all times to assault their lawns, it was almost as if they took a growth spurt, brought on by the rain, personally

Rebecca listened until she was sure the car had gone. That was another thing, she wanted a car for her own use, her independence back. She knew how to get one but would have to frame it differently to Dave otherwise he'd not stop moaning. She whipped through the chores of the morning, surprised at how good she felt and how excited she was about her new career, if it got off the ground. Once Guy was down for a while she fired up the iPad.

"I like what I've seen, especially this new work, Becca, you know I always thought we'd make a good team one day". The person on Facetime looked like he'd just stepped out of a grooming parlour.

"Thanks James, I'm very flattered. I got a real feel for the house once we got inside and now I'm ready for a new project. It's very good of you to take an interest in me, to make an offer. Working remotely would really suit me, what with Guy and the bump".

"You've earned it, but you might have to do a bit of field work too, you know, once you're settled. I'd also like a face-to-face next time you come home, we can catch up on good times past and hopefully plan more to come. Do bring that partner of yours along, if you like, I'd be intrigued to meet him. A policeman, you say?"

"I don't think so, James, he and mummy are worse than chalk and cheese, besides, he's always busy and not very fond of being away from his home base unless it's to go to a match. 'Crime never sleeps', he says".

"Pity. Any plans to visit soon? I'm hoping".

"Actually, I was thinking of nipping down this weekend. Dave and his chum Cliff are talking about going to a football match in Birmingham, or Brentford, or somewhere, so I'll be free. Mummy will sit Guy".

"Splendid, I'll book us somewhere nice for lunch, I can expense it as training. Text me when you decide. Got to go, I have a footballer who wants my attention, well his WAG does. I'll show you the design for their place when you come down, it's in your current neck-of-the-woods actually. I tried to insert a wedge of taste into their requirements but, really, he's just a northern yob who gets a ridiculous amount of money to kick a ball straight. Oh, my gosh, Becca, sorry. I didn't mean to infer that your chap was a yob, or northern, or anything".

"Don't worry about it, James, you're not too far wrong on both counts. I'll be in touch, ciao". Rebecca paused, 'ciao' where had that come from? She also realised that she'd used her Home Counties accent when speaking to James, the one honed at the posh girls' school. Suddenly the day was much brighter and yes, she'd go and see mummy on the weekend while Dave and Cliff swore at hooligans, somewhere.

She texted her intentions to Thompson but the reply irritated her immensely, the match was two weekends away, not one. She rationalized her irritation. True, it was her fault not knowing about the timing of the match or even where it was, but it would have been such a good way of killing two birds with a big rock. She also decided that she was annoyed at Dave for treating her like she was made of glass all the time although, true, she did feel that she might fracture some days. Well, she'd just talk to mummy and go anyway. She was irrationally excited about the idea of going home.

'Hi, James, me again. I'm good for this weekend. Let me know where, and when, and I'm all yours - Becca'. She re-read the text then sent it, she hoped it wasn't ambiguous.

Ten

03 August 2017

"Good course, Dave?" Ranjit had appeared in his office almost as soon as his bum had hit the seat.

"Yes, good course, but someone seems to have added a foot of paper to my portfolio while I've been gone".

"I'll leave you to it then, just checking on my star detective. Don't forget this afternoon's one. I think you'll find the intro to cyber-crime very illuminating, it's in town so you'll back to your files before you know it. Let me know if you want to do the full course, a three day job at Brunel University, in London". Thompson got it, they had to be trained but mostly they had to be seen to be trained. Some things that the job threw up couldn't be trained for, you just did your best and hoped to get it right. It was a thin line between doing the right thing and screwing everything up. Three days down south?, he was already mentally saying 'no'.

He used the fifteen minutes he had until departure for yet another course and started reading up on the Duncan's Doughnut case notes before the scheduled brief last off when the phone rang. "I just sent you details of a burnt-out house in Aspley, Dave. I suspect it might be a tit-for-tat, the home occupant was known for her work in the community and is now in Queens Med. Send Prosser or Banks, you have cyber-crime calling". Perkins made it quite clear that he wasn't playing field detective today, so he stuck his head out of the office door.

"Liam…"

Thompson explained, Prosser listened. "Does Perkins have any evidence that this might be the empire striking back?"

"He must have something in mind, otherwise he'd not have mentioned it. Not one for embellishing instructions, our Superintendent". Tilda had sidled up to the conversation, hoping to get a piece of whatever action was on offer. Prosser had noticed but had already decided to take Gecko, he still had one foot in the 'unconvinced' camp about Tilda Jeffries.

Thompson saw her disappointment. "Give it time, Marie's lot are in the same boat. I've noted Liam and his preference for Gecko as a side-kick, I'll be nipping that one in the bud, privately. How's my Johnson profile going?"

"Sorry, I got dragged away this morning for a couple of hours over an old case, Perkins said it was ok. I've made a start, I'll be ready for when the two musketeers get back. I know it takes time but I'm chomping at the bit, I'm much more used to field, rather than office work".

"Tell me about it", said Thompson, sadly, before disappearing back into his office to get his bits for yet more classroom boredom.

Tilda started pulling files for the brief and printing up copies, most of the information was of little use. Informants passing on a nibble for a tenner, some vague addresses that may or may not still be in use, a couple of vehicles, one of which would be Johnson's legal car. His arrest record was typical of a bright crook. Early, stupid stuff like shoplifting, moving on to car nicking and one for intimidation, none of the events recorded had convictions attached. Then it all went quiet as he found his feet and a way to stay off the radar, she'd seen his sort before.

Accessing some of his girls' files was pretty simple, mostly because she knew where to look. Officers not familiar with the workings of Vice might miss things, she didn't. Some of his girls had arrest records, probably users going freelance for a few extras, or those that worked the streets. Some were just photos of the 'known associates' type. One bad photo she checked twice before making a call. She printed everything up, copies for everyone, better ones for the board. When she went back into the system to check, the one she'd flagged had gone and she couldn't find any trace.

When she'd set everything up ready for Prosser's return and the brief later, she nipped to the loo. Once the door was shut and she was sure she was alone, she unfolded a printed copy of one of the file photos. It was the only one she found which included her undercover, they'd missed it after the promised database clean-up following her spell in Vice supposedly ending. She tried to place the occasion, then realised where she was and who she was with, although she had no idea who might have been the photographer. It took three flushes and a lot of careful tearing but, hopefully, that image wasn't out there anymore.

The office was quiet and Tilda was starting to get bored when suddenly the place erupted with activity as Perkins rushed into the office telling Jenny Banks something and telling her to take Elkie with her. She looked at Josh who shrugged that he didn't know. Left out of the action again, and she wasn't the only one looking pissed off by it.

The office settled down quickly, they all had their tasks even if the Boss and both sergeants were not there to encourage them. Tilda went over to Josh's desk and sat. Josh wasn't sure about Tilda either, she made him nervous, she had more police miles than he did, hard ones too. "Tilda, something I can do for you?"

"Are you as fed-up as me that we're always left indoors while the Boss's old team gets the prize?"

"Lorna and me are his old team too, but I know what you mean. I'd like to get out more but I suppose it depends on the shout. Elkie will be gone soon so that's a window to aim for. Why, what have you got in mind?"

"I thought maybe us left-behinds could have a collective chat to the Boss, air our grievances, he does reckon his door is always open. He is aware, he's not long told me so but maybe he's not as aware as he should be".

"If we're talking a polite 'excuse me Boss, but can you see your way clear' type of thing, ok, but I'm not thumping any tables and Marie's boys won't either, we've talked. You know I try to touch base with everyone, you might try it yourself".

Tilda was surprised, being told she wasn't making an effort by Josh was like being savaged by a lettuce.

"Just think about it. If we get a window it should look unplanned. Use your charm on the others to get a better feeling for it. Let me know", and she went back to her brief planning.

"What did the ice queen want, your body for an hour, sale or return?" It was Lorna who'd seen the exchange and was just being plain nosey, Josh explained. Rumours of her impending departure obviously hadn't leaked out, which was unusual, but she said she didn't think it appropriate for her to be involved. When she'd gone, Josh saw Tilda trying to catch his eye from her desk. A slight shake of the head was enough to answer the question.

"Josie Turner, how is she?" asked Prosser of a busy senior nurse. In a bed on its own, various drips were busy working on the prostrate woman, she was obviously in a bad way.

"Crispy. She was lucky, she'll have scars though and she's not quite out of the woods yet. Do you think this was deliberate?"

"I don't know, just got it, we're investigating. It is possible that this young lady worked in home entertainment, other people's, and/or hotel rooms too, if you get my drift. She might have medical needs besides the trauma care, just a heads-up".

"Understood, thanks, I'll pass that on. I hope you get the buggers that did this, it was just nasty. She could have been toast, there and then".

"Or a crumpet", said Gecko behind Prosser, who gave him a sharp look.

"No pets allowed on the ward, Detective Sergeant", said the nurse as she rushed off on her daily ward marathon. Gecko was used to be verbally abused, it was almost a badge of honour for him.

"Do you know her at all, Mickey?" Prosser showed him a photo that had been sent through, one before the damage.

Gecko looked closely. "Yeah, used to but she moved up. Not many locals swinging handbags on street corners these days. Don't blame 'em, the pimps are bastards and the coppers worse. I don't know who she worked for, I've already asked back when but people were keeping schtum. It happens, especially when one of her regular visitors has pips".

"You think she entertained police officers?"

"That was what we thought when we asked around about her, if she did, expect pressure from unexpected sources. That was how it worked in Vice. Files would wander, links not made and cases cleaned up until all you could smell was Vim".

Prosser texted Thompson, knowing his phone would be off but keeping him in the loop. 'Boss, Josie Turner was the burn-out victim, we don't know who ran her yet but I'd bet that this is a marker. She's in a bad way but we're told she's stable. Won't be doing much modelling in the future though. More at the brief later'.

"How well do you know the Boss, Liam?"

"How well do we know anyone, Mickey? When the door at home closes people can become different. His missus is nice but I hear whispers that it looks a bit rocky at present but it might settle, might just be her being pregnant. Our Jenny has a soft-spot but I'm not telling you anything you didn't know there. He's honest, thorough, sometimes inspired. I like him even when he's being a twat. I trust him. Why, what's this leading to?"

"Nothing, whispers".

"Like the one about him and Elkie when they were on stake-out?"

"No, maybe not a whisper, maybe more of a low-key proclamation".

"Proclamation, fuck me Mickey, that's the longest word I've ever heard you use".

"I have my moments. Keep an eye on the Boss, we might have to intervene at some point".

"Mickey, you do know I can make you tell me your darkest secrets if I choose?"

"I heard that, but you won't. I'll find out more, if we need to, me and you'll take care of things for the Boss, agreed?"

"I'm not agreeing to anything unless I know what it entails but thanks, keep me informed".

"Leave it with me, where are we going by the way, this isn't the way to a bacon cob".

"We're doing a drop-in on an old acquaintance".

Gecko hadn't seen Prosser in this mood before. The poor fried kid in the bed seemed to have had an effect on him, and him being a bender too. In Gecko's world, or at least the one he'd lived in before joining normal people, this wasn't right, it didn't fit the profile. When the car made a turn into a small industrial estate, one of many in Nottingham, he guessed who they were going to visit.

The noise startled Duncan Collins but he was confident that his new precautions were adequate. A second noise had him reaching for his drawer. "I wouldn't, Duncan", said Prosser, as he casually walked into the room and sat down.

"Liam, how unexpected. I heard a noise, this is just a sensible precaution. I can't even recall whether it's loaded or not".

Prosser knew exactly what Collins had in the drawer, but that wasn't why he was there. "Your chap out there tripped over and hurt himself, my colleague is looking after him now and the other two as well, nothing serious, just impact injuries from falling over. I'd get that loose carpet fixed Duncan, before you get sued for an industrial injury".

Collins could see that Prosser was angry, mostly by how very serene he was.

"Go on then, why do you feel the sudden need to intimidate me? You do know I don't always play nice, Liam".

"I just saw a young woman lying in a hospital bed, not a pretty sight now but I reckon she was once. She was the unfortunate victim of a fire in Aspley, know anything about it?"

Collins looked genuinely shocked. "Oh my goodness, I'm so sorry. The place was supposed to be empty, I gave strict instructions, they're supposed to check. Honestly, Liam, what do you think I am? I don't hurt young ladies, surely you know that. Leave this with me, please, I'll deal with it and the young lady will be looked after properly. I'm truly sorry".

Prosser didn't become any less serene. "You know what, Duncan. I think when I dig, I'll find the name 'Johnson' connected somewhere, and when I dig further, I'll find out that the person who toasted you will be one and the same. We're going to find Johnson, but if you find him first you'll let me know. We both know where we stand here, this is, as they say, non-negotiable. Explain the facts of life to your boys outside and I want a name for the fire in Aspley".

"I said I'll deal with it. I can't be seen to be a police informer, it would undermine me if that sort of thing got around. Please, Liam, you know I have my methods, I'll deal with it properly".

"Not this time Duncan, I know he's not one of yours, you lot don't work that way. Send me a name and address or we'll not leave you alone until you're wearing overalls with little arrows on them. Yes, that is a threat, yes I am intimidating you because you do not fuck with us on this scale. Send those details", and Prosser left quietly. Another crash outside told Collins that one of his boys was a very slow learner. He picked up the phone and sent the text. This wasn't finished though, not by a long chalk.

"I'm not stupid, Liam, what's going on?" asked Gecko. He was very nervous after what he'd just seen.

Prosser's phone pinged, an unknown caller. "Can you get me to this address?" and he handed the phone over.

"Does the Pope shit..., oh jeez, sorry Liam, I never asked".

"What, whether I'm a bigoted religious nut or not? No, I'm not, but thanks for being considerate".

Gecko relaxed a bit. "Twelve minutes, left at the next set of lights. How did you know where Collins was now?"

"He's got a taxi firm, legit but also a front for money-laundering. It was a lucky guess with a splash of local knowledge".

"Is he a mess too?"

"No. Mickey, nervous and very, very angry but untouched and probably making phone calls to our betters right now. I don't expect you to say anything untrue when this dollop of shit hits the fan, and it will, I know

Collins. First we'll deal with the issues in-hand, it might get naughty, are you ok with that?"

"I was born naughty, Liam. Is this the fire bomber?"

"Yes. You should also know that I have history motivating me. Back home, my sister died in a fire bomb attack. Seeing that lass on the ward just set me off, sorry I had to drag you into it".

"I wasn't dragged. I might play up to my nickname a bit but I've spent a lot of years on the street, nobody drags me anywhere. This name on the text, Malone, do you know him?"

"Despite the belief of the English, Mickey, not all bog trotters from the Emerald Isle know each other personally. Besides, just because he's called Malone does not mean he's Irish. No, he'll be a brought-in contractor or borrowed specifically for the job. After what's happened, Collins will suffer greatly for this, professionally. I expect I will, too".

"What, suffer for trying to break up a fight between three blokes, a silly fight over a card game? I know what happened, Liam, I was there, remember?"

"I appreciate what you're saying, Mickey, but don't. I lost it, I shouldn't have done and now I might lose it again, stop me if you can but I don't recommend trying".

"Liam, do shut the fuck up, won't you. Let's just pull this shit and take him to a dark place, if not, then the nick will do". Prosser laughed, he felt he'd found something of a kindred spirit although he'd never say as much.

The little hotel wasn't much more than a large house turned into units. There was no obvious sign outside, it was one of those places you'd know about if you moved around a lot, it was a place that kept itself clean and offered a bed for the night at a reasonable price, cash only. On the desk, an older man was hunched over reading The Sun. "I'm here to talk to Mr. Malone", said Prosser, showing the guy his ID. "Room?"

"Seven, top of the stairs", the old guy replied with an edge to his voice. By his disposition, he clearly didn't buy a ticket for the annual police benevolent fund raffle.

"If you touch the phone or alert Malone to our presence in any way, I will not be very happy", said Prosser, politely.

The old boy saw that Prosser's knuckles were showing signs of recent activity and made a decision. He reached behind and got an old coat off the back of the door. "Just going for a walk and a smoke. Don't make too much of a mess, it's muggins here as has to clean it up", and he left them to it.

Prosser knocked on the door, he was about to speak when Gecko chirped up. "Any laundry, Mr. Malone?" followed by a hacking cough. It caught Prosser by surprise, it was a passable impersonation of the old boy from the desk. The door opened.

"Mr. Malone, I'm arresting you for", then all hell broke loose. After some excitement, Malone was soon lying cuffed on the floor and a large knife was being bagged by Gecko, who was bleeding on the bag a bit. Prosser found a wallet. "Sorry, Kevin, I missed that bit out of the caution. Now Kevin Malone, you recognise the accent I see, good, just let than sink in a bit. Now you can struggle and be subdued, again, or you can walk quietly to the car. I'll be charging you with resisting arrest and assault on a police officer, as well as attempted murder. You'll have to hope my colleague can still rely on his fingers to accurately count, after he sees a medic".

Malone said nothing. His face was beginning to swell in a couple of places and his ribs hurt, not to mention being almost breathless from a blow to the nuts. He went into the back of the car quietly and sat motionless. More officers began to arrive, including SOCO and a few uniforms. Prosser left them to it, after a short brief.

In the passenger seat, Gecko sat holding his hand up. He had a pillow case wrapped around it but blood was weeping right through. Prosser had already called ahead and arranged for an ambulance using 'officer injured', despite Gecko's protest, it met them on the ring road. Banks and Elkie were there too, waiting. Elkie climbed into the ambulance with Gecko while Banks got in with Prosser.

"Fuck me, Liam, busy day?"

"You could say that. Does Dave know?"

"No, his phone will still be off, another course remember?"

"Right, sorry, it's been a bit confused this past hour. This might get messy, Jenny, just so you know".

In the back Malone said something in Gaelic and smiled. Prosser answered in the same tongue, the reply wiped the smile clean off his face. In the passenger seat Jenny Banks was writing a text and trying to phrase it as economically as possible. Despite having no Gaelic, she thought she understood the tenor of Prosser's reply.

Prosser and Banks arrived back at the nick just as Thompson was arriving. "I just read the text, get him to a cell, Liam, then come and see me". It was curt, Banks knew that something more was brewing. "Jenny, this will be yours for now, sorry to drop it on you. Give Malone a couple of hours, I'll come and find you later. When he gets back from the hospital, take Mickey to one side, sit him in a corner and watch him. He talks to nobody, including you. No calls, nothing. Text Elkie now, tell her he's quarantined, stress the word 'quarantined', she'll know what that means".

"Right boss", said Banks, wondering what sort of thing Elkie would have been involved in once to have used a phrase like 'quarantined' in that context.

In the office, Thompson's light was flashing like a bastard. "My office when you get this". There was no warmth in Perkins' tone. Thompson found the door open, ready and waiting when he got there, he sat and listened to what was as much of a rant as he'd ever heard from Perkins. He said nothing, just waited for the thing to end. "Well?"

"I only have your side of events, Sir. I have Prosser in my office and, until I hear his side, there is no 'well'. I have Newton quarantined by Elkie and I will find out what happened but, since when did a gangster call the shots here because if this is any of that old-school bullshit, I'll come after you for it, privately if it comes to that. I'm a Detective Inspector and I expect my Superintendent to respect that. I'll report back when I've interviewed the officers alleged to have committed an offence. If you don't trust my impartiality, give it to another syndicate and, since I don't think Collins is reporting an offence at all, expect union involvement if you try any unwarranted disciplinary on any of my officers, Sir".

Perkins looked a bit shocked, then he seemed to deflate. "Sorry, David, but we can't have bulls going around wrecking china shops at will. You know there's a balance, a delicate one. This isn't anything to do with an old school, this is to do with Prosser and Collins, I suspect some history there and for once I don't know what it is. For your information, no matter what you find out, Prosser will spend six-months demoted and on the naughty step. Sham will be acting DS, solid but no imagination, live with it. Now you go and scare the shit out of Liam Prosser. As far as I'm concerned, the matter is now concluded".

"Collins?"

"My problem".

"Then you'd better do a good job of dealing with it because if you don't, we will". Thompson was still fuming when he got back to his office. Prosser was sat quietly; he had a fresh coffee on the go and there was one waiting for Thompson too. Both had sad faces drawn on them, gifts from Josh.

"Do you need your hands looking at?"

"No, I'll be fine. I want to offer my resignation, Sir. I acted improperly; I accept whatever happens".

"Fuck off, Liam, you total dick. You're not getting out of this with a wrist slap and then walking away. You fucked up and, worse, you make me look like a twat, a complete twat, because my sergeant is a fucking Neanderthal who can't control his fists". Thompson could see Prosser bunching his fists slowly. "Go on then, Liam, have a go, here I am. You fuckwit, what were you thinking?" Each word was delivered at an increased volume.

"I lost it, I said. Be careful now, Dave".

"No, I won't be fucking careful. I want the whole story, every single thing now. Starting from when you saw that kid in hospital to invading Collins' place to the arrest of Malone, all of it". Thompson knew he could be heard outside and possibly in the cells too, it was deliberate.

Prosser looked like he might explode, but he didn't. Thompson gave it a few minutes then spoke quietly. "Now we've got that out of our systems, publicly, and I'm not a bleeding mess on the floor, come on Liam, talk to me".

"I fucked up, Dave. I saw Josie Turner lying there, badly burnt and I saw my sister. She died back home, we got fire-bombed. The Good Friday agreement wasn't instant and those who made money from the Troubles continued to do so, still do, we just got caught up in it. That was why I left or at least one of the reasons. I saw my sister lying burnt in that bed and I knew that bastard Collins was involved and I wasn't wrong. Mickey Newton had nothing to do with this, I dragged him along against his will, no matter what he says. He's completely innocent".

"First time for everything then, Liam. Ok, dead sister I get and I won't say 'sorry for your loss', it would be trite, but I am. When you got to Collins, what happened?"

"I told him not to fuck with us, that I knew he was involved in the fire-bombing, tit-for-tat, and I wanted the person responsible. He eventually agreed, I didn't hit him but I may have hinted at the possibility and that we'd show more interest in everything we let him get away with".

"Going back to his boys, three?"

"Yes, I think after I'd said who I was and that I wanted a quick word, they were happy to play cards with Mickey while he waited. Not good losers and one of them cheats, Gecko skillfully managed to diffuse the tension".

"That, Liam, is the biggest crock of shit I've ever heard so far today, at least. Malone, is there history with the name, too?"

"No, never heard of him. He was a hired hand bought in by Collins, he knifed Mickey while resisting, how is he?"

"Elkie hasn't got back to me yet, if it was too serious, she would have". Thompson flipped open the lid of his laptop and started typing. "Drink your coffee or Josh will bring another one with a questioning face on it". He could see that Prosser was shaking a bit, he probably needed nicotine. The printer did a short spell of machinery Olympics before it spat out a single sheet. "Sign this, six-months' demotion to DC for not following procedure, don't do it again. Don't speak to Gecko, I haven't done yet, now go home".

"I need to write up my report, I want to watch Malone cough".

"Go home, we'll let you know what happened tomorrow. Just so you know, there won't be a second chance and you have to thank Perkins for not stringing you up by your balls. We're done". Prosser realised there was no point arguing and he left. He didn't reply when a couple of the team asked if he was ok.

'On the way back, Boss. Gecko lost a little finger, is it at the arrest site?' It was Elkie, in a taxi. 'Quarantine intact'. Thompson took a deep breath and called Jenny in, briefing her then asking her to send Sham in.

After a limited explanation of the situation he told Sham the news. "Sorry, Boss, I don't want it. I know I'm senior but I don't want it, not yet, maybe not ever. I've got a new baby, I want to see her grow up". Sham's words hit home hard, but now wasn't the time to think about it. Thompson was disappointed and said so, but he thanked Sham for his honesty. He called Lorna in.

"I need to ask a favour, Lorna. You can say no, you aren't obliged, but I need you to stay for another six-months". Lorna wasn't sure what was going on, but she guessed that Prosser wasn't going to be wearing stripes for a while now, not after what they'd all heard.

"You want an acting-sergeant, right?"

"For six-months".

"Ok, what if Liam doesn't want to step back up after six-months?"

"Take the exam".

"I'll have to talk to people in London but it should be ok, thanks for your confidence, Sir". Thompson smiled, there was no need to mention that Sham was Perkins' first choice just yet, besides, if she was any good she'd have already guessed. The door opened and a bloodied Gecko walked in.

"Mickey, lost a finger I see. I asked them to look for it but they only found a little claw, is that yours? We're all assuming you can just grow another one, same way you can grow a new tail".

"I wish. It's ok, Boss, I'll manage, I'll get some compo but my 'Trois Mouvements de Petrouchka' on the piano is going to sound shit from now on". His bandaged hand looked like something from 'Revenge of the Mummy'.

"Can I assume you will tell me a true and accurate version of the events when I ask?"

"Absolutely, Sir. What happened was, me and Liam attended after that place had been torched and, after seeing the poor kid in hospital, we popped around to see Mr. Collins for a chat, see if he'd heard any whispers. I played cards with his lads while Liam got some information, freely given. The lads were a bit boisterous, cheats the lot of them. Then we arrested Malone and he slashed me, I wish to press charges".

"Ok, go home Mickey, sorry about the hand, come back when the doctor says you can".

Gecko sat still bewildered. "Really?"

"No, make sure you're back in tomorrow, we've not done. Liam is a DC again for six-months. You'll probably get a commendation or something for this. Lorna, that nice black girl, is our new acting DS. Be good to her or be dealing with me, anything else?" There wasn't.

As Gecko left, Jenny walked in. "Busy day, Dave. Lorna told me, she'll be good and Liam will be back, I hope, he's too good to let this be anything more than a trip up. Come on, let's go to my place, it's time we relaxed together, properly". Thompson's phone went.

"David, the young lady passed. Charge Malone with murder". It was Perkins, he sounded very angry. Thompson pressed speakerphone so Jenny could hear.

"You ok, Sir?"

"Someone's daughter just died, David. It didn't matter what her life choices were, she didn't deserve to die like that. Talk to Malone tomorrow, he won't give you anything but there will be something somewhere that will make the connection to him and the fire. We know what we're dealing with, we know who we're going after now".

"And balance, Sir?"

"Fuck balance, Detective Inspector, let's make things wobble". *Click.*

Jenny looked at Thompson for answers. "I think it's going to get very lively around here for a while", he said.

"Good, I need a bit of stimulation, there's only so many times you can look a smiling skull in the mouth and care. That relaxation, it's still available if you want it, Dave".

"Not now, Jenny, but I appreciate the offer, besides if I took you up on it, I might have to give everyone in the office a go". He hoped he'd made a successful joke of it, he wasn't sure though, Jenny had been a bit intense when she'd said it, a bad sign. His phone pinged.

'I'm popping home for a few days, when you go to the football this weekend'. It was Rebecca. There it was, home wasn't where they lived, again.

'It's next weekend, the match, not this weekend, if I go', he texted back, then 'are you ok driving?' There was no immediate answer. When one did come, Thompson couldn't detect any sort of undercurrent to the text. 'Ok, my bad, but I need to talk to my potential future boss, face-to-face, so I'll go down this weekend anyway and I'll take Guy, I'll hire a car. You'll probably have work to do anyway'. There was no hint in the text that Rebecca wanted him with her on the visit 'home'.

Thompson was relieved that she'd got something to look forward to, even though it wasn't his idea of fun. Despite the night before, there was still some tension there, things unsaid. He still hoped moving to the new home might eventually wash away her irritations, he wasn't too sure that it would wash away his, though.

After fetching a coffee, he went back to scaling Mount Paperwork. He read for a bit before a knock on the door got his attention. "Sorry, I thought you'd be gone, just a quick whip around". It was one of the contract cleaners that Thompson occasionally saw. He checked the clock, *shit*. As he drove home, Thompson replayed the events of the day. Would he have reacted the same way as Liam if he'd been previously touched by tragedy? At least they'd got Malone, even if it cost Liam a lot, professionally. Then he pondered on Jenny's offer and realised how close he'd come to accepting it. Getting Joe back was becoming a matter of priority, for many reasons.

The house was quiet when he walked in. Normally there would be some noise from Guy or Rebecca or at least a chattering TV, but this was unsettling. Rebecca looked up from her chair, she'd been reading a magazine, 'House and Home', 'Dado Rail and You' or something similar. "In the oven", was all she said, her voice not offering a hint of 'I'll get it for you' or 'how did your day go?'

He pulled the plate out with a tea towel. Straight away he could see that there was too much veg, but now wasn't the time to complain. He pulled a tray from the cupboard, loaded the plate and cutlery onto it and headed for the living room. Rebecca had gone. The TV went on, football from wherever, he'd get most of the second half. Once he'd finished eating he stacked the new dishwasher, cleaned up and went looking for Rebecca. She was in the back bedroom, the one they used as an office, well she did, and was busy. He knocked, then poked his head through the door.

"Thanks, very nice, sorry, got tied up again, you know how it is. I can tell you a bit about it if you like".

"It was much nicer, as you call it, when it was fresh, honestly Dave", said Rebecca, showing no interest in his day, his work, or his life.

"Yeah, I said sorry. What are you doing?"

Rebecca sounded exasperated. "Continuing designing the interior of our love nest". It was said quite coldly, as if 'bus depot' and 'love nest' were interchangeable descriptions. "I'll be taking another course module soon and I want some alternatives".

Thompson looked over. The sketches were done on a screen, not by hand in the traditional sense. At least it kept her occupied and happy, well happier.

"If this goes anywhere, you don't think this interior design thing will get in the way of bringing up the kids?"

"No, I need some stimulation, I'm stagnating. I told you about James back home? Well, we've chatted on Facetime and he likes what I've sent him. I'm going to meet up with him when I'm home".

"I thought this was home?"

"You know what I mean, besides, the kids will be at school soon enough and I'm not going to sit around here all day long doing bollocks all like a good little housewife. Not that the 'wife' bit has happened or is likely to, now".

Thompson went back downstairs to find another match to watch, something clearly wasn't quite right with them anymore. Since leaving their pokey flat, the extra space had created extra space between them, it was no longer cosy. The 'home' crack was bothering him even more now too, it did every time she said it, he was beginning to think it was deliberate. And what about the 'wife' thing? Ok, they'd agreed to put the wedding on the back-burner for the moment, while getting the house and the second child sorted, but it was still going to happen. Wasn't it?

The match was ok, South American prima donnas rolling around if an earwig farted on them, a ref who surely should not be allowed to drive with vision like that and a manager who would be better managing Pizza Hut than a professional football team. When he got to bed, Rebecca wasn't there. She slept in the nursery with Guy again.

Eleven

Back to 27 July 2017

After what seemed like forever, the rain finally stopped and the flooding started to subside a little. Nottingham had been under flood advisories for weeks, which was ironic as all but the blind could see the water washing over roads and even the blind would know that their feet were getting wet. The floods were breaching flood banks everywhere, making insurance office staff even busier than usual and therefore taking even longer to get around to talking to you, despite your business being so very important to them.

Scott Westbury decided to go fishing. He wasn't exactly a stranger to the hobby, having fished all over Europe as he moved around with his job. Now he was settled in Nottingham and had found gainful employment of a static nature. Fishing locally for specimen fish was now his passion and probably explained his marital status. For a Carlton resident, the whole of the Trent system beckoned, but his regular spots, places where he'd found not just fish, but a bit of relaxation too, were all done for by the floods. The Trent, usually a gentle lady of a river but with occasional hissy fits, had become a raging termagant and it would be some time, and much work, before she was back to her more controlled self.

In desperation, Westbury settled on a visit to Colwick Park. He rationalized that the long-term fish-stocking policy the council had, that would be 'wait until the river breaches and dumps fish everywhere', was likely to have freshened up the stocks in The Loop, the old course of the River Trent but long since unnavigable.

Parking at what they laughingly called a Fishing Lodge, a steel shipping container with windows, selected from the 'it'll do' range, he could see how badly the park had suffered. Debris was everywhere but the wardens seemed to have found an ancient tractor which they were now using to clear the road. Westbury had been there three weeks previously, watching, along with a lot of locals, as a part of the flood bank gave way and a bunch of starter homes for young executives got the pool they'd always dreamed about, plus all the flotsam they could handle.

In the old days, the event would have been recorded by an on-the-spot film crew, now it was all over social media with phone footage-was it still called footage? There was even some impressive stuff from drones, which caught the moment the Trent breached and the flood banks just gave up. The world had changed dramatically in a few short years, and that change was being well-documented for future civilisations to shake their heads at when they saw it. If anyone survived to see it, that is.

Inside the Fishing Lodge, the old warden fought with his computer to get it to issue a ticket. Outside, the grumble of a generator powering the building made speech difficult and that, allied to the warden being the wrong side of hard-of-hearing, didn't help. "You must be mad fishing in this", he said, louder than he needed to. Westbury smiled and handed over the correct money, it was easier. He'd dealt with this guy before, he could be a tad curmudgeonly, bordering racist. Westbury assumed he was one of many on a long waiting list for the Inclusivity Course.

"Where are you fishing? Just so we know where the body might be", the old boy asked, laughing.

Westbury laughed too, a joke, he liked jokes. "The Loop, maybe the river if I can find a safe spot. Travelling light today, specimen hunting".

"Good luck with that on the Loop, the outside lads pulled the whole fence out of there this morning. The banks gone in places and it's dangerous. If you fall in, you're on your own and don't think that the Hall Lake is now fair game just because it's a part of the Trent. It's still no fishing there until the big bosses tell us otherwise".

"I'll be careful, thanks for the concern, and thanks for the tip about the Hall Lake. If the Trent is running in, fish might be following. I can still fish from the Trent bank, legally, right? I wouldn't want to drag any of your staff away from the clean-up to ticket me, or is that the brew up?"

The warden laughed, reminding those in the tight little container that was the Fishing Lodge that garlic was a major part of whatever he ate. "You won't son, they'll be all day and more besides. Y'all have a nice day now".

Westbury pulled his lightweight rod out and set up. He was planning to be totally mobile with no keep net, he didn't like them much anyway, no good for the fish. He had a small landing net with an extendable handle and a bag containing essentials, it was all he'd need today. He had intended taking a path on the park-side of the Loop, but that had totally gone in places and the water was still lapping high up the bank. Gaps in the trees offered a few spots to cast but nothing came out, but he slowly worked his way around as best he could, undeterred.

At one point, a large dog started to trot his way. Westbury liked dogs as a concept, but unleashed, uncontrolled dogs were a bane. When the dog was less than ten feet away, a clear female voice called "Blaze, sit", and the dog stopped and sat, well there was a surprise. In moments, a lady walked up to 'Blaze' and leashed him, before continuing along the damaged path. As she passed Westbury, he thanked her, both for putting 'Blaze' on a leash and for not telling him that the dog doesn't bite.

"Oh but he does, if told to, but I could see you aren't one of the local louts so I decided not to let him rip your throat out, you're welcome". She was smiling as she said it, humour again, the day had been a riot of laughs so far.

Westbury examined the woman, critically. It was something he always did, he had no idea why, maybe it was because he'd been single for a long time. She was quite tall, maybe five-eleven, slim to the point of underfed and slightly worn. If he was asked to guess her age, and he didn't see that happening for any reason, he would say between a nicely kept forty-five and a well-lived sixty. He wondered what sort of life had happened to her for it to show so in her features. *Shit*, she'd noticed him looking.

"Natasha Ellis, I live locally. I don't think I've seen you here before".

"Scott Westbury, I live fairly locally now. I don't come here that often, no dog, but I do like to fish, you meet interesting people, sometimes".

There was that smile again.

"Bothering the fish. I've never quite understood, what do you get out of it?" It was an odd question, one Westbury had often asked himself without ever coming to a firm conclusion.

"I try to catch specimen fish out of curiosity but, like I said, it's the people that you meet when you're fishing, if they're interesting it gives you a conversational starting point".

Shit again, now he was flirting, and it got a third smile too. This was his best day for women smiling at him in a long time, he might even write it in his little fishing notebook later.

"Well, Scott Westbury, I hope we'll meet again sometime and I'll try to be even more interesting next time. I have to go, Blaze hasn't savaged any of those awful kids that hang around the toilet block yet, it's a release for him and good exercise for them when they have to run".

With another smile, a fourth, not that he was counting, Natasha was gone.

'Don't', said Westbury mentally, but his mind had set to filling in the blanks in Natasha's life story. She'd obviously been a beauty at one point, still was but now she was enigmatic too, which was the same if you didn't look with only your eyes. Should he sprint after her, give her his number, ask for hers, have Blaze rip his throat out? Maybe next time.

He continued around the Loop, stepping over debris where it remained, looking for signs of fish but also hoping to get a final look at Natasha. He'd noticed she walked very upright, as if she could balance a tray of

Martinis on her head and not spill a drop. Was that schooled or natural? It was all a part of the enigma that would now occupy his thoughts for the rest of the day and possibly into the early evening. When he got over a hill that looked down on the Loop and the park he could see her in the distance. Blaze was playing fetch with something, then they both entered a tunnel of trees and were lost.

Westbury moved on to where a small bridge led from the interior of the park and accessed the flood bank, it had tape all over it. A hand-written note had been put in a vinyl pouch and stapled to a post advising the public that the bridge had been undercut in the floods and was unsafe. 'Ok', he thought, slipped under the tape and crossed to the flood bank. It wasn't far, maybe ten yards and he didn't die. 'Elfin safety', he thought.

Looking into what they called the Nature Reserve, Westbury could see that much of it was still under water. He wasn't surprised, he'd seen on the local news that the Racecourse, a physical part of the area, was all underwater too, and that they'd had to cancel a meet. Walking the flood bank on the north side of the Loop he could see the damage. Sections had washed away and he'd had to drop down the Candle Meadow side to get around. Wellies would have been very useful at that point, his were still upside down over a radiator at home.

He was intending heading for the last section of the Loop on the Candle Meadow side. He'd seen fish activity about a hundred yards before the bridge, right where The Loop used to narrow, it had looked promising. Bits of the banks were very slippery, this hadn't been helped by the obvious wheel damage done by whatever they'd used to pull the lost fence out of the water. He passed the fence, all piled up in what was once a wetland meadow but now looked more like a scrapyard. Behind him, the row of rather bland houses all sported piles of sandbags where they'd attempted the Canute thing as water had cascaded in their direction. A couple of the houses were also burnt out, maybe the owners were going for bust on the insurance?

Westbury found the spot he wanted and cast to a ripple. Almost immediately he got a take and worked a fine Chub to the net. Worm was a banker when it came to Chub, post-floods. After taking a photo and then bagging and labelling fish scales lost in the landing net, a biologist friend was studying freshwater fish age and distribution, he cast again. This time the dog wasn't at all controlled, the old boy walking it seemingly not at all bothered that it was jumping up on someone, its muddy feet leaving their mark. He decided to make some distance between himself and the old boy, in case he was tempted to be rude, or worse.

After a couple of hours of trying new spots created by the floods, he found himself at the Hall Lake end of the park, so, out of curiosity, he went for a look. Naturally more 'do not cross' tape tried to impede him, but he gave it short shrift. About fifty yards along a route into the park, the Trent had carved the bank away and water was flowing straight into the Hall Lake.

Where the path had gone, a large channel that carried water from the river into the lake had created a slack, this was just the sort of spot he'd been looking for. A splash across the new inlet told him a bit more of the bank had crumbled and fallen into the busy water, hence the warning tape. He found what looked like a decent, stable spot and cast. Almost immediately he got a bite, a good one. The Chub, when it came towards the net, was a beauty, but his landing net struggled to quite reach and he had to lean well forward to net the fish, as he did so, something embedded in the muddy banks caught his eye, something shiny.

The human brain is a remarkable device that can multi-task if the owner is relatively sentient, not all are. What it doesn't do very well is sudden distraction, and it tends to stop paying attention to other things in order to focus on the new item of interest. In Westbury's case, it was his footing that lost out and he plunged forward into the brown water. As it closed in over his head, his brain was still processing the shiny item, failing completely to remember to close his mouth.

Scott Westbury was a good swimmer, but he wasn't so good at breathing through absent gills, which soon became an issue. He thrashed about gasping and gulping and trying to remember whether he'd left the cooker on. He vaguely noticed activity above him and heard noises, although they changed every time he went under.

"Grab it, Scott", he heard, as he came up for what his brain was starting to suggest might be the last time. He flailed and grabbed and some stability came into his life. Coughing and spitting, he clung to the lifebelt. His tackle had gone, his phone would be done for and his car key might not work at all, bless you keyless start cars. The whole event had seemed to take about an hour to Scott, but had probably only been a minute or so, and he gradually got a grip.

"Lucky you chose to go swimming early, before the little shits have been around and thrown all the lifebelts in". He recognized the voice but from where? Through dirty eyes he saw the smiling face of Natasha. Blaze sat patiently by her side as she held the rope that was attached to the fading orange-and-white lifebelt. There, slightly embedded in the bank was the shiny thing again.

'NOT NOW!' yelled his subconscious, but curiosity was already operating his limbs. He grabbed at the shiny thing and clawed his way up the treacherous bank. Once he was on the level, he laid back and gasped some more. "Thank you, I owe you at least a good meal". How could he be flirting again when he'd just nearly died, stupid testosterone.

"Come on, I'm only just in Candle Meadow, a dry bit. I think I can find you something less wet to wear and we can get some cola down you". Westbury was confused and his expression said so.

"Cola helps kill off bugs, you swallowed a lot of water. Essence of Trent is less than pure, which is why we can't sell it to the French", and she helped him up.

It didn't take long to get to Natasha's place, it was one of the houses that looked like they came out of a flat-pack. Inside it was ok, if a big doggy. Natasha led him to the bathroom where he stripped off his clothes and spent an age in her power shower, long enough for her to tap at the door and ask if he was ok. When he felt a bit cleaner he stepped out. On the floor, a pile of men's clothes awaited him. The style and bright colours were not quite to his taste, but they would do until he could get home. He made his way downstairs where he was greeted by a large cup of coffee and some hot-buttered, crusty toast.

"I don't like sushi and I suspect you won't either after today. Despite appearances, I do like a nice pasta and the place on Trent Bridge is said to be good, you can use my phone to book if you like", and Natasha handed Westbury a smart iPhone, the expensive one. "Just press five".

Without saying anything, Scott pressed five and booked a table for two for seven that evening.

"Before you ask, the clothes are my brothers, he has different tastes in many things but they'll get you home. I don't drive, so you'll have to collect me. A taxi is on the way so you can go home for your spare car keys. The park staff knows what happened". Trying not to appear shell-shocked, Westbury thanked Natasha profusely, several times, until they settled into conversation. The smile was back.

A toot outside told them the taxi had arrived. Westbury stood a moment, but Natasha was ready and handed him a small bag. "I don't know what it is but it looks valuable. Take it home and clean it up, take a photo with your new phone when you get it, I'd like to see it clean. I have some thoughts", then she gave him a light kiss and he floated out to the taxi, clutching his bag.

"Colwick Park please".

"What, that's only half a mile away, are you taking the piss?" In life you can always rely on a dose of reality from a taxi driver.

"I just want to check my car, then on to Carlton, then back to my car with my spare keys. Don't worry, there'll be a drink in it". That seemed to satisfy the cabby, although he kept casting a glance in the rear view mirror at Westbury. Given the clothes Natasha had furnished, he understood why.

"I heard you'd been swimming in the Loop, that is very much verboten, son. Why are you dressed up as one of the Bee Gees, are you ok?" The old guy in the Fishing Lodge was getting the rest of the day's allocation of jokes out all in one go.

"Staying alive", said Westbury, besting the warden on the joke front, so much so that he almost, but not quite, smiled. "I'll be an hour or so getting sorted out. If anyone hands in my lost fishing tackle, can I give you my number so you can call me?" This seemed to amuse the warden no end, his laughing ending in a hacking cough. "That'll be a 'no', then. Tell me, do you have anything about the park and the hall, you know, the history?"

The warden slowly stopped coughing and opened a drawer, pulling out a booklet. "Five quid".

Westbury paid with a damp note and left. He tried the keyless start but it was uninterested, so he fetched his spare key, handsomely tipped the taxi driver when he'd been ferried back to his car and headed home. A second shower and change of clothes had him feeling a bit better, then he filled a bowl with soapy water and dropped the shiny thing into it.

Letting things soak, he dipped into his Colwick book and read. It was all pretty standard stuff, even including a bit of tosh about a haunting. 'Local legend states that the ghost of Mademoiselle de Fay, dressed in an evening gown, haunts the shrubbery at night, looking for her pearl necklace and other precious jewels, which she lost while hiding there'. Westbury vaguely wondered whether the thing currently soaking in a bowl in his kitchen was related, or was it just a story made up to add a bit of legend to an otherwise bland building?

Natasha was waiting for him when he arrived. As she got in the car she expected to see the emergency clothes, maybe in a bag or perhaps he'd decided to give them a wash before returning them. Either way it was a good sign. They had a great evening with lots of laughs and a little bit of healthy innuendo. When he dropped her off she decided not to offer a night cap, yet. Oddly enough the chance of spending a bit more time in her company hadn't crossed Westbury's mind, it didn't work that way.

It was a couple of days before the call came, but Natasha had more or less expected it. "Hi, Natasha, it's Scott. I was wondering when it might be convenient for me to bring back Robin Gibb's leisure suit?"

Natasha was pleased. It had crossed her mind that Scott might just drop the clothes on her doorstep and run, but he seemed interested and so was she.

"This evening if you like, I'm making a Thai curry, any good?"

"Sounds great, I can bring wine".

"Terrific, a nice Californian white would be good in case you're wondering. See you later, seven-ish".

Scott reflected on the events of the past few days, then he had to rush to the loo again before rummaging in his travel first-aid kit for the Imodium. He hoped that the after-effects of rinsing his insides with Trent water wouldn't come back to haunt him at an inopportune moment. He shoved the now clean necklace into his jeans pocket and set off for Carlton Booze, hoping they might have something from the Golden State.

After a nice meal and emptying the wine bottles to a point where driving was not advisable, Scott and Natasha found themselves very compatible. "That necklace, did you take a photo?"

"Better than that", he said, and he fished his jeans off the bedroom floor and produced the piece, it looked much better not caked in mud.

"Wow, it's better than I thought. Somebody lost this, there might even be a reward. Can I try it on?"

Westbury fastened the necklace around Natasha's slim neck, it suited her. "If you want it, it's yours". Later on he reflected on his fishing permit being the best thing he'd bought in ages because if he'd not gone to Colwick, he'd never have fallen in the Trent and he wouldn't be where he was now.

Unfortunately, Imodium is only effective for so long.

Twelve

03 August 2017

John Fraser sat in the Land Rover, watching nothing but the rain. Next to him was a kid from the local school, 'Kieffer with two ffs', he'd stressed that point when introducing himself on his first day. He was on a week's work experience placement by choice, even though school was out for summer. It was complicated and involved suspensions. Colwick was a popular gig with the older kids for work experience because word had got around that Fraser had a very relaxed attitude to life. If they had half a brain, most kids got to use the patrol boat or even drive the Land Rover, off-road. That more than made up for emptying the dog shit bins and cleaning up endless bits of rubbish dropped, or dumped, by the ignoranti of Nottingham.

"This rain, Kieffer with two ffs, would you say it's just falling down? I reckon we could go for siling down myself, although connoisseurs of precipitation might argue. I'd value your input".

Kieffer wasn't used to being asked his opinion, he was also really pissed off because his work placement had been three days of solid rain so far, and he desperately wanted to do stuff like his mates had. "I don't know what 'siling' means".

"That's because it isn't an official word but, while you won't find 'siling' in the concise Oxford English dictionary, in some parts of the world, and in the case of siling we're talking East Yorkshire- although they will insist on calling it Humberside- siling is a perfectly adequate way to describe the sort of rain we're seeing. Locally we say 'plothering', but not often, now. If we headed up to Geordie land we could say 'hoying doon', the 'doon' meaning down for those that speak English, it's all a bit of a minefield really".

"My Nan would say it's bucketing it down, my grandad was more basic with pissing down. Neither ever said 'siling'".

"Your nan's not from Hull, then?"

"No, Barbados".

"Really? You don't look Caribbean".

"I lied about my colour".

"Very wise, I lied about having a Franco-Prussian lineage although it did me no good whatsoever, because here I am sat in a Land Rover with the rain siling down. Sorry we've not got exciting things for you to do yet. We do need to fix that floating log boom to stop the toy boaters straying at some point. I suppose we could put our waterproofs on and do it, although we're sure to get siled on".

"I think I'm ready to face a bit of siling".

"Come on then, let's go and find you a nice pink lifejacket. They should be orange, but they're about a hundred years old and have faded badly, sorry about that. At least the lettering saying 'Titanic' has faded too".

"If they're that old, will they float?"

"Let's hope we don't need to find out".

Launching the boat was routine, especially if you checked the bung was in before it shot off the trailer, which Fraser had. The engine could be a bit temperamental, but with effort and application it would finally catch. After backing the ensemble down the slipway, Fraser gave the boat an extra ping into the water. Not because the water was low, anything but, because Kieffer was sat in the boat and now had to row back to the jetty, it was character-building. Kieffer was soon forty yards out and asking loudly how to row. It hadn't occurred to Fraser that something as basic as rowing might not be widely known.

Fortunately it was quite windy and the boat drifted into the bank some way from the jetty. Fraser scrambled abroad and did a rowing demonstration, taking the boat far enough from the shore that he could run the engine without taking a blade off the prop. On the front seat, Kieffer sat and shivered and dreamed of a desk job, or at least one where he didn't have to wear a pink lifejacket. A cloud of oily blue smoke announced that the engine would grant the person pulling the starter cord perhaps one more performance, then they set off. It was a bit splashy out on the lake but, by now, they would be more likely to get drier than wetter. Fraser was already wondering whether this little exercise was wise.

The log boom was usually strung across a bay at one end of the lake. The people who played with toy boats there tended to need something to catch their toys when they inevitably lost control of them, much like their sanity, but the boom was elderly and kept breaking. A new set of fresh logs and decent linking chains was required, but council cutbacks bit deep, so it was always a patch-up job unless they unexpectedly came across something suitable just lying around somewhere. Things were getting so tight that the Colwick crew were expecting their jobs to go next.

Fraser expertly looped one end of the rope through a detached link on one log then got Kieffer to hand-out the rope until the boat found the other section flapping in the waves. After making a sturdy knot, the boat was eased to a central point between the logs and Fraser told Kieffer to drop the boat's anchor, then they both hauled on the ropes. Fraser kept an eye on Kieffer, he didn't want another one falling out the boat and their mum suing the council for their drowned phone. He'd told her to leave it in the office but, oh no, kids can't be away from Shagchat or whatever for ten minutes before they shrivel and die.

It was slow going, the wind was busy and the waves were now splashing freely into the boat, depositing at least eight inches of lake water into the bottom, water that repeatedly sloshed over the top of their wellies. Finally, the two halves came together and a clip was applied to the elderly bits of chain and the log boom was restored for future generations of toy boat-fondlers to enjoy. Fraser readied himself to head back to the jetty, but first there was a second initiative test for Kieffer to undertake. He sat there waiting.

"Are we done?" asked Kieffer, dripping into the boat.

"One last thing to do, any ideas on that front?" Fraser was a great believer in making the kids do the thinking at times like this, they probably never got the chance at school.

"Oh, the anchor, I'll pull it up, yes?"

"Good man, we'll make a sailor of you yet".

The anchor came in very slowly and Fraser wondered whether Kieffer was stretching the job out for some sort of sado-masochistic reason of his own. He was just about to go and hurry him up a bit when Kieffer fell backwards almost into Fraser lap, followed by the anchor and a hessian sack covered in a fair bit of sludge.

"Oh, fuck me", said Fraser, then remembered himself. "Sorry about that, not supposed to swear when we have our young guests".

"Don't worry, Mr. Price who teaches maths swears all the time, says we're all a bunch of thick shits and should fuck off and die. He's one of the best teachers we have, the rest treat us like kids".

"Education has changed a bit since I went to school. How's your stomach?"

"Alright, I'm not seasick or anything".

"No, it's not that, I have an idea that something resides in that sack that might make you jump but, if you're ok, tip the sack up and let's see if I'm right".

Before Fraser could step in with more words of caution, Kieffer held the sack out at chest height, tipping out the contents. A skull fell to the bottom of the boat, splashing into the now muddy and much deeper water, quite a bit of which went in Kieffer's open mouth. It is not wise to jump about in in a small boat on a choppy lake, you could almost call it initiative test number three.

The Fishing Lodge had the heater turned up high, which suited the desk warden as his metabolism was more dinosaur than human due to extreme age. On one of the plastic chairs, Kieffer sat in green overalls that were at least seventeen sizes too big, a mug of tea in his hand, his dripping clothing on a wire above one of the electric heaters. Fraser had briefed the desk warden to call Thompson and report another skull while he put the boat away.

"Still cold", said Kieffer, his teeth comedically chattering.

The old boy eased off his chair, opened a drawer and plopped a generous helping of something strong-smelling into the tea. "Drink that, you'll stop shivering". Kieffer drank his tea in greedy gulps and went back for a second dollop. He was giggling a lot when Fraser got back and saw what had happed. "Another blanket might have been favourite, Jack".

"At his age I was drinking half a bottle of rum a day".

"When you were his age cavemen roamed the earth and the wheel was the hot new thing" Kieffer seemed to find this hilarious.

Fraser rearranged the unplanned washing. He was hoping to dry enough of it so that Kieffer would be comfortable, if slightly damp, but at least in his own clothes before he went home. The lodge door opened and a drowned kitten walked in. "Hello Carla, still spitting out there I see".

Carla Adams didn't seem to want to chat, she was wet-through, having made the mistake of thinking she'd not get very wet nipping from the car to the lodge, she did. Fraser handed her a plastic rubbish bag. "What's up with him?" she asked.

"Pissed I'm afraid, they no longer teach children how to imbibe strong liquor in schools, the country's going to the dogs".

"He's underage, he shouldn't be drinking".

Kieffer found this all even more amusing, but then the lake water mixed with alcohol started to have an effect and he rushed off to the toilet where he yelled for 'hughie'.

"He fell in, got very cold, it was medicinal, Officer. My desk warden here probably saved his life". From the toilet, the sound of amateur yodelling continued.

"Three hughies in quick succession, quite impressive for one so young", said Carla, turning down the offer of tea and something in it. "What would be the logistics of draining the lake?"

"Ten large pumps, six weeks and no rain, and the entire park diesel budget for a year, roughly".

"Sorry, I was told to ask. Right, thanks for the offer of tea and this", and she patted the bagged-up skull. "Try not to find any more, or if you do, catch the person who keeps chucking them in, please".

"Funny you should say that, but one of the local nutters saw something".

"Surely you mean local rate payers?"

"I pronounce rate payer differently, it's my Franco-Prussian lineage, sorry. Anyway, she reckons she saw an old guy throw something into the lake. She didn't get a great look but she's sure it was an old man. I've asked for some trail cams to be fitted at strategic points for that and other sundry issues".

Carla knew what Fraser meant, once staff had left the park for the day it became a playground for the nefarious of Nottinghamshire. "That would be good, do you think you'll get them?"

"Almost certainly, they'll be very useful for filming hell freezing over and pigs flying past in formation. They call themselves the Pork Choppers, the local pig formation flying team". Just then the loudest 'hughie' of the lot came from the toilet.

"Anyway", said Carla in the protracted way that people use to humour the insane. "This will be added to our growing collection and I'll pass on the info about the old man. I'd appreciate a name for the nutter and, if you say what's wrong with 'Carla', I'll arrest you".

"Her name is Natasha, I don't know her last name but she's here daily with her dog".

"Very upright-walking lady, looks like she's on a catwalk?"

"That would be her, yes. She's local I think, maybe even Candle Meadow".

"Natasha Ellis, I know her. I'll drop by and have a chat. Got to go, has the rain eased?"

"I think so, less siling now, more cats and dogs. Ask Thompson if he's thought of doing an identification parade with the skulls on TV, might be somebody out there will recognise one of them".

"They all look the same, John".

"Skullist. I suppose I shouldn't be surprised at such prejudice from the police".

"Not really, one of ours already cracked that rubbish joke about a line-up in a briefing, so I'm just mocking your unoriginal material, must try harder", and with that Carla dashed for her car, it was all getting too surreal. Fraser had been incorrect, it was still siling down, but now with murderous intent. Inside the Fishing Lodge, Kieffer had left 'hughie' to his own devices and was now wrapped up in the Lifeguard's emergency blanket. "She's nice", he said, suddenly looking a bit brighter.

"No good for you, son", said the desk warden. "Sups from the furry cup".

"Oh, she's gay, right, well she's still nice. What? We study inclusivity at school. I might not know bugger all about rowing but I do know all about homophobes and bigots like you". Kieffer had moved swiftly from the giggling phase to the confrontational phase that alcohol often encourages.

The old boy wasn't happy, but Fraser stepped in and calmed the mood. "Come on lad, gather your soggy clothes and I'll run you home. Don't tell your mother about the reviving brew".

"She won't care, she knows all about reviving brews".

"And sorry about you getting wet and everything, hopefully no rain tomorrow, or so they reckon".

"No worries, this has been a great day so far, looking forward to tomorrow", and Fraser could see that Kieffer genuinely was. How unstimulating must life be if a highlight is falling into Colwick Lake? For the first time, Fraser had some deep understanding of why Colwick was so popular as work experience, he just wished they'd stop coming back and dumping their stolen cars once they'd left school.

Back in the Fishing Lodge the old boy was closing up. He knew Fraser would send him home early when he got back, nobody was going to be on the park in this weather. He was wrong. "Can I book a slip out please?" A slip out involved the Colwick staff hauling a boat out of the water on a large, metal cradle.

"I'll check with John when he gets back. Trouble?"

"Yes, my mate just had to tow me in, prop issues. I probably shouldn't have gone out with the river like this but I wanted to run up the engine, I've not been down a while. It might just be an 'in and out', is that still full price?"

"Three-day slip minimum, sorry, but you can talk to John about that. I'll just scribble down your name and number and he'll call tomorrow". Just then the Land Rover pulled into the park. "He's here now, you're in the diary in pencil", and he slid the plastic partition window closed, which told the customer the audience was over.

Fraser rushed into the lodge, dodging the rain. "Trouble?"

The boater explained the issues and John set up a time for the next day, before clumsily erasing the booking out of the diary. The same boater had once donated ten bags of ready-mixed cement to the park so that the wardens were able to make some of the strategic access-point bollards less able to be removed. He'd asked for nothing in return but had good-will in the bank, things sometimes ran best when employing a reciprocal economy at Colwick. There was also a note from above about a weather warning for the next day. More rain now, lagging it down perhaps in the afternoon. Looks like Kieffer's going to have another exciting time, he thought.

Despite the continuing rain, Carla decided to walk the short distance to Natasha Ellis's house from her place. She'd only just dried out from her trip to Colwick, so she donned a large waterproof and dug out her umbrella. She knew she wouldn't get paid any extra for this little visit, a detective's life didn't work that way, the clock was something that other people watched. Natasha Ellis's house was one of the identical places built on Candle Meadow when ticky-tacky was all the rage. The small fence and gate had a sign suggesting visitors should be wary of the dog, but Carla guessed it was all for show. She knocked, next door a curtain twitched. The door in front opened a crack and Natasha stood in the opening, looking a little wary.

"Natasha? Hi, it's Carla. You probably don't remember me, I used to run with the local kids years ago. I'm Detective Constable Adams now, I understand you might have information regarding a case we're working on, can I come in?" Carla brandished her warrant card, for extra encouragement.

"Carla, right, no, sorry I don't remember you. Give me a moment to put the dog in the kitchen. He doesn't bite but he can be over-interested, if you get my drift". The door closed and Adams heard the patter of dog claws on bare flooring. The door opened fully and Carla entered the wet-dog smelling house. As she went through, she made a mental note of the man's coat on the back of a chair and a pair of large trainers on a plastic tray.

"Is this about the man I saw? I already told John Fraser everything I saw, I don't think I can add anything material to your case".

"No, that's fine, I just need to hear about it directly from you, for the case files".

"Will I be named?"

"Yes. I'll just add the details as a witness statement, standard procedure".

"I'm not happy about giving my name".

"Ok, but I assure you it's confidential. Nobody outside the investigating team sees the statement and the case is unlikely to be anything more than some weirdo getting skulls from somewhere- you do know the thing your man chucked in the lake was a human skull?" Carla wasn't intending to give details, but felt that, because this Natasha Ellis was clearly nervous about police involvement, she'd give her a bit of information to stress the gravity of the situation, such as it was. She'd also talk to the computer about her tomorrow.

"No, I didn't know that. I thought it was probably a cat or something, people can be so cruel to animals. I still don't want to give my name to a statement but I'll tell you what happened and that's it, take it or leave it. I know I'm not obliged".

'Previous then', thought Carla. "No, you're right, you're not obliged", she said, subtly informing Natasha that she'd got the message.

"I know what you're thinking, I don't have a police record but I do have a past. I left that behind when I moved here and there are people from that past I don't want to deal with, I hope you understand. Carla did but was still going to have a look in the files anyway.

"I'll just jot bullet notes, off you go in your own time, everything from the beginning, please".

"I was walking the dog around Colwick Park, as I do three times a day at least. I saw a man, older, I'd say dishevelled. He was some distance from me, I was on what they call the peninsula; if you're local you'll know it. He came in from the Nature Reserve area, possibly from the Starter's Orders end where the flood bank is, or was. He walked out to where the bench is directly in front of the gate by the little bridge and threw something in the lake. As I said, I was some distance away and lost him when he turned and walked back the way he came. I went around to where he'd thrown whatever it was, in case it was a struggling cat, but saw nothing. Today I bumped into John Fraser emptying bins around the park and stopped to chat, I'm sure he thinks I'm just a local nutter or something. I remembered the incident and told him all about it. That was it, nothing really".

"Not nothing, Natasha, a lead. We now want to speak to this person in connection with the case. I wonder if he drove?"

"The gates were locked, I passed that way, so if he came in the Starters Orders way he didn't park inside the park. It was late in the day when I saw him, the wardens sometimes lock that barrier early when they can. It had been bucketing down all day, but stopped for a few hours in the early evening so I took advantage. You'll have noticed the wet dog smell, seems we get wet every time we go out. Maybe the Starter's Orders pub was where he parked, or he could have come on the bus".

It was true, the rain had been almost never ending. "Are you concerned about your property? The flood bank has held so far in places but further along its busted".

"I think we should all be concerned, Carla, biblical rain shouldn't happen, it's a myth that seems to be coming true but I'm far enough away from the water, for now".

"And you can think of nothing else? Can you clarify 'dishevelled' for me, please?"

Old clothes that looked too big for him. He had a strange way of walking, like his feet were sticking to the floor and it was an effort to drag them free".

"Like when you wear wellies?"

"Yes, like that only more exaggerated. I think he had green trousers on, it was hard to tell what shade but probably same general green colour as the park Land Rover".

It's amazing how much more detail witnesses can recall if you get their brain warmed up first. Outside the rain continued unrelenting, so Carla thanked Natasha, said if she changed her mind about being named on the statement would she call her, left a card and walked home with the rain hammering on her umbrella. Once home, Carla pinged a text to Thompson, giving him the basics as told by Natasha.

"Who was it?" asked Scott Westbury. He'd tried to listen to the conversation from upstairs, but the rooms were pretty well sound-proofed, probably a selling feature when your neighbour is just the other side of a thin wall.

"The police, about that man I saw chucking that bag in, I might not have told you. She was a local girl, I know her vaguely, she might be able to help advise about the bling you found".

"I've been reading up, it might have belonged to a lady of Colwick Hall. Seems some event years ago made them hide in the garden and her jewels fell in the lake or something. It might be treasure trove".

"Could be, if that jewel story wasn't just a tale for tourists. Besides, I've seen a bit of bling in my time and yours is more recent in design. I think it was probably nicked sometime and brought by the river, you might have to talk to Carla about it but on your own if you decided to report it, I want no part of it. Now where were we?"

"Well the music's finished, does it have to be The Bolero?"

"I've got the Minute Waltz if that helps".

"I was thinking more Dark Side of the Moon".

"How about Meatloaf's 'I'll do anything for love, but I won't do that?'"

The thick walls did their job muffling the laughter and everything else, while the woman next door was busy doing whatever thing it was that she did, besides twitching curtains.

Thirteen

04 August 2017

"Carla, Jenny, a minute, please".

He'd hung his jacket, put his coffee down, put his snap, a box of Jaffa Cakes, in the drawer and nobody had arrived. Thompson started to feel irrationally angry when Jenny arrived. "Carla will be two seconds, she's just saving something on the PC". Carla was actually a couple of minutes but Thompson had subsided by then.

"Carla, I want to shift you from Jenny's Wet Bones case to a new case, the fire-bombing. I'll need a team brief later from Lorna, can you help her with it, ok?" It was a courtesy 'ok' more than anything, so he was surprised when Carla asked to work the bones case in tandem.

"Why?" It was a very curt question from Thompson, both officers noticed.

"Local interest, I've made contact with a potential witness, I know the area and people there, and I might have something", said Carla, defensively.

"A potential witness? You've seen them?"

"Yes, I picked up another skull when I went home last night, then saw the potential witness when Fraser mentioned her. I did text you".

Thompson pulled his phone out and scrolled. "Shit, sorry, I must have had the thing on quiet time, I missed it. Natasha Ellis, I see it now, go on".

"She's adamant that she won't make a formal statement, but she told me all the details she has. I think our guy probably comes in a car or on the bus with the skulls, dumps them in the lake for whatever reason and

114

then leaves. What we need to see first are the bus-cams for the route and dates. I think they have a set period before deletion".

Thompson had forgotten his irritation. "Brilliant, is that ok with you, Jenny?"

"Why am I only hearing this now? I am lead".

"Because I have only been here, checks watch, eleven minutes, possibly only five before The Mighty Dave called us in. That is what I was saving, my write-up, which I've forwarded to you both", said Carla, calmly.

"Sorry Carla, my bad, I woke up snappy this morning, can't think why. Great work, I'd be happy if The Mighty Dave allowed you to work with us on this", said Banks, contritely.

"Speaking as The Mighty Dave himself, ok, go with it, but I need another officer with Lorna and we've got another thing to do that will require a field trip. You, Jenny, will be going to Leicester to talk to a famous footballer. Tilda will be doing the trip with you too and playing agent provocateur. Intrigued? Good. I'm not taking any questions at this point.

A light tap, which was slightly off-rhythm, indicated that Ranjit from Human Resources was outside. "Come in Ranji", said Thompson. "Thanks people, I need a quick word with our new recruit before throwing him to the wolves". As Jenny and Carla left, Jenny was going through Carla's chat with Natasha and discussing how long it was before the bus-cams got deleted.

"I told you, Simon, your boss is telepathic so watch your step. Detective Inspector, this is Simon Beresford, you've already had his file. He's yours now, apart from us needing him occasionally for HR mind-conditioning". Thompson smiled. He had grown to like Ranji, despite initially thinking he was a total dickhead after their first meeting. Ranji knew not to linger, Simon seemed to know nothing, he just stood there, waiting.

"Sit. Right. I'm 'Boss' casually, 'Sir', formally. You might, at times, get to address me as 'Dave' but not yet. You are joining a new team made of two old ones, it's a recent thing and we've only had a handful of weeks to get to know each other. You will work with Detective Constable Carla Adams. She is your boss despite being the same rank. You will do what she tells you to at all times. I'll introduce you to the rest of the team you'll be working with shortly, but in brief they are DS Jenny Banks, DS Mickey Newton, Acting DS Lorna Meikle, DC Liam Prosser, DC Josh Brady and DC Laura Knight. DS Newton is also known as 'Gecko', you'll know why when you meet him. DC Knight is mostly called 'Elkie' round here, I'll leave you to figure out why. So, any questions?

Beresford seemed to take this question as something deep and meaningful. Thompson was patient but he was also busy. "Well?"

"What time is lunch?" he said, smiling.

Thompson took it as a joke and ushered Simon into the main office. "Right, everyone, this is Simon Beresford. Ranji has delivered him to us, Carla is mummy for now but I want you all to join in. Show him where things are, make sure he learns not to piss me off otherwise we'll need a shovel and a van again and, thinking about it, a different wood to bury the body in, not much room in the old spot".

The group laughed. The little speech was Thompson's way of easing a new recruit's nerves, not that Simon Beresford seemed to have any. Carla walked over and led the new boy to the worst desk in the office, the rest had plenty to do, Simon could wait.

"Oh, I see, it's her initials, L and K, Elkie, right?" said Beresford.

"I can see that you're going to be a real bundle of joy, Simon", said Carla. "Right, let's us log on and I'll show you were the files are".

Thompson knocked and waited. Normally Perkins knew who was there knocking on his door and why. This time nothing. He waited for a count of fifty and knocked again. "Come". Thompson's suspicious mind suggested that Perkins needed to hide something from public view, hence the delay.

"Malone, Sir. I was thinking Banks and Elkie, men like him tend to relax when a woman is interviewing. Thoughts, Sir?"

"Malone fire-bombed a young woman without a second thought, David. I want you to interview, go in as hard as you can. Take Elkie, she'll read him and let Lorna observe, although I imagine you could sell tickets for this one".

"And Prosser? I had a quick word on the phone earlier, he's coming in later, after speaking to HR. I suppose he's going to be busy on courses himself for a while?"

"Cynical David, but true. We need to be seen addressing anger issues from officers, even if it's only for the benefit of those above. Keep Prosser away from Malone for now, but don't rule out employing the psychology of fear. I doubt Malone would want to meet Prosser in a dark alley, for many reasons".

"What aren't you saying, Sir?"

"Malone is a long-standing intimidation artist in his native Belfast and, as such, I expect a resounding silence from him. I forwarded his details to you, no doubt you will brief the troops before hauling him into the luxury of the interview room. So far he's not asked for representation, but don't be surprised if Silenzi appears. If he does, that will be as good as a straight line to Collins. If not, then we'll know he's cut him loose. Either way Collins is in the spotlight".

"Repercussions from Malone's boss?"

"If word got out that Collins hung their boy out to dry, yes, but don't be tempted to leak anything and make sure your team know the same. We don't want any more imports causing trouble here. When Collins gets his, we are the ones who will be giving it to him and if we can't, I'll be the one to leak it, understood?"

Thompson could see that Perkins was still spitting feathers about Collins, where he'd hardly given it another thought, home issues were at the front of his mind. He'd even briefly considered suggesting counselling or something, to try to get back on an even keel with Rebecca.

"Anything else, David? Only I think it's time we got Kevin Malone in the hot seat, don't you?"

Back in the general office, Elkie was missing, Josh mimed that she had gone to the loo. It was a piece of performance art that nobody wanted to see ever again. At the worst desk in the room he could see Carla being painfully patient with their new charge as she showed him the system. He wondered whether he should share Beresford's lineage with the group, whether it would be fair to the boy himself.

"Sorry Boss, I take it I'm in with you while we try to make Malone talk, yes?" Elkie was back and raring to go.

"Yes. Lorna, observe in case we miss anything". Lorna could lip-read very well, a skill only known to a couple of the team. Not that Lorna would do anything as unethical as lip-reading people who didn't want you to know what they were saying, perhaps to their solicitor.

Custody staff had Malone ready when they got there. He looked a bit tired and unwashed and his bruises had developed nicely overnight. Thompson marched in, followed by Elkie. They took their places, got the tapes going and made a start.

"Kevin, you do know why you're here?"

"Yes, Sir". Well, that was different. Both officers had been braced for a lengthy round of 'no comment'.

"Can you account for your movements yesterday? Starting with when you got up, where you went and who you talked to".

"Yes, Sir, I can. In the morning after a shit and a shave, sorry miss, I went to see a man about a job".

Thompson had an idea of what was happening. "And this man, did you know him, do you have a name?"

"I do, Sir, his name is Duncan Collins, he's a local businessman, Sir. You may know him". Oh deary me. Thompson stopped the tape and he and Elkie left the room. "Observe only", he said to Elkie and Lorna. "I need to talk to a man about a set-up".

"Back so soon, David?" Perkins was surprised when Thompson had knocked and not waited for a reply. Thompson for his part was surprised to see Tilda Jeffries in there. "Detective Constable Jeffries was just updating me on a case from her former life in Vice. I maintain a passing interest and she has been good enough to feed that interest. Thank you, Tilda, if you hear any more I'd be grateful for an update".

"This had better be good, David". Thompson stood aside while Tilda crept past, then explained what he thought was happening, Perkins listened.

"Put him back in a cell for now, I need to talk to people and I don't mean Collins. I might have to pass this one up to a more senior officer, you do understand?"

"Yes, Sir, but if you need me to continue with the case at some point in the future, I'm happy to".

As soon as Collins had been mentioned, he'd expected to have the case yanked and was even slightly relieved. If a nutter like Ray Frost was happy to try to kill Jock Charnley in a car crusher, what might the likes of Collins try with Prosser and Gecko, or even him? At least with nutters you know what to expect.

For the first time in a while it wasn't actually raining, merely suggesting that it might later, they'd said it would. Seeing as it was his last day, Kieffer had been allowed to mop boats out, make tea and clean up the night's excesses which seemed to have involved three wine bottles, twenty beer cans, a disposable barbecue and the remnants of a large fire that had been powered by local foliage. Just a normal night really. Then Fraser told him he'd got something a bit different for him. "Today, Kieffer with two ffs, we will be pulling a boat out of the water in the Marina. You will be in the water with me while we chock-up the boat, then we'll winch it part-way up so the owner can untangle the prop. I'm expecting maybe a nylon veg bag, or some nylon rope. It shouldn't take him long and we can roll him back in later. I have chest waders for you, what size feet do you currently have?"

"Fourteen".

"Change of plan then, we only got up to a ten. You will stay dry and I'll be in the water but you will work the winch and, if things go smoothly, you can roll him back into the water. Relaunching is a procedure which is often quite exciting, especially if the boat won't start once you let him go".

Kieffer was beside himself, at last, a proper day of doing things. Pity it wasn't going to help the computer programming career he had in mind.

In the Marina, the boat had been moved from its temporary berth by a narrowboat, broadside. It was then eased over the waiting, submerged haul-out cradle, but gently because fiberglass can react to angled metal in quite a bad way. The owner had been out on the cradle before and so knew to follow any instructions to the letter, all to be shouted clearly by Fraser, despite him being in possession of what might be called a 'delicate' head.

Fraser showed Kieffer how to work the winch, which as it consisted of pressing a red button, and then not pressing it when told to stop, wasn't too taxing. Slowly they eased the cradle out of the water and the boat started to settle, ready for the first chocks. "Ok, over to you. Watch me, if I raise my arm, stop, ok?"

"Got it. What will you be doing?"

"As the boat comes out the water, I'll be putting angled wooden blocks where I can to stop it falling over. The winch is slow, but sometimes the boats can wobble a bit until they settle. Watch me, arm up and stop", and he waddled down and into the water.

"Keep it coming", yelled Fraser, and Kieffer nervously pressed the red button. The ratio on the winch gears meant progress was comfortably slow and Fraser happily scampered over to a pile of wood several times, selecting various suitable bits before climbing into the water. At one point the water was almost up to his chest, but then he found the spot he wanted. Kieffer pressed red and the boat edged forward.

Happy that no disaster was likely and the boat now secure, Fraser walked up the slipway to the winch and unclipped his chest waders. "Nice and steady", he said, not that Kieffer could do anything else. Further up the Marina, the boater who'd eased the stricken vessel around to the haul-out cradle had tied his own boat up and was heading back over for a look. He could see the boat gradually clearing the water, but the prop was still hidden and would be for a few minutes more yet.

"I told him not to go on the river, John, but he's itching to try out the new engine. I hope the river drops soon, we've not been out for a month ourselves". The Good Samaritan was stood with John and Kieffer, intent on setting the world to rights.

"The forecast is pretty wet for the next seven days, you might end up writing the summer off until the end of August at this rate", said Fraser, aware that many of the Marina regulars were spending money on boats they couldn't use.

"This is all down to climate change, we did that at school", said Kieffer, suddenly feeling the urge to converse. "My generation will have to try to fix the problems of those who went before us, my teacher said we're doomed".

"Not quite doomed, I think", said Fraser. "But, yes, we need to change and now. This doom-monger teacher, what's his subject?"

"Religious education, and he's the careers master, too".

"I thought the religious lot were all accepting their fate as God's will?"

"I don't think he's actually a believer, more that RE was easy to teach so he went for it. He's gay for a start and he talks more Humanist values than Christian ones. I quite like him, he's another one that listens".

Fraser was starting to realise that Kieffer's thoughts on life ran deeper than you'd expect from one so young.

The helper had wandered down the slipway to get a look at the prop and drive shaft as the back-end of the boat started to clear the water. "John, here".

Fraser knew the tone. "Stop now and wait for my signal. Don't come down the slipway under any circumstances, I'm serious".

Kieffer was stunned. Fraser had been all about joking and not taking things seriously, but now there was no doubt that he had to do what he'd been told. If this was that serious he wanted to know what was going on. Fraser half-ran down the slipway until he could see what the helper saw. "What?" yelled the boat owner from his lofty perch.

"Stay there", said Fraser with no politeness. He walked back up the slipway. "Come on, Kieffer, we have things to do elsewhere", and he bustled the lad into the Land Rover where he used his radio to get the desk warden to call the police.

"What's up, what was around the prop, is it a stiff?" Fraser was surprised, Kieffer didn't seem at all upset that there might be a body wrapped around the propeller shaft of the boat they'd hauled out.

"Yes, a body and not very nice to look at either, which is why we're going to find you some lodge work".

"No, I want to help, I've seen bodies before. The skull just made me jump, I wasn't frightened or anything, it was just a skull".

"Bodies, really, when?"

"When my mum crashed the car".

Fraser's mind went back to a recent conversation with Kieffer, the one where he mentioned his mum knowing all about reviving brews. "Ok, you're a big lad but don't sue me if you have nightmares". After that, Fraser called his desk warden again and told him to clean up some mugs for guests.

Thompson listened to Fraser's description of the body, he was fairly sure that it would turn out to be a Johnson. After speaking to SOCO, he'd intended to send Lorna and Gecko to investigate, but Lorna was in with HR so he sent Prosser and Gecko instead, Lorna to follow when she'd done. It seemed odd to think of Prosser as a DC again, sergeant had been a really good fit for him. When Prosser and Gecko got there, the boat had been hauled all the way up the slipway and various SOCO people were doing what they needed to do where the mangled body was concerned. Fraser and Kieffer were keeping well back when Prosser found them. "Messy, John. This place is a stiff magnet".

"Is it one of the Johnsons? Joe Meade told me we might get some watery visitors".

"Yes, we believe so but we're not sure which one yet, Mickey is waiting for a look at a wallet. It would have helped us with the ID if he still had the rest of his face. You ok, lad?"

"Fine", said Kieffer, who was.

"And you, John, you ok?"

"Yes, fine, but the poor bloke who owns the boat is in a bit of a state. He got a close-up of the body when we fetched a ladder to get him down. Your counselling people might want a word".

"I'll get my sergeant to see to it", said Prosser.

"I thought you were the sergeant, Liam?" said Fraser, puzzled.

"No, not any more, don't ask", and Prosser went back to where Gecko was on the phone talking Thompson through how things looked.

"This one's Matty Johnson, Boss. There was a wallet in his pocket, I can see a driving licence, his photo doesn't much look like him now though. He was dead before he got wrapped around the prop, it did a bit of slicing and dicing before it stopped spinning. I had a word with the owner and explained, he felt a bit better after, must have been a shock".

"Thanks, Mickey, Lorna's on her way down. Tell Liam to brief her when she gets there".

"There's no need for her to come down, Boss, we've got it".

"She's your Boss on this one, she needs to be involved. You know the score, Mickey, Liam too".

When Thompson had gone, Gecko relayed the conversation to Prosser. "Quite right too, Mickey, by the book. Lorna's the Boss and Dave is the Almighty, don't forget that". Gecko knew Prosser was right but it didn't make it any easier. "I think young Kieffer there has more stomach than a lot of adults I know, I wonder what his story is?" said Prosser, deftly changing the subject.

"I know of his mother, if that helps fill in the blanks". Prosser nodded, it did. Lorna eventually arrived and was a bit awkward at first, but Gecko saw that Prosser had eased her in the right direction, introduced her to the protagonists and then stepped back while she asserted herself. The transition was seamless.

Lorna talked to the boat owner for a while and explained the issues. He'd be out until they'd finished their investigation but it shouldn't take too long, then she went over to where Prosser was having a smoke. "Best get back to the nick, boys, I'll follow. I just want to look at a couple of things here to get up to speed. The boss has a new case and he's called a brief for Monday. Sergeants' meeting before, Liam".

"I'm sure that won't be involving me, Lorna, busted for six months, remember?"

"I do, but the Boss told me to tell you to be there, he'll have his reasons".

Prosser didn't know what to make of that. He'd instantly accepted the demotion and he had no problem working with either Jenny, Lorna or even Joe if he ever came back. Gecko was less sure. "I thought it'd be a face-saving thing, you know, public bump down but privately nothing changes".

"Then you don't know the boss, Mickey. He'll play it dead straight but on his own terms. I don't know why he wants me there either, I do know it won't be to rub my nose in it in front of Banks and Meikle".

"I heard he chewed you out yesterday big time".

"Chewed but didn't swallow, Mickey, you'll learn"

Fourteen

05 August-06 August 2017

Jenny Banks had surprised herself in going out on a limb with Dave. It hadn't been planned, just a spur-of-the-moment instinct that something was possible, it was something she still wanted. That he'd turned her down didn't bother her either, she sensed an inevitability about the situation, she'd just have to be patient a little longer. Quite what the rest of them would make of it when it happened she didn't know or care. Only Elkie was close to Rebecca and even she was seeing cracks. Could Dave see them too?

First things first, she had to know where Joe was with her. She'd phoned a few times Saturday and left messages. It was Sunday now and if he didn't answer this call, the situation had 'Dear John' written all over it. Jenny had decided he'd get seven rings, she was surprised, and not a bit disappointed, when he picked up on six.

"What's going on, Joe?" The phone stayed silent a while, as if the person who was supposed to answer was working out something plausible to say. She filled in the silence.

"Well, just so you know, I'm not happy. I don't like not knowing where I am with someone who I thought was my boyfriend, especially when he announces, out of the blue, that his ex-wife has showed up. How ex is she exactly?" It remained quiet, then she heard a light sniff, followed by another which at least confirmed that there was someone on the end of the line.

"Joe, if you don't start talking to me now, I'm hanging up and we're done. I don't function like this and if you think I'll be the one that leaves the team, think again".

"I hadn't thought of that". Joe Lawrence didn't sound at all like Banks had expected him to. Instead he was detached, hung over possibly?

"Yes, well, you mess with me at your peril and, as for Dave, his patience is paper-thin with you now. Come on, what the fuck is going on with you?"

"Sorry, I can't tell you anything yet. Things have sort of crept up on me, what with Marie and everything else. I need a bit more time to sort this out".

"You'd better talk to Dave then, he's not an ogre, normally, but like I said, he's pissed off at you too, and it takes a lot to get the wrong side of genial Dave".

"No, I can't talk to Dave, I can't explain just yet. I'm sorry to mess you about, I can't commit to anything at the moment so we'd better take a break. Yes, we should step back a little, just to give me time to get things sorted. I'll explain when I can but not now". He was almost pleading, sounding weak.

"This is where you apologise profusely for messing me about and you keep telling me it's not me but it's you. Ok, a bit longer". The phone stayed virtually silent with just the occasional sniff in the background, so Banks hung up. 'Well, that was different', she thought as she pocketed her phone. 'At least I know where I stand with Joe for now, but Dave doesn't, yet. Technically I'm a free agent again, pending'.

"Jenny, what's up?" Elkie mouthed 'Jenny Banks' to Cliff who was sat next to her in the local pub. Elkie could count on the fingers of Gecko's injured hand the number of times Jenny had called her, socially.

"Sorry to bother you, I just needed to hear a friendly voice. I just talked to Joe, he's acting weird and I don't normally piss about but I've given him one more chance to sort things out. I just wanted to say it out loud so I could hear it myself because normally he'd be toast by now. It's not a secret that we're this close to being done, but I thought I'd better tell my friend first. I can hear you're in a restaurant or pub or something so I'll let you go, thanks for listening". *Click.*

"What did she want?"

"I think she's just told me that she's now free, and if this little wobble Dave and Rebecca have been going through becomes a genuine oscillation, she'll be poised to pick up the scraps and Joe will be history".

"Oscillation, who even says that?"

"I'm serious. You're going on this football thing with him, talk to him. Find out how bad it is between them, or if he's even noticed. I'll do the same with Rebecca when we're shopping".

"Men don't talk about that sort of thing, relationships and stuff. We're all beer and skittles and the size of the local barmaid's tits, we're very shallow really".

"Well time to get deeper. Right, dessert".

"Pudding".

"Whatever, I'm having that chocolate cake with warm chocolate sauce".

"To share?"

Cliff, darling, I love you and I'll share my bed, my money and even bodily fluids with you but don't ever ask to share chocolate cake ever again, or they'll never find the body".

"Wouldn't dream of it".

When Thompson got home Friday, late, Rebecca had already gone 'home'. The house seemed even emptier now but it was what it was. He texted to check she'd arrived safely, she texted back that she had but nothing more.

On a dusty coffee table a pile of files were waiting, but Thompson decided not to touch them until Saturday at least, then he jumped into the car and headed for the off-licence.

Saturday was much better than it had been recently. The start of the domestic football season meant there was plenty to watch, if not enjoy. He kept wanting to call Rebecca but also didn't want to appear needy. He got a text. 'Thought you might call, don't bother-now out and phone off, Guy fine, back late Sunday afternoon'.

Thompson got a text Sunday telling him they'd just left. He checked the travel web site and saw no delays, so he set about making dinner, or at least heating up the components as supplied by Sainsbury's. It seemed to go down well.

"How did it go then, the meeting with your possible new boss and everything?"

Despite being fed, Rebecca was a bit detached. "It went exceptionally well, James had barely changed. He's doing very well, has a fabulous house and very tastefully decorated. I learnt a lot".

"I thought it was a lunch thing, a business meeting?" Thompson was a bit taken-aback, he hadn't expected a home visit.

"It was, but he had an idea, he wants me to do a design for his place, not that it needs it, but it was a practical exam-thing, that's why we went back there. If I do a good job, I think I'll get taken on. What did you get up to?"

"Lazy weekend, work stuff to wade through, it's been a crazy week again. Will you need to go back, down south?"

"I might. I chatted with mummy, she picked up on my mood and she's concerned. She suggested a longer break but I said no, lots to do here. Besides, you might need me".

129

Thompson was about to answer when his phone binged. He glanced and saw a message from Jenny Banks, it would have to wait.

"No, go on, it might be important, besides, I have something I want to do for the project. I'll come back down to clean up, thanks for cooking", and she went off to the office.

'Joe and I are stepping back from each other for a while by mutual consent. Something isn't right with him but he won't talk, best plan your empire without him. See you tomorrow, Jenny. Feeling sad and lonely'.

"Problem?" Rebecca was back.

"Joe Lawrence, seems he needs a few more days off".

Rebecca said nothing, she just went into the kitchen and tidied up, then went back to the office. Through the closed office door, later, he could hear her chatting in a low voice, and laughing.

Fifteen

07 August 2017

Thompson reflected on a better morning as he drove in but the smell of petrol was there again, he'd have to get on his back and take a look, when he had time. Rebecca had been quite cheerful and even Guy was up and full of beans. He was even good with his food, maybe he was getting the hang of things. He tried to put the cheery Facetime conversation he'd overheard out of his mind, it was nothing.

In the office, the team were busy, briefs being prepped, reports written, phones used, it was how it should be. In one corner, by the worst desk, Carla was busy.

"Simon, Simon, Earth calling Simon". Carla hadn't wanted to be the one to take care of the new DC, Simon Beresford in the first place, and he'd been just as big a pain as she'd expected when he'd finally arrived. It wasn't that he was actually stupid but he seemed to move at a tangent, mentally, to everyone else.

"Sorry, I was engrossed", said Beresford, emerging from deep within a magazine he'd been reading.

The magazine that had so captured whatever imagination he had was discussing scientific techniques for tracing isotopes found during forensics. "You see, if we can isolate where something has been, then we can tie an object into any relevant crime. It works best with organic material, an example might be if you had bought a free-range chicken and wanted to know where it came from".

"A free-range chicken, wouldn't it come from a free-range chicken farm?" Carla found that she was, reluctantly, being drawn into the conversation.

"You might expect so, but define free-range".

"Chickens that wander around outside, I suppose".

"That is the important bit and the fact that they are exposed to their environment. Now imagine that chicken is moved from farm A to Farm B, then processed and delivered to your local butchers. According to science, we should be able to isolate through isotope analysis, the location where the bird 'grew up', usually based on water supply or feed. It really is fascinating".

"Simon, if I ask you a question, is it possible for you to give a concise and simplistic answer?" Carla was being nice, something had clicked in her head, something she'd not thought of before.

"I can try, just kick me if I wander, I tend to do that, my teachers at school were forever kicking me. I'm sure they thought I was at the school under false pretenses but, while I'm easily absorbed by a subject to the point of eliminating any distractions, I am not so self-unaware as to not be able to participate".

Carla looked at him for a moment, her own instinct was to kick him anyway, but she didn't. "Does that mean yes?"

"I suppose it must, however..."

"Which school, Simon?"

"Whitaker, of course".

"Come with me", and Carla led him to Jenny's desk, where she was wading through some CCTV from Carlton and trying to tie in any faces to the Duncan's Doughnuts case. "Tell Jenny what you just told me".

Beresford took a breath but Jenny raised her finger, complete with immaculate, deep red finger nail, to stop him. "A summary by an adult will do. Carla?"

"We can tell where free-range chickens come from".

"Excellent, Mrs. Tweedy will be delighted. So what?"

"Simon, does the Whitaker School have a collection of stuffed birds?"

"Oh, yes, they have many of Joseph Whitaker's old skins, Whitaker is considered by some as the father of Nottinghamshire Ornithology, although I find his collection of antique fob watches more interesting myself. Why?"

"Good and 'yes' is the answer, via my patented Beresford translator. I think I'm getting the hang of this now. Simon, does the school ever add to its collection?"

"Of course, if it has a gap and a specimen becomes available. However, the Wildlife and Countryside act doesn't permit collecting any more so new specimens are donated, usually road deaths or ringing fatalities, sometimes feline interventions. The boys know this and keep a constant vigil. Mr. Fielding is always most pleased to fill a gap".

"Carla, is this fascinating wander around a private natural history museum with the least charismatic tour guide in history going anywhere? Only I'm a bit busy". Banks was getting frustrated, so far she'd stayed well away from Beresford and even the kind and gentle-ish Elkie had kept her distance.

"When we did a look-around the school, I saw something, but I can't pin it down. It's like a bit of food stuck in your teeth that you just can't reach with your tongue. I need time to go back through my photos, whatever I saw might be in there. I've got a strange feeling it links to the Pickles case".

"Talk to Dave first, he said to leave Pickles for now and concentrate on the skulls. This idea, is it solid?"

Carla wasn't sure that it was, but Thompson said they should always speak out, even if it was only an idea, so she lied a bit. "Yes, very".

"Come in, Carla. Ah, I see you've brought Simon too, what can I do for you? Not come to give him up for adoption, have you?"

"Sir, Simon was telling me about isotope analysis as a way of finding out where free-range chickens come from".

"Lovely, does it work on Paxo, too?"

"No, Sir", said Beresford. "Stuffing would be made up of a wide range of ingredients, each bearing an individual isotope signature". Carla could see Beresford winding up his brain for another unintelligible sentence, so she stepped in.

"We could analyse the birds found in Kingston's freezer, and through isotope analysis confirm that they were taken from a local environment, Sir, possibly from a specific place. If we know who had frequented that place too, we might have something. We never ruled out any of Kingston's suppliers of birds being in the frame".

"Ok, I can see that there would be the opportunity to tie-in the location of the birds in Kingston's freezer with a specific location, but we already know that they were illegally-obtained. How would that help?"

"I don't know, Sir, but I have a brain itch. I've seen something and I'm not putting the clues together because I don't know what they are yet. Kingston was killed in a ritual manner, I think we all know that and so whoever killed him knew that too. Anyone sent by Collins because of debt default wouldn't mess about with that set up, which rules out Joyce, besides, dead people are slow payers".

Suddenly Simon Beresford started to laugh. Carla and Thompson were surprised, they'd only seen his slightly deranged smile since he arrived. "Very good, dead people default on their debts, very funny, er..."

Carla turned back to Thompson as Simon subsided once again to 'off' mode. "Sir, I need a bit of time to wade through some photos, I may even need a school visit. I'd like to scratch that itch a bit".

"Ok, get Simon to help you". Carla's look said it all.

"Right, Simon. I'm going to run each photo past our inquiring eyes, we'll examine it and say if we spot something. Let me know if I need to zoom in". Beresford sat like a Laughing Policeman at the seaside, awaiting a penny in his slot to activate him.

The first image came on the screen. "Move on". When Carla had finished, Beresford appeared to be thinking. "Interesting and, naturally, in taxonomic order. Go back to the buntings".

Carla was only casually interested in birds, she wasn't a birder and wasn't too sure where the buntings were, so Beresford told her. "Third image from the end if it helps", said Beresford, helpfully. The case in the photos had a number of small birds in it. Carla recognized the Yellowhammer, it was what the Pickles case centred on. "Zoom into the bottom right, please". She did as asked and Beresford stared at the screen, and stared, and stared, until Carla's eyes started to water but he didn't seem to need to blink. "Can we go and see the thing in real life?"

At the Whitaker School there was some confusion as to whether to allow the police in. Following their recent woes, the death of a teacher on the premises who'd been murdered rather brutally, and the subsequent suicide of the Headmaster, the school had gone into full damage-limitation mode and that didn't include having the police poking about again. Peter Fielding saw what was happening and intervened, he strongly believed in cooperation with the police. Carla explained what they wanted to see and he escorted them in.

"Ah, Beresford, I believe. Good to see you again. Finding your way in our modern Police Service, I see?" Beresford didn't seem to register that Fielding has spoken to him, until Carla gave him a sharp elbow jab to the ribs to wake him up.

"Yes. Hello, Mr. Fielding". That was it, that was all they would get but Fielding didn't seem at all surprised. Carla decided that he must have remembered Simon, of old, and expected nothing more.

Carla had pre-briefed Beresford to follow her lead once inside, but when they got to the bird room he'd just stood motionless as she examined the large case populated with dead birds. She deliberately started with the buntings, before examining the rest of the mounts just as carefully. Then she thanked Fielding for his help and they left. In the car Beresford reanimated. "I see, you started with what we were looking for, then pretended not to find it by searching the whole case randomly and in detail. I understand, excellent", and he switched off again.

"I'm sorry to trouble you, Stones, but the police have returned to the school regarding the case of Miles Kingston. I understand their name for it is 'Pickles', rather apt. There are things we might discuss".

Jeremy Stones had thought the situation would resolve itself but if Sir asked, he would respond. "Clumber is such a pleasant place to stroll, Sir. I well remember a school excursion where we chanced upon a Great Grey Shrike, you were most animated, Sir".

"Animated?" said Fielding. "Yes, I suppose I was. Perhaps I will take your advice, a stroll at Clumber, near the ford, would indeed be very pleasant. Do you think the weather will be clement this afternoon, around 4 pm?"

'Yes, Sir, I do believe that will be the case".

"Shut the door, Lorna and take a seat". Jenny Banks and Prosser were already sat waiting. A knock stopped Thompson in mid-breath and Simon Beresford walked in with a tray of coffees, but only three.

"Sorry to disturb, Boss. Josh said I should take charge of refreshments, a big responsibility. I assumed only three people, sorry, Liam, Sir, I'll get yours right away".

"Not for me, Simon, thanks", said Prosser, eager to get whatever was going to happen over and done with.

"I'll have a word", said Banks, once Simon had left, understanding that this unrequested coffee thing had to stop.

"You all know what happened, that has been dealt with and we move on. I've had to re-think the case allocation in the light of the temporary changes, so first I'll start with you, Liam. Obviously you're not leading the hot cases, but either sergeant can use you and Gecko, if he's fit. You, Liam, I want to take control of wrapping up Broomhilda and Marie's twoccer. I've got Marie's boys on it too, although I'll pull any I need elsewhere. You can say no if you want, but I want you to be lead on those cases despite being the same rank as the others".

"Will righty-ho do, Boss?"

"Good enough. Ok, thanks Liam". It was unsaid, but Prosser's part in the meeting had ended and he left.

"I take it neither of you have any objections? If you do say so now or forever hold your peace". Jenny hadn't seen this steely edge to Thompson for a while, or maybe she had but had been too busy to notice. "Jenny, you keep the Wet Bones and Pickles, and you've got the, as yet unnamed, case that I'll brief on shortly. Whether you keep it remains to be seen but I want us to make a start. Lorna, in at the deep-end, you'll keep an eye on Duncan's Doughnuts but the actual investigation there is likely going elsewhere, I'll explain more later".

"Right, Boss. Can I ask about Joe? Sorry, Jenny, but I think I'm out of the loop there".

"Joe is still on leave but I am losing patience and so are others. We may have to cope with two sergeants for the duration, although that was Perkins' original plan, just so you know. If Joe comes back, I'll make a decision on whether I keep him. Sorry, Jenny, I can't wait forever". Thompson was a bit cautious about upsetting Banks, she'd not really clarified where she was with Lawrence, what did a break actually mean?

"No problem, Boss. For the record, Lorna, Joe and I are taking a break, it might be permanent, we'll see. This new case, what can you tell me? I don't want to have a surprised look on my face when you do the big reveal".

"Understandable. Lorna, can you jot down your thoughts on Matt Johnson's discovery for me? I'll want you to tag it onto the brief about the body from Colwick, but that will then be a part of Jenny's new case, thanks". And then there was two, as Lorna left. Only two sergeants too, Thompson had already decided it was time to talk to Newton again.

"Perkins is being stranger than normal on this one, Jenny. There was a robbery a while ago in Leicester where some jewels were nicked, I mentioned it a while ago. One piece is worth eleven mill, the rest they don't seem too bothered about. Remember I said that you and Tilda will be doing a visit, interviewing the owner, be sure to use your wiles. Say nothing about this case until I say so. As for the other case, last week the three shits that jumped into the Trent were the Johnson brothers, it was in the news. They had a boot full of flat screen TVs from somewhere, but that is small beer. As we know, the stiff at Colwick is one of the brothers, Matthew. Of the two currently missing brothers, Stanley Richard Johnson, known as Ritchie, is the one we're told to be interested in, jewel-wise. He's linked to the Collins burn-out too, so it might all get confusing but we'll focus on the robbery for now. You'll need to work closely with Meikle if she has a part to play in Duncan's Doughnuts. I wish we'd called it something easier, like Crispy the Clown or something. Make sure you pool information and resources with Lorna".

"The valuable piece, I've not heard anything about that at all".

"The thinking is that when and if we get Ritchie, the rest will fall into place. It was three men who did the Leicester robbery, the Johnsons. Ritchie will be the brains here, he probably nicked it to order with a buyer in mind but your chat with the footballer, Lemmy Dowie, might change our minds about that. He went to school with Ritchie, not saying but... I have files made up for you, take a look after the brief. Tilda is your right-hand on this, let Carla run with the Wet Bones and now Pickles with Beresford, use Josh too. Questions?"

"No. Yes, how do I brief when I've only just heard about the case?"

"You don't, I do. Tilda prepped for me and Lorna will add a bit, after that it's all yours unless it gets yanked. I already did the interview with the chasers from when the Johnsons went swimming, people upstairs seem to be sticking their oar in, more on that later. Perkins and others are watching, so be careful".

Out in the main office, Superintendent Perkins was sat on the front row, which was unusual. He normally arrived unseen, put the willies up people with some searching comment and then left him to clean up the debris. Thompson deliberately sat at the back, watching. His team, his expanded team, were filling the room now. The boards were covered with images, sheets of paper and notes. He waited until the room was full and walked to the front.

"I'm just going to run through the latest addition to our portfolio, this will be an Internal of sorts. We've been given it because, well, I don't know why but they must have confidence in us, otherwise we wouldn't be given it", and he glanced deliberately at Perkins. "This is a strictest confidence case, any leaks and my displeasure will be palpable".

The team rummaged through their recently acquired piles of paper while Thompson continued.

"Most of you know of the Johnson family. Drugs, stolen property, a bit of robbery with violence and a bit of random violence too. Stanley Richard Johnson, Ritchie by preference, goes a bit deeper. Escorts, drugs, loan-sharking, things that need more nous than his brothers have, or had. On the night in question, Uniform were chasing a car that we believe was involved in a local robbery of some sort, that's all I have, nothing specific. The car shed two tyres, stopped and three men got out, right by the high wall between the Trent and the road outside the Riverside retail park. You might have seen the clip on YouTube. The men saw our boys advancing and jumped into the river. One body was found wrapped around a boat prop at Colwick today, no sign of the other two, but Joe Meade is still looking when he can and we've alerted people who work on, or by, the river. We know they jumped and weren't thrown in, we have the clip and regular CCTV, but we still have to investigate whether the attending officers were at fault and we need to be seen to investigate. There's likely to be some complaining about 'police brutality' on social media from Johnson family associates, so it's best to be ahead of the game. So, Matthew Johnson is on a slab, Christopher and the supposedly charismatic Ritchie are not, yet. Questions?"

"Why are we pissing about wasting time like this? If they jumped, they jumped".

Thank you, Gecko, your grasp of the important facts is a credit to you. We have to investigate because of the smell of one, possibly three, men dying because of police actions upsets people. Before anyone says it, it matters not whether the world is a better place without them. What does matter is whether we did anything wrong, which I doubt we did. It also matters that we are seen to get to the bottom of this in a transparent manner. Lorna".

Lorna strode to the front confidently and went through the body at Colwick situation. Perkins stood and went to Thompson's office, a clear signal that he expected to be kept company. Thompson followed, closing the door as he went through it.

"How are you dealing with the missing jewellery situation?" Perkins sounded surprised that the brief hadn't included it.

"I intend to hold back that piece of information a while, at least until we know whether Ritchie is alive or dead. Jenny is aware though, and she'll be interviewing Lemmy Dowie about the robbery, Tilda will be with her, that might shed some light. Now that I have all the case details, and I'll assume that I do, I suspect there is more to this robbery than meets the eye. I don't want to speculate in public or private yet. Any issues with that?"

"No, that sounds perfectly acceptable. I want to be kept well informed though, especially if and when the other two Johnsons make an appearance, extant or not, as the case may be".

"Is them being dead better than them being alive, Sir?"

"In Ritchie's case it may well be, but I didn't say that. Now, young Beresford, be as tough as you need to, David. Don't spare the rod". As Perkins left, Thompson headed back to the briefing and saw that Tilda had already done her bit and Jenny was now telling the floor, again, that we 'do a nice, clean and transparent investigation', that she'd already sorted out the first tasks, and that everyone was to report back to her at every step. Organised Jenny was on top of the case. She was always impressive when in full flow.

"Do we have a case name?" asked Sham.

"'Magpies', don't ask why, all will become obvious, later. Now the rest of the cases, Carla, the bones job? I know you've made progress there".

"Going to work through bus-cams looking for our dishevelled bloke as seen by a potential witness when I get them, they're a bit disorganized down at the bus depot. No other people of interest, as yet, but time has been limited on this one".

"And the dead chef?" asked Josh.

"Pickles is set to simmer for now, but Carla has a lead, potentially", and there was a ripple of laugher. "We'll get to Pickles once we've got on top of the other cases and if the lead pans out. That's all".

Thompson rejoined one of the groups discussing the briefing. Mostly the room had coalesced into his old group, Marie's group and then Josh and Beresford, with Gecko and Prosser on the periphery of everything. Banks handed Thompson a copy of the hastily-prepared actions for the new case, limited though they were. She waited while he flicked through. She knew that he desperately wanted to be more involved, but he was now management, his choice.

"Good, I see you're settling in nicely, Tilda. Jenny, Lorna, buddy people up as usual but mix and match, let's see what dynamic works. Elkie, I don't want us to make your condition an excuse for anything, I know you'd not want that, nor do I want you to not accept any limitations, is that ok?"

"Yes, thanks, Sir. I'm being very sensible. I'm off Brown Ale, I quit chewing tobacco and hung up my wrestling leotard, for now at least". The micro-group laughed, getting looks from Marie's lot.

"Thoughts on the dead shits, Liam?" Thompson could see another sub-group forming there, if he didn't intervene, sorting out Gecko might do just that. Prosser seemed surprised to be asked, but equally pleased to be able to answer. "The crafty one isn't dead, Dave, I bet. I know of him, got a friend who had to deal with him a few times. I'm surprised he was in the car with his brothers, he got the brains, they got what was left".

"You think he'll have got out then, Liam? The Trent was a real bitch that day".

"True but he was a school swimming champion and he used to run a 'Swimming with Dolphins' thing in Cornwall, it's all in the notes".

"Right, not sure whether that's good news or bad news. If he's the bright one, why get involved directly?"

"He might have just been getting a lift, Dave. He was more a con man, ran a few girls, did a bit of wheeling and dealing. I can't find any real violence charges for him, the white sheep of the family".

"Ok, good. We'll assume for now that he got out, so check his known associates, all the usual stuff. Regular reports everyone then, keep me in the loop if I need to be". The last line was delivered solemnly, Thompson found it hard to miss out knowing everything in real time.

"Gecko, a few minutes of your precious time, Jenny, a word in my office, just give me fifteen minutes". Leaving them to it, he used the pause to dig out Joe Lawrence's file and added it to the rest of Marie's boys' pile.

Gecko appeared and cautiously sat, wondering what he'd done now? "Mickey, how's the hand?"

"Sore but I'll get used to it. I don't want time off or anything, I don't want to miss what's going on".

"It's about that", said Thompson. Newton's heart sank. "I'm thinking you should step up as one of my sergeants now",

"But I want to be involved, Boss, I know I did a stupid thing but we've all moved on and Banks seems ok. What...?"

"Sergeant, you, my team. Sorry, Mickey, I can't put it any simpler".

Newton sat motionless for a moment, like a gecko about to grab a fly. "Your sergeant, me? I know I am one but I thought, well, you know. Yeah, yeah".

"Good, but I expect your reports to be more coherent going forwards, despite your debilitating injury. Will this cause problems with Prosser?"

"No, but I'm guessing you don't want me and him doing the Starsky and Hutch thing all the time?"

"Not Pascoe and Dalziel, interesting. I'm not giving you a case directly, yet, but your expertise is needed on the Johnson case, so work with Jenny".

"Does she know?"

"Nope".

"Will you tell her?"

"Yes, that's my next task. Ok Mickey, anything else you need to ask before you, er, go?"

"No, thanks Boss, I won't let you down. I'd salute but I'm not sure a four-fingered one doesn't mean something rude".

Jenny Banks walked in after fifteen minutes exactly. "Boss?"

"Dave, when it's just you and me, Jenny. What's really happening with Joe?"

"He said he has things to sort out, he took more leave I think, I suppose, HR should have cleared it with you. Do you think I should go find him, see what's really going on?"

"If the opportunity arises, it might answer a few questions. We have support systems within the force if people have difficulties, if you do see him, you might remind him of that. Are you ok?"

"Fine, Dave. Easy come, easy go and maybe I'm back in the hunt. I'm beginning to think Joe was a mistake, a refuge, there's always something lurking in the background, isn't there? We'd only been seeing each other a short time, we'd not even got to the carpet burns on the bum stage yet, not my choice by the way".

Thompson laughed, Jenny had a funny turn of phrase sometimes. "Well, I hope things turn out ok for you, if not with him then with the next one".

"Thanks, Dave, anything else?"

"Gecko is a sergeant with us now, I'm happy he isn't a complete arse. Any problems with that?"

"I thought you might, it makes sense and I'll go with sense. If he steps out of line with any of the girls I won't be responsible though".

"I was worried you might object, glad you're ok with it, get back to work then". Thompson knew as soon as he'd said it that it was a bit blunt between friends. He looked at Jenny, trying to express that it was meant as a joke, was she offended?

Jenny Banks raised her head slightly, as if an unpleasant odour had just been detected, then she turned and walked out the office silently. Later Thompson went for a pee, as he crossed the office he saw Jenny and Elkie chatting. They looked at him and both shook their heads slowly.

For most of the afternoon, Thompson was worried that he'd been a twat with Jenny. Perhaps they were less friends than before? In the end he went to see Jenny for a quiet word. "Before, what I said, honestly, it was meant to be a joke, just a joke. I'm horrified that I might have offended you, I'm really sorry". At her desk Thompson could see Elkie straining to hear.

"I'm winding you up, Dave, no offence taken, I knew you were joking. I told Elkie to play along when we saw you, she doesn't know what you said. Actually I rather liked it, you know I like it when you're firm".

"Sorry,...what?"

"Firm Dave, sometimes I need putting in my place by a strong hand".

Thompson started to perspire, he felt he was inadvertently treading familiar boards, then Jenny started laughing.

"Detective Inspector, a word in your office if we may?" It was Perkins breaking the moment. He'd already gone into Thompson's office and so didn't see the saucy wink from Jenny.

"Everything happening that should be happening, David?"

"Yes, Sir, although I feel it's nearly time to include the other information for everyone to digest at this point. Not, I suspect, that I have it all yet".

"Not my decision, I honestly don't know what is going on here. Even I get kept in the dark sometimes, despite my lofty point of observation. All we can do is proceed with caution, see what we turn up and then address the rest of it later. I'm advised that Joe won't be back for a while longer, it seems he has much deeper personal issues to deal with and I'm told that we must show our compassionate side".

"And with that in mind I have taken Mickey Newton fully onboard as my third sergeant. I think Joe will need to rethink his career, I don't want him. No objections there, I take it?"

"No, but it might be an issue if he goes to the union, I'll speak to him on his return. Your plan regarding interviewing the owner of the lost items, how is that unfolding?"

"Jenny and Tilda are fully aware of what is required, Sir. I feel they might be my best-equipped officers to extract any information we might find useful at this particular juncture".

"Why, David, I do believe you're becoming more devious by the day. Once we have his statement and a feel for the situation, we can proceed. There's another thing. While our esteemed friend Duncan Collins has moved to less-flammable if not entirely secure premises, I think your team should still quietly investigate the apparent deliberate destruction of his former premises without impinging on the whole 'Malone wants to sing for us' thing. That, predictably, will be going elsewhere".

"I already have that in hand, Sir".

"I think we would both like to be confident that any undertakings between Collins and the powers-that-be are fair in nature. I can tell you now that the old-boy network has been in full damage mitigation mode and it seems our betters feel that a change of opponent in the chess game of crime isn't advantageous at this juncture. I believe you and I have a different perspective".

"In other words the bastard will get away with ordering the burn-out and subsequent death but we in my team might find an alternative, and perhaps under the wire, way of nailing him".

"I believe that is what I said. I'll leave it with you, David, no need to report too often on this unless something significant happens, and then only after the fact. Good day to you".

When Perkins had gone it was time for a think, because Thompson had never had that type of ambiguous instruction from a superior officer before. Effectively Perkins wanted his team to look at Collins and the fire-bombing of his place, outside of the ongoing Malone case, which, as had been expected, was being passed up to a more experienced officer, he wondered who?

Fielding and Herriot, his faithful hound, walked down the road towards the ford at Clumber Park. A slim figure was already present, leaning on the balustrade, looking out over the water. Another dog was sitting obediently at his feet. Fielding approached.

"Good afternoon, Stones. A fine afternoon. Dinsdale looks to be in good health".

"Good afternoon, Sir. Yes, he's very well. I hope that Herriot is in equally fine form".

"He is indeed. Stones, I need to ask you some questions regarding the death of Kingston".

"Yes, Sir, but I've always cherished the idea of plausible deniability. Are you sure you want details, or do you just require a limited oversight?"

"I'll start with the skin of *Emberiza cirlus*. My records state it was a road casualty from near Newark, a vagrant immature bird. I sent the data to the bird society suggesting it be withheld and they agreed. What are your thoughts on that?"

"Sir, there is a small population of Cirl Bunting in the same general area that Kingston is believed to have sourced his Yellowhammers from. This is a word-of-mouth situation, given to me in confidence. I have maintained that confidence".

"Quite right too. Who knows of this?"

"My source will remain confidential, Sir, sorry. The police visit, do you know why?"

"They looked at the Cirl Bunting mount. I had naturally appended the details to the label, as far as I knew them. Now I suspect that you had involvement in procuring that specimen. Please don't misunderstand me, I do not for one minute suggest you have taken it from the wild yourself".

"Sir, it came from Kingston's freezer. When I examined the first bag of Yellowhammers, I saw it, knew what it was and its ornithological importance in the context of the county, and removed it. I then arranged for it to be presented to you, using the details you have, again, plausible deniability. Do we need to talk further?"

"Perhaps, I'll contact you if we do. Thank you for your honesty, I know that you were not directly responsible for the demise of Kingston, blessing though it is. I may be wrong, the police may not have made any connections and are just thrashing about in the dark, but I see they have Beresford in their ranks now".

"Really, is he still a little eccentric? I know you had hopes he'd emerge the other side from education as a more rounded individual".

"He remains unchanged".

After Stones and Dinsdale had gone, Fielding sat for a while, Herriot at his feet busy with new and exciting smells. The police were not idiots and Thompson had shown himself to be a formidable thinker, considering. This wasn't something for the network to address, this was something that would have to be left to run its natural course. He anticipated that more visits from Nottinghamshire's finest might be expected.

Sixteen

11 August 2017

"I don't mind driving if you get tired you know", said Tilda, as they made their way along the A453 out of Nottingham.

"Tired? It's only Leicester, I'll be fine, you just navigate, ok? I know some people aren't able to follow simple maps, I hope that's not you", said Jenny Banks, calmly.

"I'll be using Android Auto, they probably didn't have it when you started driving. I just plug my phone in, enter the destination and the voice tells you where to go".

"I know, I have the same thing but I know where we're going, just not the fine details such as might appear on a map", said Banks, quite capable of giving as good as she got. "I don't think we can expect too much from this bloke either, I've heard him on Match of the Day, it's like he swallowed a book of clichés. If he says 'over the moon' we should search him for drugs, you did bring some to plant, I hope? Were you winding me up there? Not a bad try for a junior".

"Teasing a bit, just finding my feet. You know how it is when you're a new face in a team and the old lot are so close-knit? Why has the Boss sent us to do this, do you know?"

"Because we've both got feasible vaginas and he's banking on the distraction of our pheromones tripping up our footballer, with a bit of flirting and a flash of gusset too, if it comes to that. I guarantee it would be Elkie and me, if she was viable, she's the best reader of people I've ever met. I'll have to ask her about you".

"You could ask me directly while you have my ear. If it's work-related and you've got clearance I'll answer, anything personal and I'll answer to a point, I suspect that's another reason it's us doing this. The Boss wants to see if we come back together or if only one survives". Banks thought Tilda might not be that far wide of the mark there, she knew Thompson, knew how he thought.

"Plenty of time for a catfight later", laughed Banks. "We should wait until we are back at the nick, with the guys, and sell tickets. I'm thinking about this bloke, this footballer. We might have to use tricky questions to help him along, neither of us know quite what we're after here".

"Isn't that a bit cynical?"

"Said the Vice plant who walked amongst street girls. How was that?"

"Without it sounding flippant, it was all about juggling any number of balls at once". Jenny laughed again, it was a good joke. "Seriously, I had to be careful. If the pimps rumbled me I'd have got a beating, probably raped or worse. If the girls rumbled me, I might have got a stiletto in the eye, or my face slashed. I wasn't there to find the street girls, I was there to find some missing girls, hostesses, it was a recovery operation".

"And did you find any?"

"Yes. Most didn't want to hear my words of wisdom, a few did, one in particular, but she's strong-willed and smart, and worked according to her own choices, eventually. She probably guessed who I was from the off and she'll know for sure now I've vanished. I saw signs from some of the others too so I told my handler. Eastern Europeans are not very forgiving. That was why I was pulled, that and the fact that I wasn't bringing in enough dosh for my DI, no matter how much time I was on my back". Another joke, nearly as good as the first.

"This recovery girl then, is she still on the game?"

"She was, but not on the streets. A lot of that stuff is all about business cards and having your own Internet channel with paid subscribers nowadays. She knew her stuff".

"Who was she?"

"Sorry, I can't really go into personal details. Is it true that Gecko tried to bung your lock on a training thing?"

Jenny was surprised to be asked. "It's a complicated tale but, yes, when he got a slap he backed off though. I'm surprised we got him, he isn't an obvious fit for us".

"Give him time, I think there's more to him than people think, he can just be a bit of a wanker at times. They all can, don't you find? What do you make of the Boss?"

"Solid, loyal to his staff, a bit too honourable at times but he has his moments".

"Would you shag him?"

"He's got a partner and a kid, and another coming soon. November, I think".

"So I hear, but would you?"

"Yes. You?"

"Yeah, I think I would".

For the next few miles the car was quiet, no directions came from the phone.

"You and Joe, how's that going?"

"Ok, or it was until his ex-wife showed up, now it's a non-story. I don't expect anything there and I've not been disappointed so far".

"Tricky. Why, what does she want?"

"He hasn't said yet. I'm giving him space without me in it to sort things out. Besides, he's semi-officially dumped. I have my job to think about without mooning about over a flakey man, keep that to yourself for now".

"Have you noticed that he fidgets, Joe?"

Jenny looked over to see whether this was another joke, but Tilda had a straight face.

"Nervous energy maybe. I've not know him long, we were at the 'getting to know you' stage before his disappearing trick".

"You've shagged him though, yes?"

"No, what is it with you and who's shagged who?"

"Sorry, just a nosey cow and if you had shagged him, you'd have more insights into what he's like, or on. I might take Josh for a canter, what do you think?"

"I'd put down a plastic under-sheet first". Tilda roared with laughter, Jenny joined in and they nearly missed the voice telling them to leave the motorway at the next exit.

"When you say 'on', do you think Lawrence is on something?" Banks had only just picked up on the casual remark.

"Look at the situation through your sergeant's eyes and not through your fanny. If you saw him at a party, weighed him up as being interesting without talking to him, watched him fidget like he does, what would you think?"

"Oh fuck, you're right, bollocks. I'm going to have to talk to Dave about him again and he's going to have to talk to Fiery Marie Burns, who may or may not have been shagging Joe herself. I suspect there was more there than a DI, DS relationship". The conversation ended when they turned a corner and saw their destination. The house was what they'd expected, expensive. They had to press a button at a metal gate and show their ID to a camera before the gate wheezed open. The grounds were manicured, more like a model than a real garden. As they got out of the car, the front door opened and a tall and willowy twenty-something, was there to greet them. She was wearing enough foundation for the footings of a bungalow while sporting a substantial overhang. It was two-thirty in the afternoon and she was already dripping jewellery.

As they shook hands, Tilda surreptitiously tried to read one of her many tattoos. "Do you like them, I've got the time of every goal my Lemmy scored for England, and on the other arm I've got my dead sister's name".

"Lovely", said Tilda, trying to hide what she really thought.

"Sorry, I should have said. I'm Shania-Marie, the girlfriend. Lemmy won't be long, can I get you anything, a coffee?"

"Thanks, Shania but no, we'll only need to pee on the way back if we start drinking anything and I hate motorway bogs, don't you?" Jenny watched while Tilda morphed into something resembling another footballer's wife, one who'd missed out on Roedean. "I saw Lemmy play against Man City, he was fucking brilliant, that second goal, we sang our hearts out".

"Yeah, he got Goal of the Month for that one, he'll show you his trophies if you ask. He loves meeting his fans, sorry, I didn't get your names".

Banks stepped in, "DS Jenny Banks, DC Tilda Jeffries".

"Please, come in", and she led them through to one of the large rooms off a grand foyer. The house looked surprisingly tastefully decorated, Shania-Marie saw them admiring. "It's alright but not to our taste. We've got a posh bloke doing the interior design for us, he's not started yet 'cause we've only been here a couple of months. We'll soon breathe some modern life into the place. Lemmy is in the hot tub, he's got a minor strain that's kept him from training so he's on a couple of days rest and relaxation. I'm doing my best to keep him from being overactive".

Tilda saw Jenny's face and accurately read her mind. The room they were led to was big enough to swing a giraffe around in. It looked like it had been readied for a photo shoot, lighting umbrellas and equipment were stacked in one corner. Lemmy Dowie entered through another door, wearing a club tracksuit and a welcoming smile. Shania-Marie slipped out of the same door, leaving them alone.

"Ladies, sorry for the delay, got too relaxed, you know how it is. Jenny and Tilda, is it? I'm told that Tilda, you're a fan. Anything you want me to sign?"

"A cheque?"

Lemmy Dowie laughed like he'd just heard the best joke ever, it was quite possible that it was.

Banks cut short the bonhomie. "Mr. Dowie, we're here to talk about your losses from the break-in. Normally we do serious crime, like murder, but our bosses want us to look at this so here we are. Can you run us through it? I know you've already done it with local police, but it's always better when coming from the horse's mouth".

"Sure, no problem, Jen, at least you didn't say 'donkey's mouth'", and he went into spasms of laughter again, Tilda joined in. Behind Dowie, the door had been left slightly open and Banks was sure that Shania-Marie was listening in. Dowie went through the events of the night. He didn't seem particularly troubled by it as he related the story of the three men breaking in, getting into his safe and filling a bag with whatever was in there.

Banks jotted a few questions as he spoke, but Tilda stepped in as soon as Dowie had finished. "Security, who set it up?"

"A mate at the club used a firm, they looked after him so we went with them. I think they're embarrassed that they got into the safe at all, supposed to be very difficult".

"But not impossible?"

"Nothing's impossible. Look at me, a council house shit from Broxtowe, now one of the top Premiership players and living the dream".

"I think that's what fans like me love about you, Lemmy, you're like us. You carry the council house-raised flag for all of us. We're all really proud, all my mates say so", said Tilda, gushing.

"If we can just get away from overt sycophancy and back to the robbery, your insurance report lists a number of jewels", said Banks, taking the role of the straight guy in the comedy partnership, surprisingly finding Tilda's performance quite entertaining.

"Yeah, investments. My agent said to put money into jewels and houses and you won't go wrong, so I did both. They can't tax the increase in value over time, he says. Some of the lads at the club have done the same, solid investments and inflation-proof. One day I won't be kicking a ball for a living, so we'll need a bit of something to fall back on, it's my pension plan. I sent them photos, the local plods".

"Yes, we have them, thanks, and we're actively looking to recover your property. Did you see the men well?"

"Nah, Shania-Marie saw them better than me, it was her scream that woke me up. I just saw 'em legging it over the gate. Good job I didn't catch 'em, you don't rob a Broxtowe boy and get away with it".

"Is the necklace valuation correct?" said Banks, ignoring the veiled threat of what would happen to anyone Lemmy caught nicking from him.

"Yeah, that's what I'm told, my agent and personal manager deals with all that stuff. It's insured, I know, but Shania-Marie is very fond of the necklace. Sometimes, she wears it and not much else around the house". Dowie laughed again, but not so heartily this time.

"I see. Does Shania-Marie still have plenty of bling to be going on with though?"

"Yeah, stuff for show, not the good stuff that was nicked, we don't keep her day stuff in the safe. None of the stuff nicked was her property, we've only been together a couple of years so we're at the financially-detached stage, my agent said I should be careful. I'm more trusting, I know my Shania-Marie, she's not a gold digger, just a girl from back home".

"Very wise, your agent, there are some girls who will take advantage of an impulsive character but if you know, you know. Shania-Marie, can you come in please?" Banks had raised her voice to give the impression that Shania-Marie might be busily occupied elsewhere in the house and not just loitering by the door.

"Sorry, I was just passing, everything alright Lemmy?"

"Yeah, these lovely ladies want to know how much you saw. Do you mind, girls, I need to pay a visit, this medication has me pissing buckets". Banks was about to remind Lemmy that, true, while they were 'girls', they were police officers first, but Tilda's look said 'no'. Lemmy left the room limping slightly, it looked put on for their benefit.

"So, Shania-Marie, Lemmy has told us what happened. Your turn, what did you see?"

"I heard a noise but the alarms hadn't triggered, I'm a light sleeper, I like to be there if Lemmy needs me. We had a squirrel get in a few weeks ago and I thought it might be that banging around again, so I came down to have a look".

"Weren't you concerned for your safety?" asked Banks.

"Nah, I'm not scared of squirrels. Anyway, over there behind a painting and yes, I know it's such a terrible cliché, there's a wall-mounted safe. The men were there and they had the door open. It was dark when I saw them, I screamed and they ran out of the open french windows and across the lawn".

"Any CCTV?"

"No, it was down. A power surge had blown a fuse or something. Our guy was due the next day with the new part, ordered specially, we thought one night wouldn't matter. We were obviously wrong".

Banks had been scribbling notes and Tilda could see that she was engrossed, so she went full-on with the sympathy.

"That must have been so scary, honestly, I'd have shit myself". They both saw the flinch.

"It was over so quick. We called you, the police, and they came and looked. They took prints and everything but said they wore gloves. After, we went to Lemmy's mate's place for the rest of the night, he got some security people in here and they slept on the premises. The next day, we sent the details of the robbery over to the insurers and made the claim, the security people came and fixed the alarms and doors and everything, and we came back".

"We're going to need the details of the security firm that set everything up here in the first place and anything that you can remember about how the robbers looked, what they were wearing. Did they have a bag?"

"Yes, one of them had a rucksack, I think. I'll get Cherise to send the other details over, anything else and you'll need to go through Lemmy's manager and agent, Bruno Lago, this is his card, he's in Italy at the moment. Cherise is Lemmy's PA, she's out organising the shopping, got to eat after all. Lemmy and Cherise are close, their business relationship precedes us".

"Lemmy says you're a local girl, Nottingham, Shania-Marie, which bit?"

Shania-Marie might have blushed slightly, but her fake-tanned face did a good job of hiding it if she did. "St-Ann's".

"Quite a step-up", said Banks, being deliberately pointed.

"Yeah, but we'd be together if he was a welder and I worked in Aldi's, I truly believe that. I got lucky and I know thousands of girls like you, Tilda, who would happily swap places. I know it's only been a couple of years but we'll last, I'm sure".

"You're right, I do envy you a bit", said Tilda, edging towards coy. "Lemmy mentioned that you are financially-detached, I think he called it. Is that a formal thing or just agreed between the two of you?"

"What?"

"The money, is that your choice, him not sharing it fifty-fifty?"

"Oh, right, no it was Bruno who had a talk with us, it makes good sense. I don't care about the money, I don't starve and I get to live here with Lemmy, we're very happy". Tilda was going to ask a few more questions but a glance from Banks said not to. To be fair they didn't know whether Shania-Marie had understood the implications of the financial questions. Or maybe she'd just played thick to put them off letting on that she did, and resented it.

Banks finished writing her notes. "Good, a quick look at the safe then and we'll be off. Lemmy can get back in his hot tub, thank him for seeing us and we'll be in touch".

The safe wasn't large but looked sturdy. Banks took a couple of camera phone shots of it from different angles, one catching Shania-Marie in the same picture. Just as they reached the front door, Lemmy reappeared bearing a white club T-shirt. "Tilda, a lovely name, it suits you", and he scribbled something illegible on the T-shirt. Tilda gushed and gave him a kiss on the cheek. Out of the corner of her eye, she could see Shania-Marie staring daggers at her.

As the gates swung open to let them out, Banks could see Shania-Marie still stood on the step watching them go, Lemmy was nowhere to be seen.

"Interesting. I like the WAG mode there, it wouldn't suit me but you were able to carry it off", said Banks, with the tiniest of edge.

"I wasn't convinced though, were you? With him I think what you see is what you get, with her there's something else going on. Did you notice that one of the names on her tattoos was altered? I couldn't quite read

159

it, but I'd love to know what it said. We need to look at her in detail, I see you got a photo, sneaky".

"I saw you got her talking normally too, as if you didn't really come from the rough side of town, equally sneaky. At one point she forgot she was a footballer's girlfriend and started enunciating". Banks was warming to Tilda but also aware that, if she wanted to, Tilda could be anyone she liked, she had that talent.

"I'm thinking inside job, either the lovely Shania-Marie or someone else close, a set up. Maybe this Cherise woman? Not likely to be Bruno Lago though. I've heard of him, a big agent, worth billions probably. I wonder who lives in Lemmy's houses? I heard he'd set up a trust for young people to be able to have affordable rented property, or someone had done it for him. Maybe he really is as good as his publicity".

"I read that too, he wouldn't be the first rags-to-riches kid to give something back. Dave is going to be very interested when we tell him. So, Lemmy Dowie then, super-fit footballer and rough diamond, would you?"

Tilda started laughing. "I don't think so although I bet he has impressive energy. Actually, I usually prefer the more cerebral type for anything other than a knee-trembler".

"Like?"

"Never you mind, maybe when I know you better. Any plans for the weekend yourself?"

"Going to try and see if I can sort a little personal problem out, not Joe, you understand, after what you said he's dead to me now. You?"

"I've got to see a friend about something. It might be nothing, but a friend in need and all that and, like I said, if I can fit him in I might take our Josh out for a canter at some point". Jenny couldn't see it, Josh was a lively puppy that might pee on the sofa and Tilda was using classic deflection technique, she must have known it would be obvious.

"What's your game plan, Tilda, you know, in the context of the team?"

"Upwards and onwards if I can, yours?"

"More or less the same, game on for both of us then".

The car remained quiet for the rest of the way into Nottingham. Banks thought that a mark had been made in the sand but Jeffries never gave the comment another thought, her mind preoccupied with her friend's issues. In the office only Liam remained. "Dave declared it 'poet's day', he's going to a match tomorrow with Cliff so he had to iron his replica kit or something", said Prosser, without Banks or Jeffries asking. "Interesting interview?"

"Yes, we got an insight. Tilda here particularly enjoyed herself, even got a signed shirt from the man himself".

"Really, well I'm beside myself with envy. Dave wants a full briefing Monday, and a brief synopsis by text so you can take advantage of leaving early today or you can come in Saturday and set it up, or very, very early Monday, your choice".

Banks wasn't happy that Liam appeared to be playing the boss again, considering, but Tilda stepped in saying they'd be ready and not to worry. Much later, after they'd set everything up, they walked out together. "Good luck with your thing, Jenny. Liam wasn't playing boss in there you know, just passing on instructions. If you need to talk any time, I'm a good listener. We're not rivals here and, if we were, you'd be a long way in front. Call me if you fancy going out for a drink some time, we can go on the pull together", and she smiled and patted Banks' arm.

"Sorry, I know Liam was just being Liam. I'm a bit wound up, nothing ever seems to be simple for me. Thanks for the drinks offer, I just might call you if my thing goes pear-shaped".

Seventeen

12 August 2017

James Heston was stood looking over the floating black tanks above Colwick Sluice Gates, his dog Masson busy with a scent on a nearby stump. Heston was using his Saturday to go out birding and he was looking for a year-tick Yellow-legged Gull, a bird that had been coming back to the same spot for years. Colwick wasn't his regular stomping ground, he preferred it when it had been a messy gravel pit and muddy mess, but a country park was better than nothing and he had seen some precious Notts ticks there in the past.

Eventually the gull drifted in, possibly from the direction of the nearby racecourse. It settled on its favourite green buoy and surveyed the river. As Heston watched, a human arm gracefully made an arc as a body drifted past the green buoy, unsettling the gull which flew off. Heston watched the same patch of water for five minutes before deciding to go and tell the wardens. Were they expecting anyone?

"And he's sure it's a body, John?" Prosser was surprised to hear from John Fraser, Head Warden at Colwick, he thought he'd be more likely to call the local station first, but then he remembered a certain amount of antipathy towards the local nick from Fraser.

"He's a top birder, Liam, better eyes than most and a keen mind. Yes, he saw a body. It must be another of the bad lads who'd jumped".

"Thanks, John, we'll take it from here". Prosser was about to call Thompson, but remembered something or other about him going to a football match.

It being a Saturday morning, a few of the team were in catching up, taking advantage of what was supposed to be a quiet time. Unfortunately no sergeants were there, so Prosser improvised. Grabbing his jacket, he decided to go and look himself. "Josh, we need a team to recover a potential body from the sluice gates at Colwick, get Simon to help you. Carla, you're with me". Josh looked shocked. He had no idea who to talk to.

When Beresford got back from a break, he found the room had virtually emptied and Josh on the phone talking to the duty sergeant, who was unhelpfully half-way through a potted history of the now defunct river police.

"Where is everybody?" asked Beresford.

"A body at Colwick", said Josh, taking a break from the ramblings of a bored desk sergeant.

"When you say a body, do you mean skull?"

"No, a body in the river, must be one of the jumpers. Who do I call for a boat?"

"Leave it with me".

That threw Josh because, so far, Beresford had appeared to be devoid of any common sense whatsoever, so he listened in. "Hi, Joe, how are you, Simon Beresford, we met a while back. Yes I'm on DI Thompson's team now, loving it. The thing is, Joe, and I know it's a bit of an imposition given you're almost retired now, but we think one of the bridge jumpers has bobbed up at Colwick, any chance? Thanks, much appreciated, we'll see you there."

Josh looked at Beresford in amazement. Give him something manual and he'd simply not get it, but schmoozing, the boy was a born talker when his lights were on. Beresford recognized the look. "What? My family are police, I just know my way around a bit. So what if Joe might not remember me, he's too polite to say. I do know he misses the river and I do know he's moored not far from Colwick, does no harm asking".

Josh had to agree, not every job needed a spanner, some jobs needed people who could read the instruction manual as well.

In the end it was all a damp squib. Joe had had trouble on the swollen river and couldn't look for the body effectively, the police divers were out on another job and nothing else poked above the surface despite intense scrutiny from several onlookers. With so much water charging through, the chances were that whoever it was taking an unscheduled swim was now being macerated to component levels under a steel sluice gate.

"I feel guilty after working all week, I feel I should be here, with you", said Thompson, as Rebecca shooed him out of the new house.

"You'd be on your own then, because Elkie, Guy and me are off to do some light shopping", said Rebecca, getting impatient. When Thompson had suggested to Cliff Colman that they watch Forest away, he hadn't really expected it to happen.

"If you're sure?" he said, as Colman tooted the horn on his old Land Rover for the sixth time.

"I'm sure, and I know you keep a list of grounds and that Griffin Park isn't on it".

Thompson looked surprised.

"What's that look for? Cliff is just as sad, the difference is that he has no funny little secrets from Elkie".

Thompson said nothing, he just grabbed his ancient red-and-white scarf and left.

"Not to be rude or anything, Dave, but what are you faffing about at?"

"Just double-checking it was ok with Rebecca".

"Do you have the note?"

"What note?"

"Dear Mr. Colman, David is hereby given permission to visit the big city with a responsible adult, please have him back by bed time".

"Fuck off", said Thompson, laughing. "I am not under the thumb".

Progress was slow and Thompson was wondering why they were using the old Land Rover rather than going in a proper car, but chose not to ask. It was Cliff's pride and joy.

"This takes me back, heading away to see the Reds, and to a new ground. How many now?"

"Seventy-three", said Thompson, without thinking. "How sad is that?"

"A life well-lived, if you ask me", said Colman.

"Remember that away trip together years ago, to play Villa. It was a bit of a trip, as I remember".

"Yes, with Glen and Kev. We got chased and ended up in a dead end but broke a fence and used the staves as clubs. They ran, as I recall".

"They did, good job we didn't get caught, I'd probably be working in a warehouse now and not banging my head on the upper echelons of the Nottinghamshire Police".

"True", said Colman. "Rumour has it that Brentford used to be lively, all London clubs were at one time, but I think it's much safer now".

"Think? You said there was no trouble there now. I can't afford to get involved in anything, first sign of trouble and we leg it, agreed?"

"Dave, we look like middle-aged men, nobody will bother us. We stroll in as if we own the place, have a pie, buy a programme and watch the Reds romp home four-nil, then we nip out three minutes early to avoid the rush and go home. League ground seventy-four under the belt, easy, and not just any old league ground, a proper one, Griffin Park. I read they're moving to a community stadium in 2020, so this might be our last chance".

Thompson ignored the logic and settled on the abuse. "If I look like a middle-aged man, you look like my dad".

"Fuck off again", said Colman.

As they slipped south along the M1, they saw a few cars with Forest scarves on the back parcel shelf and a couple of fan coaches tore past. "I was told to ask this, and don't get all uppity, Dave, but are you and Rebecca all right? Elkie's worried".

"I think so, we snipe a bit at each other from time to time and she's gone off at the deep end, spending on expensive stuff for the house but, yeah, I think we're ok".

"Snipe? You mean you argue. What about?"

"I should say mind your own fucking business but I know you mean well and if I talk about it to you it'll save me a grilling by Elkie. Believe me, she's much better at interrogation than you are. Work is putting pressure on us, I'm there too long and she's got tangled up with some design thing instead of concentrating on parenting. I don't mind, it's good for her to be active but maybe not now. There's also the house. I know you two are happy with yours but ours is a right shithole, we just didn't see it. She wants a lot of work doing too, expensive work".

"Shit, Dave, I wish I'd minded my own business now. That other detective, the Welsh one, you didn't, did you?"

"No, I didn't, she's a friend and colleague, like Elkie; alright, not quite like Elkie. Jenny did have a thing about me but she's got a boyfriend now and that little infatuation has ended. We talked, I know you're knocking on a bit but you remember how we youngsters have these little problems".

"And fuck off again, Dave. With Rebecca, be careful. Try to get your head into a more positive position about the house and her interests and don't treat her like a breeding unit, they don't like it".

"This latest one wasn't really my idea, neither one was until we'd got a proper house, but it happened so you get on with it. Can we go back to talking football now?"

"Ok, name the team for the first League Cup Final, first game, not the replay".

"Woods..."

"Oh, hello, I didn't expect to see you again. Well, maybe in an official capacity, perhaps". When she heard the familiar voice, Tilda had a quick look around. The coffee shop wasn't busy so nobody heard the comment.

"I thought you'd guessed about me", said Tilda defensively. "Are you keeping ok, Jenny?"

"If you mean have I rethought my current life choices? No, but I do have a plan".

"Is this a cunning plan for just you, or are other people involved?"

"If you're asking about pimps, no, there isn't one. You know I don't hang about on street corners. What were you really up to?"

"Police business. On a personal level I wanted to help girls get out if they wanted to".

"And yet you attached yourself to me, don't think I didn't notice".

"You were one of several I thought I might have some success with. Obviously, I was wrong".

"You got out at the right time you know, I heard things. Someone knew about you, a nasty accident was planned".

Tilda shrugged. "Goes with the job. I was well looked after, I had back-up".

"Why are you here, now?"

"It's a coffee shop, I came in for coffee and cake. **You** spoke to **me**, remember?"

"True, when I saw you I just wanted to pass on about their plans for you, in case you dug your high heels out again. Are you working out of Central?"

Tilda said nothing, she wasn't entirely sure that Jenny was being straight with her and she had no intention of giving her details about herself, even though this Jenny was a bit different from the other girls she'd made contact with, for a number of reasons. She also knew the question was redundant.

"You remember that bloke, that copper we met here, who was he?" asked Jenny.

"Just a copper out with his mate for a coffee. Why?"

"No reason, I liked him, nice bloke I thought. No ring, so I was going to slip him my details but I saw you'd given him an exit option. That was when I knew about you for sure".

"He's just a copper like me, I've seen him about. I didn't want to let him get into trouble, not that he would, he's a sensible bloke".

"So you do know him then?"

Tilda didn't answer.

"No matter. Look, I do appreciate what you were trying to do for me but I'm ok, honestly, I've got it sorted and I'll be fine. Who was working you? I know how it works, who was your back-up, anyone I know?"

"I was working out of Vice, I know you've not got an arrest record, I checked. My boss was my DI and me being out there was part of a new initiative. It happens from time to time, someone gets a bee in their bonnet about working girls".

"So I wasn't targeted for any reason, other than a hunch?"

"That about covers it. The fact that we didn't know all about you, like even your real name, was a flag that maybe you were new and could be helped. Look, can we not just have a coffee together like a couple of working girls, just ones working in different professions?"

"I don't think so, we might get seen then they'll try to go after me and I'll have to move again. Got to go, you watch your back, Tilda, they have long memories. Say hello to that nice bloke for me".

Tilda said she might and watched her new sort-of friend Jenny walk out into the passing crowd of shoppers, then she made a call. "She's ok but I don't think I should be involved any more. She seems to have an idea of what she wants, she's not on the streets. I think that's the best you can hope for at the moment".

"Thanks, Tilda, I appreciate it". The phone rang off.

"Hello", said a vaguely familiar voice. It took Tilda a second to realise that it was Elkie.

"Oh, hello there. Out shopping?" A quick assessment told her that Elkie was with a friend.

"Yes, hitting the posh shops. This is Rebecca, Dave's better half. Rebecca, this is our new recruit, Tilda".

"Hi, pleased to meet you. Do I know you? No, I can't do, can I? Dave's told me nothing about you but he tells me bugger all at the best of times, not that I see him that much these days".

"Rebecca, right, yes, the Boss talks about you all the time at work, nice to meet you. Sorry, I've got to be off, I'm late for an appointment. I was just on my way out".

"No worries", said Elkie, admiring the diplomatic untruth. "We're just taking a break before finding more bounty to upset our significant others with, catch you at work".

Coffee and cake was quickly organized whilst Guy had his own catering arrangements.

"Attractive girl that Tilda, there's something about her I can't put my finger on. Did Dave choose her to be on the team?" asked Rebecca, casually.

"No, he doesn't really get to choose as such. His boss, Superintendent Perkins, agrees to a post and HR fill it, or at least bring a small selection of people for it, having already earmarked their favoured candidate. In Tilda's case we didn't know anything about her until she showed up, she worked in Vice before, I heard. We generally don't pry despite that being our jobs".

"But, Jenny Banks, he did choose Jenny Banks to be his sergeant, is that right?"

"That was different. Jenny should never have left us really, that was partly my fault. It was all down to office politics and jealousy but you know what it's like and we soon put it behind us. She's settled back in well and she's with someone now, the other sergeant, Joe. Seems to be going ok", lied Elkie.

"Yes, I heard, Dave made a point of telling me. He said he doesn't know what her long-term plans are, plays things close to her lovely chest, or so I'm told. Come on, drink up, I'm going to buy some Jimmy Choos".

"Jimmy's, really? Aren't they a bit pricey?"

"I've decided I'm worth it".

Much of the rest of the trip to Brentford was spent talking about the 'do's' and 'don'ts' of kids. Thompson, with his limited experience, in more practical terms as Colman's pending issue was still in Elkie's womb. It was busy around the ground when they got near and there seemed to be a few scuffles going on. Just the usual stuff, people running around like headless chickens, a few swinging boots, playground stuff. Colman found the parking at St Paul's Recreation Ground easily enough, from there it was a short walk to the ground.

"Tell me again why we aren't in the away section car park", said Thompson.

"It gets gridlocked, according to 'Flight of the Bees', the Brentford on-line fanzine. It recommends parking a little way away and reckons you'll save half-an-hour at least. London is always busy, we could be sat for hours otherwise", said Colman, now also beginning to doubt the positive side of not being with the away fans en-masse.

The road around the rec was busy as lots of people were using it for street parking. Thompson had always hankered after a house in West Bridgford that looked over the playing surface at the City Ground but, having seen the mass of people that made movement around the area untenable on match days and as he'd got older, and maybe wiser, he'd shelved the notion. Now he was almost pitying the residents around Griffin Park on match days.

They got the Land Rover parked in a tight spot that needed much shunting to fill, they hid their scarves in the poacher's pockets of their waxed jackets and set off. All around were Brentford fans chattering in their occasionally baffling accent. As they neared the ground, the mix of people changed, became younger, leaner. Colman hadn't noticed, but Thompson had.

"This way", he whispered to Colman, just as a spotty-faced youth came up to them. "Got a light, mate?" he said with a local twang.

Thompson shook his head, but Colman said 'no, he didn't smoke' in broadest Nottingham. *Shit.*

From nowhere a crowd surged towards them. Thompson shouted run and almost dragged Colman with him. Another skinny youth slid his fist off Thompson's forehead and got a boot in the groin for his trouble. Colman got tripped and had three on him in an instant, so Thompson turned and yelled loudly "police", holding out his warrant card above head-height for all to see.

There was a surge away, briefly, and Colman scrambled to his feet, blood was running from his nose but he'd had the sense to cover his head, or at least as much of it as he could. Further on, another group were advancing but got intercepted by a bunch of Forest lads, all in plain-clothes so to speak, who waded in.

Thompson and Colman half-ran back towards the Land Rover but soon ran into another, smaller mob of older men. "Police", shouted Thompson again, hoping to buy a bit of time. "And?" drawled the Brentford accent. This time there were only three of them showing interest so Colman, who was mightily pissed off, downed one and went for the other. A melee ensued.

Behind the three, Thompson could see four uniforms approaching with enthusiasm. "Police", he yelled loudly, again flashing his warrant card in the general direction of anyone not occupied.

Thompson saw the one who said 'and' head back his way, but he fell as a night-stick stopped him in his tracks. Thompson kept his card very visible as bodies ran in all directions. Colman, after his initial success, had caught another fist to the nose and was now limping slightly. The

Brentford yobs had legged it, leaving Thompson facing four impatient uniforms. He made a point of yelling "police" again, as a reflex.

"What are you two twats up to?" said a London accent.

"We were heading for the match", said Thompson. "Detective Inspector Thompson, Nottinghamshire Police".

The uniform glanced at the ID. "Why have you parked here? This is where they ambush the stupid fans who park away from the safe end", said one of the uniforms. He had a substantial stick of unspecified issue and looked like he might suddenly start swinging it. It certainly wasn't a standard truncheon.

"It said to on the website", said Colman, using his scarf to stench his bleeding nose.

"You pair of Muppets, they set you up. Go on, fuck off out of it or we'll leave you to them".

"Hey, constable, I am a Detective Inspector, respect for the rank", said Thompson, but his heart wasn't in it.

"Sorry, Sir. Fuck off out of it now, Sir. Get it?"

They did.

They sat in silence in the Land Rover until the street emptied as the fighters hit their seats late, it was always the way.

"Never again", said Thompson. "Don't ever mention going to an away match ever again".

"You're not the one who has to tell his partner where the blood came from. Elkie's going to either kill me or laugh herself into a very early delivery room. I'm not sure which one I'm more scared off".

"It's way too early for the delivery room, she'll just pull a muscle executing a complicated Karate move on you, you can say goodbye to your knackers. Put the radio on, at least we can listen on the way home.

I'm counting that ground, I got within a hundred yards and I had a ticket", said Thompson. "You know that I should arrest you for that assault, right Cliff?"

"Not going to though, are you, or I might remember that Villa fan you hit with half a house brick that time, Detective Inspector".

"I have no recollection of any such incident, My Lord", said Thompson, laughing.

On the radio, the local radio station commentator was bemoaning Forest scoring early, a second big chance coming on five.

"A two-one loss do you reckon?" asked Thompson.

"Seems about right", said Colman, as a distant roar told them that Brentford had started having near-misses of their own. The radio got turned up to see what was happening and, to their delight, the roar was for a second Forest goal.

As they headed back out of London, they came across a bunch of youths fighting, spilling out onto the road. Colman recognised one of them as the deliverer of his bloody nose, the Land Rover veered slightly. "Don't", said Thompson. "The paperwork alone is appalling".

"They weren't even going to the match", said Colman.

Thompson shrugged. "The ills of a broken society, distilled into a montage of aggression", he said.

"Bollocks", said Colman, and they both burst out laughing.

"How was the match?" asked Rebecca. She wasn't much of a fan.

"Won four-three, good game", said Thompson. "How was the unbridled shopping?"

"Unbridled", said Rebecca, nodding to a clutch of designer store carry bags.

Before he could say anything, she said "don't worry, birthday money and I had gift cards saved up. We bought Elkie and Cliff a baby thing too. Nothing left our precious, if sparse, 'do up the new house' account this time, besides, Daddy won't let us starve". Rebecca's tone was slightly mocking, or was he just hearing it that way?

Elkie and Cliff gave thanks for the baby gift and bid them farewell. When they'd gone, Thompson tried to not look too relieved about the spending but he was. After the football match debacle he was more wound-up than ever and could feel the pressure in his head again, like before. Was this what happened to Charnley or was it just him? He'd have to ask him and soon, it was time he saw his old mentor again.

Rebecca went off to do her designing in her office, so he checked his phone and read Prosser's text, wondering who corpse two had been and hoping it was Ritchie Johnson. A short text from Banks only gave salient details of their visit to the footballer's house. That would keep. He grabbed a beer from the new fridge, then nipped up to check on Guy before intending to settle down to watch Match of the Day. Rebecca had set up the box room as her office-cum-work room and was spending a lot of time in there. He could hear her chatting and laughing with someone, probably on Facetime, she kept in touch with her friends that way. She sounded like the old Rebecca, before Guy and before responsibilities, he missed that. He didn't think there was anything in it, the chatter, but it was diligently filed away as something to watch carefully.

In the Land Rover, Cliff was desperately trying to play down the events of the day, the details of which were skillfully prised from him. "Come on, Elkie, it's really not that funny. They could have done me some real damage". Colman was looking for a bit of sympathy as his eye blackened and slowly closed.

"Kicking you in the head, I doubt it", and she carried on with her chuckle, then started a conversation with her belly. "Sorry to tell you, but daddy is an idiot. We might have to sneak away in the night and find a daddy who doesn't go fighting young men in foreign cities. I blame Durex not coping, like a demented rabbit he was, as far as I can remember, it was all a blur".

"Did you have a good time shopping with Rebecca?" said Cliff, wisely changing the subject.

"We did, well Rebecca did, I didn't spend much. We bumped into Tilda, Rebecca was a bit odd with her, I put it down to her not liking the idea of attractive women at work with Dave. Is he alright, did you talk to him like I said? Rebecca seemed a bit off over him all day. Maybe I'm reading it wrong but when I mentioned that you two might get beaten up as a joke, she just said one of you'd deserve it. It was an odd thing to say and she made out it was a joke too, but I get a bad feeling there".

"It must be the pregnancy? I'm told that women can go a bit weird when pregnant, not that my lovely girlfriend is showing any signs".

"I don't know. I do think she regrets getting pregnant again. She said she thought the house would smooth things out a bit, but I didn't even know things were that rippled".

"Dave never mentioned Rebecca once", lied Colman. "I did try to get him talking but he probably couldn't get a word in because I kept on gushing about you".

"You do know that we get taught how to spot untruths in my line of work, Mr. Colman?"

"No, honestly, he never mentioned her, nor Guy. Maybe he was just getting out of himself a bit, enjoying being a Forest fan on the road again. He's not been a regular for a while. Is work heavy?"

"It's never particularly light but we have this expanded group that he's got to herd, maybe that's bothering him. I'll talk to people, get them to make more effort with him".

"Is Dave popular, you know, as a boss?"

"We'd all do almost anything for him".

"You don't think Rebecca is going to dump him then?"

"No, I don't think so, no nothing like that. I think she's just missing out on a bit of life, or thinks she is. She'll be fine, they both will. Now, tell me again how you defended yourself from four attackers and managed to drag a semi-conscious Dave to safety despite them raining blow after blow upon you".

"Well..."

Eighteen

14 August 2017

Thompson listened while Jenny relayed the visit details; full written versions were already with him with a copy for Lorna, too. Both Jenny and Tilda were hinting that something wasn't quite right with the whole robbery, but also that the idea of a piece of jewellery being bought to offset tax or something was new to them.

"Footballers do get paid an enormous amount these days but usually in a legal way that shunts cash or assets around. I'm surprised this Shania-Marie isn't utilised as a tax offset. Maybe these properties are a part of it, a list of addresses might be interesting". When Lorna stopped talking, the rest of the room looked at her for an explanation.

"I dated a footballer, a Brentford player, a few years ago. He told me a few eye-opening things but all legal, I checked. I hear you visited Griffin Park, Dave. Have fun or did they chase you all up and down the High Street?" She laughed.

"Hooligans are only after blokes their own age, Lorna, we had a quiet game". Elkie's look told Thompson she knew differently, but she didn't say.

"Look at Shania-Marie in detail, speak to people who know her. Check for Lemmy's name on properties. He mentioned the properties are managed by an agent, did he mean Bruno? Check him too but be careful, the rich and powerful are asbestos. Oh, and find out about his PA, Cherise, do we have a surname for her?"

Thompson's phone rang. The group chatted while he listened. "Ok, meeting ended. Lorna, take whoever to Colwick Park, I'll be attending too. Elkie, with me please, Liam is already on his way with Gecko".

"Another body, Boss?"

"Sounds like it might be the same one, it's just a bit tricky from what Fraser just told me. Not sure how this is going to work, which is why I'm allowing myself out to do the risk assessment".

Lorna picked up Josh and Beresford as she grabbed her stuff. Thompson had a quick word with Perkins before following Elkie to her car. In the pit of his stomach, the old excitement of the unknown was pumping adrenaline around his system. For a while he was a cop in the field again.

They were on the Colwick Loop Road before the conversation started. "Are you ok, Dave? Rebecca and you ok?" asked Elkie, Thompson had been quiet for a while. Normally on the way to a bit of excitement Thompson could be a chatterer, especially with those closer to him.

"Yes, as far as I know. She can be a bit snappy sometimes but I put that down to her condition. Why? You spent a day shopping and no doubt subtly chatting, what do you know that I don't?"

"Nothing. I said to Cliff on the way home, she just seemed a bit unsettled when we were out, like she had things on her mind. I was going to say 'disenchanted' but I thought that might be a touch over-exaggerated and I can't see what with either. Can you?"

"I think she's getting bored, she certainly hinted at it, me being stuck at work doesn't help either. Did she tell you about the interior design thing? I don't get it myself but if it makes her happy, then great. I just worry that she might get put on".

"Yes, she talked about it a lot, the course on-line and a job offer, I checked them out for her, privately, not using us or our system. She was very upbeat about it when I told her they were legit, it sounds a good fit for her. Nothing else going on though, is there?"

"No, don't think so. Like I said, the job gets in the way a bit, well a lot, but she knew that when we got together. I think I get a bit grumpy, I try not to but sometimes she's a bit sharp. My mood doesn't improve when

I spend too much time shut up in that fucking office but, hey, field trip to Colwick, a place of very happy memories".

"Happy for you maybe but I told you before, I still have nightmares. This big slavering beast climbing on top of me, his hot breath on my neck, his hands, well, he had more hands than any human should have and his thing...well, I see female ducks at breeding time in a different way, now".

"Yes, thank you Elkie, I thought we'd dropped the whole T-bone thing".

"My therapist says I should air my fears, get things out in the open. Not that that's any sort of invitation for you to get anything out in the open, you understand. I'm now with child and my man would take it very badly".

"Elkie, really, nothing is getting an uninvited airing. Right, I'm changing the subject. What do you think of Beresford?"

"An idiot".

"An idiot? That quickly, you met him not long ago and the boy's an idiot?"

"Yup, definitely. I might also stretch to 'special' but that is only a possible".

"I was going to get him to set up Lorna's leaving drink before Liam went apeshit. I'll assume I was the last to know that she wanted to leave before. Homesick, she said".

"Lorna was intending to leave us, really? Oh shame. No, I didn't know, I don't think anyone did, she's very private but I don't hear a bad word said about her".

"I suppose it depends now on whether the job she was after will wait, and whether she enjoys being a DS with us enough to take the exam and stay. I might be telling you something you already know but I think Joe is toast. I don't want him back, I won't put up with being in the dark about one of my sergeants. I know Jenny has all but terminated him".

"That sounds fatal, she doesn't like being messed about that one, a woman scorned and all that, it also explains Gecko taking Joe's post. I'm warming to him, I think he'll be alright", said Elkie, not as aware of the Jenny-Joe situation as she'd like. "Was that psychology sending two females to that footballer's house to interview him? You know what they say about Premiership footballers, insatiable".

"Elkie, how could you think that sending two attractive, female, police officers to interview a grunt footballer might be a distraction to get more out of him. Do you really think I'm that devious?"

Elkie looked at Thompson. It seemed that the thought of Jenny Banks showing her thighs to make a man talk appealed to him, it was the brightest he'd been all day.

'We're back to the Pope shitting in the woods question, aren't we?"

"Bears, Elkie, it's bears that shit in the woods. No I thought Tilda would benefit from the full-on Jenny Banks experience first-hand and it worked. Between them they got some very interesting possibilities to look at and they got to know each other a bit. Both came back alive so it seems to have been worth the risk".

"The full-on Jenny experience, not sure I'd inflict that on a new colleague. She can be a bit intense at times, and I say that as a friend. If Joe's toast, then I'd lock up my male children of sixteen and over, at least until she hooks up with someone else".

"How are you two getting on now that she's the DS again and everything, and no doubt organizing everyone. I've not seen that much of her since we wrapped up the school case and I've barely spoken to Tilda".

"We're fine, I don't worry about the DS stuff now, bigger things afoot", and she pointed to her bump. "Tilda is interesting. Don't expect to keep her too long, she's a climber, she's sharp and more than a match for Jenny. I bet it was a fun conversation when they drove over to Leicester, I'd like to be a fly on that windscreen".

"I wouldn't, Jenny hates insects, you'd be swatted in seconds".

Elkie didn't say anything in reply, it wasn't her place, but the idea of Tilda and Jenny swapping barbed comments cheered her up no end. The pause told her what to expect.

"So, what do you make of Rebecca and this old friend offering her a job thing?"

"Classic interrogation technique, Dave. Soften them up with light talk then hit them with the main question, impressive. I think it's odd, they've not seen or spoken to each other for years but he was very soft on her at one time, her first, she said. Maybe its vicarious love".

"Classic deferring technique to talk about Jenny and Tilda when you saw the question coming and no, nothing like vicarious love or anything, it sounds like a mate offering a hand up. It'll probably never happen anyway, you know how it is, people make promises they don't intend to keep. They have spoken though, they Facetime each other, work stuff, I suppose", and Thompson told her about the overheard conversation, the old Rebecca laughing.

"Yeah, you're probably right about it being good for her, the idea of doing something different is making her relax more. Maybe being a bit off really is all part of everything going on, including carrying your child, although I'm never like that, full of beans me. I think I wear Cliff out, he's bulk ordering Lucozade".

"Well, at his age it's understandable. Just make sure his flannelette pyjamas are aired, he'll be fine".

"You looked after him at the match, I know you did. I wanted him back in one piece, and you delivered but he's not going to an away game ever again, he's too old. You too, you're grounded".

"Hey, who is Detective Inspector here?"

"You, but if anything happens to my man while he's with you, the she-wolf will come calling and no more bables for the Detective Inspector".

"No need to worry on that front, Rebecca thinks I should get nipped, not that…".

"Don't, I don't want to know. Nipping might be a good idea, stop you spraying the furniture. I know a bloke with a couple of blue-bricks, cheap".

"Thank you, very good, and don't pass that snippet on".

"Poor choice of word there, Sir. We're here".

"Thank Christ for that, you used to be so deferential at one time, what happened?"

"Well my therapist says…"

A couple of cars were already parked up on an old slipway that overlooked the floating black tanks above the sluice gate. A thick raft of debris butted against the thick chains strung between them, the chains being there to stop out-of-control boats from disappearing under the sluice gate. Presently a small boat appeared, containing two men in bright orange lifejackets, it was fighting the current valiantly. The little boat was able to pick its way along into little holes in the floating debris, disturbed bits breaking free and racing towards the gates themselves. On the bank a little way upstream, a new part-time warden with binoculars strung around his neck was gesturing for the boat to move left to the next bay. It moved over and soon the guy directing was giving the thumbs up.

"Ok, John, how do we do this?" Prosser was awful in boats, a self-confessed landlubber but, in the absence of anyone else and to show willing in the face of adversity, including Gecko, he'd taken control without thinking it through.

"We grab him then rope him up to the side, we'll ease him out and go to the river stages, number three to let them unload. I'm not doing it, bits fall off and we might lose the arm with the watch on. Best tell Dave to sort out the formalities and to stop people going down the stage until he's bagged up".

Prosser wasn't surprised at Fraser's casual approach to a body, it was far from his first. He was surprised though when Fraser yelled to look out as a large, dead tree came cartwheeling past them in the current. A branch hooked under Prosser's life jacket and lifted him up bodily, but Fraser grabbed him and the branch snapped allowing the tree to continue its route, victim-free. Prosser thudded heavily into the bottom of the boat, landing on his back. "Come on Liam, is this any time to take a nap?" joked Fraser, but his face said he was worried.

"I'm ok, just a bit winded, thanks. I can't swim".

On the bank, the whole crowd watched the progress of the tree as it rolled over the chains and headed towards the gates themselves. Tangled in the branches in a grotesque montage of a crucifixion was the body, complete with a good wristwatch. The change in weight via the addition of the body as ballast seemed to steady the tree and the cartwheeling motion slowed to a stop. By the time the tree reached the sluice gates, it was bobbing up and down like an angler's float, the tangled and mangled body flopping as it dipped.

"Now what?" asked Prosser, shaking after his brush with, if not death, then a serious dunking. Fraser was already on his radio telling the desk warden to call the water authority, they were going to have to access the gates and find a way to recover the tree without shaking the body loose in the process. Prosser almost jumped out of the boat when it reached the river stages and then sprinted for the grassy bank alongside. "Nobody say anything, I am never going in a small boat ever again". Simon Beresford had watched the whole spectacle as if waiting to be recharged. He looked at Prosser and asked whether they did this sort of thing often? It was a genuine enquiry.

"At least twice a month", said Thompson, straight-faced.

"Oh".

It took an hour to organise, but soon people with ropes and stuff had the body removed and into the water authority compound. Various support vehicles arrived and the body was eventually on its way to the morgue. Before they moved off, a few present had a quick look.

"Jeez, the fish have been busy", said Josh, not that keen on bodies.

"Not really, I can see why they called him 'Igor' now. This one's Christopher Johnson", said Prosser.

Thompson thanked Fraser for helping out and his new part-timer for his diligent spotting. Excitement over, he headed back, leaving Prosser, and Josh to finish off. "Mickey, a word".

"Boss?"

"You're the sergeant here, act like one".

"I tried, Boss, but Liam dived in. Don't worry, I'll talk to him, he just didn't realise". Thompson had listened and was ok with it, but told Newton he'd be on a self-assertion course as soon as one came up.

"I wonder how many poor sods have gone through that sluice gate?" said Elkie reflectively, as they drove back. She wasn't bothered by bodies, it was just so much meat, but the raw power of the violent river after heavy rain unsettled her.

"Keeps the fish fed", said Thompson, his mind still elsewhere.

"Sorry, Carla, I'm not following you here, but if you have an idea just run with it, just let the Boss know" Banks was busy and had temporarily dumped the Pickles case into her mental dustbin. She was trying to maintain concentration on picking through the Wet Bones case.

"Did I hear my name?" asked Thompson, arriving back from Colwick and hearing the word 'Boss', and assuming there was something he should know.

"Sir, I need to talk to people about Cirl Buntings, bird club people who might know. Would that be James Heston, do you think? I'm not really up-to-date with their current hierarchy but James was always the go-to bird man".

Thompson called Cliff, who called Heston, who said he was happy to help if he could, but he was doing a twenty-four-hour birding patch-watch at Hoveringham, a big day, and wouldn't be done until midnight.

"Big day?" asked Banks, finding her focus drifting but feeling she should show interest.

"They spend all day in one spot, or one site, one county or even one country and see how many birds they can see in twenty-four hours", said Carla. Saying it out loud she realised what a silly thing it was to do.

Banks looked blank, she didn't get bird spotting at all, never mind why anyone would spend all day doing it. She went back to working through records of missing people.

"Heston is down by the Yacht Club, according to Cliff. Take Simon and show him a tree, or something" said Thompson, his phone suddenly pinging texts like a pinball machine.

It didn't take long to get to Hoveringham. The track that led to the Yacht Club was rough gravel but well-travelled. Before the club building was a locked gate, but Heston was waiting and let them through. His car had a deck chair set up next to it and he had a cooler with drinks and food. He offered a fizzy drink but Carla thought it best not to give Beresford sugar. Suddenly he became aware of where he was.

"A gravel extraction, now sailing amenity. Odd to think that 15,000 years ago the glaciers were just receding during the Holocene Period, leaving behind a substantial alluvial plain".

Carla and Heston looked at him, waiting to see if there was any more to come, there wasn't. Carla explained and Heston listened, his face creased in concentration or, perhaps, shaped that way after years spent outside birding. She wasn't sure which.

"This is quite a difficult one because there is information not in the public domain and I'd prefer to keep it that way".

"This is a murder enquiry, James. What I'm asking, in general terms, is could the Cirl Bunting in the Whitaker School bird room be a Notts bird, yes or no?"

Heston again looked pained. "The thing is, there are egg collectors out there who would strip them bare if they found out, but you think the bird in the school collection came from Notts recently?"

"It has a label saying so. Picked up near Newark, road casualty".

"Can the origin be proven?

Carla was reluctant to recite Beresford isotope thing so just went for a yes, provided they had the right bits for anaylsis.

"Can I examine the other birds you found in Kingston's place?"

"I can arrange that, why?"

"To get you an answer, perhaps".

"You know we think Trevor Gold is responsible for the murder, any thoughts there?"

"Gold is erratic. He's passionate about wildlife and birds in particular but he's odd and I say that as a fully-fledged bird spotter myself, the oddest of the odd. If you asked whether he could do it, I'd say yes but maybe not sober. Get me access to the birds and you'll get proof of location, I don't have much more besides. You might want to consider that the location isn't just the preserve of myself and Gold".

"Did you tell someone?"

"No, but I think Gold may have, but I don't know who, just things he said, the way he worded sentences. He rings me up regularly and warns me not to tell anyone".

"Does he leave messages?"

"He does, you're going to want them now I suppose. Can I send them or do you have to take the phone, only I need it".

Beresford stepped forward. "I can strip the message off here, I have an app, I just need a verbal from you for authorization".

"Ok, let's do it".

On the way back to the nick, Carla was trying to figure out where Heston was going with it and why wouldn't he just say they had Cirl Buntings somewhere. The phone message had been a surprise though.

"If Heston finds another one in the evidence bag of birds, he'll tell you what you want to know. He's right to be concerned about Oologists, they still represent a scourge to our rare breeding species. The message is interesting but probably not sufficient, we need more. The recent images of Europa have just been released, fascinating".

"Simon, can I ask you something?" There was no answer so she did anyway. "Do you ever have normal conversations, you know, ones with a beginning, middle and end?"

"I must do, but I tend to edit out the irrelevant when I speak, that way people aren't exposed to me for longer than strictly necessary". Carla found that quite sad and vowed to try to be nicer to him, possibly.

"Boss, a turn up for the books, Shania-Marie Luckhurst is downstairs wanting to talk to us. I'll take Tilda in with me, thought you might like to watch, maybe Elkie too?" Banks seemed quite excited at the prospect of getting to grips with Lemmy Dowie's girlfriend again, with possibly the opportunity to make her squirm a bit. In the stark light of the interview room, Shania-Marie looked weird, like she'd had her face made up to star in a horror film. She was also clearly nervous. When Banks and Jeffries walked in, she stiffened as if ready to run for it. Elkie whispered that she was having second-thoughts, Tilda had also seen it and instinctively switched her accent, called her 'babe' and gave her a friendly hug. This seemed to calm her a bit.

"Jenny said Tilda was good at role play. She had me nearly convinced that she's from Bilborough", Elkie commented.

"She is", said Thompson, as the interview got underway.

"I've thought about it for a couple of days and I don't want this recording or anything. I've come here because I thought I'd better say a bit about my past. If you haven't already found out, I used to do escort work for one of those men who died, Ritchie Johnson. It was him that introduced me to Lemmy. Him and Lemmy go back a bit and Johnson manages Lemmy's properties. I know what he gets up to but Lemmy won't listen, he's pig-headed, and his mate Ritchie can do no wrong so I don't say nothing anymore. I think the three men I saw, I think it was them, the Johnson brothers". Everyone could see that Shania-Marie was relieved to get that off her possibly-enhanced chest. That level of personal detail wasn't something you normally asked about, but Elkie had already indicated that she was in the pneumatic camp.

"Did you set up the robbery, give Ritchie the access code for the safe?"

"No, I'm not allowed to know it. Only three people have it, Lemmy, Bruno and the PA, Cherise. It's meant to change regularly but I don't get involved. You might have guessed, I'm little more than a lodger there, handy to provide a bit of horizontal jogging for Lemmy. I'm in a gilded cage".

In the observation room, Thompson shrugged. "And singing like a canary", he said to Elkie. "Why do you think she's really here?"

"It sounds like the PA might be a doing more hands-on job than Shania-Marie likes, or it could be that she's being honest and wants it all out before our big police officers' boots go kicking a hole in her life".

"Does Lemmy know you're here, Shania-Marie?" Tilda's accent was getting thicker to the point of caricature.

"No, he's away with the team, training somewhere. It's just me in that big place, rattling around bored to tears. Would it fit my profile if I said I spent all day cracking one off?" Her accent was a little more polished now.

The door opened and Elkie whispered in Banks' ear, before leaving.

"Sorry, I'm going to have to go shortly. One last thing, Shania-Marie, which school did you go to?"

"Ha, she's bright that one. Oakham, I suppose I should reveal all, as they say. Daddy didn't approve of my recreational choices, but when I met Ritchie he provided options, later Lemmy was one of them".

"Are you still using?" asked Banks.

"Clean twenty-three months and counting, thanks for asking. You can drop the accent too if you like, Tilda".

"Sharp cookie, was I that obvious?"

"Not at home, no, but here I heard you outside. Then when you came in you were all 'babe' and the like and I knew. I think I've said all I can about what happened. I was never very happy about having that bloody necklace in the house, I just played up to it. You should have seen Lemmy's shorts when I was wandering around in the buff wearing just his precious necklace. It wasn't a phone in his pocket, he really was pleased to see me. Pity about the technique though, don't believe everything you read in the sports press, he's not that great in the box", and she winked at the mirror. "That one's for the boys watching".

Jenny Banks laughed, she'd unexpectedly found that she quite liked the real Shania-Marie.

"So now what, back to Lemmy and the cage?" asked Tilda, in her normal voice.

"Until this is sorted out, yes. Besides, I'm safer with Lemmy than out in the wild. I don't trust Ritchie not to rise from the dead and come calling again, I'm really hoping he's fish food though".

The door to the interview room opened and Thompson walked in. "Oh, hello", said Shania-Marie in her best flirty voice, her posture changing to 'boy-mode'. "Who are you then?" She swivelled sideways to face Thompson and stretched her long legs out, like a female spider feeling her web for prey.

"DI Thompson. Hello Shania-Marie, can I ask, when you worked as a hostess, did you mix with Johnson's other girls or were you kept separately?" Banks looked at Tilda who gave her the 'I don't know' look.

"I knew a few, but it wasn't like we'd have parties or anything. All Ritchie was interested in was the money, but he isn't stupid, I'd say he's sly. He graded his girls accordingly, educated girls like me went indoors, regular clients, clean. The thickos with a short life expectancy were outside and less well-maintained. Why?"

"Do you have any idea where Ritchie might hide, if he managed to get out the Trent alive?"

"If he got out, and I hope to God he didn't, he'd have called one of his indoor girls to pick him up, then he'd move every few days, probably using Lemmy's places, randomly".

"You've obviously given this some thought".

"Hedging my bets. Dead, I can stop worrying about Ritchie, alive and you lot need to catch him". Then she did a very exaggerated leg cross right in front of Thompson, who didn't bat an eyelid.

"Thanks for the information, Shania-Marie. Any thoughts on the new Brazilian Leicester just bought?" said Thompson, dead-pan.

Shania-Marie burst out laughing, turned to Banks and said "I like him, can I borrow him?" She'd reverted back to Lemmy's WAG.

Thompson smiled and left the interview, rejoining Elkie.

"Did she give you a nice eyeful there, Dave?"

"Sharon Stone did it better. Is she legit?"

"I think so, but she can act. The change when you went in was marked, total boy mode, mystifying, I wonder if she put her contacts in today? When it was just Jenny and Tilda we got nearer to the real Shania-Marie, she's scared".

Back in the room, Banks was winding up the interview.

"Just so you know, I'm not repeating any of this and I'm not telling you anything more, so don't come calling. Lemmy might be a thick grunt but he's a good boy really, dedicated to his career. You find those properties and you might find that shit Ritchie, if he's still breathing. You might look at Cherise, too".

Tilda took Shania-Marie out and gave her a proper hug. She seemed surprised at first then Shania-Marie whispered in her ear "Ritchie knew about you and had plans", before tottering off. When Tilda got back upstairs. she was ushered into Thompson's office to break down the interview.

Thompson sat at his desk, the door closed and the team involved in the little chat with Shania-Marie waiting. He raised a finger, indicating to wait a moment. A few seconds later, a tap on the door saw Beresford coming in with four coffees. "Courtesy of Josh, I don't know who has what but you're all detectives so it shouldn't be too taxing". He put the tray of coffee down and left.

"I thought we were going to put a stop to this, Jenny".

"Sorry, Boss, I'll move from hints to threats. Ok, what did we make of that? A performance for sure but with bits of honesty and fear in there too, a role based on reality".

"Where are we on the property list?"

"Requested by email, but this Cherise is hard to pin down and the trust isn't registered where we have jurisdiction. We need to see her in person, get some direct information and find out who she is. I don't like to not know who she is". Banks was clearly frustrated.

"Agreed. What did we get on the financials for the burn-out? If Josie Turner used banking then it might lead to others with the same system?" Thompson had been drawing a diagram on his scratch pad. In the centre was Ritchie Johnson, and all around him were lines leading to simplistic houses, each one containing a financial contributor.

"I looked at Johnson, nothing is out there in his name", said Elkie. "No bank account or credit cards so he must have some sort of shell company or use a different professional name".

"What we need is to find just one of his indoor girls, as Shania-Marie called them, and get her to talk. Tilda, when you were attached to Vice, did you meet any?"

Although she tried very hard not to glance momentarily at Thompson, it happened and Elkie saw it. "Not that I'm aware of but I still have contacts and I'll see what I can find. I have to be careful, I might be closer to a bit of retribution than I thought", and she passed on Shania-Marie's warning.

"What about Gecko, might he have an idea?"

"No, he mostly dealt with street girls. I did already ask him about Johnson's girls but he wasn't able to be helpful, not really in his area".

"Jenny, set up your actions, track down and interview this Cherise and, Tilda, you push where you can but don't get yourself into trouble. If you go out, take either Carla or Lorna with you as back-up, Josh, too, if you think he'd help. Good, thanks everyone", and Thompson closed the meeting. The rest filed out but Elkie hung back.

"I saw Tilda's reaction when asked if she met any Johnson girls and I wondered at your question to Shania-Marie about whether she knew names. It went beyond a regular enquiry, it was more personal, Dave. I hope you know what you're doing".

"I saw you'd noticed. I can't say anything yet because it's just a hunch about Tilda and someone else, it'll all come out later. Trust me, I'll find out".

"Implicitly, Dave. If you need me for anything, any little jobs that need my skills, just let me know".

"I will".

"Oh and Boss, how much did you really see when those long legs went into action?"

Thompson laughed. "Shania-Marie has a lovely smile, Elkie".

After giving Perkins a brief verbal update regarding Shania-Marie, during which he seemed wholly disinterested until Thompson mentioned Johnson and the warning, Thompson went home. He wasn't that late and he was looking forward to a bit of Guy time. It didn't quite pan out that way though.

"So I thought we could paint it all bile green and turn the spare room into a bordello".

Thompson caught the last word. "What? A bordello, what are you talking about?"

Rebecca was clearly very annoyed and Dave Thompson was desperately trying to put together earlier words aimed in his direction, hoping to pick up the thread.

"You don't listen to me, I said I want the work doing as soon as possible. Mr. Wheeler called, He can start in a couple of days, remember, we said about the roof and the extension. I said yes and got everything sorted because you're never here". That had an edge, Thompson wasn't happy about the edge, it had been creeping in gradually, or maybe not gradually, he wasn't sure now.

"I thought we'd agreed to wait until, you know, after", and Thompson pointed to the developing bump.

"No, you did but I want it all done and dusted by then. He reckons three weeks or so, then the walls have to settle, so I think a month or so should cover it. I intend to use my own interior design, as you know, but for now here won't be very healthy. I've already spoken to mummy".

Now Thompson was well and truly lost, what did Rebecca's mother have to do with anything and could she even plaster?

"I see from your face that you missed that nugget of information, too. I thought I'd visit mummy for that break she suggested, stay there with Guy until the work was finished and then come home to a shiny, clean and not roof-leaking house, and a blank canvas. Then I can implement my plans".

So that was it, Rebecca was bailing for a month while he lived in dust and shit. A little voice inside him found the idea appealing, and it worried him.

"Ok, yes, I see the sense in that and your mother does adore Guy despite his lineage". *Damn, that wasn't supposed to come out!*

Rebecca got tearful which, she'd stated several times, was a given considering her condition. "I thought we'd finally got somewhere with you and mummy, I really did. She agrees, it's best for me and Guy to be out the way, safe". *Damn, she hadn't meant to use that word!*

"Safe? It would be safe here if you didn't want to tear down the fucking walls!" *Damn, damn, damn!*

"I knew it wouldn't be long before you reverted to swearing, go on, swear all you like, get out that repressed Clifton boy. It makes you sound common". *Shit! Yes shit covered it!*

"Common? Well I am common and proud of it. You go to mummy and don't feel you have to come back until the dust settles, if you like". *Oh dear!*

Doors didn't bang because Rebecca didn't bang doors and that made it all the worse. Thompson knew that he'd gone too far, he should have just agreed, he should have listened, always, but work kept waving at him, attracting his attention. It was that sort of a job even without a tart flashing her fanny at him.

Rebecca was now calm, the sort of forced calm that hides a tempest, she was very good at it. Thompson called Perkins. "Sir, I might need half a day". Before Perkins could answer, Rebecca was asking what the fuck he was doing?

"Taking half a day so I can drive you and Guy to your mum's".

"No need, I've arranged a one way hire again, they'll drop the car off here later and will pick it up at the other end and, before you get uppity about cost, mummy paid for this one too, she insisted". And she carried on with what she was doing before, which, Thompson realised, was packing.

That was that, then. A row had winkled the information out, it had already been arranged. He'd be a good dog, wag his tail and do as he was told.

"Oh, right", he said, calmly.

Nineteen

15 August 2017

Rebecca made an early start, driving off sedately, she wasn't a fast driver. The car was almost new and put their own battered car to shame. Thompson made a mental note to run it into the garage for the back-end check, he was sure he could still smell petrol sometimes. He'd stood on the step waving like a maniac, but she'd been preoccupied with learning the switches and dials on the new car, too preoccupied to look back at him, it seemed. It felt like something important had slipped by.

"You look like shit, Dave, Sir". Jenny Banks was hedging her bets. Recently she hadn't been able to read which Dave Thompson had arrived for work and, like a good friend, she was concerned.

"My own fault, Jenny, not paying attention to everything again. I'll be fine but thanks for noticing. All good with you now?" It was an unnecessary question and neither Thompson nor Banks were sure why it had been asked.

"Er, fine, yes. Fine for now". There was something in the reply, an uncertainty. This was a surprise for Thompson because, as far as he'd cared to take notice of, everything had been fine when Jenny came back and slotted right into her old life, apart from Joe messing her about. He'd been pleased for her. Sure she'd been flirty with him a few times, but that was just Jenny.

"A quick verbal about the Wet Bones case. So far they're males only, pathology reckons not overly old either. No signs of trauma to the bits we have, Paul is doing yet another look around the bottom of that lake but we reckon we might have them all, for now. Got two more cars too that were dumped, both empty and recovered".

'For now, Jenny was fine for now?' was this something else he'd missed?

"It seems that the latest skull was placed in the water after the previous ones, maybe only a week ago. Some, we know, have been there between a year and six months. It's as if someone has a little hobby of visiting Colwick Park and chucking skulls in the lake, less serious than flashing, I suppose. Regular dog walkers, park staff, council people doing whatever they do there have all been looked at. We've also talked to people from all user groups, nothing. We'd need a DNA match to match a skull to a death if we have them in the database, then we'd be able to work back, but DNA analysis on twelve skulls, that'll be pricy and might not even be feasible. Probably best to explore other options, first".

"Ok, thanks for that. Perkins is bound to ask".

Jenny sat sideways on the desk. "If there's ever anything you want to talk about, I'm here for you, I hope you know that?"

Although Jenny's skirt wasn't overly short, Thompson was aware of her legs. "Thanks, I will, thanks. Right, must get on". Jenny took the cue to leave. As she passed through the office, several heads looked in her direction. She gave a slight shrug to indicate that she didn't know what was up with the Boss this time and carried on to her own desk.

The day was one of those where suddenly, nothing happened. The team was functioning, a few questions came his way but were dealt with swiftly and Perkins didn't trouble him. For once he got home at a reasonable time, which was ironic as there was nobody there to share his time with. After a light snack and some tea, he settled in to watch whatever football he could find, chilling in his jogging bottoms and a T-shirt. He'd just dozed off when the phone went. Waking with a start he answered but the line was dead and he didn't know the number. He put it down to either scammers or window sellers, which amounted to the same thing in his book. He had decided not to brood about his row with Rebecca, they'd had disagreements before and it had always blown over. She'd been right, the mess when the work started would be even more depressing and, although it stuck in his craw, he reluctantly agreed that mummy was right, this time. Then he had an idea, it was only early, the snack hadn't covered it, he'd go out for a proper meal and a pint.

The pub wasn't really a pub, more a place to eat where beer, of a sort, was a menu option. Thompson sat at his table sipping his one pint and devouring his Chicken Kiev. He wished he'd picked up the Evening Post or something to read, so he didn't have such an abandoned look.

"Hello again, fancy seeing you here".

Thompson looked up at a young woman. Her face had seen a little bit of life but at least the make-up wasn't trowelled on. She was dressed modestly in jeans and a nice top, no jewellery. He wracked his brain for an answer as to who this was.

"Sorry, er…"

"Jenny. We met in town when I was doing the lunchtime shift. I was with Tilda, you were with your dad, I think. You are?"

"Dave". For a moment Thompson was lost, racking his brain. His dad, in town, Tilda? *Oh, bugger me!*

"There you go, it's all coming back to you now. Don't worry, I'm in plain-clothes tonight, much like yourself".

Again Thompson looked confused.

"I'm not working. Even in my line we take days off you know, live a normal life. So, what's bothering you, it looks like you're carrying the world on your shoulders. Mind if I join you?" and she sat down.

Thompson caught a scent, nice, not overpowering. For some reason he'd expected someone like this Jenny to wear overpowering scent. It didn't change the fact that he was a Detective Inspector and she was, as far as he knew, a prostitute, but she was right and if 'they' had a night off, then so did he.

"Come on then, tell Jenny all about it".

"Life stuff really, I'm sure you get the same. Things build up, get on top of you, no release then 'woosh'".

"Sorry, do you want to rephrase that?"

Thompson frowned, then replayed his sentence in his head before bursting out laughing and Jenny joined in, she had a really nice laugh, genuine.

"There you go, laughter is a good release. So these woes of yours have resulted in a meal for one in a pub, very sad but I get you".

Throughout his career, those who break the law were criminals, but he'd always tried very hard to see them as regular people too. There but for the grace and all that. The exception was people like Ray Frost, who he'd regarded as little more than an animal. Despite the nature of what this Jenny did, and possibly why she did what she did, he found it hard to not to see her as just another attractive woman out for the night.

"Are you alone too, then?"

"Yes, I split up with my boyfriend some time back and things have taken a bit of a turn. I think he was a bad influence on me", and she laughed the sweet laugh again. "What, are you surprised I had a boyfriend? No one path leads to the dark side", and she laughed again.

"The dark side? A curious turn of phrase".

"Star Wars nut, sorry. Sometimes I speak pure Star Trek, Star Wars or Python. Some people have no idea what I'm saying half the time, it can have its uses".

"I have the same with the younger officers on my team. You here to eat too, then?"

"Yes, I just fancied a meal out and this pub has good reviews on Trip Advisor. I do like to cook but sometimes I'll chance a pub meal; not too often though, I watch the weight. Are you going to tell me your woes then or tell me to piss off? I'd understand if you did, given my circumstances. I promise not to call you 'deary', swing my handbag or show you the price of a quickie chalked on my shoes".

"Please, stay, I don't want to unload on a stranger. Oh, shit, I did it again, I didn't mean… oh, shit!" It was too late, Jenny was laughing uncontrollably and attracting some attention.

"Best shut up, Dave, you're making my stomach hurt and people are looking".

"I just meant I prefer to keep my stuff to myself. Oh god, that's no better is it. Can we just talk about the weather for five minutes?" Thompson was flustered and he knew it.

"Fine, just don't mention you've been doing a bit of DIY", and Jenny started her nice laughing again and Thompson joined in. The conversation turned lighter, littered with silly puns and jokes that only the pair of them seemed to get. After an hour Thompson started to feel guilty because he'd not thought of Rebecca once. He briefly wondered whether she'd been thinking of him at all. Probably not.

Twenty

16 August 2017

The sun streamed through the window straight into his eyes, the curtains were open. Thompson wondered why, Rebecca always drew the curtains when they went to bed. Ah. He took a breath, there was a smell, a perfume he couldn't place. It wasn't one of those overrated ones that Rebecca sometimes wore, but a more regular one that he'd smelled recently. A noise, very close by, told him why. He reached over.

When she got up, Jenny must have sensed his discomfort because she didn't hang around too long, but she didn't exactly run away either. When she'd eventually gone, Thompson had a bath. He was normally a shower man but this time a bath seemed to be the right thing to do. Then he stripped and remade the bed, washing the bedding and almost getting everything perfect. A hot wash in the brand new washer had seemed about right, but his red football socks had found their way in with the sheets and duvet cover. Everything was now pink, *fuck*.

He had another bath.

There was a loud knock on the door. Thompson threw a towel around his midriff and dashed downstairs, dripping. If this was Jenny back for anything, he'd have to explain and what, pay her? He'd been thinking about that. Money hadn't been mentioned, did he even still have a wallet?

"Dave, remember me? Pete Wheeler. Your missus wants us to make a mess for you and so here we are", and a brawny, dog-rough guy was holding out his hand to shake. Thompson shook his hand while holding on to most of a towel with the other hand and trying to clear his head at the same time. Wheeler hadn't looked so rough when he'd met him last time.

"I thought you were coming tomorrow or the day after?"

"Ah, yes, well, the last job ended suddenly when the client decided that he wasn't going to pay and I had to take affirmative action".

Thompson's ears pricked up.

"Don't worry, I know who you are and what you do. We just left the site with him lacking two fitted rear windows. We'd agreed a price and then he decided to play silly buggers half-way through the job, well two can do that. He'll be on the phone later, only it will cost him double now, nobody pisses me and my lads about. Not that an officer of the law would do that. Right boys, get set up".

This was another situation where Thompson had completely lost control. "Right, good, I'll get you a key and you lads carry on. Let me know if you want some cash to be going on with. Oh, and get your lad there to sort out those lights on your van, won't you".

"Ha, ha, I like you already. Don't worry about the cash, all taken care of. Tony, fix the fucking lights on the van". A spotty youth of about eleven shouted "yes boss" and the rest of his lads sort of fanned out around the outside of the house.

"Roof first, then we really make a mess. Once we chop a hole in the wall you might want to be somewhere else for a night or two, if you can, I'll let you know when. Don't worry about security here, Tony will sleep on a camp bed. He might look like a little kid but he's a right nasty bastard if needs be. Deborah will be here if Tony's busy, a good girl but don't go telling her I said so. By the way, she has got a cock but I don't judge".

"Right, ok then, I'll leave you to it, work to do", was all Thompson could think of. Then he thought 'Deborah, which one was Deborah?'

In a state of disarray, Thompson set off for work. He realised that he was trusting this hairy-arsed builder, who he didn't know from Adam, with the keys to their house and access to all his worldly goods, strangely it didn't seem to bother him. The traffic on the way in was busy, so he had plenty of time to reflect on the evening before, not that he wanted to. What he really wanted to was to forget it ever happened, all of it, but could he? He flipped on the radio.

Dave Thompson had long-been convinced that gods did exist, especially the god of inappropriate if meaningful music. This god, he argued, could read minds and would then feed that mind something to jog it into being stuck in a loop. It had happened to him so many times that he was now impervious, expecting it even. Nevertheless, the radio still surprised him when one of his favourites by Kirsty MacColl came on, the one about Cowboys and counting the cracks in the ceiling.

"I refuse to believe in such a stupid thing, it's coincidence", he said loudly to himself. He pressed the button for the station to change from local radio to Radio Two, surely they had a bigger audience to target. The music told him that the back end of a song that he didn't know was just winding down, this was more like it, then the mellow-voiced presenter told him that Elton John would shortly sing to him of 'sweet painted ladies who got paid for being laid', and that did for him. He vowed that he was never going to turn that fucking radio on, ever again.

"You still look like shit yet again, Sir", said Jenny Banks, as Thompson looked up from a pile of overtime claims.

"Rebecca away, builders arrived this morning, eating unsuitable food, watching unsuitable films and behaving very badly. Does that tell you all you need to know?"

"Thought it was something like that. If you want to grab a meal, I'm free any time. Attractive men eating out alone can send out the wrong signals to some women, you know. We don't want some tart picking you up and having her way with you while Rebecca's away now do we?" Thompson almost choked.

Jenny looked at him quizzically.

"Sorry, swallowed the coffee down the wrong way. Sure, a 'friends meal', yes, will anyone else be there?"

"No, just me and you. Is that a problem?"

"No, not at all, it's just Rebecca still thinks we…er, well, no, that's great, a meal, yes. You choose and I'll see you there".

All morning Thompson was unsettled and completely unable to concentrate. He kept reliving the night before and finding it hard to believe what had happened. Then he decided that nobody can ever know. Jenny the prostitute had seemed a decent sort, for a prostitute, and therefore unlikely to bring any sort of pressure to bear on him just because he was a Detective Inspector in the Nottinghamshire Police and she was a prostitute. Who was he kidding? *Oh fuck…*

Another by-product of the evening was several trips to the toilet to examine, things. He knew that most prostitutes were careful, but they hadn't been. What if he'd got a dreadful disease, a relationship-ending disease, and all because what, he couldn't control himself? He knew he hadn't even tried. He went back to his paper monolith.

"Missing Rebecca?" asked Elkie, making him jump.

"Yes, of course but the builders arrived today and now the mess starts. I didn't get much sleep, on my own as I was, alone. It felt odd so, yes, missing Rebecca and Guy".

"You should know, she called me when she got to Surrey, I'm not surprised she didn't call you, she was pretty upset. I think some distance between you two just might do the trick, provided you don't run off with an exotic dancer or something. You won't, will you, Dave?"

He realised that Elkie was gently winding him up, so he played along a bit. "How exotic?"

"Dressed only in your best Forest away kit, the yellow one from the Championship year". In his head he could still see the girl, Jenny, wandering around the house earlier. For a while she'd been dressed in only that short football shirt. How did Elkie know about that? It was surely witchcraft.

He deflected. "Was there something you wanted, Elkie? Only this reconstituted tree isn't going to process itself".

"Gecko is seeing a mate, he might have a house for us, one with Ritchie Johnson in it. He's going to call you when he's spoken to the mate and folding has changed hands. We looked for you when he called to tell us but you were in the bog again. Everything alright downstairs?"

"In the cafeteria?"

"Very good, Dave, anyway expect a call. Jenny and Lorna are both out waiting to go, Josh, Tilda and Carla are on back-up. Me and the rest got left behind like naughty kids, but I'm game for a ride if you are".

"You know what, sod the paperwork and sod everything else, let's go". Elkie was pleased to see the real Dave Thompson back, however briefly. In the parking garage a pungent pool of petrol lay on the floor below Thompson's car. Perfect.

"You better get that sorted, Dave, fire hazard and all that. We'll sit this one out back in the office then, maybe it's for the best".

The car got hauled away and the garage texted the cost, another seven hundred quid to pay out and, even though he'd get it back under insurance, it was still irritating. In his office, a disembodied voice kept telling him how important his call was until a thick Indian accent walked him through the claim. He got a rental under insurance and went to pick it up. When he got back to the office, he got the call.

"Boss, we went to an address and knocked, nobody answered so we spoke to a neighbour. Seems people were there until yesterday afternoon, she identified Ritchie Johnson, so we know where we are there. The house is owned by a trust, the neighbour rents from a different trust but knows the young woman who lives there, name of Jenny Spinner. Not seeing her on the system though".

Thompson laughed. "Jenny, I suspect that Jenny Spinner, or 'Spinning Jenny' isn't a real name. Find out what you can and we'll talk later. At least she didn't call herself 'Norma Snockers' or something".

"Sorry, Boss, I don't get it. Anyway, two things. We're doing a bit of door-to-door for old time's sake and we're eating later at a nice Italian on Mansfield Road, pick me up at six-thirty, ok?"

Thompson wondered who she meant for a moment, then realised he was going to go out for another meal but with a different Jenny, two in a row. He idly wondered whether this Jenny Spinner had a window in her diary for the hat-trick. "Ok, fine, I'll be here wading through my paper pile when you lot get back from your adventure".

The light outside pushed around the sides of the curtains. For a moment Thompson tried to remember when Rebecca had replaced the blue curtains with yellow ones, daffodil yellow. She hadn't. He sniffed.

Twenty-one

17 August 2017

Thompson appeared at his office door and beckoned Banks and Jeffries in, then put his phone on speaker. "Sorry, Ms. Belanger, I was just calling the lead officers to listen in, I hope you don't mind?"

"No, not at all. As I was saying, why are Mr. Dowie's property investments of interest? Surely the focus of your investigation must be the missing necklace, I'm sure you're aware of the value". Cherise Belanger had a lilt to her voice, it said European, her name suggested French or Belgian.

"We believe there may be a link between the properties and the theft. It's an active line of enquiry, so if you can send those addresses and details soonest, I'd be grateful".

"This has come from that stupid woman, Shania-Marie, hasn't it? Lemmy told me she'd been hinting to him that it was his property manager who was to blame. You do know she's jealous of Mr. Johnson?"

"Why would that be, Ms. Belanger?"

"Lemmy trusts his friend implicitly and Ritchie Johnson knows better than to mess with Lemmy. He got given a second a chance and, yes, we do know about his mixed past. Lemmy says everyone deserves a second crack at life and he's true to his word".

"We still require that list, so if you'd be so kind. What exactly is your role with Lemmy Dowie?"

"I'm his personal assistant. I take care of his day-to-day life so he can concentrate on the football".

"How did you come to be in this role?"

"Bruno Lago headhunted me. I'm rather good at my job, if I say so myself".

"Do you get on with Shania-Marie? Your comments suggest otherwise".

"She came in as entertainment, nothing more, but Lemmy is finding he has some affection for her. He can do better than a common girl like that, he deserves someone with more refinement and a better vocabulary".

"Like you?" chipped in Tilda.

"Lemmy and I have a professional relationship".

"So you've never slept with him then?" Tilda wasn't letting this bone go easily.

"I take care of his needs when we're away. Better me, clean and responsible, than some trashy camp follower trying for another footballer's name on their lucky knickers. I see taking care of Lemmy's needs as all part of the job".

"Surely that makes you a paid escort then, a prostitute, Ms. Belanger?"

On the other end of the line, Cherise Belanger was obviously trying hard to stay civil. "Detective Inspector, I'll arrange for that list to be sent to you but it may take a few days, I have to run it past Bruno and Lemmy first". She hung up.

"You might have cost us her cooperation there, Tilda. Care to explain?"

"She's a suspect, Sir. I'm wondering whether her and this Bruno person are working together on some scam".

"But Lago is worth a fortune, why would he?"

"Because the rich get richer by being crooks. When they get rich they get bored and play games, thinking that their money places them above the law. I don't like to see people like Shania-Marie treated like facilities, and I don't like to see the Lemmys of this world screwed over, either. What if Johnson was working for Lago and Belanger?"

"What do we know about Belanger?"

"Only the stuff on her LinkedIn profile. Josh is prepping a brief".

"Good, let's see what that list says when we get it and move Lago and Belanger up on the board from peripheral to the centre of the investigation. Thompson's phone rang, it was Perkins. The man was psychic.

The room emptied and Thompson took the call. "David, just a quick call. I've had high-ups asking why we're harassing this footballer and his agent. Are they relevant?" Thompson relayed the details of the conversation, Perkins didn't interrupt. "Good, carry on. I look forward to the briefing". Thompson's mobile started to ring, he grabbed it hoping the display would say 'Rebecca'. It didn't, it just said 'private caller'. "Hello?"

"Hi, it's me, Jenny, remember? Don't worry, I'm not stalking you or after anything. I really enjoyed our night but I felt you should know, because we were unprotected and while I am always careful, there is a risk of an STD. I'll get checked out, they do us quickly because, well, you know. Sorry, I should have called before... Hello?"

Thompson stared at his phone as if it might explode. "Dave", said Jenny Banks right behind him. She had a way of moving silently, even in heels, that could be unnerving. He leapt a mile. "Sorry", she said. "I can start knocking if you like, only we thought you were back on an even keel again".

"Sorry, no, it's me. One second". Thompson walked to the window and mouthed 'signal', which Jenny knew was utter rubbish. "Good, right thanks for that, and if I need to discuss anything with you again?"

"Dave, are you ok?" This was confusing, Thompson was experiencing a chorus of Jennies asking how he was. "Fine", he said to the phone, then "fine" to the other Jenny.

"Good, you can use this number for now", and the phone went dead.

Jenny Banks was waiting for an answer.

"Sorry, lots of things happening at once. What's up?"

Jenny dropped his wallet on the desk. "You left it in my bed". Thompson slumped into his seat and held his head in his hands.

"Ah, Detective Inspector, contemplating a dilemma?" It was Perkins, another who had a habit of materialising in his office. Both Thompson and Banks gave each other a look.

"I can see that you are busy with matters of a personal nature, however, I just wanted to say that I'm assured that Bruno Lago and his organization, in the form of Cherise Belanger, have agreed to assist us and that those property details should be with you shortly. Keep me informed", and he left the way he came.

"How much did he hear, Dave?"

"Enough to put into his archive, ready for use should the need arrive. Thanks, it must have dropped out of my pocket this morning. Look, thanks for the spare room, I do appreciate it, despite the wagging tongues. I don't want to be a problem though, for you, with any other people you might be involved with".

"You won't be, that's what mates are for. Anyway, 'Bruno Lago agrees', what is he, a fucking giant corporation or something? We should pull him and see what we can shake out". Thompson was surprised at how aggressive Banks was, she sounded frustrated about something more than Lago. So was he, but it was no good threatening billionaires, it just didn't work

It had taken a bit of organization but eventually it was set up and Carla asked James Heston to visit the police station. In one of the interview rooms, now furnished with a long folding table, was a cooler box, not at all unlike his own. It contained a number of dated bags holding dead birds awaiting inspection. He asked Carla to jot down notes as he went, she wasn't sure why.

After ten minutes or so, and with Heston asking her to put a tick in columns headed 'immature, male, female', he'd finished and had one bird on its own on the table, the rest were back in the cooler.

"Another Cirl Bunting, an immature. Can I see a photo of the one at the school?" Carla showed him. "Another immature. Assuming that these are collected from the same place, and that they are from the same brood, this constitutes the first evidence of breeding in Notts for many decades".

"Would isotope analysis confirm this has Nottinghamshire origins, if done in conjunction with a number of controls, the Yellowhammers?"

Heston was surprised, it wasn't a question he'd seen coming. "Yes, I expect so".

"Ok, crunch time. Where are they and who knew about them".

"Myself and Trevor Gold. They're on a private estate but not near Newark. Gold found them, or at least he found two adults, a male and female. He trespassed to get on, he took me and showed me. The estate is owned by some foreign company, used as a client retreat and pheasant shoot for rich people. He was there looking for illegal hawk traps, we'd heard rumours and you know how he is, but he found a singing male Cirl Bunting and called me".

"And you said nothing because of egg collectors and the private nature of the site?"

213

"Yes, that, and the fact that I'd seen a Cirl Bunting in Notts but they weren't generally available. Listing jealousy is a thing".

Carla ignored the last bit as irrelevant. She bagged the Cirl Bunting separately, selected another three Yellowhammers to join it and arranged for the rest of birds to go back in the freezer. "Come on, James, time you talked to the Boss. Do you think Gold is capable of killing someone?"

"Sober or drunk?"

Thompson listened to what Heston had to say then sent him home, with thanks. His only 'crime' had been a minor and irrelevant trespass. Now he had to talk to Perkins and try to get some analysis done.

Perkins listened as Thompson explained. "Who did this come from, initially?" asked Perkins.

"I think from Beresford, who was reading an article about isotope analysis. He told Carla who had a brain-wave".

"Very good. I have a suggestion, speak to Peter Fielding again, he has contacts at various universities, he may well have a contact in the Nottingham University Avian Biology Research Department. I can see you're wondering about his personal involvement. Unlikely, but that is not to say he doesn't know more than he's revealing. I won't tell him you're coming, this time, back foot is always a good place to put people when you want information. Please commend DC Adams for her line of thought and young Beresford for his valuable input".

Thompson took Perkins at his word, gathered up Adams and went off to try to catch Fielding unawares. He was quite sure Perkins had meant him to send someone else to talk to Fielding, but language can be so ambiguous sometimes.

"I'd like you to interview, Carla. Your intuition got us this far and I suspect Fielding won't be too keen on talking to a young woman but will cooperate with getting the analysis done as a favour. I hope he isn't the killer, this could all get awkward later".

As they approached Fielding's front door it opened and they were greeted by the man himself. "Detective Inspector and DC Adams, welcome. Tea?" So much for the back foot approach. Tea arrived along with some Nice biscuits, which surprised Thompson as he'd thought Hobnobs might be de rigueur for the teaching profession.

"Ms. Adams, I believe this is your baby, as they say. Excellent deduction, a fine product of a comprehensive education at Carlton-le-Willows, I must say. Please proceed".

"Sir, your example of *Emberiza cirlus* at the school may have emanated from a crime scene. No finger of suspicion is pointed in your direction, but we need isotope analysis of a second specimen to confirm the source location and it's been suggested by your good friend, Superintendent Perkins, that you might be able to facilitate that?"

"Tell me, Carla, do you always speak like that?"

"No, Sir, but I can if I wish. We all have the capability to act a part if we try".

"Excellent, Thompson here has recruited well. Yes, I can talk to my people at the university. Can I ask, when the dust is settled, and presumably you lot haven't 'fitted me up' and I'm not 'banged to rights', that the *cirlus* specimen might come back my way rather than be destroyed?"

Carla laughed. "You sound like an Eastenders fan, Sir".

"Never miss an episode, Carla. Well?"

"Not my decision but we can ask. As we walked in, I heard your printer chuntering away. I presume that is going to be a list of all your bird club members at school from, say, the last ten years?"

"Very, very good. Thompson, promote this young person immediately".

Thompson had sat listening and was slightly gobsmacked by it all. "I'd like to", was all he said.

Arrangements were made to deliver the Cirl Bunting and Yellowhammers to the university and Fielding invited them to call any time and assured them that it wasn't Perkins who'd gave him the "what is it called, the heads-up?", this time.

"Was that ok, Sir?"

"Carlton-le-Willows, eh? Posh school then".

"Not really, but not terrible. Can he have the dead bird?"

"He was being polite in asking, I feel sure all that has already been arranged. These people move in a different way to the rest of the world, but I suspect he knows more than we've winkled out of him. Anyone on the list of interest?"

"Kieran Joyce, we knew might be on there, Jeremy Stones is a surprise though. We've not had many dealings with them yet, the Stones family are an old firm, they operate despite Duncan Collins and he's sensible enough not to try to stop them".

"In the frame?"

"Perhaps, but outside their normal range of activities, I'd say".

"Sir, I really think this must be our last meeting. We might be away from the gaze of the city, but news seeps inexorably through cracks and into the system, you could be compromised". Jeremy Stones was beginning to wish he'd never got involved, and so was his dad. He'd agreed to this meeting on the old Gedling Pit Top, now a country park, only very reluctantly.

"Tell me the whole story, if you would, leave no details out. I would know what happened". Stones could see that Fielding had made up his mind. It wasn't a risk but to Fielding himself, there was no route back.

"Trevor Gold, a hothead, discovered Cirl Buntings in habitat in Nottinghamshire. He thinks that only one other birder knows bar James Heston, but I know too. Gold imbibes freely and in copious amounts. Since losing his licence, I've transported him home occasionally, and we've talked. He knew about Kingston- it wasn't a secret, it was in that magazine. When it was suggested to him, while in a catatonic state, that his Cirl Buntings were also for the brandy, I knew that I'd planted a seed. Later, on a park visit to exercise Dinsdale, a meeting I'd manufactured, I made sure he learned what was needed to do to gain entry".

"You told him how to break in and deactivate the doorbell-cam?"

"I told him that I reckoned Kingston was the type to keep a spare key under his wheely bin, and made sure that was the case. Then I showed him my feeder-cam on the phone. I told him about an app, 'Blink', which will deactivate a camera for one minute. I told him it was to censor the activities of a marauding Sparrowhawk, my feeder-cam is a public feed and the AI detects predators by shape and activates 'Blink' thus sparing the masses the avian brutality".

Fielding listened with increasing bemusement and Stones could see his discomfort. "Sorry, Sir, the modern world moves quickly. When I told him, I expected him to just enter, perhaps spoil the brandy and liberate the Yellowhammers, although I had been at pains to point out that removing them might result in Kingston procuring replacements. He said that it was better that Kingston knew that someone knew about his secret, and that he was going to let him know he had them and was going public. He obviously changed his plan, though".

"Stones, I am relieved to know that you did not participate in Kingston's demise but this is still complicated. Is Gold likely to tell people of your conversation?"

"No, Sir, I am very sure he knows what might happen if he did. Sorry to be so base about this but 'needs must' in my industry".

"The police are even now tying in the Cirl Bunting to the Nottinghamshire population, which is hopefully still extant. They will know who was aware of it and Gold's name will be furnished. It may be wise to see that any incriminating evidence that confirms Gold's obvious guilt is made available".

"Wheels are in motion, Sir. We'll meet no more until justice has taken its due course". With that, Stones left Fielding to digest all he now knew.

Twenty-two

21 August 2017

"He came a day or two early. After five days the roof is going well, as far as I can see, walls all marked up, outside wall footings built. He's cutting tomorrow". Thompson tried to sound upbeat on the phone, even though he wasn't. The house was the shitty mess he'd expected, or at least it was before he'd stopped over at Jenny's place as a guest. He'd go home alone tonight, and see what else they'd done.

"Send me some photos. We're all good. Look, I'm sorry to run out on you like that, I felt guilty as soon as the car door clicked shut. Guy says 'hi', mummy says 'hi', too, which surprised me". Rebecca sounded quite cheerful.

"I say 'hi' back".

"What are you going to do while he makes the real mess?" Thompson tried hard not to pause.

"I'm going ask to stay with Jenny, and Joe, they're close to work. They have a spare room, just a couple of nights Wheeler reckons, maybe not at all if they get on with it today but the rain is falling again".

"Oh, Jenny's place, right, and Joe will be there, good. Only Elkie reckons all is not plain-sailing there and she might not have told you through embarrassment. Don't be a gooseberry if they need space, get a hotel or something, just use your intuition". That was a bit loaded. The memory of a scent that was not Rebecca's entered his head from nowhere.

"Funny, she's not said anything to me but we're always in work mode these days, no socializing. Another case today, up to my armpits in bodies again" he lied.

"Well don't forget to make notes, your fans are eagerly awaiting your next novel".

Thompson laughed, he was pretty sure 'they' weren't, despite Rebecca's encouragement. "Are you keeping busy?"

"Oh, you know, catching up with old friends, people I've not seen in years. Some have moved away, as they do, as I did, but it was nice to see a few people. We're having that school reunion at the weekend, remember, I told you".

"Yes, I remember, that should be fun". He didn't really think so, he'd always reckoned school reunions were only done so those doing well could brag about it. Any featuring his old school would probably be held in 'E' wing.

"Actually we have a few absentees, just can't find them. Is it considered illegal to use the police network to find old school friends after Friends Unlimited has failed?"

"Very much so. Why?"

"Trish, the organizer-I know, I forgave her, it was her ex-boyfriend who was the crook-anyway, she reckons one of my old classmates now lives in Nottingham somewhere, which was her original neck of the woods before she was sent to a private school. According to Trish, seems she might be known to you, or at least some of your colleagues but we don't judge. It would just be nice to see her, give her our best. I can send you a photo, not recent though, do you mind?"

"Colleagues, when you say colleagues who do you mean exactly?"

"Gecko, actually".

"I see. Go on then, send me the image and I'll make a casual inquiry without tapping into the system, illegally".

"Great, sending. Say thanks to Jenny from me for helping out, and Joe. Love you", *click*.

'Ping', Thompson went to his text folder, opened the image and looked at the face, if it was who he thought it was she had much longer hair back then and looked less mature, but surely not?

"Ready, Boss", said Jenny Banks. "You ok?"

"Yes, thanks, just been chatting to Rebecca, she's good, Guy's good, everything is good".

"Good too, a week away will do her the world of good. I'm cooking tonight, a relaxing night in, ok?"

"Ok, great, on with the briefing then".

'Ping' – now what?

'I'm clean, so you should be too, unless you've been a busy boy elsewhere with a different naughty girl. Hope you appreciate that I didn't say busy little boy ;) XXX'.

Twenty-three

22 August 2017

The morning had dragged as Thompson's head sought refuge in work as opposed to thinking about his mess of a life. Liam Prosser put his head around Thompson's door without knocking. "I need a word, in private, Dave, urgent".

"Ok". Prosser sidled in and shut the door.

"A mate texted me just now, he got a call for a body, he investigated and they've just found Joe, dead. I've got no more details yet, another syndicate, Bridger's, have the job, obviously. I thought you needed to know straightaway, no doubt Perkins will tell you, officially and there's Jenny to deal with".

"Send her in, Liam, and thanks, I appreciate it". Prosser's face said 'rather you than me' as he opened the door and called Banks to go in as he left the office.

"Go on then", said Banks, sitting down. She knew Prosser well enough to have read the signs, something had happened and it affected her.

"How are you coping with the Joe situation?"

"If you mean, am I sinking two bottles of wine a night while pining for love? You know I'm not. I gave up on him".

"Sorry, I wasn't prying, you're my friend as well as a valued colleague, and nobody knows anything about the other stuff and never will, not from me. Jenny, I've got some news, Joe's been found, dead. Paul Bridger's team have it, we don't have any information as to how, why and where, or when yet. You need to contact Bridger right away. I'm sorry, Jenny, I really am".

Banks sat very still with little or no emotion on her face. Thompson briefly wondered whether she was in shock, but Jenny didn't do shock, she weighed things up, then organised them in her head to make a picture she could comprehend.

"Am I suspended?"

"Not unless I'm told otherwise. Do you want anything, anyone?"

"No, I'm fine. I'll go for a coffee first, take Tilda. No, I'll take Elkie, if that's alright?"

"Ok, I really am very sorry, Jenny". Thompson didn't know whether to hug her, hold her and tell her it would all be alright because that was his natural instinct, but his cop head ruled that level of familiarity out. Besides, he didn't think Jenny would welcome it.

Banks crossed the office, which was busy as always, and approached Elkie. "Do you have time to have a coffee and a chat? I need a friend". Without thinking, Elkie was up and following Banks to the cafeteria. Prosser watched as they went, and waited until they were clear.

"A bit more just came through Dave. He was found at the back of some shops in Arnold, he'd been hit with something heavy then finished with a knife, throat cut to be sure he was dead. The site is known to us, was he doing anything for another syndicate? Only the suggestion is this is a drugs thing". Before Thompson could answer, his door opened and Paul Bridger walked in. He looked at Prosser, who left silently.

"You've heard then?"

"Yes, just now, a shock. I have a few details but you can fill me in".

"Not sure I can say too much at the moment, my boss is talking to yours. What do you know about him, Joe Lawrence?"

"I just inherited him from Fiery Marie, seemed straight, efficient and clear-thinking".

"I was told he was involved with the other DS, Banks. I'll need to talk to her".

"Yes, I know, she's just found out, I sent her for coffee with a colleague. I told her to contact you, she probably just needs a bit of time to get her head around it, I know I would".

"You know she's a suspect, why didn't you stick her in an interview room on her own for me?"

"Because I'm not a total cunt like you. If you don't like it, then fuck off and complain to Perkins".

Bridger wasn't at all happy about being sworn at and Thompson could see that, but there was something else.

"Good, I heard you look after your own, but since I don't know you I thought I'd see for myself. Ask Jenny to come to see me when she gets back. Sorry to wind you up like that", and Bridger held out his hand for Thompson to shake, which he did automatically.

"There's a drugs angle here, Dave. If what I think happened, happened, then Jenny Banks will be in the dark about it. Does she have any vices?"

Thompson nearly paused but didn't, now was not the time to be economical with the truth, no matter what he'd just said to Jenny. "Confidentially, she likes the odd glass but nothing serious, she's ambitious to the point where she can be a bit blinkered, and she's been messed about emotionally. She was in the early days with Lawrence but he's been odd recently, she says, something to do with a wife coming back onto the scene. Marie might know more on Joe, she worked with him for years, she'll need to be told".

"Fiery Marie, I'd not thought about that. I don't know her apart from her reputation, she scares the shit out of me though. Do you want to talk to her first, soften the blow? I'd really appreciate it".

"Ok. How involved do you want my team?"

"Not at all, you need to be detached if one of your own is involved, even though she's probably only on the periphery. I'll keep you up to speed where I can but you'll probably get more from Chalky than me, you know how it works. Sorry about the wind-up again. Marie Burns, let me know, I might need to talk to her, too".

"If you do, don't go in and wind her up. Really, you should be scared".

Bridger took the warning the way Thompson had meant it, because he could remember Marie before they got to know each other. Bridger's phone rang and he waved 'bye as he walked out. 'Right', thought Thompson, 'time to talk to fiery Marie Burns'.

"And that's all I know for now, Marie. I spoke to Bridger directly, he's shit-scared of you and will want to talk to you, so it might be a good idea not to be too fiery. I know it's the news we all hate the idea of when it's a colleague but it is what it is. Jenny knows but she's hard to read, she has your edge. Marie?"

"Sorry, Dave, thanks for calling. I had heard but I think I needed you to confirm it for me. Joe was a good boy but sometimes he was a bit erratic. I always put it down to him thinking about too many things at once, but in the wake of this I think he might have used from time to time, more people do a bit of recreational than you'd think. Don't pass that on, I'll talk to Bridger and I won't bite him unless I decide he's a wanker. I appreciate the call, take good care of Banks, she needs you now".

It was ten minutes since he'd heard about Lawrence but it seemed like hours and Thompson was feeling emotionally drained. His phone went, again. Rebecca.

"It's me, look Dave, can we talk?

"I've just lost an officer, I'm a bit tied up".

"I won't keep you long. I've decided to stay at home until after the birth. I'm going private. Mummy has arranged things, I think it best and it will give us time to sort out the house. Come down and see Guy if you like, just call first. Sorry to drop this on you but when Mummy suggested it, well it seemed so obvious. Dave, are you there?"

"Ok, I see. Can I get back to you? Like I said, I just lost a team member to a crime, I'll call you later".

"Before seven then, bye".

Thompson slumped in his chair, it took a moment before he realised how quiet it had gone, he opened the door and looked out. In the office a numbness had descended, even Beresford was quiet. "You've heard then? We can all expect to be interviewed, be honest when asked is all I'll say there. The details of what happened to Joe are scant at present, but it was a violent death. I expect Jenny will be taking a few days off while process happens, but I'm promised we'll be kept in the loop and we will get to the bottom of this, meanwhile, idle speculation won't do any good. Most of us barely knew Joe but he was a good lad..."

The faces looking at him told him all he needed to know. His team understood, so he trusted them to be professional.

"David, my office, please", said Perkins, quietly in his ear. He hadn't even seen that he was there.

"You said all the right things there, David. There is no question of Banks being involved but procedure has to be followed. I'm getting updates, but at present only isolated details, not much else. People must prepare themselves, Joe Lawrence might have had a darker side and this might not be straightforward".

"Was Lawrence a user?"

"That is the suggestion from multiple sources. He was being monitored, the way you all are. He may have made bad choices, recreationally, I don't think anyone is suggesting dealing here. How is Banks?"

"Stoic".

"And you?"

"Me, fine, busy but not too busy to take on anything else. I know this is Bridger's case but if there's anything we can do, say so. My lot will want to help".

"You know it can't work that way. Look after Banks, she may be stoic now but she'll need her friends".

"Is that all, Sir?"

"The other things, the extant Johnson, anything to know, recent?"

Perkins' attitude always changed when he asked about the Johnson case, he was trying to hide being needy but Thompson's spidey senses had seen it clear as day. There was something there not being said.

"No, Jenny is, or maybe was, leading there". Thompson wasn't ready to discuss details at this point, it also occurred to him that losing another sergeant was probably going to create logistical difficulties for a while, he'd have to give Gecko Jenny's cases.

"Good, well, keep me appraised at all times".

As he made his way back through the now busy but not quite so noisy office, he reflected on the meeting. Perkins had always maintained an air of greater knowledge in all things, it was his way, but the Johnson case made him almost apologetic when he asked about it. Why?

Then something else hit him hard. Rebecca hadn't asked who it was that the team had lost, not even to check it wasn't Elkie.

He dialled Rebecca again, it was unlike her not to answer, where the hell was she? The fifth time he got no answer he left a message. He tried hard not to sound anxious, frustrated, angry even, but it was a losing battle. "Elkie", he shouted.

"Out, boss", said Josh, through what sounded like a mouthful of foodstuff. That reminded Thompson, he needed to eat something.

In his drawer he'd got a Kit-Kat, a Mars bar and some Prawn Cocktail crisps, it was like being seventeen again. "I'm going out for a walk and to grab some food", he said to nobody as he passed through the office. He glanced at Josh who appeared to be trying to eat a huge burger of some sort, his belly rumbled louder.

The café was ok, not quite upmarket but not a greasy spoon either. This would do and he'd have something healthy, he'd promised. He settled on macaroni cheese and garlic bread. Glancing around he could see that the clientele were on the smarter side, he felt a bit out of place in his three-day old suit. Elkie had already called him 'Worzel'.

"I'm beginning to think you slipped a tracking device in my handbag" The voice was in his ear but his nose told him who was speaking.

"No, just lunch, Rebecca's still away, got to take care of myself. You, er, are you working?"

"No, not until later. My Only Fans crowd get their one hour of action before bedtime, settles them in for the night after a bit of wrist action", and she laughed.

Thompson wasn't sure what she'd just said but smiled weakly anyway.

"Are you going to invite me to join you?"

"Sorry, of course", said Thompson, casting an eye around the room in case another officer was in. There didn't appear to be any, but he was acutely aware that a senior police officer having a jolly lunch with a lady of the night, never mind anything else, might be frowned on in some quarters. Perkins' disappointed face popped into his frontal lobe.

"So, how have you been?"

"Good, yes, fine. Thanks for the message, by the way, a relief, obviously. It never crossed my mind, probably not thinking straight".

"My bad, I should have been more aware but I got a bit carried away too. I don't usually, you know, get carried away when I'm working, but I wasn't working, it was real and I just went with the moment".

This was rapidly becoming the most difficult conversation that Thompson had ever had, at least until Rebecca found out.

"Sorry, I'm a bit forthright, say what I think, this is fairly new ground for me too. It did occur to me that the way we choose to earn our bread might not be seen as compatible, it's just that I really like you and I have good memories of that night. If you say so, I'll just slip away and never bother you again. I'll delete your number from my phone and that will be that, I don't want to, but it's your choice and I'll respect that".

Inside Thompson's head, the man with one child and another on the way was screaming to take the offer and run, but another part wouldn't let him, the part that had had a delayed reaction to Rebecca not caring when told he'd lost a team member. He could even picture her saying she hoped it was Jenny Banks. "No, it's ok, if I can ever help, let me know. I won't break the law though, just to be clear".

Jenny's eyes started to moisten. "I knew you were different. Look, if you need to find me, I like to walk the Grantham Canal at Tollerton sometimes. I wander through the farmland enjoying the nature, it gives me, I don't know, maybe renewal. Join me sometime, if you can, as a friend, a real friend. Just text 'canal' and a time and I'll know, although I do change the phone regularly. Then she leant over and kissed him lightly, her perfume again filling Thompson's head and trousers. He watched her go with mixed feelings.

"Hello, Dave, I didn't know you came in here".

Thompson's stomach hit the nice laminate floor with a resounding thud. "Jenny, I thought you'd gone home with, you know, and everything. If

I'd known you were still around I'd have asked you to come with me for lunch".

"Really?" said Jenny Banks, lighting up as if someone had stuck a three-pin plug in her flue.

"I presume Bridger has done his thing?"

"Yes, I can't talk about it though, the case. Don't get me wrong, it was a shock, but you know me, I'd already airbrushed Joe out of my memory. Now it's just somebody else's case. I'm fine really, I don't want time off or anything".

"It might not be my choice or yours. Please, join me now, have you been here long?"

"No, I just walked in and saw you sat on your own, so I thought you wouldn't mind being with me, in the circumstances". Thompson said he didn't, that he was there for her, all the genuine platitudes he could think of. Jenny, for her part, started chatting away pretty much as if nothing had happened but Thompson wasn't noticing what she was saying, instead he saw a phone that wasn't his on the table, it was under his copy of Four-Four-Two.

"Excuse me, sorry to bother you. I was sat here earlier and I think I left my phone behind, somewhere". It was Jenny, the other Jenny, she'd come back. *Oh shit!*

Jenny Banks looked at the other woman, then smiled at her. Having completed her critical assessment, she lifted Thompson's football magazine, retrieving the phone and handing it over. Thompson realised he didn't know her last name, his new Jenny. Not the old Jenny, not that he'd ever had the old Jenny, as such. *Oh, Jesus!*

"Thanks, sorry to bother you, must get back on the job, don't want people starting without me". Thompson started coughing, Jenny Banks was considering the Heimlich, but he took a mouthful of coffee and recovered a bit.

"You ok?"

Thompson nodded that he was. His choking gave him time to get his thoughts together. Jenny One had said she hadn't seen Jenny Two, if she had, why would she lie?

Banks watched the other woman walk away. "Personal Assistant that one I'd say, or in Marketing, something professional. Did you sneak her phone under your footy mag to get to talk to her, you crafty old devil?"

"No, of course not", said Thompson, coughing a bit more.

Jenny Banks leant over and gave Thompson a light kiss, exactly like Jenny Two had done. Then she used her finger to wipe something away. "Lipstick, gone now". *Oh fuck!*

After ordering what was the most complicated salad Thompson had ever heard of, Jenny turned to him with a look in her eye. "Well?"

"Fine now, yes, thanks".

"No, you know what I meant".

"No, not really". Thompson hoped that he could stupid his way out of whatever was now happening.

"Rebecca, you two, what's really going on? You've had a face like a smacked arse forever. Elkie is saying nothing more, none of my other spies have anything for me so I came to the horse, hoping to persuade it to use its mouth".

"Rebecca", the relief was there in Thompson's voice, if you knew where to look. "She's gone to her mother's while we have builders in, an extension and a roof. It looks like she might stay away a while now, she called while everything was happening and I couldn't talk, I was more concerned about how you were. It looks like I'm back to being single again for the duration". *Bugger!* That came out wrong. Jenny cocked her head as if trying to hear a shepherd's whistled commands.

"I know all that, you said it before you sullied my spare bed for two nights. No, there's something more, something you're not telling me. How can I understand and help if you don't tell me?"

"She's not answering her phone now and she's stopping there, in Surrey, until she sprogs, that's what I meant by staying away a while. I got a bit ratty after she called and told me, I left a curt message, more than curt. I'm just worried it's over".

Jenny Banks had a look that sometimes was almost as good as an autopsy, she appeared to see everything.

"I see, right. I assume that builder of yours has given you the ok to move back in now, so I'll come over later and cook, keep you company, we can talk over old times. You know I need you, Dave, a friend who understands. You know this is all bravado about Joe, we can be miserable together and console each other in our hour of need, yes?"

Thompson reluctantly leapt from the wok clean into the tandoor oven and agreed.

Around mid-afternoon, and after beginning to lose the will to live over the paperwork mountain he wasn't making a dent in, Thompson got the call he was dreading. He answered, expecting to get the chance to explain, but was surprised to be talking to Rebecca's mother. The 'conversation', which was entirely one-sided, lasted four-minutes, twenty-one seconds, he'd checked when mummy had gone. He'd never heard her swear before, it sounded odd her using 'f-words' and even a 'c-word' once, all delivered in a posh accent. It was like when Rebecca said 'bollocks', it just didn't sound right, didn't seem to mean the same, like she was using a word she didn't fully understand. His instincts had been right all along although, in retrospect, he shouldn't have gone into Clifton mode and told mummy where to go, somewhat impolitely.

"Boss".

Thompson looked up, Gecko stood before him. "Did you just scuttle down that wall?"

"Ha, good one, Dave. No, I just thought I'd pass on something. My mate in Vice told me that they are doing a sweep, on-line tarts who get their tits out for a fiver and drop their drawers for fifteen. He told me they was monitoring sites and I thought I'd tell my mate Dave, he might know people who would like to know".

"What are you talking about, Mickey. It isn't illegal is it?"

"No, but they're usually on the game, soliciting, and that is, it's just that people have been seen with certain people, might be innocent, might not, just saying, alright?" and he left the room as if he'd just spotted an incautious Bluebottle on the office wall outside. Nothing about that conversation had made any sense to Thompson, why was nothing ever simple?

To take his mind of things and to appear busy, he sorted his bits of paper, made sure they sat just right on the desk, edges squared up, piles neat. When he was satisfied, he got his jacket off the back of the door and left. It was hard to get a signal in the garage he parked in, but he tried, two bars. 'Canal, 6:30?' He looked at the message for a full five minutes before deleting it and going home.

In the house the builder was going great guns. The roof was nearly finished and they were in the process of removing some of the scaffolding. The part-built extension was sheeted up and the windows were leaning against one wall. There was still some dust, but they'd obviously tried to clean up a bit, he was grateful for that. After a shower and a change of clothes he sat on the sofa looking at his phone, then he texted Rebecca apologizing profusely and asking if they could meet, to talk, he'd come down. It didn't seem enough but it was all he had. The doorbell rang.

"I bought a red and a white. I also cheated and picked up a curry, hope you don't mind". Jenny Banks breezed inside without waiting for the formality of being invited in. Thompson caught her perfume as she went past, Jenny One and Jenny Two wearing the same fragrance was surely against the Geneva Convention. He closed the door, someone made a note that it was 19:06 and settled in to wait.

"Did you change your perfume?" It was an odd question in Thompson's mind but he'd felt compelled to ask.

"You noticed? Yes I did. I don't want to smell like Rebecca, I thought it might upset you if I did".

"That's very considerate, but I'm not sure I'm worth it".

"You are, Dave. Look, I don't want to worry you but there's a guy in a Range Rover out there, I think he's watching someone, maybe you".

"Have you had a bang on the head, Jenny? Why would anyone be watching me?"

"Have you pissed off Collins again recently?"

"I hope so, but he wouldn't bother me at home, we understand each other, as Jock Charnley might say, or we did before Liam".

"Maybe I'm wrong then. Is there a back way out?"

"I'm missing part of a wall, will that do? You can go around the tarpaulin, the extension has no door yet, or most of a wall come to think of it, why?"

"I'll sneak up on him, flash my warrant card, see what he's up to".

Before Thompson could say anything she'd pushed through the side of the tarpaulin covering the hole, seconds later the screeching started. Thompson rushed through. Banks had someone in a head-lock, she said her name was Deborah and she was swearing at Banks in a most unladylike manner. She was giving her a run for her money, almost getting free. "Let her go, Jenny, she's one of the builders".

Banks let go and Deborah pulled back, looking around for something heavy. Thompson stepped in. "Deborah, sorry about that, this is a colleague, how long have you been there?"

"I got the short straw, every night since we started. They said I was to sleep here, keep it safe for the policeman, so I did. Don't worry, I sleep heavy", and she gave Thompson a look, before glancing at Banks.

"Ok, right, well thank Pete will you but you can go home now, I'll keep an eye".

Deborah shrugged, grabbed a nicely-patterned shoulder bag and went out through a gaping gap in the wall where a door would soon be.

"Sorry, Dave, I thought he was breaking in".

"He?"

"Sorry, she".

Things were reaching boiling point inside Thompson again. "Right, Jenny, would you sort out the food, please? I want to speak to a man about a Range Rover.

In the car, the time 19:17 had been neatly written as someone of unspecific gender had left the property, it was one of a couple of brief notes in what was obviously a new pad. Turning to put the pad on the passenger seat was unfortunate timing, as the occupier of the Range Rover didn't see Thompson approach from the rear, he only heard the door open followed by the sensation of his body hitting the road. "Speak".

The face full of tarmac that the watcher was currently enjoying wasn't really conducive to social intercourse. He could feel that the person who'd put him there was strong and that resistance was probably futile. Thompson lifted him bodily to his feet. "I said speak".

"Barton Montague, private detective, I've been watching you".

"Why and how long, and is that really your name?"

"Today, since you got home, and no".

Thompson looked inside the car and saw the pad. He threw Barton to the floor, retrieved the pad and read. He held it up so the few entries were visible. "Explain".

"The time your young lady arrived, the time the other young, er, person left".

"Keep going".

Barton Montague was looking worried, so Thompson hauled him the short distance to his house and dragged him inside. "Are you from Collins?"

Montague looked confused, that would be a 'no' then. "I'm a friend of Rebecca's, er, friend".

Now it was Thompson's turn to look confused. From the kitchen, the noise of food preparation had ceased. "Jenny, can you come here please?"

Banks walked through. "Dave?"

"Tell this Barton Montague character who you are, please".

Banks flipped open her ID, Montague slumped slightly.

"Did Rebecca tell you to spy on me?"

"No, it was my friend's idea. Look, I'm sorry, I know it was wrong but she's upset, and everyone's upset, and I thought I could help with proof".

Thompson let go of the slightly-built Montague, his anger being replaced by confusion.

"I think, Dave, that this man thought you might be playing away while Rebecca is staying at her parents' house. Am I right, Barton?"

"Yes, and no. If you were, my friend thought that might be a good reason for Rebecca to further rethink her choices, in terms of partner, I mean".

Thompson punched him, quite hard and in a bit that would easily show. Banks never moved.

"Out".

Montague ran for it, his blood tracing spots on the floor and on the steps outside.

Dinner was muted. Thompson didn't really feel hungry but he ate anyway. Banks didn't feel like drinking but she drank anyway. The second bottle went down much easier, the third, dug out of a cupboard and a bit rough, needed virtually no encouragement at all.

It was dark when Thompson woke, the pain in his right hand told him that something wasn't right there. His head was a bit fluffy, but not too bad. The room had a fug of wine and curry about it, Chicken Tikka Masala, his favourite.

"You're awake then?"

"Yes".

"About time, I nearly started without you".

Forty-five minutes later, two cars drove off. In a shaky hand, the time 06:02 was written with 'both' appended next to it.

Twenty-four

23 August-25 August 2017

The next few days were not terribly productive for anyone. Bridger's team interviewed everyone, but spent most time talking to Marie's boys. At work, Banks had started to keep her distance, trying too hard. Thompson just stuck to his office. Another call from mummy had told him where he could put his request to talk to Rebecca, in person. It shouldn't happen this way, he thought. He was considering driving down and banging on the door until they had no choice, but there were laws for that sort of thing. Besides, he wasn't getting a lot of time to chew things over, Jenny was very demanding away from work.

After four nights the visits stopped and he was relieved when Jenny One said she wouldn't be there. Then he'd had a text asking if he fancied a drink, as friends. He answered 'yes' and they did.

Twenty-five

26 August 2017

"Why do I get the impression that you don't want to be seen out with me?" Although she was only half-joking, Jenny Two had a point. Dave Thompson had picked obscure pubs out in the sticks for each of their 'friends' evenings out. This one looked like only a couple of locals ever used it, he wasn't too far wrong.

"It's not that I don't want to be seen with you. I'm still fighting with it all. I told you all about my situation, warts and all. It would help if this mysterious and complicated story as to why you earn money the way you do, or did, I'm not sure now, came out".

"I see, yes, you're right. I didn't want to go to deep with you, so to speak, because I didn't expect anything, still don't really. I've been a bit surprised by all this, welcome though it is".

"You do understand, my job, it's important to me but, it seems, so are you now but I need something solid".

Jenny was quite touched, that was one of the nicest things anyone had said to her for a long time.

"Right, fullish disclosure. I met a bloke, we got on and lived together. He seemed ok at first, a bit full of himself but I'd been a bit reclusive for a while. My first and at the time only long-term boyfriend had died, a motorbike accident, and I was feeling pretty low. I was also in debt, no insurance pay-out and a big mortgage I couldn't afford".

"What, here?"

"Yes, more or less, Chaddesden".

"I'm guessing you borrowed money?"

"Yes, from the smooth guy. He was cool at first but then he wanted more money back than had been agreed. I had to find some money, he suggested I entertain some people he knew. A slippery slope".

"And you paid him off, Why continue…, you know?"

"No, I didn't pay him off. The interest grew and I could see that I'd never escape the way things were going. Then I started to freelance, found a small group of customers, then I found the Only Fans thing, built up a following and then dropped the in-person customers. I made some money, a lot of money, and sent it to him with a solicitor's letter, one of my ex-customers did me a favour. That did the trick, debt-wise, but I had to move too, so I went to Carlton. I got a nice flat, changed a few things and went exclusively Only Fans. I trained in computing so it was easy".

"So you don't work the streets, that explains why I didn't find you".

"You looked me up?"

"Part of a case, remember".

"Yes, Tilda, I didn't think she was legit, I said as much to her when I bumped into her in town recently, same place we first met, actually". That was news to Thompson.

"And now, what are your plans?"

"Well they were to save more money, move on, rejoin the real world somewhere, then two things happened".

"Two?"

"Yes, you, if this is real, and now my money-lender ex has gone missing. I'm hoping he drowned like his stupid brothers. That would mean I won't have to keep looking over my shoulder all the time".

Thompson nearly asked Jenny to repeat what she'd just said. If dating an escort was bad enough, he found he couldn't even think the word 'prostitute', how was he going to deal with her being tentatively linked to someone in an active case?"

"Can I confirm, the money-lender and abuser, was he Stanley Johnson?"

"Stanley, he doesn't like being called that, he calls himself Richie, his middle name is Richard, or so he said. I should have realised that you must know he's missing, it was your lot that chased the toe-rags into the Trent, good riddance".

"This complicates things for us further. I'm not sure what to do at the moment. I'm not sure we can see each other until the case is over. I need advice".

"Is that your nice way of saying I'm dumped?" She'd hoped that getting everything out in the open might be cathartic for her and fill in a few gaps for Thompson, but it wasn't looking that way now.

"No, not dumping you at all, please don't even think that, it's just that my team are investigating the Johnson case. If I'm seen to be influenced in any way, and I can assure you that I won't be, it might prejudice the whole thing in court, if we get that far. Just so you know, the toe-rags had a car full of stolen gear and jumped instead of just giving themselves up. Only Stanley, sorry, Ritchie, is still missing, he's out there alive somewhere and I'd like to find him".

"I'm a keeper then?"

"Yes, but with complications".

"What's life without a few complications? It's not like you're a dyed-in-the-wool Forest fan is it?"

Thompson looked shocked. Chaddesden, she'd said Chaddesden, *oh no!*

"What?" said Jenny with a surprisingly innocent face, considering.

"Tell me you're not a Derby fan, please".

Jenny started laughing. "Gotcha!"

The little joke was just what they needed to break the tension. Thompson relaxed a bit and Jenny, who'd looked close to tears at one point, was back to being fun.

As they drove back into town, Jenny told Thompson that her old number was dead now and that she'd be in touch later. He didn't ask how much later and she didn't say.

Twenty-six

29 August 2017

"Jock, how are you. Thought I might pop round, need an ear". Dave Thompson had taken a couple of days after his last Jenny Two date to decide what he was going to do. Jenny Two's comments about the mortgage pushing her into penury had him thinking. If she wasn't coming back then Rebecca probably didn't want the house, mummy would call in the financial help and he couldn't afford to keep the house anyway. He would be the only Detective Inspector in the force living in a cardboard box on the embankment. Then there was Jenny Banks herself and the fact that Jock didn't know his relationship with Rebecca had gone tits up.

"Dave", said Jock Charnley, opening the door and stepping aside.

"You look well, the pressure of the job being gone seems to suit you".

"I've been hearing things, Dave. Rebecca and you, is this true?"

"Straight to the point, I shouldn't have expected anything less. Yes. Seems she was disenchanted with me, went home while the house was being updated- for her, I might add, and, reading between the lines although her mother had been quite specific, got together with someone else. Thinks I'd been playing away, which, at the time, I hadn't, she blinked first. All a bit of a mess".

No tea had been offered, no biscuits, no hospitality at all. It was as if Charnley had decided to see what answers were forthcoming before hospitality was a possibility. There was a short silence. "Sorry to hear it, Dave. I won't ask if there's any way back, you'll have explored the options, I know you. The 'at the time' bit then, is it relevant?"

Trust Charnley to pick up on the one clue he'd cleverly left in the sentence.

"I formed a relationship with a woman after, Jenny, but it's complicated".

"Banks?"

"No, but maybe. I don't know how things are going to go. I met a Jenny, I call her Jenny Two, Banks is Jenny One. Jenny Two was a sex worker, she's associated with a case I have now. I can't think objectively so I thought I'd ask you".

"Fuck me, Dave. When I left you were a well-behaved young man that virtually any mother outside of Surrey would be happy to have courting her daughter. Now you're hooked up with a tart and a detective. You should stop writing detective stories and take up writing farces".

"Delicately put, Jock. Ex-tart, and not really a tart as such. Jenny One is a complication".

"Has union taken place with both Jennies?"

"Yes".

"Have you thought of putting something in your tea, try bromide. I think the Army and Navy store have it as surplus". Charnley was laughing at his own joke, nothing changed or so it seemed.

"Seriously, Jock, I need some objectivity here".

"Ok, Jenny One, reliable but intense, in the force so one of you would have to move. I see her being infatuated, I don't think you are, step back there if you can. Jenny Two, complicated as you helpfully pointed out. Happy to ignore past misdemeanours but has more baggage than a footballer's wife on World Cup duty. Who makes you laugh, who makes you feel more like who you really are?"

Charnley had a point. Both relationships could be doomed, but Banks was least likely to succeed, either way there he'd lose a friend. Jenny

Two was the one and he decided that if she ever called he would both tell her and find out her real name. Yes she made him laugh, they were similar, got on, bounced off each other. Had he and Rebecca ever truly done that?

"I can see you have lots to think about. Carole is back soon, you'd better go, she loves Guy and Rebecca, she'll be upset when I tell her, it'll be easier if you're not here. I hope I've helped but in the end it's down to you, Dave".

"Yes, thanks, you've helped. Carole, she's ok?"

"She's better than ok, Dave. I hope you find a Carole, maybe one of the Jennies is your Carole, I hope so".

The five-minute audience with his old mentor had given Thompson some clarity. Jenny One, no, he had to put a stop to that. Jenny Two, ok, issues there but not unsurmountable? The old Thompson would have said 'definitely not', the new world-weary version was less decisive but willing to give it a go.

The office was quiet so Thompson ploughed on with the paperwork, every action seemed to cost a tree its life. It was almost a relief to get summoned to Perkins' office.

Tilda was surprised to see Gecko sitting alone in the cafeteria. She knew he must eat sometimes, but assumed he made his own arrangements. "Mind if I join you?"

"If you like. Actually I could do with a bit of advice, you might the person to talk to first".

"First, what are you talking about, Mickey?"

"The Boss wanted me to dig and ask questions, find out about certain people, so I did and I got a list, it's in my pocket now". Gecko's tone made it sound like this list of his might be wrapped in a hand grenade, one with the pin out.

"Why the reluctance to give it to him?"

"One of the names on the list, I think you know her".

"Ah, right. Can I see the list first?" He passed it over.

'Not sure what to do, what do you recommend? I don't want to drop the Boss in anything. I'm just finding my feet here, I like it and I don't want to screw this one up, he's showed faith in me".

"How about if you took it to a more senior officer first, I'd be happy to come with you, moral support and to vouch for you. I've been telling people not to misjudge you myself".

"Really? I appreciate that, you know better than most how baggage can follow you around. Who had you got in mind?"

"Superintendent Perkins".

"We don't really get on, me and him. I was amazed he let me move across in the first place, he's not slow to ask favours, though".

"You might have misjudged him then, maybe he has faith in you too. He can be a bit intimidating though, I can see why you might be scared of him".

"Scared, who said scared? Come on then".

Outside Perkins' office, Gecko let Tilda knock, at her suggestion. He didn't notice the knock, he was more worried that he was starting to sweat. "Come", said the voice of doom from inside.

Tilda eased Gecko inside with a hand in the small of his back. "Sir, DS Newton here has something he needs your advice with. Its sensitive information and, at present, known only to me, him and you, once you see the list of hostesses run by Ritchie Johnson".

Perkins' expression didn't change. "DS Newton, you were wise to come to me with it. Tilda, thank you, if you don't mind". Gecko looked nervous as Tilda left him alone.

Gecko passed the list over and Perkins scanned it without emotion. "I see, am I correct in thinking that one name on this list might be contentious?"

"Well, yeah. You know who I mean, right, Sir?"

Perkins made a show of reading the list again. "Am I to presume the ultimate destination for this document is DI Thompson?"

"Yes, Sir. I was just pondering whether he needed to see the full list".

"Luckily I have DI Thompson coming here for a meeting shortly. Is this the only copy of the list? I see that it is handwritten".

"Yes, Sir. I felt it wasn't the sort of thing to leave on a computer where it might be accidentally discovered".

"Where did this list actually come from?"

"I compiled it personally, from multiple sources, Sir".

"I see. Please leave it with me, Mickey. You did right to come and see me first, but I see no issues with the list and I will discuss it DI Thompson when he arrives. Good day".

Tilda was adjacent to Gecko's route back to his desk, not that he used it much. "Everything ok, Mickey?"

"Perkins is dealing with it, thanks for your advice, delicate".

"Great, best forget it then, agreed?"

"What are you two planning?" Thompson was on his way to Perkins' office after being summoned, and passed Tilda and Gecko in subdued conversation.

"Mickey was telling me he just gave Perkins a list of escorts run by Johnson. He was going to bring it straight to you but Perkins intervened. What's he up to, Boss?"

"Nothing, as far as I know but, thanks for that, I'll try to look suitably surprised when he gives it to me. Anything on there I should know about, Mickey?"

"Not for me to say, Sir. You asked for a list and I've pulled in a lot of favours to get you one".

"Much appreciated, Mickey, thanks. I'd best get on, he'll be waiting".

When he'd gone, Gecko looked at Tilda with renewed respect. "Clever, Tilda. I just hope we did the right thing".

Thompson nearly got to knock before 'enter' was called from within this time. "David, DS Newton has managed to procure a list of known escorts in the Johnson stable, I'm just printing you a copy now". Behind Thompson a small printer disgorged a single sheet. "If you would". He reached over and read it.

"Is this complete?" asked Thompson.

"As complete as it's possible to be given the reluctance of people to disclose such information". Thompson read it again, she wasn't on it.

Only one name on the list was known to Thompson, Josie Turner, the girl murdered in the burning house in Aspley but there was no Jenny Spinner either. The dilemma here was did Jenny Two lie about being associated with Johnson, or had the list been doctored? Would Gecko know if he checked it through with him and, more importantly, would he tell him? Thompson left Perkins' office with much on his mind.

"Boss, still here, I thought you had a home to go to?" It was Carla who didn't know the full details about Rebecca yet, but she had an idea that all was not well in Thompson's world.

"Pixie, sorry, Carla, I'll drop the Pixie moniker, I don't think it suits you now, not with the size of character you have. I could do with a bit of character myself".

Carla sat down. "Need an ear, Dave?"

"You might say that".

The bar was trendy without being loud, It was a place people went to talk and drink, not drink and talk, and pull. Thompson had a half of something gassy and awful, Carla a fruit thing, non-alcoholic.

"Honestly, this is lovely but you really don't have to listen to me you know, you're young, you should be out and copping off".

"I'm meeting Melanie here later so no need for me to 'cop off' as you call it. Go on then, Dave, shock me".

Thompson couldn't help himself, he had to get it out.

"Rebecca's left me, gone back south, hooked up with an ex, we're done and dusted".

"Oh, sorry to hear that, Why?" It was a typical Carla question, to the point, nothing fluffy about it.

"She thought I was having a thing with Jenny Banks, I think. I wasn't, but we are perhaps now closer than is good for us. Rebecca was always a bit of a fish out of water up here".

"Go on".

"There is a bit more. I did meet someone else, after, well before but not really, now I don't know. You can see why I'm confused".

"This new person, no problems there or a tangled web of intrigue?"

"Who taught you to read situations and ask the most awkward bloody questions imaginable?"

"You did, actually. Well?"

"Yes, there are some issues but I'll work through them. Carla, I'm sorry to dump this on you, I know I don't need to ask you to keep it to yourself. Anyway, enough about me, Melanie, how's that going?"

"Just sex at the moment, Dave, not sure there's much more there but we'll see".

Thompson felt distinctly uncomfortable, he'd expected more just a 'fine' or something. "Right, good, well, I'll go now and you can enjoy your...er".

"Sex?"

"Did I hear sex on offer?" Melanie had arrived, she kissed Carla and then turned to Thompson. "Have you set us up for a threesome, Carla? I'm game".

"No, this is Dave Thompson, my boss. I told you about him, remember?"

"THE Dave Thompson?"

"Yup".

"Of trophy fame?"

"Yup".

"Oh my God, Dave, I'm honoured. I've won that trophy myself a few times. I wonder, can you help a girl fulfill a dream and give me your autograph? I'd prefer it in lipstick on my left breast it it's all the same to you".

Thompson laughed and started blowing on his hands to warm them up. "Hang on", he said. "Can you hear a jingling sound? It seems to coming from your knickers, Melanie".

"That will be my friendship rings. Carla, you said you wouldn't tell anyone".

"She didn't, detective remember, I guessed. Enjoy your campanology later you two. Night, Carla and thanks for listening".

"Sure you don't want a tug yourself, Dave?" asked Melanie. Carla was now hoping he'd just go away before Melanie got even more graphic.

"I'll be fine, thanks", and he left them to their evening.

"Too much?" asked Melanie when he'd gone.

"I might get used to it", said Carla, wondering whether she would.

Sat in his car looking at his phone, Thompson suddenly felt old. Carla and Melanie seemed so assured with who they were while he flapped about in the wind. He didn't know what had happened to him, but at least it wasn't affecting his work, yet.

Twenty-seven

29 August 2017

"Three dates in then Dave, it's not something I expected". Jenny Two was dressed casually for what Thompson had described as a quiet meal in a country pub.

"Dates, ha, it seems so teenage to talk about dates. I'd not thought about how many. I never asked you whether this was ok, you know, yet another pub out in the sticks".

"Away from prying eyes again, I thought to myself, but that's fine. I doubt I'll see anyone I know in a pub in Nottinghamshire but you might and they'll know Rebecca and you'll have to explain and it just gets in the way. Who else knows about me?"

"I've not been exactly advertising. Most people I know are also friends with Rebecca, so probably only Carla and then without details".

"Is she hot, this Carla?"

"Is she hot? Wow, what can I say? If I had the equipment that might interest her, I'd be right in there".

"Right, I get it, how's the tattoo?"

"A bit sore but looks good, subtle. Sorry but I don't remember you having any, it was dark though".

"I've only got the one".

"Let me guess, something discreet, personal".

"Actually, no, more business. It's a barcode on my bum, if they scan it with their phone it takes clients straight to my Only Fans site".

Thompson gripped the wheel. "You do know I'm joking, right?" and Jenny Two laughed that laugh. She was a good laugher, Thompson thought, especially when he made one of his crappy jokes.

The pub was deliberately country-moody. Not overly lit, clean menus, clean cutlery, it was nice. Thompson ordered a steak, a big one. He'd not eaten a good cooked meal for a while, the house was still brick dust and banging about after some delays. Jenny Two had surprised him on their first meal together by revealing that she was a vegetarian. He'd refrained from making any pork-related jokes.

"Well look who it is, bought yourself a tart for the night have we?" An obviously well-heeled, equine-featured woman was talking to Thompson but he had no idea who it was.

"Sorry, do I know you?"

"Honestly, call yourself a policeman? Bethany Peason-Balding, Rebecca's friend. How is your pregnant wife and child these days?" It was said loud enough that the whole pub had soon bought into the sudden arrival of entertainment.

"Not sure, we speak through intermediaries at the moment, her choice even though she chose to play away first with James. Bethany, I remember you now, we met once or twice. I'm surprised you're out, what with eight kids at home to look after and all before you're thirty. I suppose you left them with Nanny". It was a hard comment but now that Thompson remembered the bossy Bethany, he didn't much care, besides, he had no Rebecca in his ear to make him be nice to her. Behind Bethany, what was obviously the husband hovered, he didn't seem to want to get involved.

"You brought it on yourself. Poor Rebecca, she deserved so much better than you and now she's found it, still I see your tart is more your level". Thompson could see Jenny Two had a mouthful of food, but he was pretty sure that once it had gone, she'd have a mouthful of words instead, this should be fun. She swallowed.

"Excuse me, I don't know you, and you don't know me. I could be a work colleague", said Jenny, with steel-edged politeness.

"But your voice and base appearance says tart. You two probably deserve each other. You do know he dumped his wife for one of his detectives, make sure he pays upfront, he's a runner".

Jenny smiled ever so sweetly. "I do hope we deserve each other, but at the moment we're just at the shagging each other senseless stage in our relationship. You have eight kids, really? Wow, somebody got unlucky eight times" Then she addressed the husband. "Was it you, you poor sod? I hope you kept your eyes closed, or found a bag to put over her head, you could lose an eye to that overbite". The guy behind Bethany was clearly hoping the ground would swallow him up.

"Michael and I are in a genuine loving relationship and the fruits of our union are our lives. Yes we have eight children but at least we can afford them".

"Eight little bodies forced out of your dry fanny, honestly, how on earth do you even swim? Just a suggestion dear, this world really doesn't deserve to be flooded by your retarded horsey genes. I suggest you buy yourself a cat and keep your tights on in future".

Bethany didn't know what to say but Michael finally stepped in and dragged her away and out of the pub.

"Well, that went well", said Jenny Two, shovelling another fork full of something green into her mouth. When she'd finished masticating, she looked at Thompson, waiting for an explanation regarding the 'dumped for a detective' remark. When it didn't come, she shrugged and went for the next load of rabbit food.

As they drove back to Nottingham it was quiet in the car for a while. Thompson broke the tension. "Shagging each other senseless stage?"

"I may have exaggerated a bit. Wife dumped for a detective, I know I don't have the right to ask, but do I have a rival?"

"No, it's a convenient stick for Rebecca to beat me with, she's convinced that I shagged one of my female colleagues because I know some semi-intimate details about her and she had a thing about me".

"Complicated, not that I'm judging, work is work for both of us. What's this detective's name?"

"DS Banks".

"That's not a name, that's a rank. Come on, name".

"Jenny".

"Oh".

Jenny Two's little hatchback was still in the pub car park where he'd picked her up, unmolested, not that joy riders would get much joy out of it. Thompson half considered looking for the plate details but decided against it, he wasn't in the mood, he wasn't sure what mood he was in.

"Sorry about Bethany and everything. Will I see you again?"

"Your life's a bit messy at the moment, Dave. Sure you don't want to sort things out a bit first?"

"Messy doesn't cover it, but I'd rather you made it messier than not".

"Maybe. That number you have for me doesn't work anymore, I'll be in touch. Don't bother trying to trace the car by the way, it's borrowed, mine got done a while back. I get a newer one next week. Take care of yourself", and with that she was out and into her car and away before Thompson had moved. He drove home not sure whether it was for the best if things cooled naturally, or maybe he'd just tell them all to screw themselves and go and do something else with his life.

The house was dark and the smell of fresh plaster still keen, paint would follow. Thompson's heart wasn't really in it anymore, though. In a couple of months he'd gone from having a partner and a kid to being a sad cop who'd allowed things to wash away from him. He made a cup of Horlicks and sat watching late-night telly. He heard the front door go. "Don't mind me, been out?"

He didn't stir from the sofa. "Yes, went for a meal with a friend".

"Female?"

"Yes".

"Oh, ok. I'll be waiting for you when you've finished your Horlicks".

The thought that the two women in his life were both called Jenny amused him briefly. He drained his cup and climbed the stairs.

In a different car everything had already been noted. 'Arrived, 22:48. Banks'.

Twenty-eight

30 August 2017

Dave Thompson didn't much like that he had to drive along Brian Clough Way to get into Derby. It wasn't that it was called Brian Clough Way, it was that it was in Derby and he thought that Nottingham should have named something bigger and better after the great man, maybe West Bridgford. Fasildad, Dad to his friends, had been surprised when Thompson had called but he'd justified the visit as part of his investigation into Ritchie Johnson's network. That he was actively tending his own network too was just a bonus, he'd always liked Dad, someone he knew ran deep.

"Dave lad, a bit thicker in the middle, don't let it get out of hand now you're single again. Yes I know, I heard". Typical Dad, he didn't mince words if he felt it appropriate.

"You're looking exactly the same, how come your wife's delicious fancies don't stick to your bones?"

"I keep very active, I work out. Don't look so shocked, I never sit still".

"The team send their regards, the ones that know you. You heard about Marie and the bigger team? If you ever fancy coming back and I have a DS post, I'd be happy to have you back".

"I'm aiming for DI myself, Dave. I never thought I'd have the chance but things are less, well, regimented, here in Derby, but thanks and if you ever cross the Rubicon, I could use a good officer, even one who struggles with the language".

Dave laughed, the sparring had been fun but he had things to ask. "Ritchie Johnson, I understand he had girls in Chaddesden?"

"When you called out of the blue I assumed this must be something about that. Yes, a shit if ever I met one and yes, he had three girls here. Two on the street, one by order only. I heard he's missing, nicked some jewels we're not supposed to know about and then jumped in the Trent. I do know his two street girls were taken on by another pimp when he vanished, junkies the pair of them. The hostess cleared out some time before, I only know a bit about her but I'm guessing she's the one who interests you?"

'Yes, part of an inquiry".

"She has a powerful friend. I don't know any more but if we tried to visit her she was never there. I heard she might have moved your way. We don't want to talk to her or anything, one of the officers did recovery work and she was one of her targets, but you know that, you've already spoken to Tilda".

"Is there anything going on here that you don't know about but suspect, Dad?"

"No, and I know you're the same, or was. I don't have anything else for you, Dave, except you might want to look closely at the nicked jewels, something not right there and there's something else. That footballer's girlfriend was one of Johnson's at one time but got out, and the only way out from Johnson is by paying a lot of money. Good luck with everything, remember me to Jenny Banks", and he gave Thompson a look that went right through him.

"Great to chat and thanks, and it's great to see you getting on. I always learned a lot from you, the sharpest officer I've ever worked with".

"Really, Dave, you'll make me blush. Here, the wife sent these, even Gecko might try one. She iced one with little flies, specially".

Thompson laughed and shook Dad's hand before setting off to say hello to another old mate, as he was passing. He got that networking was just a way of using the resources available but it seemed a bit cynical and

Dad didn't seem to buy into it. Still, that had been a most interesting conversation and certainly not one that he'd trust to a phone line.

As he drove back to Nottingham, taking the scenic route through Long Eaton, his phone kept pinging so he pulled into a quiet layby to catch up. Mostly it was just the team confirming things they'd been told to check. One was from Perkins wanting an audience when he got back. As he read, he was aware of a car opposite, but he ignored it. While sending a few replies he got distracted by the car opposite flashing its headlights at him. Oh, one of those places.

As he wound down his window, the car opposite started up and crept his way. Thompson eased his magnetic blue light out and set it flashing. The guy opposite nearly lost control of his car as he tried to hit escape velocity. It cheered Thompson up no end.

Back at the nick he went straight to Perkins' office. "Nice trip, David, how is Fasildad?"

Thompson wasn't surprised that Perkins knew where he'd been, it wasn't exactly a secret. "Dad's in fine fettle and I got some interesting information, especially about one of Johnson's escorts. He says 'hello' to everyone on the team so I suppose that includes you, Sir".

Perkins had reacted very slightly, he'd tried not to but Thompson knew what to look for.

"Glad to see Fasildad's doing so well, Derby suits him. When I arranged for his involvement there I suspected he would do well, despite his loss here being heavily felt. You should be sending people out to do these little chats, David, not just wandering off alone, good job we've got a tracker on your car".

Thompson was thrown. That was possibly a joke, possibly.

"I also wanted to tend my network, personally. I know there are organisations that have a better, or at least more readily-available system, but I've never much liked secret societies, especially ones that seem to operate for the benefit of their members more that to uphold the laws of the land". He wasn't sure why but he suddenly felt quite combative.

"Networks can be made of many different threads, David, only a fool dismisses a thread because it offends whatever social conscience he might carry. The secret is to know where the line exists and not step over it. Honestly, David, if you show interest it's not closed to you. More than one comprehensively-educated boy has done well with the right contacts".

"I'll have to give the situation due consideration then".

"Very good. Anything I should know?"

"If there is, it will be in my dutifully-completed daily reports, Sir".

"And you, David, are you ok? I know your domestic world is, and pardon my French, a shit-show in places, I've been there myself so I have an idea of what might be in your head, but there is always light at the end of the tunnel, even if you can't quite see it yet. As a police officer, and I don't mean the nine-to-five type but officers like us, it's important to have a partner who understands, who can live with the unremitting unpredictability of this life and that isn't necessarily going to be somebody in the same line of work. Remember that when you next decide to consider putting down roots".

This was shaping up to be one of the stranger conversations Thompson had ever had with Perkins, and it made him realise how little he knew about the man who seemed to be shaping his career.

"Thanks for the advice, Sir. I have a brief to attend, so if you'll excuse me".

Perkins went into his 'ignoring people like they are shit on his shoe' mode and Thompson headed back to his office. Had Perkins really suggested he not get too involved with Jenny Banks?

Working in downtown Nottingham had lots of advantages, especially when you were preparing for the arrival of a baby, albeit some months away, and was busily in the process of making your new nest your own. Elkie took advantage of the chance, whenever she could, to pick up bits and pieces and she'd become keen on finding interesting nick-nacks for her new home. Cliff wasn't quite so bothered. A few books, his music collection and the garden and he was happy, but Elkie always had an eye out for the eclectic. She was well aware that she was nest-building

Mansfield Road arrows north from the city and has numerous businesses right through to Arnold. Most are the standard newsagents, estate agents, restaurants and a few book shops. Then there's the odd shop that you think can't make much money, but that is often worth a browse, it was in places like this where you find curios. Inside, the shop rambled with narrow aisles set over four floors, each stuffed with bits and pieces, some of which defied description.

Elkie had not long found out about the shop via Liam and his erotic figurines, this was only her second visit and she'd only made it to the third floor so far. She'd been on one of the upper floors looking at various interesting items when she'd casually looked out and had been surprised to see something in the postage stamp-sized park next door, it was Tilda sat on a bench, smoking. At first she thought that she, like herself, had found a quiet place for a while, an escape, then Superintendent Perkins joined her and they sat and had an animated chat on one of the old benches dotted around the park.

Elkie had taken time to warm to Tilda when she'd joined, part of the reason being that she was just too amiable. At times it was almost as if she was a method actor, flawlessly portraying someone she wasn't, it was just a hunch. Elkie had, eventually, scrubbed the idea and just put Tilda's disposition down to a mixture of nerves and confidence, and then got on with her as well as anyone. She was good officer, very intuitive and able to read situations, much like Elkie herself. When she'd mentioned her mild misgivings to Jenny Banks, Jenny had suggested that she was jealous of the new, cool girl in the team, someone almost a facsimile of herself.

Elkie watched the odd meeting for the whole five-minute duration, before both parties left through different exits. She knew from experience that Perkins only showed any one of the five or more cards he was playing at any one time. He was a shrewd operator who bridged the gap, as Dave had said, between us and them. When they'd gone, she bought a piece of African art and had a chat with the store owner, an eccentric of the first order with a huge ginger beard and all-weather sandals. In her minds-eye, he was exactly what the owner of such a shop would look like.

Later the same day Elkie was sipping a coffee in the cafeteria, she'd felt the need to get away from her desk, the office had been a bit loud. "How much did you see?" asked Tilda, taking the seat opposite.

"Sorry, see?"

"You were in that junk shop on Mansfield Road at lunchtime, I saw your car parked up. How much did you see?"

Elkie was trying to decide whether there was menace in the request. If there was, she wasn't worried, even pregnant she could handle herself. She tested the waters. "I saw a curious thing actually, I saw a team member and colleague consorting with the enemy, then I thought perhaps it's sexual, but I quickly dismissed that. Perkins isn't like that and I don't think you have a daddy fetish, so I thought this must be something else".

"Did you tell anyone about it?" Now Tilda was less threatening, more pleading.

"No, I haven't decided what I was seeing. If we were spies, I'd say it was almost a drop, but we're not, we work in the same place with ostensibly the same goals. So, you tell me what it was so I can decide whether I take it to another place".

"You mean Dave, right? Good. I'll confide in you, I won't ask you to swear to secrecy but you might want to after you hear what I have to say".

Now Elkie was very intrigued, what the hell was going on here?

"You know I worked Vice, well I had a specific job there that I was put in to do. I was reporting directly to Perkins, I still am and I'm still doing the Vice job. I can't reveal the details, but it has to do with personnel and it is quite complicated. Don't worry, I am very dedicated to the team, but there is an issue and I'm still involved in its resolution. I thought I'd done with Vice when I came here, but it seems I haven't, yet". Tilda took a gulp of her drink, hot chocolate by the smell of it, and awaited Elkie's position.

"Is someone on the team going to be personally harmed by your task, and are they breaking the law?"

"No, on both counts".

"Ok, but if they are and what is happening isn't justified, you won't like us much. You do realise that?"

"I know, it's a fine line but, I promise, the career of anyone in the team will not be affected by it".

"You know, I know next to sod-all about you, just the vague bits we got fed when you arrived".

"I'm new and yours is a hard group to break into, no matter how outwardly welcoming you all are. Do any of you invite colleagues to their homes for dinner?"

Elkie realised that Tilda was spot-on but, true, there were reasons why. Thompson and herself had only just moved house plus babies were, or had been, involved. Prosser lived his own life, Carla too. Josh nobody knew anything about and Lorna intimidated everyone when she was there, even though she was a sweet as anything. Jenny was in a strange place now with the steel bars back up, keeping almost everyone out. As for Marie's boys, as everyone referred to them, they came to work, they did their jobs, they went home.

"I never thought of it that way, you're right".

"It's fine, people live outside of work, I know that, but I was told this group had something else, a core of togetherness, here at least. I've not seen much of that".

That was true too, at one time they worked hard and they ate a lot of cake and laughed, recently the cake and laughs had been in short supply. Elkie remembered that it had been Fasildad's influence that had fostered that sense of real togetherness and he was now a detective sergeant in Derby. They'd kept it going, but it had slowly petered out.

"I'm sorry, you're right. I think the group dynamics changed but, yes, we did laugh a lot and eat cake and bond, I see that now". Although Tilda had been right, it didn't stop Elkie from thinking that flagging the group's transition from fun-loving, to head down and grafting, had been nothing more than a clever diversion by Tilda. She'd been on that course herself and even used it as a tactic in the field, before washing up in Nottingham.

"My on-going project for Perkins then, safe?"

"Safe, shit, look at the time, Dave will blow a gasket", and Elkie rushed back to her desk where heads were down grafting and a not a cake crumb was to be seen. "Right", she said, clapping her hands. The 'Charnley impersonations' tin was passed smartly from desk to desk before arriving on hers ready for her contribution. She laughed. 'We're not a lost cause then', she thought, 'the laughs are still in there, somewhere'.

Twenty-nine

31 August 2017

Carla breezed into the office smiling and waving a USB stick. "Due to cutbacks and people who were supposed to manage the system being off sick, I've got six months of bus-cams to enjoy. It took a while because they are disorganized beyond belief, but here it is".

Jenny Banks barely looked up. "Josh, Simon, Carla will set you up with your share. Carla will brief".

Carla was quite surprised that she had suddenly been catapulted into a supervisory role. On the down side, Simon Beresford would need what was required drawn in cartoon form to understand what he was looking for. She copied the files, divided them up almost equally and they settled down to hours of watching people getting on and off a bus. Occasionally there might be a bit of argy-bargy between a couple of passengers, but the tedium would be otherwise unbroken.

Three minutes in and Beresford shouted "Bingo", and tried to high-five Josh, who ignored him.

"Go on then, show me", said Carla, trying to keep a hint of enthusiasm in her voice. Beresford slid the play bar back a few minutes and the scene unfolded. A little old man carrying a green Asda bag was shuffling down the bus, it looked like he was wearing wellies the way he was moving. He had a large coat on, clearly bigger than required, and a flat cap, otherwise he was a generic old man.

"Make me a print and keep looking, I need his face. Note the time he got off and then search every bus calling at Colwick daily within that one-hour time period for each week we have. If he's just chucking the skulls in the lake he's probably getting back on a bus between half-an-hour and an hour later, keep digging".

"Why, I thought we'd got him?" said a disappointed Beresford.

"We might have, but we need to know how many times this has happened, then we'll know roughly how many skulls he might have pitched into Colwick Lake and we can work back cross-referencing the dating. We also might, at some point, get his face on the cam. Josh and I will send you our files while we go and see a lady about this".

"Can't I come too?"

"No, Simon, there's deep water nearby and no adult is willing to supervise. If you find any more, make them into bite-sized clips and send them to my phone. Bite-sized means small, so that my data plan doesn't go to rat shit and the phone isn't tied up downloading something as lengthy as Lord of the Rings, the extended version, got it? I'm giving you a big responsibility here, Simon, don't let me down?" Carla knew that she'd laid it on thick, but Beresford responded well to conning with praise and, besides, she more or less had what she needed. She grabbed the still from the printer and went for a ride.

"He's not that bad really, you know, just a bit of a product of his education and he excels in other areas. We're just a required stepping stone, he told me". It was Josh, defending Simon despite all the evidence.

"He's only three years younger than you, old man".

"Yes, well, he hasn't been exposed to life much. Stick with him, he'll get better".

"Not my choice, that's up to Dave. I don't think Simon is detective material, I'm amazed he got this far, maybe he has hidden depths".

"Where are we going by the way, to see the Colwick wardens?"

"No, Natasha Ellis, I called, she's in. Watch out for the dog, it's a ladies dog".

"A ladies dog, is that even a thing?"

"A ladies dog is trained not to like men, to protect their mistress aggressively, so don't piss it off or move suddenly. I've already had to visit her once before when it took a bollock and part of a penis off a bloke who'd tried to grope her".

"What, no way, really? I'm stopping in the car", Josh said, squirming in his seat. Then he saw Carla silently laughing.

"Boys and their toys", she said, laughing louder.

"It's ok for you, you don't have bits that, er, dangle".

"How do you know? I might not always have been a girl". That shut Josh up and he just sat pale and worried.

Natasha was waiting for them when they got there. "What's up with him", she said gesturing to Josh, who was making himself very small in the passenger seat.

"Nervous around dogs. I just wanted you to take a quick look at this, could this be your old man?"

Natasha had to fetch her glasses from inside, she didn't invite Carla in but only part-closed the door. Carla turned and did the fingers to mouth and frightened face thing for Josh, he shrank further. Natasha only took a short while before she was back and wearing something Barry Humphries would have been proud of as his alter-ego, Dame Edna. She peered at the image. "Yes, that's him, right size and shape at least. I suppose he's got a skull in that bag?"

"Seems likely, ok, thanks. Nice glasses".

"My brother's pair, or one of them. I should get some of my own really but too vain. Men don't make passes at girls who wear glasses. Not that that would bother you".

"Is it that obvious?"

"No, but I hear whispers and I have been around gay people all my life, you get a decent gaydar after a while. 'Be who you are' is my motto, not that I need to tell you". The door was shutting before Carla had turned to walk back to the car, which she thought either suspicious or that Natasha had had a bad experience with the police before. A different coat was on the coat hook, something or nothing or her brother's too?

Back in the car, Josh was happier now that the door had shut and the chance of meeting a dog that could open car doors had gone.

"She said 'yes', now we go to the park and see whether they know him there". As they walked into the Fishing Lodge, the smell of fish was overpowering. The dividing door between the staff and public areas opened and a young man came out carrying a microwave. Behind him a grumpy-looking John Fraser was stood shaking his head. "John, a word please".

Fraser bustled them outside, despite the presence of spitting rain. "Sorry, our new part-time warden was microwaving an old trout he found in one of our freezers. I told him not to, but this one still lacks social awareness. You'll smell like a tart's week-old drawers if we stay in there. What's up, Carla?"

"This man, do you know him?"

Fraser examined the image. No, not seen him before. Is this Madam's chap?"

"Yes, she thinks so. Ok, I'll leave you to your fumigation, if you remember him later, call me. No more skulls while we're here?"

"No, nothing, maybe we have them all now".

On the way back Josh asked if that was how Fraser always talked like?

"Oh, the tarts reference? Yes. As I understand it he speaks from experience".

Inside the Fishing Lodge, the smell was hanging no matter how much cleaning solution the kid was being made to apply to all surfaces. Fraser left him busy scrubbing and went for a ride in the Land Rover.

"Hello George, how's things?" An old fella looked up, taking a moment to focus on the Land Rover before carrying on digging. Next to him was a virtually round guy who appeared to be watching over what the old fella was doing.

"Hide the silver, Kenny, the Colwick boys are here", said the rotund supervisor. It was a jokey greeting and not at all related to the occasional re-appropriation of council materials and equipment for use at Colwick Park that had happened before after unscheduled visits. George walked over while Kenny carried on digging.

"What brings you here, John?"

"Your boy's been busy, what have you got him doing now?"

"He's moving topsoil, making a big pile over there, why?"

"Surely a machine would do that in minutes?"

"Yes, but a machine misses things, stuff in the soil. What's up?"

"I think our Kenny there has been visiting Colwick on his own".

"Probably when I have a day off and nobody else keeps an eye on him".

"Only we've been finding skulls in the lake there and we think Kenny here has been the supplier".

"Oh fuck me, I wondered what he did with them. I thought he'd reburied them quietly, he does that, there's cats and dogs he's found on the roads of Nottingham buried all over here now. Is he in trouble?"

"No, I doubt it but you might want to pop down Central and talk to Dave Thompson, nice bloke, understanding. He has the skulls now and they're wondering where they came from".

George nodded, it wasn't the first time he'd had to deal with one of Kenny's little incidents.

"Don't mention me though, they came on the park today with a bus-cam photo and I recognized Kenny straight away. I thought I'd give you the nod first, so you can deal with it at your leisure".

"Very thoughtful, John, I appreciate it. At the back of the shed over there is a set of wrought iron railings, they came from your place years ago, the hall. Help yourself but I didn't tell you about them. I think someone has scrap in mind for them".

"I will, I'll come back. I'm going to go through town on the way back now, past the nick, can I drop you?"

"Kenny, come on, we're going for a ride in the Land Rover", said George.

"To Colwick?" said Kenny, optimistically.

"No, bring it with you though".

Wilson walked over to an old trailer with a rotting tarpaulin on it, retrieved a ratty-looking ASDA bag and climbed into the back of the Land Rover.

"Why do the council keep him, George?"

"They don't, they finished him three years ago, but he still shows up for work every day. I just keep an eye on him, he's a good digger and he enjoys it so why not? Poor old sod has nothing else in that home, they just sit there like vegetables. Our Kenny might be a fairy cake short of a picnic, but he deserves better".

271

Fraser understood the situation as George chatted on the way in. "At one time every local council had a few Kenny Wilsons in their ranks, people who wanted to do, be a part of, just feel helpful, but that went when Thatcher ripped the guts out of the community that was the council. Still, bound to happen one day".

"What happens to Kenny once you can't supervise, George?"

"Stuck in the home waiting to die, John, but don't worry, while I can I'll look after him".

Parking on double yellows outside the nick, Fraser disgorged his passengers while a traffic warden looked at them, briefly, then found more interesting people to bother. "Come on, Kenny, it's time to speak to a nice man about your little hobby", and he led the trusting Kenny into the nick.

"Boss, we have somebody in the interview room, he was brought in by a council worker, George Davis. He says he has something to tell us. I had a brief word, you'll want to hear this".

Thompson had managed to get most of the words into his head as Prosser had delivered them quickly, more heavily-accented that usual and without the need to breathe. He shut his laptop and followed Prosser down to the interview room. Inside, Jenny was talking to a little old man, his age exaggerated by his lack of teeth and hair, in front of him was an ancient-looking ASDA bag. Next to him sat a rotund guy in a green bib-and-brace, older still. "Kenny Wilson and George Davis. Kenny worked for the council", whispered Prosser, as if those behind the glass could hear him. They listened in.

"Nothing to worry about, Kenny, tell the nice woman about how you were looking after the sailors". George Davis was clearly steering Kenny in the right direction.

Thompson turned to Prosser, the question on his face must have been very obvious. 'Sailors?' he mouthed. Prosser nodded for Thompson to watch.

"It's not right", said Kenny. "They were men of the sea who served their country. They deserved to be in the right place, sailors all, they belong in the water".

Thompson still hadn't joined up the dots.

"And so you decided to help them, Kenny, to put them where they needed to be, yes?" Banks was being very gentle. Gone was the sparky Welsh woman who was always playing the dragon, instead she was almost holding this Kenny's hand.

"Yes, it was only right. Now they're happy, all of them".

"How many, Kenny?"

"He won't know, miss", said George. "He can't count very well. How many did you find?"

Banks opened the file in front of her. "Twelve so far, thirteen with this one".

"You can check then, what sailors they had in there. He's been working at Rock Cemetery for the last six months, shovelling dirt, I had to put him somewhere. He gets confused and wanders off. When he was officially on the council we had to fetch him from Doncaster one day, he'd got in a van and drove it, nobody knew he could drive. It should be in a file somewhere. Mr. Perkins was very nice about it, wasn't he Kenny?" Kenny looked confused, George raised his voice a little. "I said Mr. Perkins was nice, about the van and Doncaster, wasn't he, Kenny?" Turning back to Banks, George continued. "He doesn't remember very well either. I don't know where he got the idea about the sailors, but when I heard from the Colwick lads about the skulls being found, I guessed and brought him here. I did right, didn't I?"

Jenny had already figured out that this George was Kenny's minder, of sorts, and that he was nervous, and that he could talk the hind legs off a donkey if you let him.

"Yes, you did the right thing, we can check like you say. Take Kenny home or back to work, thanks for bringing him in, George, we'll take it from here. Do you need a ride?"

"No, I can talk to someone at Eastcroft Yard, we'll get picked up, thanks for being so kind". George bustled Kenny out, the old boy looked bewildered as he went but George kept talking to him, guiding him, as if he was a five-year-old.

"There you go, boss, no black magic, no serial killer, just a confused old boy thinking he's doing right by some dead sailors. Perkins will be pleased", said Prosser.

"Indeed he is, DC Prosser, very pleased. David, please commend DS Banks and her associates for her handling of a delicate situation. The skulls will need to be repatriated, quietly, and our lords and masters can relax. My office when you have moment please, Detective Inspector". Perkins left the room quickly, the way he always did.

"Broke something, Dave?"

"Not that I know of. Thank the team as Perkins says, get Beresford to deal with the repatriation, it will occupy him, even he can't be outwitted by an empty skull".

"Your wish is my command, Dave, but don't blame anyone but yourself when he gets it wrong".

Thompson was too worn to laugh, he was feeling decidedly tired. He settled down in his office to read the rest of the notes for the Johnson case, there must be something he hadn't seen yet. The light on the phone started flashing.

"Take a seat please, David. Nothing to worry about, I merely would like a verbal update that includes all the things you won't write down".

Thompson weighed up his options. He'd have to give the boss some information, but he really didn't want to drop Jenny Two into the conversation. Best to be cryptic, then. Decision made, he picked his words very carefully.

"So far, Sir, I have an informant who doesn't know much about Johnson's current situation, more they have some historical information. We've spoken and I have a couple of possible places to look but these people move about and I doubt he'll be anywhere obvious now. We were too slow getting that list of properties and too many obstacles appeared from elsewhere, distractions such as Joe's death".

"And your source for this historical information, is she reliable?"

"Yes, they are. My informant is no longer associated with Johnson, I'm confident of that much. I'm not asking my informant to get involved anymore though, this information was a favour to a friend".

"Good, right. Your informant seems well-informed. Thanks for the update, David, I've got every faith in you, I hope you know that?"

"Er, yes, thank you, Sir".

"And David, on a personal level, I'm very sorry to hear confirmation about your domestic situation. I've said before, such things can be very painful but light may be at the end of the tunnel, chin up, man".

That was a surprise, "Er, right, thanks. I'll just go back to the present century, shall I?"

"Present century, very good, David, very good". Perkins turned off the unexpected charm and went back to a sheaf of papers.

As Thompson made his way back to the office, he ran the conversation through his Perkins filter. One thing stuck out, why did he say 'she' when he was at pains not to mention gender? Not for the first time Thompson reckoned he was only seeing half a menu here. Where might he look for the rest?

"Ok, boss?" asked Jenny Banks, when he got back to his office. She'd noticed the expression and followed him in. It was something she'd seen before and it usually meant the Thompson brain was busy joining up all the important dots.

"I think so, yes. You?"

"I'm fine. Look, I need to talk to you, away from work. I can come over or we can meet up, I really need to clear something up, ok?"

"Sure, yes, come over if you like. I have a set of doors now, no builder to roll around on the floor with. Anyway, I have a favour to ask, too". The little misunderstanding with Deborah seemed long ago.

"I'll be there around seven, I'll bring pizza and beer, see you then". As she left, Jenny closed the door slowly, as if trying not to startle him. There was a knock. What now?

"Boss, a word, please". It was Elkie, she looked worried.

"Sure, please sit".

Elkie sat but said nothing. "We can try a mind-meld if you like, but I'm crap at it", joked Thompson.

"What, oh, Star Trek isn't it? No, it's about Rebecca. Obviously I know what's happened, you're my friend and so is she. I don't know all the details but it was shitty what she did, is doing, and I just wanted you to know I've decided to privately take your side in this issue, but I'm not bailing on Rebecca. Have I put my faith in the right person?" For the normally-confident Elkie, she sounded desperately unsure.

"I don't think sides is the right thing to do. We were probably rockier than we thought, it had nothing to do with anyone else, initially. If we'd been right, then things wouldn't have happened and she wouldn't have formed an attachment back home. If I thought there was still something there then I wouldn't have moved on either. You should know that I have moved on".

Elkie seemed shocked, everything had happened in a very short period of time, then she had a thought. "Jenny?" she asked, in a voice louder than she'd meant. Thompson had a mental image of Jenny Banks, perking up her ears at her desk, before rolling her sleeves up ready to storm the office.

"I meant I've accepted the situation with Rebecca and decided, in my own pragmatic way, to get on with the rest of my life. If that includes relationships then good, if not then I'll become a mostly serene but occasionally frantic old man with blue balls".

Elkie laughed, a laugh of relief. "Ok, good then. Oh and I was thinking of taking some time after the birth, quite a lot really, ok?" Thompson had been expecting it, a new baby, a lot to do and think about. She'd soon find out that it wasn't all rose-scented poo, but he knew Elkie and she'd do whatever was right.

"Sure, after all, you've got the maternity and Cliff will only be away from you when he's queuing at the post office for his pension oh and on bingo night, too".

"Don't be cruel, you know he uses that new-fangled direct deposit thing to put his shillings into his building society and he's going to Bingo Anonymous to give up, he's doing great, just one relapse. Seriously though, as long as you're ok".

This was more like it, the almost eternally cheery Elkie was back.

"Thanks, Elkie, I appreciate it".

His office went quiet so he dialled and waited. "Hi, Dave Thompson. I have a question, you can tell me to bugger off if you like but it's about police personnel, their details. Where in the archive might I find paper copies?" Thompson listened and made a note when given a reference. "Cheers. I appreciate it", and he hung up. When he had a spare minute he popped down to look something up, just to satisfy his own, personal curiosity. It did.

Thompson checked his phone and read the text from Rebecca again, it must have been hard for her to write and he felt sorry for her. At least he was going to get to talk to her properly, without mummy sticking her oar in. He'd had no other private calls again, none for a while now and the number he had was dead, as she'd said it would be and as he'd expected it to be. It hadn't stopped him trying it, though.

Thirty

01 September 2017

Thompson read the email from Fielding. At least now he wasn't going to have to play that game with him again, the one where the teacher thinks he knows all the answers and waits for you to show your intelligence by trying to find out what they are. Isotope analysis had confirmed the natal site of the Cirl Buntings tested, and all the Yellowhammers supplied, as being sourced from one and the same place. What he now needed was to put Gold at the murder site, at or around the time of Kingston's death. What was it Carla had said about bus-cams? He opened the office door and wandered out to find Carla. "Carla, the bus-cams, the delay that got us the ones from the Colwick route, is it city-wide? I was wondering about looking at them for the Pickles case".

"I can ask but I'd say yes, they couldn't find their arses with both hands there. I'll go find out and get the videos for 9th to the 15th of June if they have them, Simon isn't going to find this in three minutes flat".

"Good, let me know when you get back, I want a case brief for the full team including the new information, include the stuff about the bus-cams. Time we finished off Pickles, I think".

"But, Sir, what about Jenny?"

"Not your problem".

Thompson told Jenny to organise the team, with Carla briefing, for when she got back. He thought she might argue, but she didn't, she just said it was good experience for her.

Carla was nervous but tried hard not to show it. "Ok, Pickles. Miles Kingston was killed sometime around 12ᵗʰ June of this year at his residence in The Park. He died after being drowned in his own brandy, while simultaneously having bird seed of the budgie feed variety shoved down his throat, this might have been contributory to his death. Without rehashing everything, although it is all in your briefing notes thanks to Jenny, the prime suspect is Trevor Gold, he's the one on the board without a gob full of bird seed". The room laughed, Carla relaxed a bit.

"Simon here had an idea and between us we've found forensic evidence that links the birds Kingston had for his pickled thing to one particular location in Nottinghamshire. This location has a rare species breeding and only two people knew this as fact, one was Trevor Gold, the finder".

"Can we place him at the collection site? Knowing where something is won't be enough, it just shows he's been there and as it's not the crime site it is circumstantial".

"Thanks, Jenny, quite right. We now also have a set of bus-cams from the route that passes near the murder location, and we'll be viewing them looking for Gold. He didn't break in so there's a key somewhere, also the site's own doorbell-cam, and those around it, all failed to record anything. As the house remains isolated as a crime scene we should be able to retrieve the data from the doorbell-cam if it writes to a local micro-SD card and see whether it had any issues. Questions?"

Nobody had anything, Pickles had been pushed to the background for a while and most needed to read the notes to get it back to the right place in their brains.

"Carla, did anyone check Gold's phone after he was arrested?" Beresford hadn't spoken up during the brief, but something was obviously on his special mind.

"For something other than calls and texts, you mean?"

"Yes, there's an app called 'Blink' and it can interfere with cams for up to sixty seconds at a time. It was removed from sale recently after people misused it, but it works and if Gold had it on his phone, that would explain doorbell-cams not seeing him enter or exit, yes?"

"Brilliant", said Carla and kissed him on the forehead. Beresford went bright crimson. "Come on, let's talk to the boss".

Carla and Simon walked over to Thompson's office and stuck their heads around the door.

"So if we can show that he knew the location for the buntings, and took their collection personally, the killing would be a revenge. If we find this 'Blink' thing on his phone, and if we find him anywhere near on a bus-cam, will that be enough? We have no DNA, no fingerprints and no witnesses who saw Gold on or near the premises. It seems a bit thin to me", said Thompson.

"DNA, Boss, yes we do. Wasn't it followed up, who was lead?" Carla knew she was right, she'd read the sheets several times before briefing.

"It was Joe, before he disappeared. Come to think of it, I don't remember seeing much follow up. Simon, if we get access to Joe's account, can you find things?"

"Oh, yes. Quite easy, the algorithm is actually quite interesting, most computers...".

"Yes, that will do, Simon. Carla, we need to check Joe's correspondence re Pickles. Anything he had, I should have been on too, but I saw no DNA results at the time. Fingers crossed, everyone".

Carla and Simon went back to the main office and Carla started splitting up the bus-cam video between herself, Simon and Josh. It was boring, but every little bit of information would help. Jenny got in touch with IT. They needed to get access to Joe's data and see if there was any DNA information on there.

The guy on the other end of the phone sucked his teeth. "It will take a little while, we are up to our necks in it here".

'This is a murder enquiry, please do what you can. You should know that Superintendent Perkins is getting very anxious". The IT guy said he'd do his best.

The latest bird club meeting had been pretty good. A talk about a trip to Costa Rica with lots of images. Carla hadn't intended to go, but Melanie was back in Bristol visiting her folks and her brother, who'd just had a baby. She'd asked Carla to go with her but it was for a long weekend and she didn't have the holiday days to take one, so there she was at a Friday night meeting, it was something to do.

After the talk, the speaker was selling home-made videos of the trip. Carla bought one, hoping she might persuade Melanie to take an exotic trip with her. She also kept half-an-eye on Trevor Gold, he'd noticed her there and wasn't very happy about it, the beer fuelling some unnecessary comments in her ear. She wasn't worried, she could deal with the likes of Gold. The speaker was happy to chat a while and painted a rosy picture of Costa Rica. She asked him about other things there besides birds, holiday stuff, and she was surprised at the variety of things on offer. Gradually the crowd slipped away and she set off to walk home, it wasn't far.

She'd not gone far when she became aware that someone was further up the road behind her. Probably someone from the Social Club walking home too. She tried not to look back but became aware that the footfall was getting closer, then it stopped and so did she.

"Hello Carla, looks like you picked up a fan there, that mouthy twat Gold from the club. I persuaded him to walk the other way while I walk you home. How are you?" It was Dale Brown.

"Dale, you didn't hit him, did you?"

"No need, there rarely is. What's up with him?"

"Just a mouthy twat who doesn't like the police much. Thanks for the offer to walk me home but I can look after myself, you know".

"I don't doubt it but there are some funny people out there, friends look after each other, answer questions if they can".

"What do you want, Dale?"

"Hypothetically, and I'm not sure what that means, if a person had an incident, perhaps a fire, and that person thought that someone was naughty and that naughty person was missing presumed dead but they wasn't sure, how would that person find out about that. Sorry, I've been practicing this all day".

"Are we talking about your boss?"

"Just a person".

"Are you suggesting that the person knows for certain who caused an accident?"

"I think so, and if the person who caused the accident was dead, how could they confirm that?"

"You know I won't tell you anything. Besides, I thought your 'person' had their own people well-placed to answer hypothetical questions?"

"He did but there's a glitch. Sorry Carla, Mr. Collins knows I know you and he asked me to approach you. I told him you'd decline".

"You said 'decline', really?"

"No, I said you'd tell me to fuck off, but it's the same thing".

"Fuck off, Dale".

"I understand, I won't mention it again and if Johnson shows up I hope you lot find him first. Anyway, I see you got your car done and I see you have a new partner. She looks nice, I hope everything's going ok".

Carla didn't ask how Dale knew personal things about her, he did and that was that.

"Yeah, it's going well, thanks for asking. Do you know Natasha Ellis?"

"Why?"

"She seems to be a fish out of water, just curious. Well, do you know her?"

"Fuck off, Carla, with the greatest respect".

"I'm worried about you Dale, you seem to be developing a personality".

"Who said I never had one in the first place. Here we are, enjoy your volleyball. Don't forget what I didn't say about finding Johnson first and if Gold gets to be a problem, let me know and I'll use stronger wording. Night Carla", and he walked off into the night. Carla watched as he went, he no longer seemed to lumber but now strolled purposefully. Interesting. Once indoors, she pulled out her phone and dialled Thompson.

"Boss, just a quickie. It's just been very strongly hinted to me by a reliable source that Duncan Collins now knows for sure Ritchie Johnson torched him, just as we thought. He's looking hard too, the suggestion is that we would do well to find him first. Sorry to bother you". Carla wondered why her boss was in bed before ten, then put it out of her mind when Melanie called asking how she was and what she'd been doing, an hour flew by. Later she laid in bed trying to turn her brain off, she wondered whether Melanie was something more, after all.

"Sorry, I had to take that", said Thompson not really needing to explain.

"That's fine, work will always be like that, goes with the job".

Thirty-one

02 September 2017

As the miles slipped past Thompson was deep in thought. Jenny Banks had been quiet, deliberately, no mention of the urgent thing she'd wanted to discuss. He appreciated the consideration. Once he'd dropped her off he'd set out on the scary, final bit. It had to be done. As always the motorway service station was busy. Parking was easy enough but it was time-limited, he'd have to trade a kidney for a sandwich or something, just to get a receipt. He wasn't sure how Rebecca was getting there, but he hoped her new friend wasn't involved. Police officer or not, sometimes you just want to nut someone.

He could see Rebecca's head in McDonalds, she was looking out of the window, he could still leg it if he wanted because she didn't seem to have seen him. The queue was small, so he got a shake and some nugget things quite quickly although he wasn't a McDonald's regular so he wasn't sure what was quick and what wasn't. He paused when he got his order, then walked calmly over. The restaurant had about twenty people in it and he'd identified Rebecca's driver as one of two people.

"Hello".

Rebecca looked up, she was teary, he wasn't surprised. Probably couldn't blame the hormones for this one.

"I nearly ran for it", she said, before wiping her nose on a napkin.

"Me too, but thanks for seeing me now. I know lawyers are supposed to be our mouthpieces but we've always been able to talk. I know we are done and that saddens me more than I can say, but I think I understand".

"I don't. I thought we were permanent, in our own idyll, but it seems not and that's as much my fault as yours".

286

Thompson resisted saying that he wasn't the one that had pissed off, but he thought it and he knew that Rebecca would know he had.

"This new guy, who is he really?"

"James Poole, my first love. It seems I never left his affections and he never left mine although I didn't know it until we met up again. Until then I thought we were still solid, you and I, just having a few hiccups. Once I met up with him, I knew straight away that all the bickering and moodiness was real and not just little instances of temper. He's a good man, you are too, and I don't think I'm a bad person. I just fell into the wrong slot and didn't realise".

Thompson was saying nothing deliberately, he wanted Rebecca to let him know where things went wrong, how bad he'd been, he wanted to compare notes. He also wanted to know details, access to his kids, the financial arrangements, that sort of thing. It was his practical nature, he wanted things in black and white.

"And you, I think of you in that house with the mess. It never became home and I know I didn't give it a chance to, either. The work was to turn it into ours, mine really. I'm sorry we came to this and that you are going to have the messiest part. You have open access to Guy and Psycho when he comes. We can bring him up, you can come down when you like or we'll meet in the middle or come up to you. No time constraints but your own"

Thompson wondered whether that was a clever dig at his job and the time it consumed. If it was he decided not to address it.

"I'll need time to finish the house, make it more sellable, then I can pay your dad back and you your half of any profit".

Rebecca looked at him coldly. She knew that this was Thompson the pragmatist, it's all done and dusted so we might as well get on. She'd hoped for another last glimpse of Dave Thompson, the man she fell for, but it seemed he was now some way in the past.

"No problem. Are you seeing Jenny then?"

"You know I am, your watcher saw her".

"What watcher? Sorry Dave, I don't know what you're talking about".

Thompson knew she was telling the truth. "A guy called Barton Montague claimed he was a friend of yours and was outside the house making notes on comings and goings, I clouted him".

"Nope, not from me, I wouldn't do that but I think I might know who might. Comings and goings?"

"That's what he said. Don't worry about it. For the record, Jenny Banks and I formed a relationship. Not serious, more supportive for now. Joe died".

"Oh, poor Jenny, I'm so sorry, I didn't know, we don't get provincial news. Is she ok?"

Thompson was reminded of a conversation, the one where Rebecca hadn't asked who'd died. She's been so self-absorbed in chasing her own happiness that it was almost as if she didn't really care, he put that aside too. "She will be, so will I and I really hope you are. From what I can see, he looks a steady enough bloke, your new man. It must be love if he's willing to take on another man's kids. Who does he support?"

Rebecca laughed, she sounded just like she used to and it jolted Thompson. Then she realised what he'd said. "You know which one he is then? I didn't think it wise to have him sat here, I had a daft idea that you might nut him. Oh, and Crystal Palace".

Thompson was relieved, at least it wasn't one of the London teams that fancied themselves. Palace were a proper club, well-respected in football circles. His phone went, he glanced at it and then apologised. Rebecca waved him away, they were done now anyway. He walked out to the car park, calling the sender of the text as he went.

"Did I get the timing right?"

"Yes, Jenny, perfect, just leaving now. It went ok, at least we're talking. Have another coffee and I'll buzz you when I get there".

Back at the car someone had stuck a leaflet under the wiper. It proclaimed that 'Jesus Saves' and Thompson couldn't help but think, 'yeah, but Kane puts in the rebound', he loved that old chestnut. He watched the BMW pull up to the door and Rebecca get in. The driver eased out the car park and even used the indicator, surely a first for a BMW driver. He set off back up the M1 to the next service station where Jenny Banks was waiting for him.

"You're quiet, not surprisingly".

"Not because of Rebecca, I was trying to figure out who might be watching me. That guy you saw and I thumped, he was not one of Rebecca's, so who was interested enough to want to know what I was up to?"

"Duncan Collins?"

"I was thinking closer to home, I was thinking maybe either ACC Osbourne or Perkins".

"Why would either of them get someone not on the force to spy on you? What aren't you telling me?"

"There'll always be odds and sods for a DI's ear only. I don't honestly know why either might do this, I'm just speculating. Perhaps it is to see what we're up to?"

"Really, you think we're that interesting to the Nottinghamshire Police? No, something else is going on here and if you don't know, you don't know. If that guy's there again, we should have a more frank conversation with him".

"We'll see".

"Did you tell Rebecca about us?"

"Yes, and I told her about Joe. I told her we were supporting each other through a difficult time".

"Supporting, ok".

"Aren't we?"

"Yes, of course we are, it's just not how I might choose to describe us".

Thompson was relieved to see the motorway exit ahead. He was more bothered that he was being watched than where he was in his relationship with Jenny One. Then he made a mental note to never refer to her as 'Jenny One' outside his own head.

Thirty-two

04 September 2017

Thompson strode out of the office and took his place at the back of the room, standing in almost, but not exactly, the same spot that Superintendent Perkins tended to occupy when he mysteriously materialized in the room. Whether it had been deliberate, or a subconscious way of marking his territory he couldn't say, but he did get some degree of satisfaction when Perkins showed up and had to pick a different spot. At the front, a large image of the missing necklace was the only thing on the board.

Jenny Banks waited while the room settled, she'd seen Perkins and so had decided against verbal encouragement to shut up. "I've just been notified that the official investigation into the death of Matthew and Christopher Johnson is complete and all involved have been exonerated. The 'Magpies' case regarding Ritchie Johnson now becomes ours, therefore I can talk about our prime interest. This, people, is what the burglars who broke into a private residence were after, and it's opened a whole new can of worms. It's a necklace, as you can see, but it is a very valuable necklace thanks to the sparkly things embedded in it. Anyone on the floor care to chuck in a valuation?" Banks was trying to engage the room and, while she'd got their attention, they didn't seem overly interested in a shiny bit of tat. She knew they would be when the numbers came out.

"Five grand". Harvinder rarely said much, so Banks was surprised when he guessed first.

"No".

"Are the jewels real or is this a paste piece, pretty though it is? Is this a trick question?"

"Not paste, Carla, but good to be suspicious".

"Twenty-five thousand pounds", said Josh, hoping to have the winning bid.

"No, anyone else want a go?"

"It's a relatively modern piece comprised of nine blue diamonds, and eighteen yellow. The original piece once belonged to Elizabeth Alexeievna, formerly known as Princess Louise of Baden. She was the wife of Alexander the First of Russia. The diamonds gave the original piece a Russian name which roughly translates as 'Light of the Earth' in English. Many referred to the jewels in their original form as a part of the Russian Crown Jewels. It was lost when the Romanov family were executed by the Bolsheviks, but the diamonds resurfaced in Switzerland, in their current form, after the Second World War. The piece we see here was sold at auction to an anonymous bidder in 1989, it may have changed hands privately since. Allowing for the rate of inflation and appreciation, thanks to the quality of the blue and yellow diamonds, the value now would be, conservatively, around eleven million pounds".

A pin dropping, had it happened at that moment, would surely have shattered eardrums but, when he'd finished speaking, Simon Beresford just reinserted the insipid smile he usually wore. The room stared at him, aghast. "What? I'm a history buff and I intend to work in this field when I've done serious crime". Then he went into what Elkie had termed 'brain saving mode' once again. Thompson noticed Perkins was having trouble stifling a laugh.

"Good, right, thanks for that Simon. I'll bring my earrings to you for a valuation later, genuine Argos, I believe". The room laughed at Bank's joke, more out of relief than anything. Then the chatter started, '*eleven mill? Hell fire!*' Banks let it run a while before reigning them in. "We think Ritchie Johnson nicked it to order and we need to find him and ask nicely if we can have it back. The item in question is the property of Lemmy Dowie, yes I can see that you footy fans know the name. There is the possibility of murky goings on here so we've done backgrounds on everyone, and I still want to know more about Ritchie Johnson and his operation, everything, see the previous profiles as a starting point. I prepared the actions, let's get digging people. Oh, and one final thing, no blabbing to anyone".

At his desk, Beresford had gone back to his war with things manual, he still hadn't mastered which cupboard to go for various snack items. He seemed completely unaware that he'd surprised people, an odd fish if ever there was one.

Perkins had gone and Thompson was relieved to not find him waiting in his office. He was surprised when Beresford just wandered in, as if he'd mistaken the office door for the one to the loo. "Simon, impressive knowledge there, can you provide the background for Jenny since you have intimate knowledge of the diamonds?" Thompson knew that there would now be a short pause.

"Oh, yes, sure, Sir. I realise I'm a useless bag of shit, as Liam calls me, but I seem to have difficulty focusing if a subject doesn't grab me".

"And serious crime and the way we have to fight it falls into the 'not grabbing you' category, does it?"

"Yes. The trouble is, to get to the right place to employ my obvious talents, the Arts and Antiques Unit in London, I have to work Serious Crime. My advisor reckoned about two years would be enough, but I can't see me wanting to do that or you wanting to put up with me, so I thought I might ask, if you were by any chance contacted by the senior officer on the AAU in relation to a position, that you might give me a reference?"

"Is that likely, me being contacted?"

"If I ask the right person, yes".

Thompson saw the sense in Beresford being a square peg in an equally square hole and it would, theoretically, free up a post in his own team for someone more wired into reality. He also saw that relatives in high places could, if they wished, circumvent procedure where promotions and transfers were involved.

"Obviously I'll discharge my duties here first, although I would appreciate having fewer names, just Simon will do. I do like the idea that I can block out the background noise of the office noise by having a brain-saving mode though. Very witty, I do like Elkie".

"You have to expect a certain amount of piss-taking. Even I get it and I'm supposed to scare people".

"But you do, Sir, and they all have the greatest respect for you. I know I'm a bit different and I don't take offence, although Liam's use of Gaelic when cursing can be confusing. Thanks for the chat, Sir"

"One thing, Simon. The diamonds were worked into the necklace. Why?"

"To move them, get them away from their Romanov history. Left in their original form, eleven million pounds would be half the value of the piece to a collector. These gems have a shady past, finding the piece, if we can, will only be the start of the investigation", and he wandered out.

Carla and Josh went back to the bus-cam footage. It was tedious in the extreme, but it had to be done.

"it would really help if we had a better time of death estimate", said Josh, scrolling through the footage for the local buses.

"I know, but the Pathologist said that the bath full of brandy really messed with that. We've just got to do the best...hang on, I think I've got him. Yes, here he is, Trevor Gold, just getting off the bus outside The Grove. What time is that?"

Josh bounded over to her workstation. Looks like around 10 pm on 11 June. Wonder if we can find him leaving, too. I take it he doesn't drive?"

"Banned, my fault I called it in when he was pissed one night". Carla scanned on. "Here he is again, boarding a bus around 11.30 pm on the same day. He looks a bit worse for wear, I bet he drank some of the brandy he used for Pickles, did we blood test him? Looks like the driver didn't really want to let him on, he might even remember him. I bet they don't get a lot of belligerent drunks boarding buses at The Grove".

"Well, that places Gold in the vicinity. If we can get some DNA results from the house, we'll be laughing".

Thirty-three

05 September 2017

Fresh from a morning's Inclusivity Course in Derby, Jenny Banks walked around Victoria Centre in a bit of a daze. She was nominally shopping, she wanted a couple of new suits for work, something hard-wearing, well-made but with a bit of style. Then it struck her, style was missing from her life. Not just style, but whatever she'd expected from a relationship, she was surprised it had taken her so long to realise it. She wasn't in love, she'd been infatuated and, in her case at least, the infatuation had passed. Now all she had to do was tell Dave.

Shopping for decent suits was always a chore. Manufacturers produced such a dire choice, thinking that the smart professional was likely to wear some brain-dead designer's dreadful creation, instead of thinking along more practical lines. Jenny always thought along practical lines, or at least she had until the thing with Thompson, now she was again.

"Hello, somebody stolen your last Rolo? You look miserable, I thought you and the boss were finally getting it together. Everybody knows by the way". It was Lorna, Jenny's fellow sergeant-in-crime.

"I've just got things on my mind, Lorna. You shopping for suits, too?"

"No, I'll wait until I go home, more choice, nothing frothy. Honestly, who would wear this shit?"

"I was thinking exactly the same", and the two detectives got into chatting as they walked the stores, disparaging just about everything they saw. One shop did have something that Jenny thought might do, but not in her size, and the assistant didn't seem mentally equipped for substantial questions. In the end she came away empty-handed. By the time they got back to the nick, both had learned a little bit more about each other, not intentionally, but Jenny and Lorna hadn't spent a lot of time together and so a bit of light digging was natural.

Back at her desk, Jenny was in pensive mood. Lorna had painted a quite different picture of London police work. She'd thought it all male-dominated, misogynist old farts running departments with little room for women to progress, but Lorna was very optimistic that, once Prosser was allowed back in the sergeants' fold and she could move back, that she could forge a niche. It was food for thought.

"You look miserable". It was Elkie who could be a bit too perceptive sometimes. Despite some rivalry between them, Elkie was just about the closest female friend Jenny had ever had, and she'd been girding her loins to ask Elkie her opinion on what to do. Elkie was also Dave's friend too, and his ex-girlfriend's, she was just too nice sometimes. Jenny had no idea how she carried it off, she couldn't, not in a million years.

"I have a dilemma, that's all. You know me, never plain-sailing. I'd appreciate a chat sometime, you know, when you have a minute".

"No time like the present. Come on, let's grab a coffee, we can chat".

"I only just got back from that course and lunch. Dave wants some files looking at. Oh, you know what, sod it, come on then".

The cafeteria was still serving lunchtime meals and Jenny was surprised when Elkie got a plate of chips. "Starving, I only just had lunch too but I fancied some chips".

"It's allowed, get away with it while you can. Your bloke won't mind a few pounds at his age".

"Actually, I never put on an ounce, no matter what I eat. Something else about me to piss people off, don't think I don't know how I wind people up sometimes, not my fault. Anyway, your little Dave Thompson problem, talk to auntie Elkie".

Jenny wasn't surprised that she'd suspected all wasn't right. Elkie had a sixth-sense, or something.

"I don't think Dave is the one and I want to let him down gently. What with Rebecca and everything, I'm worried that the stress might break him. I'm pretty sure it was infatuation for me, besides, I think I want a crack at London and he'd never move there, not that they'd have him". It was a pretty blunt assessment of the Thompson you saw, accurate, but blunt. It was very Jenny-like.

"Do you think the Mighty Dave is head-over-heels?"

"Well, no, but we're finally together-sort of-and now I don't want to be. Like I said, I don't want to break his confidence, I do care for him, but he's not the one. There might not even be a 'one'".

"What, are you thinking of having a pool of men or something and dipping in when you're in the mood for a fresh one?"

"Actually that sounds quite appealing, but no, I think I want my freedom again, and I want to lower Dave back to grim reality without tears".

"My advice, tell him straight, he's stronger than you think. He'll get over it, he might be a bit shitty to be around for a while but you'll be gone south by the sound of it and I'll be busy pushing a kid out of my fanny. I'm taking as long as I can for maternity and even then I'm undecided what I want to do after. Tell Dave, it's not like you are shacking up together, are you even being exclusive?"

Jenny ignored the question, she was but... "I know you're right, it's so unlike me not to be decisive. I'll talk to him".

Thompson sat in his office sorting papers into piles. He'd recently acquired one of those multi-pens with different coloured inks and he was more pleased about it than a Detective Inspector should be, as he colour-coded different sheets. He knew that he was evading the issue that was bothering him but it was easiest for now. The knock yanked him back to reality. Elkie pushed the half-open door and walked in, she turned and closed the door behind her, a sure sign that what was to be said was private.

"I just thought I'd have a chat and pass on some news. Rebecca did her first design for a customer and they were delighted. Guy has more teeth now and is keeping the new man awake, and Forest have sacked the manager, again, and a new bloke is coming in".

"What, really? Shit, I missed that, who is he, do you know?"

"I made the last one up, just to see where your thoughts lie. What's bothering you, Dave?"

Thompson tried to hide his disappointment at no managerial change. He already knew about the first two things. Despite what people thought, he was still in touch with Rebecca and they chatted, he even talked to his boy after a fashion. Things with Rebecca were now pretty cordial, especially with some serious geography between them, and he hoped they always would be. He did have a problem though and who better to talk to than Elkie?

"You know that Jenny and I have been, er, together a few times?"

"Shagging, yes. She did a pie chart for us all to follow your progress, you know, blue for performance, red for stamina and green for technique. Very revealing, she's run out of red".

"Lovely, I hope people see me in a different light now, then. Joking aside, obviously I really like Jenny and she's been a brick with all the split and everything, but I don't think it's working. We both seem to have lost a bit of sparkle, more me than her, obviously", he said, thinking on his feet while sitting down.

"I did wonder whether you two were suited, or whether you were just fascinated, infatuated even. Do you think it has run its short, but lively, course then?"

"I do, but I want to let her down gently. After her last two blokes she's been through the mill a bit, I'm worried that us splitting, not dumped, splitting, might damage her confidence beyond repair. Do you see?"

"What about you, will you be ok?"

"What? Yes, Clifton lad. It takes more than my world falling down around my ears to knock me out of my stride".

"My advice is to let Jenny dump you then, talk her into a place where she can see that the sparkle has dimmed, where she's in control and makes the decision. Are you sure this wasn't just a casual thing rather than an actual relationship? You don't live together, you've just bounced up and down together a few times but that's about it. Have you even been exclusive, has she?"

Thompson now had enough doubt in his mind to follow Elkie's sensible advice. He'd not been exclusive but he wasn't going to say so, he wasn't going to mention Jenny Two at all, if he didn't have to. "I think so, thanks Elkie, it really helps to bounce this off you". Taking advantage of his own decisiveness, Thompson asked Jenny into the office.

"How was the course?" It was a standard question, expected, and Thompson already knew the answer.

"Ok, some interesting bits, nice bunch, we paired up and did role-play. I expect you did too when you did yours?"

"Yes, although I had a burly DI from Stoke as my partner, definitely not my type but a Port Vale fan so not all bad".

Jenny nodded, she always did at football references, not that Thompson could see it. "I had a guy called Terry, from London, quite a laugh".

Thompson nodded himself. Jenny was a fun person usually, he wasn't surprised that others saw that too. "Sorry you had to go to Derby for yours, I can get someone to wash the car for you later".

Jenny looked blank before it clicked, oh, football again. "No need, no sheep on the road or anything, just a normal Midlands city, although I suspect the locals' arms are longer than normal, which would explain their knuckle-dragging. I saw Dad, he's well and say's 'hi' and that he hopes things work out with everything. Did you see him recently?"

"Yes, I went over for a con-flab, bits to discuss and to network a bit. I'm told I should".

"What things does he want to work out?"

"The Johnson case I suppose, that's what we mainly discussed. He told me he's aiming for DI, he'd be good".

"Yes, I think you're right. I'm a bit tired after the course, Dave, I'm going home and after a shower I'll have an early night, I'm due. I'll see you at work tomorrow.

Half-way through watching an old Forest season video, Thompson's phone rang.

"Dave, it's Jenny. Listen, we should go out somewhere quiet, turn our phones off, have a meal and a chat. I've been trying to do this for a while but what with Rebecca and everything, anyway, there are things to discuss, remember I mentioned it, is that ok with you?"

"Yes, sure, I'll book a place and we'll talk it through. Night". The phone went dark as the connection was severed. Behind him, the recently plastered wall and unpainted doors that led through to the extension-cum-conservatory were waiting patiently, another few weeks and Wheeler said he could get the paint out. He wasn't ready for bed himself yet, he was only halfway through the season and he still had a pile of papers to get through. He tried another number, still nothing.

Thompson wasn't in the best frame of mind when Bridger called him at home, but he appreciated what was happening and was happy to organize a meeting for tomorrow.

Thirty-four

06 September 2017

"I'm DCI Paul Bridger, my team are investigating the death of Joe Lawrence, who some of you knew well and some were getting to know better". Thompson watched for the look in Jenny's direction, it didn't come. If it had and he'd thought it accusatory, he'd have intervened, DCI or not. "This won't be pleasant and I don't intend to dress it up as anything other than it is. Lawrence was found dead in Arnold at a known drug run. We checked and he wasn't there officially, leading us to conclude that something else was happening". The room started to chatter quietly.

"People, the DCI is here as a favour, keeping us in the loop, he's not obliged, show some respect please. You can yap amongst yourselves later". Thompson had been quite blunt deliberately.

"Thanks, Dave. Lawrence died from a combination of a blow to the back of the head, followed by the severing of the carotid artery in his neck. Death would have been quick, he was probably unconscious from the blow when the coup-de-grace happened, and he bled out very fast".

The details were known but they sounded more raw coming from Bridger, more intrusive.

"The death of a colleague is always a shock and there is a strong feeling that retribution is required. I advise people not to visit the site and not to carry out their own investigation". This time he did look, at Marie's boys clumped in one corner of the room. "It is understandable but, please, don't get in our way. Investigations are proceeding and we anticipate an arrest shortly, we have CCTV, which is being examined and enhanced. The suspect is known to us via the National Drugs Intelligence

Unit and is being actively sought, that brings me to the more difficult bit".

Bridger took a moment, engaging with each set of eyes in the room, it was deliberate.

"Joe Lawrence was a drug user, cocaine mostly but we identified other substances, both in his system and at his residence. There is also strong evidence that Lawrence had links to organized crime, as an informer, although we are still investigating in this area. We know that organized crime has officers in their pockets and we're weeding them out. I know it's hard on you as officers of the law but those are the facts. We've completed our interviews with all who worked with Lawrence or had any sort of relationship with him, inside and outside of work, and are satisfied that he operated alone. I just want to thank everyone on the team, and your DI, for your cooperation and I'm sorry to be standing here telling you this today. Thank you".

Half the room turned to look at Marie's boys. Some probably wondered how you couldn't know, but Joe had been a part of the team and it was the team trust that he'd used and broken, not how he was with one individual, whatever their relationship.

Thompson chatted to Bridger a while, the times they'd talked he'd seemed ramrod-straight and Thompson appreciated that. When Bridger had gone, Thompson took over.

"Joe's gone, he let himself get led astray, we don't know how. On a personal level, I liked him, he was very likeable and loyal to Marie, despite what happened. Don't for a minute think he ever put one of you in danger, these things don't work that way. His death shows that even the good can stray, the thing is, we might not be aware ourselves that it's happening. If any of you ever feel things slip, speak up before it's too late. If Joe had come to us this wouldn't have happened, look after each other".

Thompson was back with his now diminishing piles of paper when Carla, Josh and Simon arrived, breathless. "You need to hear this, Boss, and so does Jenny. It's the Pickles case, I think we've got him".

Striding the three steps to the door, Thompson yelled "Jenny!" She looked up, startled, then made a bee-line for the office.

"Boss, Sarge, I think we've got Gold", said Carla, excited. "Me and Josh spent some time going through the bus-cam footage and we found him arriving at The Grove at 10 pm, the night before we found the body, and then leaving again about 90 minutes later. The bus driver remembers him, he was pissed and he didn't want to let him on board".

"Good work, you two, but we still need to place him inside Kingston's house".

"Simon can help there, Boss", said Carla, grinning.

"I finally got access to Joe's computer today. There are DNA results on there, taken from the house. One is a match for Trevor Gold".

Thompson and Banks looked at each other. It was frustrating that Joe hadn't shared the forensic results but he had obviously been going off the rails for a while. More worrying, why had the data not also been sent to Thompson, as SIO, as procedure required? That would need some follow-up.

"Go get him. Jenny. Take Liam, he can help if Gold needs a firm hand".

The knock was loud but Trevor Gold didn't hear it, he was so pissed that a bomb could have gone off and he wouldn't have heard it. When Prosser saw him slumped through a window, entry was made and an ambulance called. Gold would face questions when he recovered, backed up by forensics. He wasn't going to walk away from them this time.

Thompson headed up to Perkin's office.

"News of Johnson, David? It seemed to be all that Perkins was interested in now.

No, Sir, but we do have what we need to convict Gold of the Pickles murder. He's being arrested as we speak. A mix-up delayed DNA evidence reaching us but we have it now, along with additional evidence providing motive, notably that Gold was protective of some birds that Kingston had illegally obtained".

"Good work, congratulate the team, especially the key players. Do you ever wonder if it's all worth it, David?"

"In relation to what, Sir?"

"In relation to all the precious things we can lose through dedication to the job, sorry, just ignore me, I'm being maudlin, it's nothing. Carry on with the good work".

"Sometimes, Sir, yes, I do".

The Indian Restaurant was nice enough, a bit generic but it was recommended. If the worst came to the worst at least they'd have a decent curry. They were travelling independently, Jenny had suggested it. She had a thing later.

"You look nice", said Thompson, as Jenny took her seat

"Thanks, have you ordered?"

"No, I was waiting for you. That's me, a bit plodding at times, you might say one-paced. I've always been surprised that you ever found me attractive, a high-flyer like you".

Jenny was onto it immediately, this had Elkie all over it. She'd set them both up, the bugger.

"You know what, Dave, I won't order, I'm not stopping. I don't think this is working, me and you, and I think you feel the same. We're both so scared that we might hurt each other fatally that we've been to the same oracle and been given the same advice. Friends?"

Thompson laughed. "Friends, always I hope, we work better that way. Go on, I'll get a take-away, there's a match on telly later. I can even fart when I want".

"Too much information, Dave", and Jenny laughed before strolling out.

On the way home, the curry in its little foil trays sat patiently on the passenger seat, it was cooling rapidly. His phone had rung and the number wasn't one he knew. He'd thrown the car into the first spot he could find to take the call, he'd only just made it. "Hello, Jenny?"

"Just thought I'd call, see how you are?"

"I've been better, are you ok? I've been worried. I know you can take care of yourself, but still..."

"Yes, I've been busy, I'll tell you all about it when you've sorted out your case and we can be legal. I hope it's soon. Anyway, that's all, just letting you know I'm still alive".

"Visit me, at home. Fuck the case".

"Ok", *click*.

The light streamed in through the open curtains, followed by a dark cloud passing over and with it the threat of yet more rain. Thompson sniffed, then felt the warm body. He padded downstairs in his boxers and returned with two cups of coffee. Jenny was just waking up.

"Dave, I've heard whispers. I don't have anything for you but Ritchie is active, it's one of the reasons I went dark. I don't think he'll look for me, but he might and he has a lot of eyes and ears out there. This has to be a bit random between us until you get him, I hope you understand". He did.

Thirty-five

07 September 2017

Simon Beresford came into Thompson's office the next morning. He seemed preoccupied, nothing new there, but he had something on his mind that he wanted to share.

"I was thinking, Sir, about the missing jewels. If they do get found, if lost, or seen, if not lost, their worth might not be known. We should go public, show them an image of the necklace without commenting on the value and see what happens. At worst we've made them too hot to handle, at best they'll reappear somewhere. It might shake things up a bit".

Thompson was astonished. Beresford was sounding lucid.

"Simon, great thinking, let me just run it past the boss".

Sheila Wright was surprised to get the call from Chalky Perkins and even more surprised that he stood her lunch, albeit a modest one. "Go on then, Leroy, spit it out. What do you want?"

"Ever the perceptive one, Sheila. You are no doubt aware that a robbery took place at a footballer's residence in Leicester and that the owner would like his property back for sentimental reasons".

"Sentimental, Lemmy Dowie? I'm old enough to remember him when he was a little shit breaking into cars and nicking radios. Odd how he never found his way to Borstal like the rest of the shits. No doubt the rich football club chairman was quick to protect his investment".

"Really, Sheila, such cynicism in one so lovely. Anyway, we haven't called them Borstals for years, they are Young Offenders Institutions now. It lacks a little something, in my opinion. That aside, we want to release the news of the theft in an attempt to inform but not titillate, and we'd like you to help us out with that".

"What makes you think they'll go for it in the editor's office? You know the paper is run by teen dickheads now, don't you?"

"As I understand it, Mr. Dowie and his life-partner, Shania-Marie, would like to talk to someone exclusively about the theft and how much the family heirloom means to them".

"Whose family? The only way Dowie has an heirloom is if he nicked it. Tell me more about this exclusive though, you have my journalistic senses stimulated".

"I was thinking photos of the lovely couple, including one of Shania-Marie bedecked in the missing necklace. A local boy makes good but has a heart-felt sorrow sort of thing".

"And you can deliver that, guaranteed?"

"I can, and we will get an image of the missing jewel out there without seeming to be begging the public for help. I understand these things are called 'win-win' situations".

"Is the robbery linked to the Johnson brothers, at least two of which are no more?"

"We believe so".

Sheila Wright didn't believe a word of it but she didn't much care either. She'd do the story, but not for the paper, she'd do it in one of those glossy magazines that stay-at-home women read and make something on it, freelance.

"I should say that whatever august publication the story and the images appear in is of no consequence to us, does that give you any clarity of thinking?"

"It does and thanks for the lunch, I'll miss our occasional chats. I'll be in touch for the contact details for Dowie and leave you to get a suitable image arranged for us, they presumably have one. Preferably something tasteful and without Dowie's girlfriend's tits drawing the eye too much. Fancy a drink and a curry one night, as friends? A catch up, no tricks, no record. Promise".

"A suitable photo will be procured and, you know, I think I would".

Thirty-six

12 September 2017

"Of course, the use of one of the footballer's houses to hide in isn't likely now, is it, because Johnson is sly and will know we've made that connection, his breathing space has gone,. So we can presume that not all the houses used by Johnson were somebody else's, leaving the possibility that Johnson owns houses himself now, but registered to whom? Sorry, I was just thinking aloud". Carla had become used to Beresford randomly talking, whether it was about how evolution might have happened or the benefits of having a flexible mobile phone plan, but this little bubbling up of a molten lava idea was relevant. She searched and came up with 72 properties registered to a Johnson in Nottingham; that was a lot of leg work. She started to filter.

Thompson sat in his office, bored. He'd cleared the paper torrent, bested it, finished it off and put it to bed. Sure, it was only until the next arrival but, for now, his desk was clear. His phone pinged and his heart skipped, his Jenny? But the number was unknown, as was the address. What he did know was the name that preceded it, Ritchie Johnson.

"Liam, Gecko, Tilda with me. Jenny, take Josh and Simon and he passed over the address. Lorna, Carla, Elkie, sort back-up and then attend. Go". When Marie's boys got back from lunch the office was empty.

Across the city, a white SUV of the inexpensive sort was pulling out of an industrial estate. Inside two men sat quietly, one drove, one navigated.

The flat was in a part of a complex, large and busy with a lot of parked cars. There was only one road in but there was plenty of ways out, especially for the agile. Thompson looked at Google Maps as Prosser drove. "Put a couple of cars on roads by the railway tracks at Netherfield and get one on Vale Road, Colwick". He dialled, "Sorry to run out on you, Sham. Take the boys for a drive, be around the train bridge at the bottom of Douglas Avenue, where it crosses to Colwick and wait for directions." He dialled again. "Sir, we got an address and are out now, everyone. I'll report when I have him, Johnson".

The cops shut down the access road and everyone moved into Whimsey Park on foot. The flat was registered to a Ms. J. Johnson. Thompson tried not to think about that.

"Pull out, but drive around a bit. Try to guess where he might go, what direction". The SUV did a U-turn, like everyone else who was being prevented from getting into Whimsey Park, so they went down Douglas but cops were there too, then they drove around to Netherfield, same situation. "Pull out then, if they get him at least we'll know where he is". The SUV went back to the industrial estate.

Inside the flat a phone rang. "Cops everywhere, Ritchie". Johnson looked out the front window, the road outside was quiet, he couldn't see anyone, nor any cars moving, it was like a snapshot. He gave the girl instructions, grabbed his rucksack and went out the back door.

"Hello Ritchie".

313

In an instant, Johnson identified his route, ran and flattened a woman, blonde, short hair, familiar, then he leapt, crashing through a thorny bush before rolling down a steep bank. He was instantly up and running, stumbling, sore. He ran a couple of hundred yards hidden by trees and brambles but he could see cars moving ahead, so he doubled back up the hill, hauling himself into a back garden, then cutting through more gardens before coming out into a small cul-de-sac.

The house was empty, it looked like it had been for sale for a while, and it was easy to get inside. Johnson made a call then waited patiently, the pain in his left arm keen. It took her ten minutes to get there and she followed his instructions to the letter. She backed up to the house, then stood on the drive, taking pictures.

"Police, who are you?" The woman explained that she and her husband were thinking of buying the house and she was taking more photos, to make plans. She showed her driving licence and she was checked out, she was legit. When the cops had gone elsewhere, Johnson climbed into the boot of her car and she drove away. She got stopped again, showed her driving licence to uniformed cops and a few phone shots of the house. She said she'd been checked already, mentioning the officer by name, and then went on her way.

"Vanished, Sir, one injury, Jeffries, she's at the hospital now, fractured cheekbone. We think someone warned him from the estate when we shut the road, he might be injured himself though, he fell quite a way. The site was too big to contain, another five yards closer and we'd have secured the property, he'd have had nowhere to go. People are still searching, an empty house some distance away had been broken into, recent signs of occupation, forensics are there now. We have the woman from Whimsey Park but no comment, as expected".

Perkins was angry, Thompson could tell because he was being nicer than usual. Whichever way you dressed it, the slippery Johnson had done it again.

Thompson wasn't in any better mood than Perkins, barking orders when he got back to the nick. An hour later he'd calmed down a bit, he felt exhausted, emotionally drained. The house was registered to a James Johnson, it was one of three in Nottingham with the same registered name, all three shared a bank account. Another set of bolt holes had closed and the account was locked.

Thompson did the debrief himself, everyone was back and he wanted a fuller picture. "Johnson got away again but the information was good so perhaps whoever sent it might know where he is now and give us another go at him. Burner phone, so no idea where it came from, but it came directly to me so I have to think that one over. Tilda is ok, battered though. Had it been Liam he'd run at, or me, he'd be eating his dinner through a straw now. Don't blame Tilda, he went for the smallest and caught her before she could take him, it happens. An empty house on Russet Avenue has been identified as where we think he holed up, we'd have needed a hundred officers to cover that area properly. Thoughts?"

"Sir, we spoke to a woman on Russet, she was taking photos of an empty house there, number 28", said Sham. "Maria Poletz. She said she was buying the house, taking pictures. We checked, she came back as legit, her driving licence confirmed her ID".

"There you go, Sham there's our getaway driver".

"I know her", said Gecko. "She was a hostess in Wollaton, dropped off the radar a couple of years ago, we assumed she'd gone home but we didn't look too hard. She was not really wanted for anything".

"So Johnson was collected by one of his girls, or ex-girls, who dropped off the radar and we don't know where she is now either, terrific. Find a photo of this Maria, stick it on the board, send it out for attention", and Thompson stomped off to his office. An hour later, Tilda was back. She had a lot of bruising and a lump like a golf ball on her cheek but she was ok.

"Sorry, Boss, I nearly had him but he had momentum, you saw".

"Not your fault but we have to debrief and everything. I read your statement, just sign it and we're done. Are you taking time off?"

"No, I want Johnson even more now, Sir".

"David, your mystery message sender, any ideas?" Perkins had called and Thompson had obeyed.

"No, Sir, I have many contacts and the relevant ones are all aware of our priorities. If this was one of them, they'll tell me at some point and probably expect me to be generous. You know how it can work".

"Indeed. I just thought you might have more idea. Burner phones will be the death of this nation, we simply can't police if one of our tools is removed like that. Very well, keep looking, find this Poletz woman, although I expect Johnson to be no longer in her company. Very slippery".

"You can't stay long, Ritchie, they'll find me if I hang around for too long, one of them will join up the dots. You have another place?"

"A few but there's one I'm interested in, one under the radar, they won't look there because they don't know where she is and neither do I, yet.

Been doing well I hear, telling tales. I'm owed some back pay, time for her to settle up properly. One last little job for you, take this and put it on this car when you see it parked here, keep checking, it might take a few days", and he showed her the spot on the map "Call me when it's done".

On an industrial estate in Nottingham, a conversation was taking place. "With nowhere else to go, Ritchie Johnson will start turning over old stones looking for somewhere to hide. This address came to me recently thanks to one of our people, you know what to do. The young lady must not be harmed though, that is of utmost importance, anyone harming her will regret it, briefly. Our other little problem, do we have people in there?"

"Yes, it's in hand".

Thirty-seven

25 September 2017

Johnson's fresh disappearance added to Thompson's recurring headache, Jenny Two. For a short while after Jenny Banks had called it a day with him, she'd appeared randomly at his place, spent the night and was gone the next morning. She always came and left by cab and he'd not wanted to be so obvious as to try tracing the cab and her, or at least wherever the cab picked her up. No Johnson meant no active case, sort of. No active case meant he could ask Jenny Two to...what, move in? Yes, he'd like that, despite then having more baggage between them than Imelda Marcos on tour. Then things all went quiet with her. After nothing for two weeks, Thompson knew something wasn't right. Had she decided to vanish too after Johnson had got away again? He was sure she'd sent the address.

Later that day he was doing the dreaded visit to the solicitor. Everyone had said it was for the best to get it out of the way. For Rebecca, for Guy, and Psycho when he came, not so long now.

In the solicitor's office his guys explained everything to him. In the end Rebecca's parents had been ok with him and he was determined, when he visited Guy and Psycho, to be adult. The office had an air of depression but he wasn't sure that it was generated by the office but from the people within.

"All done?" asked Jenny Banks, as she closed her laptop.

"Yes, all done. Do you mind, Jenny, I'd like a bit of space. I appreciate you coming with me and it helped, really it did, but seeing the details in front of me in black-and-white got to me a bit. I could do with a bit of introspection time".

"Sure, no problem. Should I come over as a friend later? No, perhaps not, I have things to do anyway. Don't get too drunk, you're still the boss, remember". Thompson assured her that he wouldn't and she slipped off. He had no intention of getting drunk at all. He started to walk around Nottingham.

He found himself in the Hockley coffee shop where he'd met Tilda and Jenny Two the first time, he had no idea how he'd got there but at least the car was in the work car park nearby so not far to walk. His introspection didn't last long, a group of loud girls were on a nearby table and talking men in graphic detail. He made his way to the car and sat a while. It was getting late and Thompson decided not to head back to the office, instead he'd go home with the dust and the memories all around him. He'd put music on, get a paintbrush out and make a start, then he had an idea.

It was raining lightly when he pulled up, but not enough to put him off. The parking spot probably only had space for two cars, three if they were on the small side. The one currently there was just a little hatchback that he didn't recognise, he jotted the number down out of habit. The path was a bit muddy but nothing to worry about, it was partially covered in some sort of topping, not unlike the stuff they had at Colwick. At first Thompson wasn't sure which direction to go, the path led both ways. Then he remembered, only one led to open countryside, he set off.

A few Mallards had quacked excitedly when he'd appeared, but soon realised that he wasn't bearing edible gifts and had gone back to browsing the floating weed. He could see some way along the old canal before it bent to the right. A few benches were set at intervals, the grass around them threatening to engulf them after a growth-spurt caused by the rainy spell. As he walked, he rehearsed what he'd say, he'd been doing it since leaving the car park although he didn't know whether there would be anyone to say anything to.

As the towpath turned he saw a figure in the distance, sitting motionless on one of the less engulfed benches and not looking his direction. His pace quickened until he reached the bench, then he sat.

"I wasn't sure you'd remember".

"Detective brain, I remember virtually everything, I'm afraid. You didn't call, I waited, I was worried. Then I thought you'd made a decision to vanish and I didn't expect to see you again".

"I thought for a long time about it and decided that we might not be right, that I was putting you in a difficult position, that I was more aggro that I was worth. Then I changed my mind, woman's prerogative. I thought that if there was anything in it, you'd find me, you'd remember, and you did. I wanted to see whether you'd remember. I decided that this would be a natural test".

"How many times have you waited here?"

A few, it doesn't matter. Now what?"

"I still have a case to solve, well several actually. I have a mess of a life to sort out including selling the house, finding a place to live, child-maintenance. You'll be inheriting a lot of loose ends".

"Life is just a collection of loose ends. What do you want, Dave?"

"You".

There was no stopping the tears, from both of them, then the laughter.

"I don't know who you are though. I've been calling you Jenny Two, because I knew Jenny Banks, Jenny One, first. What's your family name?"

Jenny took a deep breath. "I don't know if you're ready to know, I don't want to spoil the moment. If I say, it might be the death knell for us".

Thompson was confused. What could spoil the moment? "You didn't marry Johnson, did you?"

"No, I never married, My maiden name, if that's an appropriate term in my case, is Perkins".

"Perkins?, really, I know a Perkins, Superintendent Perkins, he's my boss. I'm never quite sure where I stand with him", said Thompson, setting up the conversation.

"Yes, I know, he's my dad".

"That's something I've suspected for a while now". That statement even surprised Thompson as he said it, but it was true after all. The guy watching his house, that he'd thought had been employed by Perkins or ACC Osbourne, well now he was pretty sure he knew which one it was.

Thompson and Jenny sat quietly for a while, side by side. This would take some consideration. Not just the 'boss's daughter' aspect but had he been set up to play a role? He wasn't at all sure there, he had to ask.

"Was this, us, a set up? Did your dad plan it all to get you away from Johnson?" He knew it wasn't a fair question, but it was preying on his mind.

"Not by me, but I think dad hoped you might 'rescue' me, as he calls it. Neither of us planned anything, I fell for you before I knew the connection. I thought he'd asked you to drag me away from my life, I asked him and said he hadn't, that was why I visited you. I thought we might be ok and we were, but I decided I was being selfish. I told dad to back off or I'd vanish again, he did, it upset him. It was then that he decided to retire, so he wasn't appearing to influence you".

"He's retiring? I didn't know that. And just so we could be together?" It was the first that Thompson had heard of it, he was shocked.

"I think so, nothing else makes sense. So I've been coming here hoping, and you came. Under the circumstances, I'd understand if you marched off and that was it, I won't die-well, maybe a little bit, but I'll understand".

"I'll need to wrap up the case first, before we can move on. I said before, I can't do anything that will prejudice the case against Johnson, when we get him, and we will".

"I had hoped my text would have been enough, but he got away again, so we wait, yes?"

"I knew it was you, I won't ask how you knew where he was. He's in a corner now, but I can't see any other way for us until we have him, sorry".

"Ok, my number changes again soon, I'm staying dark, I'll text you. Bye, Dave". As she walked away Thompson wanted to chase after her, tell her it would all be alright but he didn't know whether it would be. It was sometime after she'd gone that he realised that the goodbye was meant to be final, and when no texts came he knew it, he'd blown it.

Thirty-eight

26 September 2017

"You wanted to see me, Boss?" Tilda Jeffries had been expecting this. She'd been walking a difficult line and leaving a heavy footfall, now what the future held for her came down to this conversation with her boss.

Thompson looked up to see a nervous officer, he was fine with that, she was right to be nervous and she wasn't the only one who would be asked difficult questions. "Sit, please, I'll be with you in two seconds". Thompson finished messing with some papers, mainly for psychological effect, and turned back to Tilda. "I'm thinking you know why you're here so we're going to have a talk, a calm and considered one where you will answer my questions, truthfully. If you have a problem with that, there's the door".

Outside, the office had heard Tilda being called in and had heard Thompson's calmness of voice. They'd heard that tone before. Even Beresford got that something was happening and made no noise. Jenny Banks looked at Elkie, asking what was going on without speaking, but Elkie gave nothing away. She'd had her part to play, now it was up to Thompson.

"Earlier this year my mate, Cliff and I were in a coffee shop on Hockley when you and a working girl joined us, do you remember?"

"Of course, I made sure you knew what was happening so you could exit quickly". Tilda wasn't sure why he'd started with that, they'd discussed it before and Thompson had even thanked her for reading the situation and allowing him to get out and away.

"Good, was that a set-up?" Ah, so that was where this was going.

"No, I was with the girl, Jenny, a sex worker, and we were getting to know each other, lunch together, I was supposed to have a plant if she met a customer but neither had showed. I'd been sure to be visible to her, I was looking to get closer".

"This Jenny was one of your intervention subjects?"

"I can't really discuss that, Sir".

Thompson waited a moment, then picked up the phone. He pressed a shortcut button and then handed the phone to Tilda. She held it slightly away from her ear, afraid of what she might hear. After a couple of seconds she handed the phone back. Thompson didn't smile.

"Yes, Sir, she was. I had a number of targets and was careful not to favour any one so as to arouse suspicion. Jenny was just who I happened to be with when I saw you and Cliff. I knew who you were and so, when Jenny started showing interest in you as a potential client, I did what I did to extricate you. It was a gamble but I explained it away as me recognising you, following a visit to the nick. Part of my cover saw me visiting the nick a few times".

"Is Jenny her real name?"

"One of them, yes".

"And the others?"

"Not for me to say, Sir, not relevant".

Thompson accepted this, but went straight into the next question. "Perkins. Explain his relationship to you, professionally".

"He had an interest in my work and asked to be kept informed. My boss had me appraising him of various situations, meeting remotely. Elkie witnessed one such meet and I persuaded her to not mention it".

"Elkie would've understood, I see that. She's an experienced officer and even though we are friends as well as colleagues, she'd be good as her word".

324

"I was told that when I told Perkins we'd been seen. He said to trust her and to trust you".

"About that, how much influence did Perkins have regarding the subsequent actions of Jenny?"

"I'm sorry, Sir, I don't know what you mean by that".

"Did Perkins push this Jenny, via you, in my direction? Accidentally bumping into each other again, that sort of thing".

"You think this is about you?"

"I seem to be involved and I want to know whether that involvement evolved naturally or whether it was cultivated".

"You think Perkins, helped by me, pushed wayward Jenny towards you deliberately, intending what? That you'd ride in on a fucking big white horse and carrying her to safety, Sir?"

Thompson was on the back foot. Is that what he meant? It wasn't what he intended this meeting to be about, all he'd wanted to know was whether he'd been used as bait before deciding what to do.

"Tilda, I know Jenny is Perkins' daughter. I don't know why she ended up where she did in life but, yes, I wanted to help, if I could, and if that included having to learn to ride a 'fucking big white horse' as you called it, then, yes, I would".

Tilda laughed. "How the hell did you get to DI with a morality chip like that? Honestly, Dave, I'll state very clearly, if anything happened between you and Jenny, subsequent to our meeting in the café, neither I nor Perkins had anything to do with it. He's her dad, do you really think he'd risk pushing her further away by behaving like a total cunt?"

"Ok, I accept what you're saying. Where do we go from here?"

"Me and you will have trust issues for a while, but we'll get over them, given the chance. You know Banks is out of here as soon as she can? I want to stay, I'm starting to feel my place is here. Ask Perkins to see my

325

real file, not the neatly-trimmed one you got from HR. If you'll have me I want to wear the stripes, Jenny Banks' stripes. What about you?"

Thompson hadn't thought that far and said so, instead dismissing Tilda for now. Anyway, what about the news that Jenny Banks was definitely planning to leave? He could see the sense of it and she'd as good as said it without actually saying it. Things would continue to be a little awkward there, for a while anyway.

The tap told him Elkie was there to apologise.

"Sorry, Boss, operational decision not to say anything, I thought, think, we can trust Tilda".

"No apology necessary, I'd have done the same thing. Tilda, would she make a sergeant?"

"Does the Pope sh…"

"Yes, ok Elkie, I get it. Thanks".

"I wasn't sure who else to talk to", said Thompson, as he sat in the food court in the Victoria Centre.

"Hell fire, Dave, nothing is ever simple with you, is it?" Cliff Colman had just sat through most of the story and Thompson was waiting for advice.

"Don't mention this to Elkie, I'll talk to her myself. The thing is, it all boils down to what should I do?"

'Do you believe in kismet, Dave?"

"That green frog from the Muppets?"

"No you twat, kismet, it means fate, what will happen, will happen. Your destiny is set by the stars".

"Don't be silly, I'm a Virgo, I don't believe in that crap".

Cliff could see the silly jokes were Thompson's way of deflecting. "You've asked me for my opinion so here it is. You have a thing for this different Jenny and she sounds like she's Thompson-tolerant, not all are, so I say find a way to contact her, meet her and commit and if things work out, there is your little green frog working. If not, you tried. Now I have to vaguely like you and leave you".

Thompson thanked him for his sage advice. "Always welcome from one so old and learned", to which Cliff had retorted with industrial language. When Cliff had gone the phone was out and he texted. 'Canal, 45 minutes'. He'd made a choice.

Duncan Collins was in a very poor frame of mind, his situation made worse by the constant prodding of his underbelly by the police. He himself had been stopped six times recently, it was harassment, deliberate. "Do we know where is now?"

"Yes, on the move".

"Ok, do it then, somewhere quiet. The car's outside, you know what to do".

Normally the romantic ending has fluffy white clouds, kittens playing with a ball of wool in the background or maybe waves lapping over writhing bodies. It was absolutely pissing it down when Thompson pulled into the little parking spot for the canal, his was the only car. Undaunted he walked to the bench, their bench, not that they'd done much more than sit on it. He sat and waited, hopeful. After half-an-hour he got up and walked back, hoping maybe she'd not got the message yet for some reason.

As he reached a point where he could see his car, he noticed another car had just arrived. Two people got out and one sprinted across the road running full-pelt down the tow path towards him. Jenny. Another person was out in an instant and sprinted across the road after her, a male, but he couldn't see who. In what seemed to take an age, a large SUV hit the chaser and he span up into the air, twisting with a strange balletic grace. Jenny had kept running without looking back. Out on the road, the SUV had stopped as Thompson started to move forward, then it backed up before driving off at speed.

When Jenny reached Thompson she threw herself at him, causing both of them to go over into the path verge. She was shaking and bleeding from a cut on her cheek. One eye was closing and she was frothing blood from her mouth. "Dave, it's Ritchie", she yelled, painfully.

Thompson dragged them both up and walked her quickly to the road. Johnson was a mess lying on the road, his face compressed by a tyre mark, but Jenny didn't look away, not once. "Is he dead?"

"Sit in my car and stay there", he said, leading her over the now clear road. He opened the back door and eased her in, then he went to see whether Johnson had survived, unlikely given the mess. He hadn't. He called Perkins.

Climbing into the back of his car, Jenny was crying and looking even bloodier. "An ambulance is coming, Johnson is dead, no sign of what hit him so I'm going for a professional hit. Talk to me, if you can".

"He showed up at my place an hour ago with a gun and demanding money. He did this to me then saw your message, he guessed I'd sent the message about where he was hiding and dragged me out. He never said anything on the way. We got here and I bolted, hoping you'd still be here, that I'd reach you before he caught up with me. I know he was going to kill me, maybe you too".

"My colleagues are coming, there'll be questions, your dad might be involved. Why did he hunt you down?"

"He said he thought I'd told Collins he'd fire-bombed him. It wasn't me though, it was a girl he had in Aspley, she died in a house fire. I knew her, sort of. I don't know how he found me, I've been very careful. I'm so sorry to drag you into this, Dave. Just dump me for your own good, I'm toxic".

Lights were flashing outside as Prosser, Gecko and Carla showed up. Behind, Perkins had Josh, Lorna and Beresford with him, no uniforms yet though.

Thompson got out to make a statement, this had to be by the book. "Later, Dave", said Prosser, busy with his phone.

Perkins gave him an apologetic look before climbing into the back of the car with Jenny, Thompson just stood there dripping. He noticed Gecko looking around the car Jenny had arrived in, so he went to see what he was up to. "This is Jenny Perkins' car, I checked the registration, it's her new one". Then he put on gloves, laid on his back in the muddy parking area and started to feel around under the car. "Thought so", he said, and he handed Thompson an Apple Air tag, which he deposited in an evidence bag. Then he kept looking. "Ah ha!" he said and he pulled out another one. Thompson stood rooted to the spot, but Beresford walked over and took the bag with the tags off him, then he climbed into the back of Perkins' car.

"Been having fun, Dave?" it was Lorna looking less than glamorous in her dripping cagoule.

"Not really. How much do you know?"

"Bugger all, Prosser just took over and dragged us all out here, said you had been involved in a traffic".

"In the back of the car is Jenny Perkins, our beloved Superintendent's daughter. She was on the game, worked for Johnson but got away. Tilda

329

was supposed to intervene and get her off the game but things got complicated when the situation involved me to some extent. I arranged to meet her here to complete the rescue, but things went a bit pear-shaped when Johnson found her and found out I'd be here. He has a gun, I think that covers it. Tell nobody this until after formal interviews".

Lorna nodded, she understood why. "These books I've heard that you write, Dave. Do you have to play the lead in all of them?"

"Seems so, I should have told you all earlier, confided, it was just a bit delicate".

Uniforms and ambulances started to arrive, things got cleared up and the whole circus decamped back to Central Nick. Beresford drove Thompson's car with him in the back, while Jenny and Perkins went off to hospital. "It's not normally so high-octane is it, Sir?

"No, Simon, today was just one of those days".

Beresford seemed to go back into stand-by mode for the rest of the ride in and Thompson just concluded that it took all sorts. His phone pinged with instructions for when he got to the nick, this wasn't going to be much fun.

Thompson sat on the wrong-side of the interview table while Paul Bridger got set up, an officer he didn't know sat with him. Bridger introduced her to Thompson, but he immediately forgot her name.

"Before I start, Dave, this is just to get a witness statement over the death of Ritchie Johnson. I don't think you're implicated, but transparency in all things, as you know. What I can tell you is that your man Simon Beresford has tracked down the phones that the air tags reported to. Both are burners, but one was in Johnson's pocket, so we know how he found Ms. Perkins in the first place. The other last sent a signal to the Carlton area twenty-seven minutes before the incident and we have an idea who might be involved there. Right, you know the drill, just tell me what happened today, no need for extraneous details regarding anyone else, and the machine went on.

A couple of hours later, Thompson was back in his office, still damp but trying to work normally. The door opened and in walked Perkins, followed by Jenny. She'd looked better. "Look after her for a bit, David, I have to speak to the ACC", said Perkins, before turning and leaving.

"I was told I couldn't visit", said Thompson, by way of an explanation.

"I know, dad said, and he said we should sort things out, baggage and all".

"Somebody will have to interview you again, formally. Are you ok with that?"

"I know, dad said. I'm feeling a bit woozy, they gave me some strong pain killers but I'm ready. Any idea who will do it?"

"No, I suspect straws are being drawn by whoever is available for the privilege. They don't know who you are, but you're possibly a suspect, and connected to me, that's what's making them nervous".

Despite her bruises and light-headedness, Jenny laughed. "Maybe instead of scaring them with Perkins, I should use my registered business name. Can I do that?"

"Please tell me it's not Madam Fifi or something worse".

"No, professionally I'm Jenny Rogers, that's why you've never been able to find my Only Fans site, Detective Inspector".

Thompson blustered that he'd never tried and never wanted to, but Jenny was laughing again although her jaw was aching. "Calm down, ask someone if I can use my work name".

Thompson thought for a moment, then picked up the phone. "Jock, sorry to bother you, can I ask something?" and he asked and listened, before hanging up. "He says yes, but your real name has to go on the statement too, but you can do that at the end, that way no hint of bias can be suggested".

Outside Thompson's office a debate was happening, quietly. Lorna was pulling rank, in that she considered herself lower than Banks so not in-line for the responsibility. Elkie said they'd draw straws.

Thompson really needed time to process everything, but he knew it wasn't available because today might be the day that shaped the rest of his life. This was it, a second chance, take it or lose it, he made a decision. "How big is your place, a flat in Carlton, right?"

"Two bedrooms, usual facilities, red light outside and customer parking. I own it now. Why?"

"Have your entertained there?"

"No, I was only joking about the red light and the parking, it's my home. I had a workroom for the Only Fans, but I've not been very active there recently, it's more of an office now. I'll be losing subscriptions but I don't care, I've been doing some software development work too, gaming stuff. I just got my first formal contract".

"What happens if I were to move in? Obviously I've got the odd loose end to tie up, my place to sell and everything but, all the same".

"Do you think you might?"

"If invited but, be careful, you do know what you're getting". The lightest of knocks told Thompson they'd decided who was doing the formal interview but, from the tenor of the knock, he wasn't sure who, then Jenny Banks walked in. "Boss, we need to interview Ms., er ?"

"Rogers, pleased to meet you although we have already met".

Banks was struggling for the right words before she'd drawn the short straw, now she was completely lost for words so she went with a grunt.

"It was in a café a little while ago. I'd left my phone on a table, it was under this gentleman's dirty magazine. You were there with him when I remembered and came back for it. I assumed you were lovers from the way you kissed him".

A light went on in Banks' head, along with a certain amount of discomfort. "Right, I remember now. It was a football magazine, wasn't it, Boss?"

"Yes, Four-Four-Two. Jenny, can you take Ms. Rogers and interview her regarding the incident with Ritchie Johnson, please".

"Are you observing, Boss?"

"Not without a subscription, he isn't", laughed Jenny Rogers.

"She's a bit woozy from medication but says she's ok. No, I won't be observing, I'm a witness too, remember, but expect attention from above".

"From above? What, God?" laughed Jenny Rogers.

"Sounds about right", said Banks. "Come on then, Ms. Rogers, come and tell me all about it".

In the interview room, Jenny Rogers accepted the offer of coffee and went through the sequence of events for the tape, from Ritchie Johnson accosting her at her flat and hitting her, to him seeing the phone message to meet, sent by Thompson. As a jealous and dangerous ex-boyfriend, he'd been furious and had intended her and Thompson harm.

"Rogers isn't my real name, I adopted a business name, I write games software. I was hoping that it would make it harder for Johnson to find me, after I dumped him."

Jenny and Elkie listened sympathetically, but Jenny hadn't had the chance to tell her everything and they still hadn't made the Thompson connection, assuming Jenny Rogers was a contact offering information in the Johnson case, hence the canal meet.

"Will Dave be in trouble?" asked Jenny Rogers.

"No, but we have to do an investigation and you two chatting before this formal interview might raise eyebrows, but since our Superintendent seems to know all about it, we're not worried. I think that's all we need, Ms. Rogers. Finally, for the tape, can you please give me your real name?"

"Yes, of course, my real name is Jennifer Sarah Perkins", then she watched Banks go slowly pale.

The door opened and Superintendent Perkins walked in. "Sensitively-done, Detective Sergeant, my thanks. I'll take care of Jenny now, if you have no objections".

"No, Sir. Thank you, Sir".

In Perkins' office, Jenny was watching the little diver in the fish tank go up and down as she waited for her dad, he came back with food and drinks in hand. "Sorry, love, bits and pieces to tie up. Here, I thought you might be hungry, how are you now?"

"Aching, the drugs are wearing off. Are they all shit-scared of you?"

"Some are, but those in that particular team are made in the image of their leader and they have a rebellious, independent streak, I encourage it".

"I see, what now?"

"I'm sorry, what do you mean?"

"Do I get yet another lecture about my life choices over civilised coffee and sandwiches? You must have a good few years of disapproval stored up and ready for release".

"No, Jenny, nothing like that. I'm just glad I'm not seeing you on a slab, my greatest ever fear. I freely admit that that that would have done for me, finish me. Can I ask, and of course it is your business and your business alone, what about David Thompson?"

"Will he lose his job if his image deviates from his leaders'?"

"When I said his team are made in the image of their leader, I meant him, not me. I just facilitate and have done so for a while now. No, he won't lose his job but, putting it in plain language, a living on immoral earnings charge in the future would change that situation".

"Then don't worry dad, he's moving in".

Behind Perkins the little diver went up and down, up and down. He watched it intently until the tears had stopped. "I'll leave you to get on then, I'm sure you're very busy, I know I am". Perkins didn't turn to look at his battered and bruised daughter as she left the room.

In the cafeteria Thompson was sipping coffee on his own, Tilda slipped in next to him. "Ok Boss, all's well that ends well. Jenny is in with Perkins, Jenny Banks has gone all a bit less assured, I quite like it, and the rest of us are gossiping wildly. Only a couple of us know what's really going on and the true nature of the situation will remain untold. You know I can keep my mouth shut, Gecko too".

"Thanks, Tilda, I appreciate it, but it will get out, these things do, not that I care. How did the interview go?"

"Great, the whole story came out, mostly, but nothing before Johnson accosted her. They still think Jenny is a contact of yours, not a girlfriend.

I'll leave that one to you but I suggest you get her to go back to using Perkins".

"Perkins, surely that has more stigma than Rogers around here?"

"Oh, Dave and you're one of our sharpest minds. 'Jenny Rogers', think about it".

Thompson did think about it, then he started to laugh.

Back in his own office, Thompson found Jenny waiting for him. "I was going to come looking for you", he said.

"You'll need this, then", and she popped a slip of paper in his top pocket. "My address", said his Jenny. He told her he had lots to do, she kissed him and said she'd see him when he got home. She slipped out of the office and Thompson followed her out, watching her go.

"Right", said Thompson, clapping his hands together. "Team meeting in twenty, situation update and sod off with the Charnley thing, that ends now. Josh, coffee and cakes please, on me".

In twenty minutes, the gathered masses were busy drinking their drinks and eating their eats. The room went quiet as Thompson walked back in, he instantly got everyone's attention. Just as he filled his lungs to deliver, Perkins appeared ominously in his regular spot. Slightly disconcerted, he made a start. "Most of you only have bits and pieces of the story, so I will tell you the version that you will take as gospel and then we are done. Jenny Perkins' statement is on file for you all to read, the blanks that require filling are that we are an item and have been for a few weeks. Very sadly, my relationship with Rebecca ended by mutual consent, we just became different people and were adult enough to recognise it. We remain friends and I will continue to be active as a father and friend. Jenny Perkins and I are at the beginning of our relationship, the past is the past. There will be a full, official brief on the Johnson case in thirty minutes, if you would, Jenny".

Banks was a bit rabbit-in-the-headlights at the news, but nodded 'yes'.

"Thanks and back to work, then. Elkie, a word in the office after".

"If I might, Detective Inspector", and Perkins stepped forward. "Excellent work across the board recently, even though the odd bump was required to be negotiated", and he looked at Prosser. "I have been taking stock of my situation and have decided it is time for me to embrace the freedom of retirement. Work has been ongoing to seek out a replacement, someone capable of delivering the sort of shock and awe in my officers that I have been responsible for over the years, this is where you laugh". A titter went around the room. "I'd just like to thank you all, personally, for your efforts in keeping the good and the great of Nottinghamshire secure in their beds. Good day to you", and he marched out.

Thompson went off to his office and the team hubbub got cracking on digesting the cake and debating the latest news. Elkie closed the door and sat.

"I know you find yourself between two stools here, but what I said about Rebecca and me is true. We've talked quite a lot, more even than when we were living in the same place, we're good with things. I hope you are?"

"You know I am. I'm just sad about it all but this new girlfriend, isn't it the 'fire and frying pan thing' again? And what about our Jenny. Did she know?"

"Not the full story, and she won't, but I feel I owe details to you, as a friend. If you don't want to know, say so and I'll shut up".

"I know that Perkins lost a daughter and, in part thanks to you, he has her back and she's with somebody he respects. Is there anything in the narrative that changes that, fundamentally?"

"No, I suppose not, but there are details which may or may not get out, things you might not approve of, details that some already know".

"It's not for me to judge, Dave, and I won't. I hope this Jenny works out for you".

Thompson had missed the ping on his phone but not by long. 'I decided to pop into our café and wait for you, it seems the right thing to do'. It was his Jenny.

It would have been quicker to walk to the coffee shop, but Thompson wanted the car to be nearer, so he drove and found a street parking spot. In the café he could see Jenny reading a magazine, he smiled when he saw it was Viz. "Just catching up on the adventures of Buster Gonads, glad I never met him professionally", she said, noticing him. She kissed him and not just a peck. Thompson sat down smartly.

"How is this going to work, the nuts and bolts?" asked Thompson.

"I don't know, didn't you have a Meccano when you were a kid? I suppose we'll just fasten bits together until we've made something. My past, if you want details I'm willing to risk it, you know, the body count".

"I'd be lying if I said I hadn't thought about it, but I won't ask you yours and you don't ask about mine, in case I win, I am from Clifton after all. Your on-line stuff, I don't think I can be associated with that and, yes, I know what you do".

"I asked dad, not because I intend to carry on but because I don't want your career biting the dust. I'm the new Jenny Perkins, Jenny Rogers is history, even at the risk of hundreds of fans being utterly distraught".

"Hundreds?"

"Many hundreds. It got me away from Johnson and allowed me to step off the slippery slope. I don't regret it, I don't regret where it's taken me".

"You might change your mind when I tell you everything, including about Jenny Banks. I didn't realise you saw the kiss".

"Shall we go home and talk about it all then, and I won't be changing my mind. You do know dad might hug you for rescuing me from a life of sin?"

"Rescuing? A bit strong, besides, I was hoping there'd still be a bit of sin in your life, just not with anyone else. As for the other thing, life is all about risks, I'll take my chances".

It was early evening when Thompson's phone rang. "Sorry, I've got to take this".

"Copper's daughter, remember? We'll eat when you get back".

Natasha Ellis was sat in the dentist's reception waiting for a check-up and clean. She was idly leafing through the latest glossy piece of shit looking at the lives of 'stars' she'd never heard of, them getting paid for passing on their diet tips and how to have more orgasms. Towards the back of the magazine she came across a piece about a footballer, a Nottingham boy, and his current girlfriend. She flicked through, mildly interested until she went white. There, around the neck of the heavily made-up woman, was the same necklace currently hanging around her own neck. She'd decided that she quite liked it after she'd pronounced that it was fake, Scott had been pleased to gift it to her. She searched the article for a valuation, but none was given, it just said it was a heirloom. Looking at the couple she reckoned the only heirlooms this pair might be involved in was a dose of crabs, she texted Scott. 'I just saw a photo of the necklace on the original owner. What do we do?'

'Give it back I suppose. Explain the finding, call that young detective. I found more than treasure that day'. Her laugh out loud made the others awaiting dentistry look her way, he was so full of shit that boy but why was he always so laid back as to be horizontal? Something about the whole necklace story wasn't sitting right with her but there was no way that she was getting involved. Maybe Scott was right, maybe she should talk to Carla, test the water. She nicked the magazine, figuring they wouldn't miss it.

"Ooh, I like your necklace", said the dental hygienist. "It looks really familiar, did you get it from Vic Centre?"

"Yes, Chisholm Hunters, a gift from my new boyfriend. Not expensive but I like it".

"I can see why, now sit very still while I just…"

"Natasha, I was surprised to get your call, what can I do for you?" Carla Adams was stood on the doorstep, in what could best be described as a party dress. Next door the curtain twitcher was active again, it was an occupational hazard for the police. Natasha gave her a look. "Sorry, out ballroom dancing later, it's not all about fitting up minorities and banging them to rights in the police these days".

"Come in, please. I put the dog away, there's someone I want you to meet". Carla followed her into the still doggy-smelling house. On the sofa, a guy was sat, casually sipping from a cup. "This is Scott, Scott Westbury, my boyfriend. Scott?"

"Hello Carla. I found something on the park and I think you might be looking for it. I was fishing a couple of days ago and hooked this. It was caked in mud so I put it in a bowl of soapy water for a while and when I cleaned it up, I could see that it was a necklace, then Natasha read this", and he held up the magazine recently liberated from the dentists. "We saw the photo of the girl with the missing necklace. It looks very similar but I'm not sure. It said Notts police were involved, so we called you".

Carla knew a pile of made-up gibberish when she heard it. "Can I see it then?"

Natasha opened a sideboard drawer and passed over the missing necklace. Carla examined it, before deftly popping it into an evidence bag and then into her glittery clutch bag. Then she looked at Scott for a while, letting him know she saw him, and that a bit of the story needed work. "Ok, thanks. I'll need a formal statement from you later, Scott, no ifs or buts. I'll just take your details now. Oh, and thanks, Natasha, you did the right thing calling me".

They both seemed relieved. "I'm just glad the lass will get her necklace back. I reckon it's just cheap paste but, out of interest, what's it worth?"

Carla had expected the question and she was fairly certain that, had they not seen the photo, they'd have kept the necklace, in ignorance. "Eleven million pounds, give or take", she said and she pulled her phone out.

A high pitched noise came from both Scott and Natasha.

"Dale, it's me, Carla. Can you sit with me while I drive into work, please, just as a favour?" Then she called Thompson, explained what had happened and that she was bringing the piece in and to call Beresford. "Don't worry, I'll have security". Thompson didn't ask what type of security, but made an educated guess.

"Thanks, Dale, I wouldn't normally ask you for this but I needed your protection and I can also use this as a demonstration of my faith in you".

"No problem, Carla, you saved me a taxi fare, but what are you talking about?"

"I just recovered a piece of missing jewellery, an expensive piece. I didn't want to chance getting mugged, so here you are, my chaperone".

Brown wasn't any clearer in understanding what Carla was up to, he just said he was happy to help. She dropped him well before the nick before heading to the parking garage, it wasn't his favourite place. Taking a deep breath, she strolled into the department. At the back of her mind 'eleven million pounds' worth of jewellery casually sitting in her little bag seemed to be screaming for attention.

Thompson followed her in, Beresford arrived by taxi. Perkins was already waiting in Thompson's office. Easing on latex gloves, they waited to see the piece. "I wouldn't bother with the gloves, it's been in soaked in soapy water for days and handled by Ellis and Westbury, they scrubbed it clean. I only used an evidence bag for effect", and she plonked the necklace down on Thompson's desk.

They all looked at it a while, the impression was that it might explode. Carla recounted the version of the discovery that Westbury had furnished, without saying she thought it was mostly bullshit.

"Simon, please take a look, your expert opinion is required", said Perkins, as entranced as anyone.

"Not an expert, Sir, but an enthusiastic amateur", and Beresford picked up the necklace, turning it over a few times. Extracting it from the bag, he produced, from somewhere, a little thirty-times magnification hand lens with a built-in light. After a few minutes of perfect silence while he examined the piece, he went "hmmm. I need a container of water large enough to hold the piece, a few inches deep minimum".

Thompson looked at Perkins who nodded. "This way, if you please", he said. A conga line of police officers followed Perkins to his office. They arrived just as his toy diver had recently surfaced and was now drifting back sedately to the bottom of the tank. Perkins opened a flap in the lid. "Proceed".

Beresford eased the necklace into the water and let go. It didn't drop like a brick, instead falling at a rate even slower than the diver had managed. "One for our friends in Serious Fraud, I think", said Perkins, hooking the necklace out with his little net and dropping it back into the evidence bag. "I'll put this somewhere safe".

"What just happened?" asked Carla, entertained by events but not a little confused.

"All the gems in this are paste, real diamonds sink to the bottom much quicker", said Beresford. "Sorry, I thought that was common knowledge. It also explains how the Trent current carried it so far, instead of burying it on the bottom somewhere".

Perkins clasped his hands together. "Right, very good, back to your respective homes and activities, whatever they may be. Lovely dress, Carla, enjoy your ballroom dancing. Excellent work, Simon, please write up a short note for your DI to include in his report, you too, DC Adams. If there's nothing else that requires my attention then I must away to a curry house on Mansfield Road to meet a friend".

Thirty-nine

27 September 2017

Thompson awoke to a familiar scent but the curtains were a mystery. A part of him was asking whether this was real. Breakfast contained a lot of fruit and muesli, but he ate it without complaint or making gerbil comments. His Forest away shirt from the Championship winning season had never looked better.

The drive in was different, but ok. Jenny said she had some tidying-up to do without specifying what she was tidying. They were going out later to buy office furniture for each of them, the spare bedroom was going to be their joint office and she'd promised to give it a good going over with the 'Shake and Vac'. On his phone was a new photo of Guy. Rebecca had promised that he would see his boy growing and that she'd try to send a photo at least once a week. Pete Wheeler had also been in touch, all done and dusted, thanks for your custom. He'd have to sort something out there.

He casually flipped the radio on, they were playing 'Lady Marmalade' the original version by Patti LaBelle, he laughed and let it play. Before leaving the parking garage, he arranged for a large box of Thornton's chocolates to be sent to Wheeler for his lads, then, on a whim, he added a small but tasteful bunch of flowers for Deborah alone. Now for the fun.

The day after the day before had everyone in the team walking on eggshells around Thompson. He was aware, but decided that things would eventually settle and soon enough normality would resume. Josh had brought him a coffee with a big question mark on it. Lorna had given him the sort of look that you give someone who'd discovered they'd left their winning lottery ticket in the pocket of their jeans and they'd just come out the washer, and Tilda had tried to hug him, unsuccessfully.

The light on his phone had stayed resolutely off and that worried him more than anything. It was nearing lunchtime when people plucked up the courage to interact, he'd actually enjoyed the peace of the morning. His office door that he'd been deliberately keeping closed, opened. "Dave, can I have a word?" It was Jenny Banks, who had what you might call her bounce back.

"Come in, anytime for Jenny, you know that".

Jenny sat and waited while Thompson shifted new bits of paper. "What can I do for you?"

"I want to transfer to London, I've got an interview and I'm asking for a reference. Terry, the bloke I met on the course, we're a thing now but I'm worried about you. You're seeing another Jenny and I'm concerned you might just be rebounding, I don't want to see you hurt, again". It was lengthy statement made up of many strands that needed unpicking.

"Ok, first the move. Get the job, put your notice in and I'll write you a reference. I'd never stand in the way of the ambitious. Terry, pleased for you, I hope you're happy and this relationship doesn't go tits-up, too. My Jenny, she went a bit wayward but we seem a good match, she just happens to be called Jenny. No matter what you think, I'm not a serial shagger of Jennies. I appreciate the concern but I'm fine, you're fine, everything is fine".

Thompson's answers, some of them, took the wind out of her sails and she felt a bit stupid now, he saw her discomfort. "It took a real friend to ask about this though, and I appreciate it".

"Ok. Good, we've all been talking along the same lines. Expect Elkie next, then maybe Carla and I think Lorna might chip in too. Prosser might want to hug you and Josh has a cup already made for you with 'I love Jennies' on it, the little bastard. I think Marie's lot are baffled".

"My lot, Jenny, my lot". Banks smiled and walked over to him until she was very close. "Did I ever tell you that you were a nice, gentle shagger? I liked that", and she caressed his cheek. Thompson started to blush, she then blew gently in his ear. He wasn't sure what the hell was going on, then Banks yelled "Yes, still got it, we have a T-Bone situation", a cheer came from outside. Thompson gave it five before answering the inevitable, a summons from above. He didn't die, he just went to see Perkins.

"David, Jenny has been in touch and filled me in on the details of, well, things. I won't pretend I'm not happy that events have worked out the way they have, I hoped, naturally, but I assure you I exerted no undue influence upon you. In fact I was at great pains to be sure to try to warn you off. Gecko passed messages, hurdles were placed. I know you will be good together, despite everything, she's a good girl".

"Leroy. Sorry, that name just doesn't sit right with me, Sir. If I thought for a moment that there had been any 'guidance' from anywhere pushing us together, Jenny and I would not be where we are now and she feels the same, we've talked. As for past lives, who is truly without sin?"

"In private I go by the name of Roy, or Chalky, David. Few use Roy but you may do so, outside of work as it will be soon. Now you'll have to excuse me, I have people to see but, David, honestly, thanks". Before him, Thompson could see an approving dad. That it was his boss too and a man he'd been indoctrinated to distrust was irrelevant. He was a dad first and Thompson respected that.

"One thing about this has bothered me though, Sir, perhaps you can clarify. Gecko procured a list of hostesses associated with Johnson and Jenny wasn't on it, any idea why?"

"My bad there, David. He gave it to me in handwritten form and you know Gecko. Sadly his recent injury did nothing for his legibility. Then, in my haste to furnish you with said list, I inadvertently mis-transcribed a few of the names when I typed it up. Not deliberate, I assure you". Perkins then went back to his paperwork so Thompson left.

When he got back to his office he was greeted by a waiting Tilda.

"Do you have a minute, Sir?" He invited her in. "Jenny just told me about her move, impending or otherwise, so I thought it was time you saw this. As I said before, I'd like to apply for her job", and she handed over a folder, not at all dissimilar to the one now residing in Thompson's desk drawer.

He opened the folder, taking in salient details, again. "I see, well you are qualified, I see you passed the exam with flying colours. Why didn't you apply elsewhere when a post came up?"

"I hadn't finished my job".

"Have you now? I don't want a sergeant who works for more than one boss, like it or not".

"All done, Sir. I just hope we get a decent replacement for Superintendent Perkins though, it can make or break a team and there are a few dickheads out there that I wouldn't want to serve under". Thompson knew what she meant. Names were already being bandied about after Perkins' little speech, he was apprehensive himself. He waited. "Was there something else, Sir?"

"I was wondering what part you really played in the events between Jenny, and me?"

Tilda admitted that she'd tried to keep an eye on Jenny and then relayed the conversation they'd had regarding him, when she'd not given his name or work location to Jenny, despite her asking. Her focus had always been to get Jenny Perkins away from her chosen life. She hadn't known they'd been seeing each other until Johnson had died, but hadn't ruled it out. Thompson had decided that, if she'd even hinted at playing a part in what went before with Jenny, she'd have been out the door, but she didn't and Thompson could see from her record that Tilda Jeffries would be a catch. "Thanks Tilda. I'll put your name forward, good luck. Oh and this, I forgot to ask you. My Rebecca, as was, was involved in a school reunion or something and she wanted to trace a class mate, she sent me this", and he passed over a print of the old photo.

Tilda looked at the photo. "That Rebecca was your Rebecca, really? What a small world it is, Sir. I won't be going to any reunion though, I was a fish out of water at that school, I hated it and they weren't slow to let me know where my place was. Why did they think you'd be able to find me? Rebecca must have known you wouldn't use the system".

"They said you'd perhaps have been of interest to Gecko and his former department at some point, looks like your cover story was better than you thought". Thompson tried at first to read Tilda's damaged face, but then decided he didn't want to.

A group message told him the time that they were all to expected be present, the time at which they would say goodbye and good luck to Superintendent Perkins. Thompson checked his watch, if he got a wiggle on he'd be back in plenty of time. "Simon, with me".

The chance for a drive had appealed and Thompson was quite interested to meet Lemmy Dowie. He might play for Leicester, but he also played for the Three Lions too and that mattered. He was less pleased to have Simon Beresford sat next to him but needs must. There was no rapport there and Thompson's attempts to engage Beresford in conversation had fallen flat. He was only taking him because Perkins had made it a condition of Thompson himself going.

"Hello again, Dave isn't it and this is?" Shania-Marie had met them outside, she'd been gardening by the gate when they'd been let in.

"Hello, this is DC Simon Beresford. Promise me no gymnastics today, Shania-Marie, I nearly put my back out last time".

She laughed out loud and had a twinkle in her eye. "Spur of the moment but your face, how did you keep it straight?"

"While I was admiring the view I was reminded of my boss, who can be a bit of one". She laughed again while Beresford appeared to be confused, not getting the base reference.

"Come on up, we're in a bit of a state, the designers are doing their thing in there, just ignore them".

Inside the house, people were busy. For one horrific moment Thompson thought he might bump into Rebecca with a tape measure and an iPad in hand, and his baby in her belly, but he didn't. Lemmy Dowie appeared in a track suit, initially he seemed subdued but he perked up a bit when the talking started and any mention of football was seized on.

"Go on then, Dave, who do you support, black and white or the Garibaldi?"

"Been a Red all my life, always will be and got the tattoo to prove it. Beresford looked shocked.

"I'll show you mine if you show me yours", and Lemmy took his tracksuit top off, covering a tattoo on the top of his arm with his hand. "Come on, it's only a laugh". Thompson slipped his jacket off and eased his shirt over, covering his tat the same. "One, two, three" and they did the big reveal, they had almost identical tattoos. The atmosphere relaxed.

"If you're here, a Detective Inspector, that means bad news, right?"

"Yes, Lemmy. We recovered the necklace, but it's a fake, the jewels are paste. This is Simon, he's our arts and treasures expert. Simon".

Beresford slipped into Antiques Roadshow mode seamlessly, explaining the history of the jewels to blank faces and explaining why it was paste but making the point that, while the jewels were fake, it was a very good fake. Thompson was quietly amazed, it was as if he'd been switched on at the mains. Once the information had been relayed, Beresford went back into sleep mode.

"We think that there is a scam going on and your agent and others are involved. Serious Fraud have the case now, and the necklace too, but you'll get it back when they're done. Sorry to be the bearer of bad news, Lemmy. I was told to ask after Cherise Belanger?"

"History", said Lemmy. "I changed my personal management team because I can, I'm not stupid. The necklace was probably a rip off from the start, an insurance scam or something by Cherise. She found it, had it valued and everything, I'd bet she was waiting for the eleven mill to hit the account before legging it. I'll answer any questions I can from the fraud boys but good luck finding Cherise though. The necklace, who found it? I'd like it back after, it still looks good in the right setting". It was hard to tell but Shania-Marie was possibly blushing.

Thompson explained about the guy fishing, where Natasha lived, how she'd seen the photo in a magazine after their interview and had called them straight away. Lemmy listened intently.

"Decent, very decent. I know Candle Meadow and the park, I used to play Sunday football on the racecourse, cut my footballing teeth there. These people, they get the reward then".

Thompson was confused. "Reward?"

"I decided to give a reward to the finder, if they deserved it. I didn't make it public nor nothing because there'd be all sorts of chancers talking bollocks. Can I give you the cheque and leave it to you? Just don't broadcast it, a strict condition of the reward". Dowie vanished for a couple of minutes before returning with a cheque book and handing it to Shania-Marie. "Who to?" This was outside Thompson's experience.

"Er, Natasha Ellis. Lemmy, you do know you've been done for eleven million quid?"

"Yeah? Oh well, crying won't change that now, will it? The rest was insured so we'll get a bit back. Anyway, I've got more important things to think about now".

"The World Cup?"

"Yeah, that too, but me and Shania-Marie are having a baby and it isn't going to go hungry with them baps to feed on, is it?"

Shania-Marie blushed again, possibly and yelled "Lemmy, really, what are you like?" Then she wrote out the cheque, folded it and gave it to Thompson.

Shania-Marie walked them out to the car and Thompson congratulated her again but hoped she wouldn't ask if he had kids. Lemmy had gone off somewhere to run on a machine. "Tell me, Mr. Detective, what else did you notice?"

"Two things, he's obviously improved on his box play and you can't sign a cheque if your name's not on the account".

Shania-Marie roared her dirty laugh again. "Clever bugger. Thanks for coming, he'll be happy as a pig in shit giving that finder a few quid, and he's always happy to meet another Forest fan. His team mates take the piss over the tattoo, but he doesn't care. He wants to wear the red shirt one day, wouldn't that be something?"

"If we ever crawl out of the Championship with enough cash to sign him, it really would be something. I might even go back to having a season ticket for that".

On the way home, Beresford suddenly reanimated, there really was no other way to put it. "I see what you did, you befriended the people first to make the news more personal, you bonded. Right, got it". Thompson remembered the cheque and pulled it out, opening it up with one hand. He nearly left the road when he saw how much.

As leaving dos go it wasn't wild, in fact the leaver was only there for half-an-hour, it was the fourth such 'drink' he'd attended in his honour. People were always awkward around Perkins and he could see it but he played his part, as he had ever since Thompson had known him.

"Retirement or some cushy security advisor job, Sir?"

"I'm done, David, you know as well as most what this job has cost me. I only hope it was worth it and I made a difference. I'll miss our chats, at work at least, I do hope you two won't be strangers".

"We won't, besides, you can't have enough mentors when you're scrabbling up that slippery pole".

"To be honest, I wouldn't bother if I was you, but I won't try to sway you, I do pity you though. Collins might be still out there but probably not for long and you'll have a power vacuum. There'll be plenty trying to fill it and all the mess that entails. Good luck with that".

"We'll manage, we always do. Well, best of luck, Sir", and Thompson offered a hand which Perkins shook gently. The party carried on, despite the guest of honour having gone. Cases had been solved and, sure, there was the new and expanding mountain of paperwork to scale and work to finish up, but that would do later, then there was the issue of who would follow Superintendent Perkins. Big shoes to fill.

Thompson was having a laugh with Elkie about something and nothing. He'd looked for Jenny Banks but was told that she'd excused herself after giving Perkins an unexpected peck on the cheek, probably deliberately leaving lipstick. He presumed Terry awaited, somewhere.

Ranjit came in, making a bee-line for Thompson. "Dave, just thought I'd drop by to see how things went here. I know you've been a bit apprehensive about your new Superintendent but good news, wait no more". Thompson looked past Elkie and Ranjit as someone with a walking stick came hobbling through the door.

"Dave, meet Marie Burns, your new Super".

"Dave, how's that shit lot in Garibaldi doing, still got a striker than couldn't hit a barn door? Anyone going to get a lady a drink? Liam, you rough old paddy, how's it hanging? Elkie, triplets or have you been eating all the pies? Josh, can someone wrap him up for me, I'll devour him later. Carla, if I had a vagina I'd bang you myself. Oh, hang on..."

Thompson took Sham to one side. "I've never seen her like this before, what gives?"

"This is the real Fiery Marie Burns, you're hers now and she'll look after you but it won't be comfortable or fluffy. Expect worse than this, or better, it depends on your point of view but give as good as you get and you'll be fine, she loves it".

"Come on Thompson, show us this famous cock of yours, or have all the girls here already had the T-Bone experience?"

"Marie, oh shit, please tell me it's not you. Still got piss-flaps like John Wayne's saddlebags?"

The room suddenly went deathly silent and Thompson was about to splutter an apology when Marie started laughing like a train. "I said he was alright this one, despite the shit football team". The room relaxed, relieved. Thompson's phone pinged, he read the message.

"Liam, with me. Sorry Marie, duty calls..."

"Hello, Carla, I didn't expect to see you again. I'm still not signing any statement, if that's what you're after".

"No, Natasha, how's it going with Scott?"

"Great, it's going great. So, why are you here?"

"I came to bring you your finder's reward for returning the necklace".

"Really, what reward? I don't remember any reward being mentioned".

Behind her Scott had appeared and was looking over her shoulder. "Hello, Carla, nice to see you again".

This reward is on the strict condition that it is not made public or you lose it. The footballer and his partner just wanted to show that they appreciate your honesty in returning their necklace", and Carla reached into her bag and handed over the folded cheque.

Natasha opened it and started making little whimpering noises, Scott just said "Nice. For real?"

"Yup".

Pardon?

Because I now live in Canada, a proportion of my writing has to be understood by Canadians, however, the Thompson books are pure Nottingham and with that come all the quirks associated with dialect and social reference. Where I can, I'll explain here what some words mean and also explain, again if I can, some of the references used. By and large much in the book is self-explanatory, but I appreciate that some readers will not want to read a manky book, they'll just get mardy about it and get a monk on later. The Thompson books are also written in English so none of that 'gray' malarkey and lots of extra L's and U's, not to mention barely a frickin' Z (pronounced 'zed', not 'zee').

ANGEL DELIGHT: Staple food of many children in England.

BAPS: Breasts, there are many such words out there.

BENDER: slang for homosexual.

BOGS: means toilets. A more polite version is LOOS.

BOLLOCKS: Items associated with the male gender unless they're eunuchs.

CAGOULE: a thin, packable waterproof coat that can make the wearer look a bit of a tit.

CARRY ON SUPER: Refers to a series of bawdy UK comedy films which might not get past political correctness nowadays.

CLARKSON: refers to Jeremy Clarkson, presenter of Top Gear and self-confessed Petrol-head.

COB: A circular bread roll that, if soft, is also called a BAP, I know!

COCK: A male bird, often a chicken.

'CRACKING ONE OFF' is another term for self-satisfaction, at least for males.

DICKHEAD: A silly person.

DIY: Do It Yourself in reference to home renovation work.

EASTENDERS: a soap, set in London.

FANNY: in the UK, refers to a woman's front bottom, not her bum.

GARIBALDI: A nickname for the mighty and much-beloved Nottingham Forest, due to the red colour of their shirts.

HAZARDS: on a car these are the four-way flashers.

IN SPATE: Not in the North American lexicon, according to Microsoft Word. Means flood but perhaps with menace.

KNACKERED: Tired, exhausted.

MANKY: Broken, not quite right.

MARDY: Not happy about something, sulky.

MONK ON: Angry at someone over something they did.

MRS. TWEEDY: a lead character in the excellent 'Chicken Run' animated movie. If you haven't seen it, your life is immeasurably poorer.

NICE: a type of cheap biscuit, flavoured with coconut. HOBNOBS are more for royalty.

OFF-LICENCE: a liquor store

PAXO: a ready-made stuffing for chicken (cooked ones).

POET'S DAY: Piss Off Early, Tomorrow's Saturday.

PONCY: A bit on the soft side, possibly with ideas above their station.

ROEDEAN: an expensive, private and very posh school for girls. Not a place for the average Clifton girl.

SCALLY: A lower class person of nefarious outlook and actions. Ooh, hark at him!

SCROTE: A scumbag, lowlife, abbreviation of the word 'scrotum'.

SILLY SODS: People who are victims, such as poor sods.

SPROG: A child. TO SPROG: to give birth.

STAIR RODS: metaphor for rain.

THE SUN: a publication that purports to be a newspaper, one that decent-minded folk avoid.

THE SWEENEY: a TV show from the 70's, about hard-drinking, rough-house London coppers working for the Flying Squad of the Metropolitan Police. Often repeated, even today. The name comes from Cockney rhyming slang-Sweeney Todd –Flying Squad. The main character is DI JACK REGAN.

TOP: to 'top' someone is to kill them.

TOTTY: An attractive female.

TWAT: Unflattering expression that somebody might be a vagina, or an idiot – I don't know why that one is in use in that context, but it is and I won't be a twat about it.

TWOCCER: A car thief. Taking Without Consent messed about with.

WELLIES: rubber boots, as invented by the Duke of Wellington so his feet didn't have to have direct contact with France.

WORZEL: relates to a character from UK children's TV called 'Worzel Gummidge', look it up.

YOB, a nasty, disruptive youth with no class. Actually 'boy' backwards.

Meet the Author

Mark Dennis is a native son of Nottingham; indeed he is 'Clifton Made', having been brought up on the erstwhile 'biggest Council Estate in Europe' during the 60's and 70's. Having escaped from Clifton, he shares a similar opinion of the place as his hero, Dave Thompson. He also shares with him a lifelong allegiance to the Garibaldi heroes, the Tricky Trees, otherwise known as Nottingham Forest Football Club-being based in Canada makes no difference to someone who proudly remembers the European Cup double.

In a varied career he has worked in a fabric warehouse, for a number of supermarkets, been a council vehicle mechanic and, for 15 years, a warden at Colwick Country Park. He is an avid birder and naturalist, never happier when out-of-doors and scanning the bushes, an interest that was first fostered during childhood rambles in the countryside around Clifton (escaping even back then!) and since fed and nurtured by birding at home and abroad.

In 2003 he and his wife, Sandra, emigrated to Canada, settling in Montreal, Quebec, where he made serious efforts to see all of his new country's birds. In 2015, they upped sticks again, to a new home by the sea in Nova Scotia. New birds, new places, and the spare time to get his creative juices flowing resulted in the publication of 29 books, to date-11 novels. 4 birding memoirs, 2 site guides and 12 birding travelogues (the latter co-authored with Sandra). Spending hours behind a keyboard might seem counter-intuitive for a birder, but he sits right in front of a picture window with an excellent view of the feeders and the binoculars are always ready for scans of the yard-that yard list won't build itself.

For more on Mark's books and birds:

https://markdennisbooks.wordpress.com

https://capesablebirding.wordpress.com

Fiction by Mark Dennis

The D.I. Thompson Nottingham Mystery Series

Coldhearted

Laboratories are safe, or so you'd think. Not this one, not for Marie-Eve Legault. Is her death a crime of passion, a revenge attack or has the 'mafia' come to call? Can DS Thompson unravel the mystery whilst dealing with a nutty boss, a pregnant girlfriend and an overwhelming desire to write a best seller?

On The Fly

There is more to becoming DI than being a good cop, which is why Dave Thompson finds he had more than enough tidying up to do when his old boss retires. When a body is discovered on a local nature reserve, is it just the tip of a particularly murky iceberg? This is where Thompson will earn his real DI's spurs.

Spiked

Dave Thompson is feeling the strain. At home he feels cramped, at work he feels put upon, in his head he's struggling to decide what is right and what is wrong in his life and his work-load keeps getting heavier.

When a sports teacher at the private Whitaker School for Boys is found dead, and in rather grizzly circumstances, he gets the case and it turns out to be a pretty tangled web of lies, deceit and intrigue. Things about the case might appear a little complicated, but Thompson is a thinker and, given time, he will get there.

The Howey Cross Nova Scotia Birder Mystery Series

The Frigatebird

When a notorious birder is found dead in Nova Scotia, the list of suspects is already available on-line, if you know where to look. Sergeant Howey Cross has to juggle an expanding caseload against a baffling murder, and he has to learn 'birder-speak', otherwise how will he understand what on earth is going on?

Nor'easter

Howey Cross investigates the disappearance of a number of young women from Queen's County, even though it is outside his jurisdiction. There's a storm coming, the largest ever recorded, but the tail might be even more dangerous, it might bring the dreaded nor'easter.

Sea Glass

Howey Cross investigates an old case as a favour to his boss, Gordy Cole. Life is changing for Howey, not least because he now has twins to think about, he calls them the 'terrors'. He's also torn about whether to push his career in Halifax, or to take the unknown road and move to King's County. Birds appear with regularity, conundrums too, as Cross finds that life is no longer the simple affair it once was.

The Collector

Howey Cross is at something of a cross-roads in his life. Two young children, a new home and job, and now his partner, Moira, is seriously ill in hospital. How can he keep his family on an even keep and still manage to make his mark in the Kentville Police? Luckily, he has good friends in Darren, Hinzi and the Nova Scotia birders, who are always ready to help.

There is a sinister undercurrent in the birding world. Rare birds are disappearing from their find sites, more precipitately than might be expected. Then there are the Friday Birds, rarities that always seem to disappear before the weekend birders can see them-is it just coincidence or is there a Collector operating in the province? And can the projected Wildlife Crimes Unit actually be established and get the backup needed to make a difference?

The Harvesters' Galaxy Series

The Harvesters
Kerry Peters lives an ordinary life in Corner Brook, Newfoundland. She likes a beer and, sometimes, the company of her boyfriend Gary, although she is sure that he's not the one.

After a heavy night of drinking, she wakes up in Transit, naked. The staff there tell here they've sorted out her little problems and that she's ready to go on, but 'go on' where, exactly? Kerry didn't know it but she's one of the Harvested and, after that fateful night, nothing is going to be the same. Not for Kerry or for anyone.

The Elementals

Kerry Peters is dead-but you can't keep a Newfie down for long. Although she was cheated out of her fated role as Ruler of the Galaxy, due to the aforementioned 'dead' thing, she is not destined to enjoy her eternal rest. No, Bernice has other plans and needs Kerry's help.

Kerry awakes once again in Transit-it seems strangely familiar. The Harvesters' Galaxy is under threat, an evil force has taken control and whole planets are being destroyed. Someone needs to attract the attention of The Elementals, the beings who set the whole thing up in the first place, and get them onside. Who better to do so than a former Ruler of the Galaxy...

Comic Fantasy

War and Peas

Best describes as alternative history, or maybe not, War and Peas tells the tale of the battle for legume supremacy in Eastern England in the early 1970s. It is a complicated tale of love, honour, loyalty and flares. Things were different back then. People knew what to expect from life; a forty-hour week, beer on the weekend, and two weeks in a caravan on the coast and all that might bring. If you were lucky, you would end up in Mablethorpe, Jewel of East Lindsey, with its exotic pubs, endless sands, donkeys and mushy peas-truly, heaven is a place on Earth.

But Heaven is under threat from evil-doers from the west. The Men of the Parched are on the march and the Podsters of the Mushy Pea must fight to uphold the supremacy of the one true pea. Life, in Mablethorpe and in England, may never be the same again.

Non-fiction by Mark Dennis

Birding Memoirs

Going For Broke

1984 in the UK-'Big Brother', the Libyan Embassy siege, Band Aid, the launch of the Apple Mac and the start of the Miner's Strike. None of it matters when a birding Big Year is in sight. In the days of no mobile phones, no pagers and no dial-up 'Birdline', all rare bird information has to be obtained by phoning a little café in Norfolk and hoping one of the customers will pick up...

A young birder on a shoestring finds his way the length and breadth of Britain, finding birds and maxxing out the credit card. He really is 'going for broke'.

Twitching Times-a UK Birding Life

Mark Dennis started birding in the UK as a child, but he really started twitching, going for rare birds, in 1981. From then to 2003, when he left the UK and moved to Canada, he birded his local patch, his county (Nottinghamshire), and the UK, going to see rare birds when he could. Here are his birding memories lifers, memorable birds, occasions and people; and an entertaining swing through the UK birding scene.

Park Life

Colwick Country Park-a haven of peace and tranquility in the midst of the urban sprawl. Well, maybe...

Mark Dennis spent 15 years as a warden at Colwick, the best years of his working life. It was a dream job for an avid birder and naturalist-essentially spending most of his waking hours on his own local patch and being paid to do so. However, there were downsides, the 'members of the public' who also shared the space.

Dog walkers, anglers, boaters, 'twoccers', even a murder...they all made sure that there was never a dull moment for a busy warden. Still, there were also birds.

Butterflies, dragonflies to fill the quiet times. Not that it stayed quiet when a National rarity turned up...

The Seven Year Twitch

'Relentless in the pursuit of birds'. That was the lighthearted claim of Mark Dennis on his arrival in Nova Scotia in 2015. To be fair, a new province, alive with birding possibilities, would take some learning, and what better way to learn than through twitching? Living on Cape Sable Island, in the south of the Province, birds were found everywhere, and it didn't take long before Nova Scotia, and even Canada, ticks were presenting themselves for appreciation and admiration.

Further afield, twitches were undertaken to the furthest reaches of the province, seeing both new birds and new places. Some were undoubtedly a bit mad, but that was all part of the fun. Seven years on, the fun, and the birding, in the beautiful province of Nova Scotia, still bewitches-and the ticks keep on coming.

Birding Site Guides

Cape Sable Island-a Birding Site Guide

Cape Sable Island juts out into the Atlantic Ocean at the very tip of Nova Scotia. The island is joined to the mainland via a causeway and there the magic begins. For the birder, Cape Island is a must-see place in Canada. Whatever season you choose to visit, there will be birds. During fall migration, there are masses of shorebirds. In winter the wharves are loaded with gulls, and alcids haunt sheltered spots. Spring brings the only Canadian American Oystercatchers and summer, the nesting Piping Plovers. Come when you like and Cape Island's birds will be waiting.

Yarmouth Birding-a Site Guide

The county of Yarmouth offers some of the finest birding in Nova Scotia. Located at the extreme south-west of the province, birds migrating north in spring often make their first land-fall there, while fall birds migrating south can accumulate in considerable numbers at the various birding hotspots found in and around the town of Yarmouth.

This guide is designed to help the visitor find the sites. Finding the birds is a different thing altogether, but if you go to the right places at the right time you stand every chance. If you are planning a quick visit or a leisurely weekend of birding, this guide will prove invaluable in making your birding trip a success.

Birding Travelogues-
with Sandra Dennis

Eastern Australia - a Tour

Three Trips to Costa Rica

Cuba - ¿Que Bola?

Panama - Canal to Coast

Down Mexico Way

Ecuador - Andes and Amazon

Northern Belize

Que Giro! - Brazil

Egypt - Ancient and Modern

Another World - Travels in North America

Back in the US of A - Family Travels in North America

Birdin' USA - More Travels in North America